*Eternal Truth* by Glenn Scott Delves

Email: eternaltruthbook@gmail.com

'At least I didn't kill anyone today.'
'You say that like it was a difficult task?'


'All our dreams can come true, if we have the courage to pursue them.
–Walt Disney


'But what if our dreams are nightmares?
And they pursue us relentlessly, eternally, until we give in? Then we lose the ability to dream, because we have become the nightmare. We are the monster in someone else's dream, or even worse, their reality.'
- Glenn Scott Delves.

For my two boys Caden & Mason.

*Missing you comes in waves, and tonight, I'm drowning.*

**Prologue.**

*January 1952, west of Crandon, Wisconsin.*

The chase was pointless. But after all, a deal was a deal. Maybe not with the devil himself, but perhaps the next best thing. The raging storm in the forest's darkness did nothing to change the odds but he pursued his target on foot regardless, even though the deck was stacked in his favour, and always was. This was no challenge. This was merely a game. This was a change, something to which he was previously immune. And this was unprecedented. The tide was turning because of something new.

Or perhaps someone new.

Trying to be someone he had always wanted to be was intriguing. The overbearing temptation will reveal all in time, probably ending in failure. Why would this time be any different to countless others? Possibly, because for the first time in his life, someone had faith in him. He had given a more than generous head start to his prey, although the distance between them was increasing by the second, giving his prey the illusion that the threat had passed. False hope. Time was up.

Moving at such speed made the surrounding forestry become a blur. Branches struck against his head and torso like the lashes of a whip, tearing the sides of his face and drawing blood. He came to a sudden stop. Now focused on his target, the only movement was his tongue licking the trickle of blood that ran down his face. Like the closing of a zipper, the deep lacerations on his right cheek slowly healed and vanished. Headlights approached from the darkness. He was no longer alone. Someone else was out braving this storm.

\*\*\*

*It's 10.39pm and you are listening to WRNW 97.3 'NOW' Radio broadcasting live across Milwaukee and the state of Wisconsin, bringing you the very best in music and entertainment this side of the Rocky Mountains. For all the lucky ones snuggled up at home for the night with nowhere to go, well then I gotta say, I envy you. For all those people who are outdoors and exposed to the storm right now, please try your best to get home safe and in one piece.*

*Yes sir, Storm Dixon is causing heavy damage and widespread power outages in most areas. Heavy rainfall and winds reaching up to 60mph are making travelling of any description inadvisable. My advice, people, is to get indoors, put on a pot of coffee and stay there. More updates on tonight's storm coming up with the news at the top of the hour; do not touch that dial!*

'It won't be long now, just hold on.'

'Do you think I have a choice in all this? How about we trade places?'

'I love a sense of humour; I'm so glad I picked a wife with a sense of humour. By the way, I think Gerard is a great name if it's a boy.'

'Oh, come on! Gerard? After your father? I thought we both agreed that would never happen?'

'Well, I gave it some more thought … look, I know you're against it, but I was thinkin' it might be a nice idea, with his death last year and all?'

'Okay, first of all, keep your eyes on the road! And secondly, he had a drink problem and used to beat you,

Bob. I don't wanna be reminded of your father every time I say that name. Anyway, I'm sure it's gonna be a girl.' Clare smiled despite her pain. The windshield wipers struggled to keep up with the sheets of torrential rain and the headlights did little to light the road ahead. A moment later Clare's smile was replaced by a look of intense discomfort.

'Oh God, here it comes again!' She leaned forward to put her hand on the dashboard, trying to ride out the pain of another contraction. Bob reached across to hold her other hand in support, keeping one hand on the wheel. A lightning flash gave a burst of light to the road and surrounding forest.

'Breathe! That's it, Clare, breathe! Long, slow, deep breaths, in through the nose and out through the mouth … remember what the doctor said …' Bob tried his best to appear calm as he struggled with one hand to keep the car from swerving as it tackled each gust of wind. The road surface ran like a black river of tar with the surrounding evergreens buckling in unison from gale-force winds. The drainage ditch on both sides of the road had filled rapidly from the hours of non-stop rainfall. Visibility was poor, the headlights barely giving enough reaction time to avoid colliding with debris.

'Keep your goddamn eyes on the road!' Clare hissed through pursed lips. 'Don't worry about me!'

'Jesus, of all the nights you have to go into labour it has to be tonight …. We're the only goddam car on the road, nobody else is stupid enough to be out in this. Or maybe that's a good thing; maybe the hospital will be empty because of the storm? Hey! Maybe we can call the baby Dixon after the storm if it's a boy?' Nervousness caused him to ramble on.

'Just please get us there in one piece, Bob – oh God … I think my waters just broke!'

'Oh crap, hold on, shouldn't be too much longer.' Bob released her hand and returned it to the wheel, trying to focus his full attention on the road ahead but struggled to keep his eyes on the centre white line that disappeared into the void. The rear wheels threw up a spray of water into the air behind them like a jet stream that vanished and became one with the rainfall.

Something caught his eye up ahead, barely visible through the build-up of condensation on the window.

'Did you see that?'

'See what? Are you kidding me right now? I'm kinda busy or haven't you noticed?' Clare grimaced through the pain. The dark outline of a solitary figure standing under the trees now came into view, seemingly unaffected by the chaos of the raging storm. Whoever it was seemed to be watching the car. For a split second Bob thought he was seeing things. Who would choose to be exposed to the elements on a night like this? Was it just his imagination?

'What the hell was tha–' As he glanced at his wife, a large moving object caught the corner of his eye but too late. By the time his brain had processed the movement in order to react, the impact had already occurred. A loud crash sounded outside the car, loud screams within. The object rolled up onto the hood, smashing into the windshield. The car swerved across the road, tyres screeching and sliding on the surface water. Bob pulled the wheel to the right, desperately trying to steady the vehicle and correct its course. The car slid sideways on four wheels as again Bob hauled on the steering wheel.

From a deadly combination of speed and sharp turns on the wet surface, the vehicle overturned and began to roll, shattering the windows on both sides. It came to a stop with the driver's side facing skywards, the passenger side now exposed to the drainage ditch underneath. A low hissing sound escaped from the overturned engine, which was leaking steam that melted into the rain. Twenty feet from the wreck, a large deer lay dead. A pool of blood diluted the rainwater surrounding it and ran into the ditch.

Clare lay semi-conscious with her back against the door that was now slowly sinking into the mud below her. The pain in her right leg, trapped and badly twisted under the front seat, snapped her back to reality. Bob lay on top of her, his face planted in the mud over her right shoulder, pinning her in position.

'Bob? Bob? Bob …!'

She screamed out in pain and terror as she forced his head up from the mud, desperately hoping for a reply. His open eyes stared blankly ahead into the rising water level behind her, his pupils fixed and dilated; he was making no attempt to breathe. With her hands supporting both sides of his face, she pulled it close to her own, and began to sob uncontrollably. Mud slowly surrounded her inside the wreck, as she watched the water level continue to rise outside and press on the already weakened glass. She looked up to the sky, beyond her dead husband through the driver's side window, while the rain pelted her face. Upstream from the wreck, a wooden log caught in the rapid flow made its way rapidly towards the overturned car, heading straight for the front window.

Striking the car with speed, it forced the broken windshield in, on to Bob's lifeless body. Clare's entire body went rigid as it was submerged in the icy water that now poured in, almost instantly filling the car. She let out a scream of bubbles muted by the freezing water. This was it, she thought. She stopped and let go, staring through the water towards the sky, ready for the inevitable. Thoughts of her life filled her mind; the unborn child she would never get to see.

Through the wind, rain and water, she felt the car jolt, and saw the dark outline of a figure standing on the side of the car above. She reached out wildly, her hand barely breaking through the water's surface, past Bob, feeling air on her fingers again. She saw the figure grab the buckled driver's door, ripping it from its hinges, and throwing it up into the air as if it was made of cardboard. The urge to breathe became too much and she opened her mouth and inhaled, gagging violently as her lungs filled with water.

The weight of her husband suddenly lifted from her, and she saw his body being pulled through the newly formed opening in the vehicle's side. The driver's seat was next to be ripped from the vehicle, freeing her trapped leg. A hand plunged into the water, gripping her clothing to lift her seemingly without effort from the doomed wreck and lay her flat on her back on the road. She coughed and spluttered, spewing water into the air. A steady flow of frothy blood seeped through her shirt from a puncture wound in her left lung. She knew her injuries had to be life-threatening. Every breath caused intense pain, but her contractions had ceased. The trauma had become too much for her baby.

The stranger stood over her, watching silently, as if contemplating, or struggling, on his next move. He started to walk away, but then stopped. He came back and knelt by her side. She opened and closed her eyes in a daze, faint from the shock of blood loss and hypothermia. Something brushed against her mouth, and she could taste something running down her throat. A familiar taste, almost metallic.

In the space of that moment, the pain vanished. She felt at peace. A contraction dragged her back to the present and she felt the baby kick again, flooding her with overwhelming relief in the utter chaos. She held her arm above her face, attempting to block the rainfall. The dark figure silently watched.

'Thank you ... who–' She was cut off by the blinding headlights of a car. When she looked back to where her saviour had stood, there was nothing but the overhanging trees above. Whoever had saved her life was gone. The headlights of the approaching car lit up the scene of devastation. A car lay on its side, in the flooding ditch. A door hung trapped in the branches of a tree above. The body of a man lay face down near the centre white line in the road. A disfigured deer lay dead behind him, next to a car seat. A heavily pregnant woman lay on her back.

'Oh my God, are you okay?' said a female voice. Her male companion examined the man lying face down on the tarmac.

'Are you in pain?' said the good Samaritan.

'Where is he? Where did he go?'

'Who are you talking about, dear?'

'Somebody ... saved me ... he saved me and my baby ... where did he go?'

'There was no one else with you when we got here, did you bang your head?' said the woman.

'I need to get to a hospital; I need to have my baby before I die! My baby's coming! But I'm wounded ...'

'What wound?'

Clare pulled up her shirt to show the puncture wound, hoping she could stay alive until they got her to a medical facility. 'But ... I don't understand ....' The man was removing a blanket from the trunk of his car to place it over her dead husband. Another contraction hit her; the contractions were getting closer together, a sure sign that birth was imminent.

'Jack! Help me get her to the car!' the woman shouted.

Clare looked down at her left side, above her baby bump. The pain was gone, along with the puncture wound. All that remained was some blood surrounding a hole in her white shirt. No signs of trauma; no scar tissue of any kind. She and her baby were alive and well, and she was back in labour. It was like her injury had never happened. An injury that she had seen with her own two eyes. An injury that seemed to have vanished without a trace along with whoever had saved her and her baby.

## Chapter 1

*Present day. Tallant, Wisconsin.*

The silence woke him.

If he could have gone back in time and chosen not to sleep that night, he would have taken the safer option rather than face the recurring nightmare again. Waking bolt upright in his bed, breathing rapidly and raising both hands to his forehead, Scott quickly realised the nightmare wasn't real; that feeling of relief and the welcome sense of innocence came rushing back, knowing that no harm had been done.

This time.

'Damn red eyes,' he said out loud to the empty room.

He glanced at the bedside clock. Sunset. He had slept right through the day, which for him was nothing new. His bedroom was small and basic with no windows. It housed one bed pushed tight to the wall with a locker next to it. On top sat his watch, and the silver bracelet that he valued above all else. An antique bookcase towered over the end of the bed, filled with handwritten journals. Over

500 volumes, some much older than others, their age easily distinguished by their colour.

Not exactly your average 17-year-old's bedroom but, then again, Scott was not your average 17-year-old. No TV, no clutter, and most notably no smartphone glued to his hands 24 hours a day to feed a constant social-media addiction. He picked up his bracelet and spoke to it.

'What could we do if you were here?' he asked, not expecting a reply. With no need to hurry, no agenda or schedule, time became his ally, a too familiar ally. The lack of light in his room did little to hide his pale complexion, hypnotic blue eyes or the dark mess of hair on top of his head; besides, vanity wasn't his thing.

He placed the bracelet around his right wrist, pushed himself up and began to get dressed. Choosing what to wear was no big chore, as most of his wardrobe was the same. Days changed but his clothes didn't. Blue denim jeans, black buttoned shirt, black Adidas trainers, and a black leather jacket always left hanging open, showing his belt buckle. Another day of boredom awaits, he thought.

He stepped out into a dimly lit living room, where a grandfather clock ticked away in the corner, breaking the silence, its pendulum swinging from side to side. An old iron candle chandelier hung from a chain in the ceiling. The place he now called home was a single-storey dwelling, with a high, flat roof. The building had only one window that was covered by a blackout blind next to the door leading to a miniature hallway, and from there, the outside world awaited.

Although it was compact, the house had been home to both him and his mother for many years. It had the appearance of an antique shop, frozen in time. But not this time. More like the century before last. The room was lit by a small lamp on a coffee table positioned between two brown leather chairs facing a large stone fireplace. Cracks in the leather were clearly visible; there was no point hiding it, or any of the other out-of-place furniture that time had forgotten. The only people living here were Scott and his mother, and it's not as if she cared.

Her bedroom door was in the corner to the left of the fireplace. It stayed locked. Same as always. Scott never ventured in there. And she respected his bedroom boundary. Almost like a mutual understanding. Not that he ever wanted to go inside, God knows what he might find. Halfway across the room, he stopped. Turning towards his mother's bedroom door, he closed his eyes and listened to the silence. He knew she was in there; he also knew the exact time she got home, having woken during the early hours by his predatory survival instinct. A vibrational hum in his chest when she approached, like a heads-up alert. But the warning could be ignored in this case.

He shook his head in disapproval, let out a deep breath and headed for the front door. Stepping into darkness, he slammed the door behind him, rattling the remains of a broken lantern hanging to the right of the doorway. His eyes locked onto it for a moment as if he was reminiscing, a smile escaping before he snapped back to the present. Above him, a stone arch was engraved with the letter 'M', half hidden by cobwebs from years of neglect. The freedom he felt outside and away from his mother was like dropping a backpack that weighed a tonne.

The remaining days of September were creeping in, bringing a hint of yellow to some leaves along with darker and colder nights. That welcome scent of pine in the air, and the sight of gravestones beat the silence and dreary atmosphere of the house any day. Scott had often smiled to himself, reflecting that there was more life and fun in the cemetery than on the other side of that front door. After all, living on the inner edge of a five-acre cemetery surrounded by a stone wall had its perks. No noise, no gangs, plenty of privacy, and of course, the night sky with no light pollution to interfere with a view of the stars.

Tallant cemetery is on the south-western side of the town. Locals argued that in a town with a population of approximately two thousand people, too large an area was wasted on the dead. Some suggested it would be better off rezoned as a park or playground. But the cemetery was protected as a heritage site. Not that this stopped the occasional homeless person wandering in, usually seeking shelter in the overgrown tombs and mausoleums that hid in a central patch of forestry, dilapidated and out of sight. Intrepid teenagers tested their courage late at night, daring who could go furthest into the five acres of blackness without turning back in fear.

Lying north-west of Green Bay, Wisconsin, just south of Chequamegon-Nicolet National Forest, the town of Tallant began as a logging camp in the early twentieth century. It's served daily by the Empire Builder train service, with a direct route from the city of Portage just south of Wausau, a regular rival for the Tallant Titans, the town's only high-school football team. The Portage Panthers are invited back yearly for homecoming to battle it out on the field the night before the homecoming dance. To date, the Panthers have never won a game on Tallant soil, hence the continuing annual invites. A win against old rivals always lifts the town's spirits ahead of the homecoming dance the next night.

Football aside, Tallant is a town with a rich history, and like most rural towns its folklore goes hand in hand with its legends that are still told today. It is a relatively quiet place, apart from the occasional missing person reports, which are mostly put down to misadventures in the forest. Some are random animal attacks, hikers missing on the mountains or accidents on the glacial lakes within. Even with all its flaws, Tallant was home for Scott. And had been for a long time.

Hands in his pockets, he turned left towards the old wrought-iron gate that separated the living and the dead. As he got close, he noticed it was locked, with the usual wrap-around chain that Toddy Coventry the groundskeeper always put in place at dusk, to stop traffic entering after a certain hour. The carnival was back in town for its summer visit, attracting people from far and wide during the warm evenings. The cemetery represented free parking for thrill seekers, to Mr Coventry's dismay. Each year the fairground is temporarily situated at the edge of town on an area of waste ground owned by a local family, the Cartwrights, not yet given planning permission. Something, no doubt, that Governor Cartwright would soon remedy.

Scott stepped through a small pedestrian gate built into the main gates, to the usual sight of traffic heading home for the evening as the shops were closing. He stopped, looked left, then right. Where to tonight, he wondered. His solitary skills took practice, but loneliness with no friends was probably for the best. Who needed friends when he could vanish into the pages of a book? TV wasn't his thing, his mother had never bought one; even if she had, it probably wouldn't be used. The movie theatre on Main Street or listening to music at home was a regular diversion, but not tonight. He needed something to write about in his journal. Empty pages from days of sleep made for boring future reading. He knew from experience. For as long as he could remember, he had religiously updated it daily, often glancing back through the pages, wishing he could return to the certain points in time when the ink touched the very paper he was holding. Not only did he miss the people and places, he missed the person he was back then. His past was forever locked in regret, for both the good and the bad.

The diner again, he guessed. Open until 1 am, his usual time to visit was midnight, when it was mostly empty. But there was always a welcoming face, partially because he had gotten to know the staff from frequenting it so much. Especially Gerry the manager, who regularly told Scott about his woes as he sat watching the world go by. Scott headed in the direction of Main Street, across the plaza with its fountain and benches, and stopped at the town-hall clock tower, which had recently become a museum. Watching the evening rush of commuters, he felt a lump grow in his throat. That clock tower brought back emotions he didn't know how to handle. The memories were vivid, almost like they'd happened yesterday. He wrapped his hand around the bracelet on his wrist and continued past the obelisk monument dedicated to some of the town's early settlers, who had died in unknown circumstances.

**Chapter 2**

Trevor's Diner sat on the corner of Main Street and Fourth Avenue. Right next door was the Enchanted Florist where Carol worked as a florist by day, and as a psychic medium at night. She also dabbled in Wicca and was known to tell lovesick teens that the roses she sold were enchanted with a love spell. Handy being situated right next door to Trevor's, with all those awkward first dates. Autumn was Carol's favourite time of year, with her annual display of pumpkins on the footpath and her love for the feast of Samhain, celebrated by the ancient Celts as a festival marking the beginning of winter. Halloween was a few weeks away yet, so the pavement remained bare. Trevor's was a must for nervous teenagers who used it as an icebreaker for dating. But it didn't permit groups of more than four teens, due to a history of rowdy incidents. Hence Gerry the manager, sitting next to the jukebox by the door with a view of the TV set always on above the cash register.

Gerry was a short but stocky man with a bald head. He wore a long black coat which he thought made him look taller. Now in his mid-sixties, in his youth he had worked and trained as a boxer when Trevor's was a boxing club, founded in 1962. Until a fatal incident involving reckless driving gave him five years behind bars. It was all common knowledge to the townsfolk, but Scott is one of the few people Gerry confides in, and Gerry has told him the tale personally.

Mid-sixties or not, Gerry wouldn't take crap from anyone, especially oversized teenagers. Several times Scott had watched him throw troublemakers out on the street. On one occasion, a brazen fellow tried to hit Gerry, who responded with a left hook that sent him flat on his back to the floor. But Gerry had a soft spot for Scott. It's almost as if he had respect for Scott, or maybe he just feels sorry for him? This kid who always comes in by himself, sits alone, eats his ice cream alone, and leaves. They became friends over time, a friendship and a time which Scott remembered in far more detail than Gerry did.

Scott turned onto Main Street, passing the old movie theatre and Manor apartment complex next to it. Almost facing the movie theatre was the Tallant US Parks Department building. This small one-storey red brick building sat on its own plot of land, a stretch of grass to the left, and a carpark that spreads from the front, around to the right side of the building. The park ranger's job in Tallant was a busy one due to the sheer size of the forest surrounding the town, and there was only one park ranger and one secretary/receptionist.

Scott halted at the corner of Main Street, a familiar feeling coming over him. One he had not felt for a long time this far from home. The vibrational hum in his chest. The kind you might feel standing too close to a speaker at a rock concert. Something wasn't right. Getting this feeling required caution and observation. He knew how to play it out, for this feeling also brought anger and hatred, but no remorse. He looked around as he stood still, trying not to make it obvious. Seeing nothing, he continued towards the diner where he could already see Gerry in his usual spot by the door.

Scott uttered some words under his breath for no one else to hear. 'Hello, my old friend.' Gerry had seen him and already had his hand on the door to welcome him back for another milkshake and chat about boxing.

'You know what? You're the only kid I'm happy to see walk through that door.'

'Hey Gerry, what's up?' Scott took his usual seat, making note of the man in the black hoodie sitting alone with his back turned to him four tables down.

'Would I be right in sayin' you don't even wanna look at a menu?' Scott smirked and looked over at Kayce, the waitress, who had also seen him come in.

'The usual?' asked Kayce. Scott gave her a nod of approval. Kayce was a heavy-set woman in her late thirties. She wore the traditional Trevor's uniform, a pink and white striped dress that went to just above knee height. Seeing

Scott, she knew there was no need to take down the pencil from behind her ear.

'One chocolate honeycomb milkshake comin' up,' she smiled and continued down along the tables with a cloth and spray in hand. Gerry sat on the stool facing Scott with his back to the door.

'Almost every night you come in here, you never try somethin' new?' remarked Gerry.

'I've tried them all, this one is my favourite.' Scott pointed to the photo in the window facing the street. 'So anyway, what's wrong with the other kids who come in here?'

'Really wanna know?'

Scott shrugged.

'Because most of them are brats with no manners. Take you for example, what age are you, 15, 16?'

'Uh, 17,' Scott grinned nervously through his teeth.

'Okay, but you're very different to most of the 17-year-olds who come through that door.' Scott smiled and folded his arms on the table, getting ready for what was coming next. He had all the time in the world to listen to Gerry ramble on, and it's not as if he had anywhere to go.

'How so?' Scott replied.

'Because they have no respect for their elders, that's what's wrong with the world today, but you, it's like you're an old head on young shoulders; you got manners, and that goes a long way with me.'

'I do appreciate that, Gerry, but surely everyone has skeletons in their closet,' Scott added, dropping the smile. He felt the usual guilt he was accustomed to when talking to Gerry. There was so much more to their acquaintance than Gerry knew; much more than Scott was ready to tell him. But now was not the time or place.

'Who are ya tellin' kid?'

Scott knew exactly what he meant.

'And besides, you're seventeen, you've barely lived! What skeletons could you be hidin'? But you'll understand how tough life can be when you grow up.'

Scott shook his head and dropped his gaze to the table in front of him. Gerry leaned in Scott's direction and lowered his voice.

'Hey kid, I know that everyone has problems, and I don't mean to pry, but you're so young, and you seem like a nice kid. I never see you in here with friends. Where's your mom and dad? In fact, come to think of it, I never seen you outside this place?' Gerry sat back, seeing Kayce approach with the shake, setting it in front of Scott with a smile and a wink.

'Thank you,' Scott said, as his eyes returned to Gerry. He picked up the long dessert spoon and started to dig at his milkshake. Scott had always avoided talking about himself and his situation by changing the subject back to Gerry. Throwing in a spontaneous question about boxing usually did the trick. But maybe he owed Gerry; after all, he was the closest thing he had to a friend.

He took a deep breath. 'What if I just don't have any friends, my dad's not around and my mom doesn't care what I do or where I go?' An uncomfortable look rolled over Gerry's face as he realised this answer was more than he'd bargained for.

'Okay, Scott. But don't forget, we all got our demons.'

Scott tore open a straw, stabbed it into his shake and began to slurp. He looked Gerry in the eye. 'You don't know the half of it … but I couldn't have put it better myself.'

# Chapter 3

The arrival of six teenagers was a welcome sight for Gerry, mostly to escape the awkwardness of Scott's last remark. He stood up, gave a quick 'I understand' smile then went outside, leaving Scott sitting alone to finish his milkshake. He watched through the glass as Gerry reminded the group of the maximum-of-four rule. One of the six stood out from the others as the spokesman of the group; chubby, wearing a check shirt, denim jeans with cons, and a baseball cap turned backwards over a head of messy brown hair.

As a family of four was greeted by Kayce at the cash register, a news bulletin commandeered the TV in the background. A blonde woman in her late twenties read from the teleprompter.

*Seven people have been arrested and one released without charge in a joint operation by the state police and the FBI in Green Bay earlier today. They carried out the arrests after an anonymous tip-off led police to the basement of a house on Monroe Road, where it's believed a bizarre sacrificial form of witchcraft was being performed on five people held hostage and previously presumed missing. It's not yet known if the incident is related to the state-wide search still in operation for the three school children who went missing last week from two separate areas of Wisconsin. This and more coming up on News at Nine. Stay tuned!*

The father paid their bill, and the family left, oblivious to the newsflash. As the door opened, Scott heard Gerry say, 'Don't be cheeky.'

'We won't start any trouble, mister,' Check shirt replied with unconvincing swagger. Gerry let them enter on condition they break into two groups that stayed apart. Two of them walked off, not happy with this outcome. Three of them entered, walked to a table down the back, leaving the loudmouth standing outside with Gerry.

'I guess your buddies don't like you that much either,' Gerry remarked. The kid responded with a cheesy grin. During this interaction, Scott kept a close watch on the black hoodie, who still had not moved. Gerry stepped back in and headed toward the four who had just sat down. Check shirt watched him for a minute, then snatched the opportunity to step inside, hoping he wouldn't be noticed. Slowly he edged his way down towards his friends, pausing at each table along the way, trying to blend in with random strangers.

Scott smiled watching the feeble attempt as he finished the last of his shake. Gerry started for the door again but when he turned, he made eye contact with Check shirt. Realising he'd been rumbled; Check shirt began to walk backwards the exit until Gerry caught up with him.

'Just where do you think you're going?'

Check shirt looked around desperately. 'I'm just sitting with my friend here.' He slid into the seat opposite Scott.

Scott couldn't help but grin when he looked at Gerry. Gerry was about to say something, but something stopped him. He looked at Check shirt, then he looked at Scott. Check shirt tried to look innocent, waiting for a reaction from the manager. Finally, Gerry gave Scott a nod, then silently stepped back outside. A subtle effort to help Scott make a new friend.

'Phew, that was close, what a douche! All I want is ice cream; you'd think that guy was a club bouncer.' Check shirt was talking to Scott but staring down the back towards his friends. Scott said nothing, knowing he was being used as a patsy. Again, Check shirt glanced at Gerry, then down at his friends, contemplating another attempt to join them. Gerry opened the door to allow another family out, then entered and spoke to Kayce, pointing a thumb in Scott's direction before returning outside. Scott waited to see how the scenario would pan out. Eventually Check shirt turned and looked at him properly for the first time.

'Peter James, or PJ, if you like, PJ the DJ, should you ever need music supplied at an event. What's your name?'

'Scott, Scott Maglace.'

PJ looked puzzled. 'What the hell kinda name is that? I mean, where's it from?'

'Actually, I'm not sure' replied Scott, trying to avoid the topic of his made-up name.

'How come I've never seen you in town before? Or at school?' queried PJ.

Scott wondered how far to let this go before leaving, but anything was better than going back to the cemetery. 'I've been here for a while … I don't really go to school.'

'Sweet! How did you pull that one off? Home-schooling?' PJ suddenly noticed that Gerry was gone from the door and stood up. 'Gotta go.'

'Sure thing,' said Scott. 'More for me.'

PJ halted, looking confused. 'Whaddya mean, more for you?' Scott nodded in Kayce's direction. 'Two free shakes are on the way, and I only need one.' Scott had his full attention now.

'How do you know that?' PJ narrowed his eyes, suspecting a prank. But all joking aside, free milkshake was free milkshake. Scott pushed his empty glass to the side and spoke.

'I heard the manager ask Kayce to bring two shakes on the house to this table.'

'Ha, ha, ha hilarious, he's about a mile away from this table, no way you heard that over the jukebox!'

Seconds later, Kayce appeared with two shakes in hand and placed them on the table. 'On the house, Scott, for you and your friend here.' PJ quickly sat back down and looked at Scott with his mouth hanging open in amazement.

'Thanks, Kayce.' Scott replied. With a nod of approval, she left to serve another table. 'Anyway ...' Scott continued, 'it was nice meeting you.'

'Wait, I mean ... I'll stay to, ah ... no point letting this shake go to waste, right?' PJ had forgotten all about his friends and was now engrossed in the free shake. 'So where ya from, Scott, isn't it?' he said as he ripped open a straw and stuck it into his shake.

'Right here in Tallant.'

'Yeah, I gathered that,' PJ tried not to look overly sarcastic, considering the free shake.

'Oh right, yeah, over near the cemetery; what about you?'

PJ stopped slurping, took a breath, and licked his lips. 'Eastbrook Lodge, you know it?' Scott knew exactly. It was a private housing development in east Tallant, all detached homes; pricey. They made his home look like a parking garage.

'Here.' PJ slid a business card across the table. *'PJ THE DJ!' ALL EVENTS COVERED!*

'Thanks.' Scott opened another straw.

'Oh, and give me a like on Facebook for a 10 per cent discount!'

'I'm not on that,' Scott said.

'Okay, Twitter then,' with a slurp.

'I'm not on that either.'

PJ stopped slurping. 'Instagram? Snapchat? Uh … LinkedIn?' he said, shaking his head, eyes wide in disbelief.

'Nope, nope and nope.'

'Jeez, Scott, what the hell is wrong with you?'

'I don't have a phone either.'

The straw dropped from PJ's mouth and landed back inside the glass. He stared across the table in shock. It was the first time in history he'd met a teenager without a phone, period. For once he was lost for words. He raised both hands to the sides of his head in confusion and uttered the words 'But … why?'

Scott finished the last of his shake. 'Because I don't need one and never have.'

'So, what do you do with yourself, then? I mean, it's obvious you work out, you know, from the way you look.'

Scott gave him a confused smile.

'No! I didn't mean it that way!'

Scott laughed for the first time in what felt like years. He leaned in close to PJ, giving him a suggestive wink.

'Stop it! You know what I meant! It's just, you look like a guy that chicks would go for, ya know?' PJ felt his face burning. He took the straw from his glass and lifted the rest of the milkshake to his mouth, hoping to disguise his blush. He knocked it back and pushed his glass to one side.

'I don't know how to answer that but, thanks, I think?' Scott jested.

'Yeah whatever, listen, you see my friends down the back? We're headed to the fairground after here, you wanna come? I owe ya for the free shake,' PJ offered. Scott looked down to the friends, who were just standing up to leave. The tall thin one brandished an angry face while paying, as if he was being overcharged. Kayce looked as if she was used to it. They settled the bill and looked at PJ, the tallest of the four nodding to the door.

'You comin'?'

'Yeah, be right there.' PJ stood up. 'Well, ya comin' or not?'

'Perhaps another time, PJ.'

'Okay then, suit yourself, but we might be meeting up with some girls after. Your loss!' PJ stood up to join his friends waiting at the exit. Gerry opened the door, gesturing for them to leave. He glanced sympathetically at Scott, alone again. Scott picked up a menu from the empty table next to him, opened it and began to read, pretending he didn't notice the black hoodie exiting behind PJ and his friends.

# Chapter 4

Amdis stood before the ancients. It was ten years to the day that she last stood where she stood now, and they expected answers. Within this stone hall lit by flickering torches, shadowy onlookers on the balcony that circled the room overlooking her. Two figures stood either side of another figure at the top of a series of steps leading to an altar. With hands by her sides and head hung low, she avoided eye contact and waited. Intimidated and alone, she knew what was coming.

'Every ten years we have summoned you to the Great Hall, and each time you argue your case to no avail.' The figure in front spoke, the voice was cold and detached, echoing back into the darkness. 'For over two hundred years you have stood where you stand now, and time is running out. This matter is of grave concern to all of us. Including you! Or have you forgotten that you, too, are one of us?'

'I haven't forgotten.'.

'The one that should not exist is nonetheless the chosen one and is to take his place here amongst the ancients to lead us against the dangers ahead.'

Amdis raised her head. 'You don't understand, Draven – there are ... complications. There is no regard for our ways, and little attention given to your concerns, either. There is no interest in coming here, now or ever. I have tried reasoning in vain.'

'Well then, perhaps we should try a more … persuasive way of reasoning?'

Raised voices echoed from one side of the chamber to the other. 'We have tried already, you know well that every scout we send never returns,' offered another hooded figure. Amdis again dropped her gaze to the floor, trying to hide a slight smile within the nervousness. Draven took three steps from the altar, raised his arm and pointed a thin finger in her direction. 'If this is true, Amdis, if our own kind have been killed, then punishment is required!'

'I know nothing of this, but I will endeavour to find out.' Bowing her head again, she turned and made her way through the door, unchallenged.

The figures converged on the centre of the hall.

'Send more scouts.'

'We know that she is covering for him and lying to protect him.'

'If she is willing to do that for him, what is he willing to do for her?'

'Perhaps she is the bait we have needed all along.'

# Chapter 5

Leaving Trevor's, the four companions started for the fairground, unaware they were being followed. Instead of turning right down Main Street, they made a left, past the Enchanted Florist onto Trail Street on the western edge of town. From here, the vast expanse of the Chequamegon Nicolet National Forest runs parallel to the road as far as the cemetery. Several forest trails used during the logging days still exist, hence the name Trail Street. Evenly spaced oak trees line the route from Fourth Avenue, with wooden benches positioned facing the forest scenery and the mountains in the distance. The seasons change, but this street is always busy with backpackers and ramblers who used the car park, just off the street itself. Camper vans, off-road vehicles and quad bikes are a regular sight in the mornings, returning later to collect exhausted hikers. The further north one travels into the forest, the steeper the terrain becomes. Gradually, the greenery and trails disappear and the stony tracks to the foothills of the mountains begin.

  After dark, the car park empties. The camper vans and off-road vehicles that occupied it during the day are replaced by vehicles with tinted windows, alloy wheels and subwoofers that echo the sounds of bass into the edge of the forest. It's a magnet for young couples to 'park' because of the absence of street lighting and a good view of the stars.

'So, who was that guy you were sitting with in Trevor's?' Dan Cartwright spoke with an air of authority. Almost the opposite to PJ, he was tall, thin, and clean-cut, fond of showing off clothing brands that most teens his age couldn't afford. Being rich in a town like Tallant helped one get by almost everywhere but being the nephew of the Governor made it game, set and match. Family money and the resulting sense of power made Dan Cartwright the unelected leader of the group. The only one stupid enough to challenge his authority was PJ.

The others flocked to Dan like moths to a flame, some using him for his easy money and some taking advantage of being close to the girls he seemed to also attract. PJ often felt it was unfair that he had to give up his spare time to work as a part-time DJ while Dan just inherited wealth for doing nothing.

PJ didn't turn around to answer. 'Just some kid, seems okay, got me a free milkshake.'

'Free milkshake? Why does he deserve a free milkshake?' Dan questioned, annoyed. PJ knew where this was going. Governor Cartwright frequents Trevor's from time to time and gets free food and drink. Dan thought he should be entitled to the same privilege just for being his nephew. He even questioned Kayce on one occasion for bringing him the bill in front of his friends, reminding her of who he was. It didn't work; in fact, she added an extra soda, which she'd forgotten about, to the bill, much to PJ's delight.

'Don't know, think the manager is his friend or somethin' … why do you care? You got plenty of dough to buy shakes for all of us, but you don't bother,' replied PJ.

Dan liked the fact that PJ remembered he was rich, but not so much the smart answer implying he was tight. He stopped walking and stared at the back of PJ's head. The other two also stopped, switching their gaze between Dan and PJ, who still hadn't realised he was now out in front walking alone.

'What I do with my money is my business, your lack of money is your business, smart-ass! Just remember that when you're getting free rides at the fair!' Dan barked.

PJ turned to face the group, mentally rolling his eyes. He'd stuck his foot in his mouth again, threatening his chance of free rides at the fairground. Unlike the milkshake dilemma, the free rides were guaranteed. Nothing to do with being the Governor's nephew, but by being a Cartwright by birth. For the past ten years, the Cartwrights have been running the fairground and were responsible for its annual visit. Surprisingly enough, it seemed to get a longer than usual temporary licence to use the waste ground. The longer it's in town, the more money it generates for the Cartwrights.

He'd also learned that staying in Dan's company kept regular DJ work coming his way. 'Okay, my bad, I'm sure you've considered buying stuff for us lots of times, but hey, it always tastes better when it's free! Right guys?' He tested this sucking-up approach, hoping the others would chime in. No reaction. Dan stared at PJ and shook his head. PJ grinned back at him through clenched teeth, hoping this awkward moment had an end in sight. Dan intentionally brushed his shoulder against PJ's as he took the lead. The others followed, shaking their heads in disapproval. For a moment, PJ stood alone facing the opposite direction. He noticed a dark figure in the distance heading towards them but, thinking nothing of it, turned to catch up with the others.

As they approached the forest car park, they crossed the street to see if any familiar cars were parked up near the start of the trails. People stood outside their cars, smoking in groups, some drinking beer, while others left a space between cars for privacy.

'Hey PJ, is that your mom's car I see parked with the lights off?' Dan couldn't help himself after the earlier comments. The others laughed, glad not to be on the receiving end of the joke. Sometimes Dan didn't discriminate, making fun at anyone's expense to make himself feel superior.

'Wait, what day is it?' replied PJ. He stopped and held his finger to his temple pretending to be thinking. 'No ... that was last night, tonight is crossdressing night; she's with your dad, helping him with his makeup and suspenders.' PJ being PJ was always ready with a comeback. Dan gave a sly grin and kept walking, giving PJ some relief that he'd taken this one on the chin.

As they neared the end of the street, the small stone wall that separated the road and the forest became the larger eight-foot boundary wall housing the northern pedestrian gate to the cemetery. It was locked, but two iron bars were bent out of shape just big enough for someone to fit through. Dan grabbed the iron bars and shook them as if testing the locking mechanism. 'So, whaddya think, guys?' Keeping one hand on the bars, he turned to the others for a reaction. 'Will we take the shortcut?'

They looked at each other, half afraid to admit that they hated the idea. Luckily for them, PJ spoke first. 'Are you crazy? It's pitch black in there! And besides, what's the point? It only takes about five minutes off the journey.' He gave a logical reason not to go in, rather than alert Dan that he hated the idea.

'Guys, there are four of us,' Dan commented. 'I mean, I already know that PJ is chicken, but don't tell me you guys are a bunch of pussies too?' Dan knew in his heart of hearts that if he was alone, there was no chance in hell he would enter the cemetery at night. Not that he'd admit that to the guys, who looked up to him. His sense of self-importance brought a false sense of bravery with it. And anyway, who would mess with the Governor's nephew? He put one foot through the bars onto the gravel within and lowered himself to fit through the gap at the widest part. Once inside, he stood up and brushed off his expensive jacket.

Taking three steps away from the gate, he turned to face the others, presuming they were right behind him. None of them had moved. Dan pointed his finger into the blackness in frustration.

'I'm gonna sit on that bench near the fountain, and whoever doesn't come join me can forget about the fair and go home! Bunch of pussies!' He stormed off into the darkness, each step crunching on the gravel. Concerned about losing the respect of Cartwright and free rides at the fairground, three of the others took turns getting through the gate, against their better judgement.

When they were through, PJ stepped up and grabbed the gate with both hands, pushing his face between the bars and protested, 'Guys, this is stupid, what's the point of going that way when we can stay on the street? It's almost as quick! Anyway, what would you care if anything happened to Scrooge in there?' At that moment, PJ's phone began to play 'The Bad Touch' by the Bloodhound Gang, a ringtone he'd been using for the past year. He got a kick from singing the chorus out loud to any female in his vicinity when it rang. He pulled it from his back pocket to see an unknown number on the screen. The trio ignored him and vanished into the cemetery on their mission to follow the leader.

'Yeah, this is PJ?'

'Peter James, this is Rebecca Chambers.'

'What the ...? How the hell did you get my number?' Rebecca is the girl at school involved in everything, mostly for credit from teachers and the vice principal. From after-school arts and crafts to drama and the chess club, with her pigtails, black-rimmed glasses and straight A's, she is the classic stereotype of the high-school nerd. Once upon a time PJ had asked her out, but got shot down, leaving him with a bitter taste in his mouth and some wounded pride. The guys found out the next day and never let him live it down. But Rebecca was one year ahead of PJ, and even though she secretly thought he was kinda cute, dating someone younger in school was out of the question.

'From your business card? Who even has those anymore? I saw it on the school notice board.'

'Okay but I thought I was too young for you? Anyway, I'm not interested anymo–'

Rebecca cut across him mid-sentence. 'Stop talking, PJ, that's not why I'm calling. I'm on the homecoming committee this year and I'm trying to organise a DJ for the night. Are you available?'

PJ backtracked. 'Oh right, uh, of course! Yeah, sure thing, I'll do it.'

'But you haven't heard the date yet, how do you know you're available?'

Realising he may have sounded a little too desperate, he tried to backtrack further. He knew full well that he would do the job no matter the date. He also knew he had nothing else booked for the next two months. A good job at the homecoming dance could secure more homecomings and prom nights.

'Yeah, yeah, cool, that's a valid point; where and when's it on?' PJ felt like a fool but couldn't help it. Rebecca made him nervous.

'The school recreation centre, dummy, where else? October 31st, it's a Saturday.'

'Hang on till I check my schedule to make sure I'm free,' PJ lied. He held the phone away from his mouth and walked in circles outside the gate to kill time, pretending to check a non-existent schedule. He stuck his face through the bars again hoping to see the others waiting at the bench. He didn't notice that the sounds of footsteps on gravel had stopped.

## Chapter 6

Dan Cartwright sat in the cemetery with nothing but the sound of crickets and the rustling of leaves for company. Headstones and obelisks surrounded him, barely visible in the limited moonlight. He was nervous. Every sound drew his full attention, snapping his head left and right to investigate. Next to the bench, a stone water fountain modelled as a flame from a candle trickled water down from a hole in the top, filling up an oversized basin beneath, which overflowed into a larger one at the bottom. Right now, all he wanted to hear were the footsteps of his friends. But if they didn't follow, he'd wait until they left, then go back the way he came in, pretending he'd taken the shortcut alone.

A twig snapped behind him.

'Hello ...? If you guys are fooling around you better get your asses out here so we can get to the fair, it's getting late!'

Everything became still.

The crickets stopped chirping; the leaves above became motionless.

A dead silence, but something was different. He felt a presence. The moon retreated behind the clouds and the hair on the back of his neck stood on end. His heart raced as he realised that he was being watched. No footsteps were heard on the gravel path, yet he knew that something was close, focusing on him from the darkness. Now he knew the mistake he'd made trying to look brave in front of the others. Maybe PJ was right. This shortcut wasn't worth it. Keeping still, he hoped the moment would pass and the sounds of nature would return. But the sound he heard instead was unexpected.

From the dark emptiness right in front of his face, a deep growl bellowed..

## Chapter 7

'Hello? PJ? Are you free that night or not?'

PJ turned from the gate and kicked a stone alone the ground; he reckoned enough time had passed now. 'Yeah, I had something else on that night, but I think I can reschedule that to help you out,' he lied.

'Okay, fine, how much will it cost?'

'A thousand dollars?' PJ the joker.

'Don't you think that's too much?'

'Of course it is, only a cheap conman would ask that much.'

'We were prepared to pay two hundred dollars.'

PJ's eyes widened. 'Surprisingly enough, I'm prepared to take it: will we seal the deal with a kiss? Or twenty dollars in cash? Either way you lose,' PJ the chancer.

'Just don't let me down, PJ, that night is as important to me as it is to you.'

Call ended appeared on the screen. He added the unknown number to his contacts and put the phone in his rear pocket before turning back to the gate. He shook his head and spoke to himself. 'The things I do for a few free rides, oh well, may fortune favour the foolish.' Gary and

Brad approached the bench where Dan Cartwright was waiting walking in a closer formation than usual. Just ahead, they could make out the faint shape of a figure sitting on the bench. When in range, Brad spoke.

'Dan? You ready? PJ is back there on his pho …' Brad stopped mid-sentence, then all three stopped dead in their tracks.

'Dan …?' No response.

'Dan? Are we going now?' Nothing.

Gary pulled out his phone and turned on the torch app, pointing it at the bench. Dan Cartwright was sitting with both feet raised off the ground, heels tight against his buttocks, his arms wrapped around his knees with fingers interlocked. He rocked back and forth, staring into the blank space ahead of him.

'Dan, are you okay?' Gary moved the light closer to Dan's face. Dan jumped, like he hadn't noticed them approaching. 'What, what is it? What's wrong?' he shouted as he snapped back to the present. 'Get that damn torch out of my eyes!'

Gary lowered the light keeping it turned on. 'You seemed zoned out or something, are you okay?'

Dan didn't know what had happened before the guys arrived. Realising he looked a little worried, he put on a brave face and changed the subject. 'Where the hell is PJ, it's getting late.'

'He's back at the gate on a call,' said Gary.

This was the opportunity Dan needed. A prank on PJ would deflect the unwanted attention from himself. He stood up and ran his hand through his hair, struggling still to look calm. 'Let's go, PJ will follow us, but we'll be long gone when he gets here; let him make his own way out alone, smart-ass deserves it.' Dan wanted payback for the comments about his dad, comments he pretended didn't bother him. They made for the southern gate leaving PJ to fend for himself.

Back at the other gate, PJ put one foot through the gap between the bars and lowered his body down to squeeze through where the gap was widest. He took a deep breath and held it, finding it more difficult to fit through than the others. 'Stupid skinny show-offs!'

On high alert, he scanned the vicinity as he made his way through the dark. A bench came into view. An empty bench. 'What the fuck …?' He stood between the bench and the fountain, peering into the dark for signs of life.

'Em, guys ...? Guys?' He cursed. 'Damn it! I'm so stupid; I should have known Cartwright would pull a stunt like this.' He pulled his phone from his back pocket again, the screen lighting up his face while he searched for Cartwright's number. He didn't notice his surroundings becoming silent. The gravel crunched behind him.

Assuming it was one of the guys, he turned around. A black hooded figure stood right in front of him.

'Holy shi–' He didn't get to finish the sentence. His phone fell to the ground as a cold hand grabbed him roughly by the throat with such force that he couldn't speak or breathe. His face began to turn red, and a deep growling sound turned his blood cold. In defence, PJ's hands clasped the hand and wrist of his attacker, as he struggled against asphyxiation. He started to panic. He reached out with one hand, scrabbling to grab the hooded figure, his other hand still desperately struggling to remove the hand around his neck. In response the grip grew tighter and lifted him with ease, his feet dangling in mid-air. In all his seventeen years, PJ had never felt terror like this.

Unexpectedly, the cold hand suddenly released him. He fell back on the gravel, lying in shock on his elbows, trying to catch his breath. The deep growl emanating from the darkness was now replaced by another, even more terrifying. Dominant with power, like a lion's roar. The intensity vibrated deep into the surrounding trees.

But then something happened that he wasn't expecting. He was grabbed and pulled upwards and stumbled back to his feet. He was dizzy, but not from lack of oxygen. It was something else. His eyes were wide open, but he stared blankly ahead like he was intoxicated or lost in a waking dream. What was the present became distant memories; those memories became flashbacks. A dark hoodie and a dark shadow. And like a dream, those memories faded, as if they'd never happened.

The dark outline of a person faced him, waiting.

## Chapter 8

Scott stood opposite PJ, grinning uncomfortably in the light from PJ's phone, which was illuminating them from the ground. PJ's tunnel vision vanished, and he snapped back to the present, looking confused. 'Okay ... what the hell just happened?'

Scott replied without hesitation, his answer already prepared. 'I changed my mind and thought I'd join you; it's a nice night after all.' Still with the grin.

'Scott? Where in the hell did you come from? What the–'

'I ran to catch up with you guys. What did I miss?' Scott picked up PJ's phone and handed it back to him.

'Okay ... I'm confused? Last thing I remember was the bench and the guys pulling a fast one leaving me on my own. Then I see you in front of me?' PJ scratched his head. He checked his phone screen for cracks, then placed it back in his pocket.

'Yeah, you were just standing here, like you said, when I arrived – so let's not waste any more time, let's go!' Scott gestured toward the southern gate, trying to change the subject. He took a few steps, hoping PJ would follow.

'Weird, but okay ...?' PJ stared in Scott's direction. 'Besides, we need to catch up to the ...' PJ stopped as if hitting an invisible wall. 'What the fuck? Am I seeing things?' He retraced his steps back to where he'd dropped his phone. He pulled it from his pocket and turned on the torch app.

Scott rolled his eyes. 'It's getting late, PJ, we should go.' His words fell on deaf ears. PJ was scanning the area, holding his phone in front of him. His mouth opened wide in confusion. The bench that Dan Cartwright had mentioned was smashed to pieces, scattered along the gravel path and grass. Some pieces smouldered as if they'd been burning.

'What the hell happened here? Okay, shit's getting really weird now, man.'

Scott turned back. With both hands still in the pockets of his jacket, he kicked one of the broken boards from the bench up onto the grass.

'Are you sure? Cause I just got here, and it was like that. Must have been some disgruntled homeless person?' A piece of the bench was in the lowest tier of the fountain, bobbing up and down. PJ moved closer and shone his light into the shallow pool.

'Why is the water red? It looks like ... blood or somethin'?'

Scott stared at PJ from the corner of his eye. At that moment, a train whistle echoed in the distance. PJ turned, his torch lighting up Scott's face. Instinctively, Scott turned his head away. Seeing his reaction, PJ pointed it back at his feet.

'Somethin' really weird's goin' on here, Scott, and I'll get to the bottom of it, but in the meantime, let's catch up on the others, that was the nine o'clock train; we'd better hurry before the free rides are gone.' No longer alone, PJ switched off the torch and headed south. With darkness for cover, Scott smiled, thinking more conversation would help distract PJ from the bench incident.

'Are you sure we're going the right way, PJ?' Scott played dumb, for something to say. He knew every nook and cranny of the cemetery and could walk it blindfolded without fear, day or night. The town too. He'd often impressed Gerry with his knowledge of Tallant as it was when Gerry was young.

'Sure we are, we can't get lost; I've been here before. I'm guessing the guys will meet us there. I was half thinkin' they might have been watching us to scare us or somethin'. I'm still half expecting them to jump out from the dark any minute, knowing Cartwright.'

Scott knew they were alone. The cemetery was empty now apart from the dead. Nearing the southern gate, he became uneasy. They were about to pass his house, just inside the boundary walls. He desperately hoped his mother had taken off for the evening. Meeting his mother in company was an absolute nightmare scenario. These encounters had never gone down well in the past. But on closer inspection, the light seemed to be off. Usually a reliable sign that she'd left for the evening although, sometimes, she would be sitting alone in the dark when he got in. Nothing was ever said. Not even raising her head as he passed to enter his bedroom. That and the stink of what she'd been drinking, which Scott detested. He was now within range to tell if she was in there but his chest felt still, no internal hum. She was gone.

PJ pointed at the house as they passed. 'Imagine living in a graveyard. I bet the "M" above the door stands for "Munsters"; bit of a fixer-upper, isn't it?'

'Yeah, weird, I guess,' Scott mumbled, relieved as the southern gate came into sight.

'Aw man, don't tell me it's locked?' PJ was referring to the chain Mr Coventry had put in place.

'It's just the main gate that's locked to stop traffic entering, the inner gate is open.'

'How do you know?' As PJ finished the sentence, he put a hand on the inner gate releasing the latch to let it swing open.

'Lucky guess?' Scott shrugged. The street busy with evening traffic earlier was now busy with pedestrians. Mostly groups of teens and couples, all drawn to the lights and sounds of the fairground. First Avenue is the southernmost street in Tallant. It's neglected, aside from those who use it for accessing the cemetery, or people out powerwalking, making the most of the summer evenings. It's lined with derelict boarded-up two-storey buildings, awaiting demolition.

Years back they'd demolished a large zone with the aim of building a water park, but a lack of investors and planning permission had stopped that idea dead in its tracks.

'So, is it just us and your other friends from Trevor's?' Scott asked.

'Nope. Gonna be some girls from school here, too. At least four of 'em!' coughed PJ, trying to clear his throat.

'You okay?' Scott was genuinely concerned; no acting needed this time.

'Why are my neck and throat so sore?'

'I'm not sure how long I'll stick around for, PJ.' Scott felt his mission was complete, PJ being safely through the cemetery. He wasn't sure a new friend was a great idea right now, especially after this evening's events. Probably best that tonight remained a random, one-off encounter.

'Lighten up, man, we just got here! And didn't you just hear me sayin' there'll be girls? Let's see.' PJ started counting on his fingers. 'Amber, Charlotte, Gwen and Nikky; Amber has a thing for Dan, so I think they might try to hit it off, anyone else is fair game.' A note of jealousy in PJ's voice.

The crowd density increased as they approached the gates. Flashing lights, music and the smell of popcorn and cotton candy filled the heavy summer air. In the distance, voices screamed in unison as a roller coaster looped the loop. Couples young and old walked hand in hand, some lucky ones exiting with oversized teddy bears hooked under one arm. Cars stopped next to the entrance dropping off teens in groups like clockwork in motion. Arriving full, leaving empty, until the pickup later that night.

Dan, Gary and Brad sat to the right of the entrance, on a plastic seat used as a bus stop at one point. Dan sat on the backrest with his feet on the bench, posing, the others sat either side. A group of girls passed by, giggling among themselves.

'Hey bitches!' PJ shouted as they got within earshot. Scott stopped behind him.

'Peter ... James, I hardly expected you to show up after the cemetery?' taunted Cartwright slyly as he jumped down and approached them.

'Yeah but ya know what? Nothin' scares me after a night with your mom.' PJ couldn't help himself and was rewarded with a smile from Scott.

'Always the smart-ass, eh James?' Cartwright scowled.

PJ removed his baseball cap, tipped it in front of him and gave an exaggerated bow. Unimpressed, Dan stared at Scott then back to PJ. 'So, who's the newbie?'

'Oh, this is Scott, he took the shortcut through the cemetery with me so I didn't have to go alone like you'd planned.' PJ turned to Scott. 'Scott, this is Dan Cartwright, and Luke, Brad and Gary.'

The other three nodded one by one.

'Ah, the free milkshake boy, right? How did that happen? You and that stupid manager got somethin' goin' on?' Cartwright teased. The guys chuckled behind him.

PJ shook his head at Scott. 'You'll get used to Cartwright's arrogance.'

'Shut it PJ! Do you know who I am?' Cartwright smirked. Scott hesitated as if unsure how to respond. He looked at PJ, then back at Cartwright.

'No, but from what I'm hearing, everyone knows who your mom is, though.'

PJ burst into a fit of laughter. That was the last response he was expecting from the new quiet guy. Even the other guys joined in the merriment. Dan Cartwright was fuming. He turned and gave them daggers, showing his frustration.

The laughing stopped, except for PJ. He slapped Scott on the back as a sign of approval and continued to giggle, testing Cartwright's limit. Dan stepped up close to Scott's face, squaring up to him, eye to eye. Scott didn't move a muscle. He already knew fear, and intimidation. This was neither.

'I hate smart-asses, Scott. When I was younger, my mom taught me to be seen and not heard.'

'Look, Daniel, if this is about your mom again I …' Scott couldn't help himself. Cartwright grabbed Scott's jacket, lifting and pulling him in his direction, his eyes locked on Scott's. Scott's feet didn't move as he stared calmly back at Cartwright.

'I don't think we're gonna get along,' Cartwright said.

Scott clasped his hands around Cartwright's, and began to squeeze, effortlessly. Dan's knuckles turned white from a tighter grip than he was expecting. Scott's demeanour remained emotionless. Colour began to drain from Dan's face. The cool demeanour of the alpha male now became an expression of panic. The metacarpals in both his hands were now at breaking point. Still no reaction from Scott.

Realising in shock that he couldn't take any more pain, Dan released his grip from Scott's jacket and tried to shove him backwards, like it was his choice to do so. Scott didn't budge as he removed his hands from Cartwright's. He placed his aching hands into his pockets, hoping the feeling would return sometime soon.

From one side of Scott's mouth, a grin appeared. 'I'll try not to lose any sleep over it.'

# Chapter 9

The tension between Scott and Cartwright died a quick death with the arrival of a white pickup truck, the green lettering on the side announcing 'U.S. Park Ranger'. Park Ranger James Brennan's hat sat with pride on the dashboard while Buster, a fully grown German Shepherd, took the centre seat between the driver and his passenger. Scott stood close to the wall, distancing himself from PJ and the others, letting Cartwright mingle with his minions. With boredom setting in, he turned away from the group and looked towards the attractions. Tonight's events had taken up more time than he'd expected, and he'd broken one of his rules in the process. He was too involved now and waited for an opportunity to make his exit.

The rear door of the pickup opened. Three girls stepped out brandishing awkward smiles at the guys who'd jumped forward to close the door behind them. The front-seat passenger remained locked into conversation with the ranger, hand signals traded between them as the girl sat and listened to another lecture from her father.

'Is that Daniel Cartwright I see again out there?'

'You know it is, Dad.'

'I thought we talked about this?'

'Yeah Dad, we did!'

Brennan put the truck in park then turned sideways to face his daughter. 'And did we not agree that you'd stay away from him?'

'No Dad, I said he's my friend, and it's not just him and me, anyway, we all meet as a group.'

'You know I don't like that boy or his family.'

'Yeah, you told me, what's so bad about him anyway?' A curious look on her face.

'I just care about you so much, sweetie, and, well, there are things about his family that you don't know, and trust me when I say, I hope you never find out.'

\*\*\*

Amber, Charlotte and Gwen stood in a semi-circle facing the guys. After a quick status update on Instagram, Amber's eyes lifted from the screen to meet Dan Cartwright's. She smiled looking back to her phone, pretending he had competition for her attention.

'Took ya long enough to get here,' said Dan.

'We had to wait for a ride, Nikky's dad wasn't home till late, some animal attack on a hiker or something? He wouldn't say much on the way over,' Amber replied, barely glancing up from her screen.

Scott was still facing the fairground with his hands in his pockets. He turned his head to the side, intrigued by the conversation he'd heard over the loud music and noisy crowd. Obviously Amber Sheridan was to the girls what Dan Cartwright was to the boys. The unelected ringleader. The loud one who called the shots, and the others followed. With her long black hair and brown eyes, she got her sallow skin and good looks from her mother's Hispanic side. She wore a grey long-sleeved wool sweater exposing a bellybutton piercing and navy skin-tight jeans.

'Another one?' Cartwright continued the conversation. 'My uncle says people risk their lives going on stupid adventures into Chequamegon-Nicolet, it's not for amateurs. Too much weird stuff with people seeing scary shit, it's all reported to his office almost weekly.'

'Maybe your mom should just stay at home then?' PJ jumped in. He stood next to Cartwright, smiling as he spoke, waiting for a reaction from the girls. Amber flew to Cartwright's defence, seeing PJ as little more than an annoyance.

'What's the matter, PJ, jealous his mom's out of your league? Speaking of which, where's your date for tonight? Oh, how silly of me, I forgot! Rebecca shot you down, more than once if I recall. Even nerds don't want you. And what the hell happened to your neck, by the way?'

The group laughed. Cartwright leered at Amber and nodded in approval. Brad sucker- punched him below the ribs, pushing him into Gary, who shoved him back while grabbing the baseball cap from his head.

'C'mon guys, it's not funny, give it back!'

They tossed the cap back and forth between them, as PJ tried to grab it. Cartwright shook his head.

'Fetch, PJ!' Without looking, Gary threw the cap over his shoulder into the air towards the boundary wall. Scott still stood with his back to the group. The others laughed while PJ ran to try catch it. With his gaze not leaving the attractions behind the wall in front, Scott removed his right hand from his jacket pocket. Timing it to perfection, he held it up, for the cap to land in his grip. He said nothing and remained still.

PJ stalled a moment in confusion. 'How the hell? How'd you do that? I mean, how'd you know it was gonna land right there? Or that they even threw it in the first place?'

'Lucky guess,' replied Scott, blandly. He turned to hand the cap back to PJ, who slapped it back on his head in its usual backwards style.

'The animal attack that the girl mentioned, did this happen today or yesterday?' Scott enquired, trying to sound nonchalant.

'Wow! Firstly, Scott, what the fuck with the baseball cap? Secondly, how the hell could you have heard what they said from over here?' said PJ, baffled. Amber was deep in conversation with Cartwright until she peeked over his shoulder; something catching her attention. And she wasn't the only one. Charlotte and Gwen noticed it too. They both looked at Amber, as if to say, do you see what we're seeing? Gwen waggled her eyebrows. PJ was speaking to someone. Someone new. Someone hot.

'Em, Dan, who's your new friend? Aren't you gonna introduce us?' Amber gestured in PJ's direction. Cartwright didn't need to turn around. He knew who she was talking about. A look of frustration showing in his demeanour. All eyes were on the new guy and Cartwright couldn't stand it. Another rooster in the hen house. Cartwright realised which way the wind was now blowing and had to change tact.

'That's just Scott, he hangs out from time to time … so you guys all set for the fair?' Dan changed the subject, trying desperately to get Amber's attention back. As much as she liked him, he didn't remember her looking at him that way.

'Isn't he gonna come over and say hi?' said Charlotte.

'Oh, he's from out of town, just here for the night, think he goes home tomorrow,' Dan lied, letting them know Scott was just a temporary attraction.

'Yeah but he must wanna say hi, though, even if he has to leave so soon?' Gwen shared Charlotte's concern about not getting to know this new hot guy.

'Yeah … sure, okay.' Cartwright approached PJ and Scott, leaving the girls whispering to each other. Gary and Luke were now invisible to them, with Scott getting their full attention.

'Scott my old pal,' Cartwright put his arm behind Scott's back onto his shoulder, pulling him so their shoulders were now touching, knowing the girls were watching, but gripping his shoulder tightly. 'Why not come say hi to the girls, I told them we're old friends, it's nice to be nice, right?' he said, with a fake smile.

Scott glanced over, seeing all three girls smiling back at him; one of them waved awkwardly and tittered. He didn't return the smile. PJ looked back and forth from Scott to the girls, then back to Scott, and shook his head in bewilderment.

'Sure thing "ole pal"; by the way, how are your hands holding up?' said Scott.

The fake smile vanished in an instant. Cartwright looked back at the girls. To his dismay, all eyes were still on Scott. He leaned in close and hissed, 'Just play nice, Scott, and remember –Amber is mine.' Cartwright released his grip on Scott's shoulder and returned to the group, leaving Scott alone with PJ.

'Could you please tell me what the hell is going on?' PJ asked.

'What do you mean?' replied Scott.

'Those girls over there are totally into you!'

'So?' Scott hadn't the slightest interest.

'"So"? Get your ass over there and piss Cartwright off big time by moving in on Amber Sheridan. Even as we speak, she's staring over here, and it's not at me. Unfortunately.'

'I'm not interested, PJ, but I'll go say hi, then I'm outta here.'

'Holy shit, Scott, are you insane? If girls were looking at me like that, I'd …'

'Scott! Come over and say hi to the girls,' shouted Cartwright.

'Let's get this over with,' said Scott as he headed for the group, leaving PJ alone. PJ scratched his head. 'I think I'm gonna go insane?'.

Scott shouted back over his shoulder, 'You're far from insane, my friend!'

PJ ran to catch up. 'What is it with your ears, man? You hear the impossible.'

Back at the group Dan Cartwright stood between Scott and the girls.

'Girls, this is Scott.' All three eyed him up and down.

'Scott, this is Charlotte, Gwen and Amber,' Cartwright continued, over-exaggerating the last name. Scott didn't care, his lack of interest visible on his face.

'Nice to meet you, guys, have fun tonight, I gotta go.'

The girls exchanged a glance of confusion. Cartwright chimed in, delighted with Scott's decision. 'Sure thing, we'll catch up soon, Scott.'

PJ's jaw almost hit the floor. He was dumbfounded but Scott's mind was made up. As he moved to leave, the front passenger door of the ranger's truck opened.

'Eleven o'clock, Nikky I mean it, big day tomorrow, your grandma's coming, remember? Don't have me back here looking for you.'

The entire group heard James Brennan's stern words, making Nikky regret her timing. 'Okay Dad! I get the message.' She rolled her eyes at her friends as she stepped out to join them. Buster took her seat, sticking his head out the window, his attention fixated on the group. He started to growl.

'Buster, what is it, boy?' said the ranger, noticing Dan Cartwright. He closed the window and reached across to pet the dog. 'Yeah, boy it's okay, I don't like him either.'

With long blonde hair in a high ponytail and deep-blue eyes, Nikky stood out a solid mile from the others. She wore a white T-shirt and spandex pants that stopped at her ankles above a pair of Adidas sneakers. As she approached, she tied a black sweater around her waist by its sleeves. Nikky was the quiet secluded type. Even though she was in a league of her own, she didn't know it, but her friends did. Getting attention wasn't her thing; besides, Amber Sheridan took it instead. Amber was used to getting attention, but she wasn't getting it right now from somebody new. All eyes were on Scott, but Amber was the one who noticed where Scott's eyes were drawn to, and it wasn't her.

Scott was suddenly seeing the world in a different light. Those eyes. He'd seen them before, but where? He watched events unfold in slow motion as she approached. Each step bringing her closer. Each step retrieving a memory. Each step testing his sanity.

He was lost in the moment.

So lost, he could hardly focus.

**Chapter 10**

Nikky Brennan checked a notification on Instagram. Amber had just uploaded a selfie at the fairground gates, getting 21 likes. After adding a like of her own, Nikky noticed the girls had their backs turned to her. Wondering what had their attention, she scanned the group, spotting the usual suspects before checking her phone again. Another glance revealed a new face next to PJ. This new face was staring in her direction. Her blue eyes connected with the stranger's. Behind her, the pickup truck drove off as she joined the group. Girl hugs ensued.

PJ made the introduction. 'Nikky, this is my friend –'

Scott stepped forward, cutting him off mid-sentence, his eyes still fixated on Nikky. 'Scott, Scott Maglace, nice to make your acquaintance.'

Nikky blushed. 'Hi back, I guess,' her simple nod bringing a small smile to his face. 'Hey guys!' she shared to the group. 'Ready for the carnival, Scott?' Nikky broke the ice.

'Scott was just leaving, busy day tomorrow, isn't that right, Scott?' Cartwright seized another opportunity to get rid of this unexpected rival, placing his hand on Scott's shoulder. Scott looked at Cartwright's hand pointedly and Dan dropped it back to his side. 'Actually, maybe I can stay a little longer, it's a nice night, after all, Cartwright,' putting his own hand on Cartwright's shoulder in return.

'Great, the more the merrier,' said Dan sarcastically but pulling his body away from Scott's hand. Gesturing for the group to follow, he turned and started for the entrance. Pleased with his answer, Nikky joined the tail end of the group, leaving Scott and PJ alone, PJ now grinning from ear to ear. 'I thought you had to leave?'

'Change of plans.' A smile escaped from one side of Scott's mouth.

PJ tapped his chest while they followed the group. 'You should listen to me more often, my man, PJ always knows best!'

Scott threw a question to PJ he was sure he already knew the answer to but needed to ask. 'About Dan Cartwright, PJ.'

'What about him?'

'I assume he's related to the Governor?'

'The same, he likes to play on that, too, or haven't you noticed? Why are you asking anyway?'

'No reason, just curious.'

The box office had four separate windows adorned with flashing lights. Cartwright skipped the line and went straight to the door at the back of the security booth. He knocked and waited. When the door opened, he held up his hands while mouthing the 'Ten'. The door closed and reopened a minute later. Cartwright returned with ten red wristbands and handed them out to everyone except Scott and PJ. He waved two wristbands in front of them as if considering his options.

'Best behaviour, boys, my uncle's making an appearance here tonight so don't make me regret this; here …' He threw the wristbands at them and headed for the security checkpoint.

'What a dick.' PJ picked up the wristbands, giving one to Scott. 'C'mon, let's catch up before he tells security we stole them.'

PJ and Scott were the last ones through the checkpoint. A fast-food stall stood between them and the group. Twenty yards past the stall Cartwright stopped next to a map showing the list of attractions.

'Where to first, guys?' he asked, taking the lead as always.

'Hey Dan, two dollars says PJ's first stop is the food stand,' Brad shouted, for everybody to hear. Everyone laughed except Nikky. She stood at the rear, keeping a lookout for PJ and his interesting new friend.

'I'll take that bet,' Gary replied.

'Guys, guys, let's try to be grown-ups in front of the girls,' Cartwright winked at Amber. 'So, on that note, I'll raise it to five bucks his sorry ass goes straight to stuffing his face.'

Nikky watched as Scott grabbed PJ by the arm. 'Get food later, PJ, besides, it might make you puke after the rides.'

'No way, I'll take the risk. Gonna grab some cotton candy, you want some?'

'PJ, trust me, if you leave it till later, I'll buy it for both of us, how about that?' Scott offered.

'Hey, now you're talking my language, it's a deal.' PJ seemed happy with the outcome. A free milkshake earlier and now more freebies. He liked this new kid. Brad and Gary were disappointed with PJ's decision to boycott the food stall, ruining their bet. PJ and Scott caught up to Nikky.

'Hey,' said Scott.

'Hey back,' she smiled.

Cartwright spoke. 'Bum deal, guys. Nobody wins.'

'Wins what? What you guys talking about?' PJ looked confused.

'Never you mind, Peter James,' sneered Cartwright.

'Whatever, man. I say we hit the roller coaster first, it's supposed to be bigger than last year.'

Cartwright wasn't impressed. He was supposed to call the shots and make suggestions, not PJ. But it was too late, PJ's comments got approval from the girls. The majority had spoken. If he objected now, he'd look foolish.

'I second that. C'mon, Dan, let's try get the front seats and leave these losers behind.' Amber grabbed Cartwright's hand and took off. The others followed, Scott, PJ and Nikky at the rear.

'Well, c'mon guys, better follow our glorious leader,' said PJ.

Scott and Nikky made eye contact again and smiled. They strolled on behind, in no hurry to catch up. Scott was first to break the ice this time. 'Who are you really, and what were you before? What did you do, and what did you think?'

'Excuse me?' Nikky looked puzzled.

'It's a line from one of my favourite movies.'

'Oh, I wasn't expecting a question like that!'

'So, what were you expecting?'

'I'm not sure, but not movie quotes. Also, nobody introduces themselves like you did at the gate, not our generation, anyway.'

'Maybe I'm an old head on young shoulders.'

They passed a clown handing out multi-coloured helium balloons to kids.

'That's not a bad thing … oh wait, can I switch sides with you? I hate clowns.' Nikky moved, placing Scott between her and the clown, watching him until he was out of reach.

'You're scared of clowns?' Scott grinned.

'Terrified, don't get me started, a bad experience at my seventh birthday, which I will not be going into right now with you,' she jested.

Scott looked behind them. 'I think you're safe now.'

'Gee thanks, you're my hero, what would I do without you?' she smiled in sarcasm.

'It's been a while since somebody called me that,' he mumbled.

'Really? So tell me, Scott – Maglace? – what does scare you, then? And who else called you their hero?'

'Very good questions, which I will not be going into right now with you,' he smirked; like for like.

'Touché, Scott, touché.'

'Quid pro quo, Nikky, quid pro quo.'

'What does that mean?

'It means something for something, or question for question in our case.'

'Okay, I see where this is going. I get to go first.' She stopped walking and shifted to face him.

'Knock yourself out.'

'So, where are you from?'

'Not far from here.'

'My turn: why do I feel like I've met you before? Your eyes look so familiar … from … long ago.'

'Well, how come I've never seen you about town? Or at school? Or maybe we've met in a previous life?'

'Perhaps.' A target stall had grabbed his attention.

'Sounds like that person was special to you?' Nikky tested the waters to see if the mysterious person she reminded him of was still a part of his life.

Further ahead, PJ noticed Scott and Nikky lagging behind. There was now enough distance between them for his plan to hatch. Looking back at the food stall he spoke to himself. 'Now's my chance.' He would get two lots of candy, one right now, and one later from Scott.

'That was a long time ago.' Scott rubbed the silver bracelet under his leather jacket.

'I guess people come and go in our lives all the time, some leave a bigger hole than others ... I know how that feels. I lost my mom a few years back.'

'Sorry to hear that, Nikky.'

'Thanks. Anyway, it's just me my dad and brother, and occasionally my grandma, but that's only once or twice a year.' Nikky's phone vibrated. Amber again.

*'Well? What have you found out? Need gossip! Meet ya in the restroom in two xx'*

Nikky looked up to see Amber looking back with her phone in hand. 'Scott, can we continue this when I get back? Girl stuff.'

'Sure thing – just one more question?'

Nikky spun back to face him. 'Go for it.'

'Do you prefer teddy bears or goldfish?'

'What?' In confusion, she started to walk away. Five steps later she turned back to face him.

'Teddy bears.' She reached into her pocket and took out a keyring with a rabbit's foot and tossed it at him. 'For luck.' She winked.

# Chapter 11

'Bless me, Father, for I have sinned, it's been … well, a hell of a long time since my last confession.'

Amdis sat in the darkened confessional box tucked away in the shadows at the rear of the Priory Catholic church on Main Street. Apart from the priest who was waiting opposite, the church was now empty, the regular attendees gone home for the night. Only the poor or desperate ventured after dark, seeking forgiveness, refuge, or both.

Father O'Malley sat sideways in his seat with his back to the wall, his face and white collar barely visible in the light above his head. Fumbling with a set of rosary beads on his lap, he slid open the hatch to see a blonde woman in her mid-thirties, resting her head in her hands. The priest spoke in a deep voice that sounded tired and scripted after years of repertoire.

'The main understanding is,' he said, 'that you made a conscious intention to show up here today; being a sinner we all carry sins with us, they weigh us down until the weight becomes too much of a hindrance. Confessing our sins to God relieves us of that burden.'

'Yes, Father, it's true,' she replied. 'I made an effort to show up, but my sins are too great to be forgiven.' She leaned forward, resting her elbows on the wooden ledge, with interlocked fingers covering her face.

'Everyone sins, my child. As the old saying goes, heaven would be empty if God didn't forgive us our sins, so you're not unique.' He glanced to his right, seeing only the lower part of her face through the mesh.

'I understand, Father, but I'm more *unique* than you realise.'

He remained silent, partially from boredom, and partially because he'd heard this speech countless times in the past. Everyone thinks they're unique, and that their sins are worse than the last occupier of the box. He readied his usual response and awaited his cue.

'The moment you asked for absolution, God forgave you. Now do your part and leave your guilt behind.'

'I didn't show up here for forgiveness, Father, and I've no guilt for what I've done, now or in the past.'

He stopped fumbling with the beads, his look of confusion lost in the dark. 'Forgive me, but why have you come here then?'

'I've killed people, Father, many people, over a long period … without remorse.'

Father O'Malley dropped his rosary beads. This was not the usual run-of-the mill parishioner's cry for help. 'You have … killed people?' he uttered, now giving her his full attention.

'Yes Father, but not in the last seventy years. I've lost count of the many innocents I've killed before that.'

'Seventy years? But you're only in your thirties?' He entertained her statement, now contemplating a mental illness and feeling some relief.

'Let's see – I was born in the year 1082 so add another 900 years onto that figure, Father, and by the way, I don't mean to brag, but I look good for someone who's over 900 years old, if I do say so myself. My powers of seduction would be wasted on you nonetheless.'

'I think we may need to get you some help, my child, but don't worry, everything will be okay in time. Tell me, are you a patient of a doctor here in Tallant?' He felt sorry for her, now certain that his initial diagnosis was correct.

In the little light available between them he suddenly noticed something peculiar. Inside her open mouth, white fangs hung from her top row of teeth in place of incisors. Her tongue moved from one to the other, tipping the ends of each as if testing their sharpness.

'Thank you, Father, but I'm not the one who needs help ... you are.'

**Chapter 12**

After Nikky had left for her gossip update, Scott made his way back to the target stall he'd noticed earlier. A large trailer adorned with stars and stripes and flashing lights, it had six bays calculated to grab the attention of the weak-minded who were willing to part with their dollars. Three bays held dart boards, the remaining three were decorated with giant playing cards stapled to a green felt background wall. Small teddy bears and stuffed goldfish hung along the rooftop as runner-up prizes; the giant ones sat underneath on the floor covered in see-through plastic for the winning contestants with a keen eye.

On his approach, Scott noticed four kids trying their luck throwing darts at two boards at the right side of the stall. One bay remained vacant. The attendant, wearing a tight yellow T-shirt with a name tag, 'Cindy', stood watching each shot, pretending to feel the kids' pain as they lost another two dollars. . Scott waited a moment to watch another feeble attempt. Two darts hit the board, with the last falling to the ground below.

'Ouch! So close this time, boys! How about another three darts? Next one could be your lucky shot!' Cindy cried enthusiastically as she put their last two dollars into her cash belt. The boys searched their pockets but came up empty-handed.

'Out of cash? That's too bad! Go ask your parents for more! Move along now, guys, and let someone with money take a turn.' Her sympathy lasted as long as their cash flow. Scott stepped forward.

'How much did these kids spend trying to win?'

'Oh, give or take, maybe twenty dollars? But that's the luck of the draw; wanna try your luck?' Cindy replied. 'Win a teddy bear for that special someone?'

Scott scanned the dart boards. Without looking in her direction, he pulled two dollars from his pocket and held them out to her.

'Thank you, sir, and the very best of luck!' Taking his two dollars, she placed three darts on the bench between them. The four unlucky kids waited to watch his efforts. Scott picked up a dart, threw it into the air and caught it, testing its weight and balance. Holding it in his right hand in front of his face, he prepared for his shot. He stared at Cindy who stared back, waiting for failure and another two dollars.

Without lifting his eyes from hers, he flung the dart in one swift movement without blinking. Without looking at the target behind her, Cindy began her scripted speech.

'Hard luck, my friend, two darts left …?' She looked at the board mid-sentence. The dart was buried deep into the centre ring of the board.

'Bullseye!' the kids cheered in unison.

'How did you …? But you – you weren't even looking?' Frowning, Cindy reached under the plastic to grab a giant blue bear. Scott took it and tore off the plastic cover, tossing it into a nearby rubbish bin. Putting the bear under his arm, he turned to walk away until one of the awestruck kids tugged at his arm.

'Hey mister, you still have two darts left!'

Scott turned and picked up the remaining darts and threw them in rapid succession at the board without taking his eyes from the kids, resulting in another loud cheer. Two more bullseyes. 'Let the kids have another go,' he said, winking at his audience of four as he walked away.

Two stalls back, PJ stared wide-eyed in amazement at what he'd just witnessed.

## Chapter 13

With the giant teddy bear under his arm, Scott made his way past the house of mirrors towards the roller coaster. PJ appeared from behind, out of breath, his face flushed and still eating his ice-cream cone.

'Hey, hold up!' he said between breaths.

'I thought you were with the others?'

'Em, yeah I was, I just had to go back and check on something.' PJ wiped his mouth with his sleeve.

'I see you went back to the food stand,' Scott smiled.

'Forget about the food stand, Scott. I wanna know more about the target stall.'

'What do you mean? I got lucky,' said Scott, showing him the oversized bear.

'Three bullseyes in a row? That's more that luck my friend,' PJ brandished a look of suspicion in Scott's direction.

'I've got a dart board at home,' Scott lied.

'No, Scott, no you don't, that isn't gonna wash with me. I was watching the whole time. Nobody gets three bullseyes not looking at the board, that's impossible.'

***

Charlotte, Gwen, Amber and Nikky made their way back from the restroom.

'So, basically, nothing happened, and you don't know Jack about him?' Amber quizzed Nikky, sounding relieved. If Scott wasn't interested in her, she didn't want Nikky to have him.

'We just started talking then I got your message. He seems nice, though, not what I expected,' Nikky commented.

'What did you expect?' said Amber.

'You know how hot guys are always so big into themselves; he seems to be respectful or something.'

The four girls stopped at the roller coaster. Over Nikky's shoulder, Amber saw Scott and PJ approaching but continued listening to Nikky with an artificial smile, glancing between her and the teddy bear that was getting closer. She guessed who it was for, and it wasn't for her.

Before they arrived back at the group, Scott looked at PJ, 'Later PJ, I promise, now's not a good time, okay?'

'I'll hold you to that,' PJ stabbed a finger into his chest.

Amber seized an opportunity for attention. She stepped towards Scott with her arms outstretched for the bear, pushing Nikky aside. 'Aw Scott, you shouldn't have, that's so nice of you! How did you win it?'

'I was just thinking the same thing, Scott. It must be difficult to win a bear … or two … or three, even?' added PJ suspiciously. Nikky spun about and began to blush, realising Scott had meant what he'd said before she'd left him.

'Afraid not, Amber, I promised this one to Nikky.' Scott held the bear in Nikky's direction. She took the bear and held it up for inspection, grinning.

'Wow, thanks, Scott!'

'I'm gonna be sick! Get a room you two,' said Amber, deflecting the rejection.

The roller coaster thundered by, getting louder on approach and decreasing as it rounded the bend. Cartwright was standing halfway up the queue with Luke, Brad and Gary.

'Cartwright's held our place in the line; c'mon guys, hurry up!' PJ took the lead with the others following.

'Actually, PJ, I'm going to sit this one out, I'll wait here.' Scott put his hands back in his pockets, now free of the bear. PJ gave a thumbs up and followed the girls. Nikky stopped and glanced back to Scott.

'Don't let me stop you from having fun, I've been on hundreds of these things, the novelty wears off after a while,' Scott said, gesturing for her to go ahead.

'I think you're right; I'll give it a miss too. I doubt that they'd allow bears on.' She winked at Scott, glad to have another few moments alone to chat. 'You wanna go for a walk instead?'

'Sure, where to?'

'Anywhere, let's see what this place has to offer.' They distanced themselves from the roller coaster and headed further into the park. With her bear tucked under her left arm, Nikky started the conversation this time.

'So, have you got brothers and sisters or are you an only child?'

'It's just me and my mom. My father's dead. You?'

'I've a younger brother, it's mostly just the three of us at home, unless my grandma visits, which is tomorrow, actually. We live in Eastbrook, you know it?'

'Same place as PJ, nice place,' he offered.

'Dan Cartwright lives there too; we all meet up after school most days.'

Scott didn't want to hear anything about Dan Cartwright. He knew enough, more than she did. He steered the conversation away from that topic.

'So, tell me something else about you, all I know is that you're frightened of clowns.'

'Isn't that enough information for a girl to divulge to a stranger?'

'I saved your life from your last clown encounter, that must count for something? Or does that still make me a stranger in your eyes?'

'That depends, what else can you save me from, Scott?'

He smiled. 'Quite a lot but clowns are my specialty. I have my limits, though, I can't protect you from everything, much as I'd like to.'

'What's your weakness? What can the brave clown killer not protect me from?'

Scott stopped next to a vending machine before answering. 'Time … you want a soda?' he reached into his pocket for change before she could respond.

Nikky looked confused but replied, 'Sure, thanks.'

Scott fed the machine some coins and retrieved two cans from the drawer below. He cracked them open one at a time, handing one to Nikky, easing her one-armed dilemma holding the bear.

'How thoughtful, thanks.' She raised the can in his direction. He tapped it with his own.
'Here's lookin' at you, kid,' he said, before taking a sip. As he raised his arm to drink, she noticed something flash silver on his right wrist.

'I like your bracelet.'

'Thanks, a gift from an old friend,' he said uncomfortably.

'You know what scares me, but you never told me what you're afraid of?' she asked, changing the subject on seeing his reaction to her bracelet comment.

'There's a famous saying,' Scott said, '"We can easily forgive a child who's afraid of the dark, the real tragedy of life is when men are afraid of the light." I always liked that quote.'

She stopped walking and turned to look at him. He stopped and looked back.

'You've sidestepped another question … but you have a way with words, Scott, I'll give you that.'

Their stroll continued, past a coffee dock and close to the boundary wall. Music and screams faded away into their new surroundings. In the shadows near the wall was the funfair graveyard, where the remains of broken carousel horses, cracked Ferris-wheel roof umbrellas and overturned dodgems whose purpose was no longer to please the crowds but to be gutted for spare parts like an organ donor lay scattered. Some were half covered in plastic, while others were left some to rust in the elements, victims of time, reminding Scott of Shakespeare's 'Well, we were born to die'. Most of us anyway, he thought.

A tent sat in solitude at the end of the pathway, a small wooden sign hanging above a draped doorway. The words 'Fortune Teller' were carved in a 'ye olde English' font. A triquetra l embroidered into the drapes could be pulled apart into two separate pieces that re-joined when closed to form the symbol of the holy Trinity in pagan and witchcraft beliefs. Flickering torches burned at the entrance.

'I guess this is the end of the road – oh, you want a coffee?' Scott suggested, nodding towards the coffee dock.

'Nope. Follow me, this should be fun!' Nikky had just spotted the tent. She turned to face him as she walked backwards towards.

'You ever been to a fortune teller before, Scott?'

He paused before answering. 'Yes, but it's been a while; have you?'

'Just once, this time last year. My grandma knows a lady in town who reads tea leaves. Even my dad joins in for fun. She doesn't charge, but we still pay her. My grandma likes it. Do you believe in that kind of thing?'

'You'd be amazed at what I believe in, Nikky, but fortune tellers are not one of them.'

'Has anyone ever told you that you're very mysterious, Scott?' she twinkled.

'I play my cards close to my chest until you get to know me well enough to learn my deep dark secrets.' He winked with half a smile, hoping she wouldn't dig any deeper right now.

They were standing before the flaming torches.

'Deep dark secrets, again with the mystery. You know how to keep a girl on the edge of her seat, Scott. I must warn you, number one, I like a challenge, and two, I don't give up easily, oh and three, I don't scare easily, either!'

'Apart from the clown thing? I'll keep that in mind.'

The occupant of the tent gawked fearfully at the black vase on the shelf next to her, listening to the sound of voices outside. Her warning system had been triggered. The single sunflower that had been in full bloom and perfect health a moment ago had shrivelled and died before her eyes.

## Chapter 14

Carol let out a slow breath as her heart slammed against her ribcage. Never in her fifteen years of practising Wicca had she felt this scared. But she steeled herself, telling herself that she was ready for this moment, regardless. She was a thin middle-aged brunette with dark eyes ringed by dark makeup, and wore a purple gown adorned with pagan symbols. Under a matching headscarf, her earrings mirrored the symbol embroidered out front. She was sitting behind a small circular table covered by a red cloth that touched the floor.

A deck of tarot cards sat next to a crystal ball and a black candle threw shadows onto the canvas behind her. Two all-weather folding chairs faced the table, waiting to be occupied. A shelf held a variety of spell books and ingredients, along with a vase supporting a dead sunflower. She watched a hand come inside to grab the cloth door and pull it apart before two figures entered. The moment she feared had arrived and she held her breath. The candle flickered as she stood to see two teenagers. One face was familiar. The other …

'Carol, is that you?' Nikky spoke with surprise in her voice after her eyes adjusted to the candlelight.

'Nikky?' Carol exclaimed in relief.

'I was just talking about you! I had no idea you were doing this again like last year!'

'It helps pay the bills, you know; say, how's your grandma? I haven't heard from her in a while, when is she coming back to Tallant?' Carol almost whispered now, avoiding eye contact with Scott.

'Believe it or not, she arrives tomorrow.'

'That's nice, I must drop over and say hi. We got a fresh batch of her favourite flowers in today at the shop. Her order hasn't changed all these years. Sunflowers with a single purple tulip for the cemetery.'

'Really? I didn't know that.' Nikky sounded surprised.

'She never told you her favourite flower?'

'No, I mean I didn't know she visits the cemetery; I didn't think we had family buried there. Hey, this is my friend Scott, by the way.'

Scott didn't say a word, he nodded and kept his hands in the pockets of his leather jacket. He scanned his surroundings, paying special attention to the dead sunflower on his right.

Carol had to drag her eyes from Nikky to try to look at Scott. She instantly regretted the decision. When her eyes met his, they pierced his soul. Except where one's soul might be found, there was nothing. Lifeless, like a doll's eyes. She was used to reading people, but not like this.

Scott stared back, unblinking, for to her what seemed like an eternity.

'Hello, Carol, I think your sunflower needs a little water,' he said, breaking the silence.

'I think my sunflower needs a little sunlight, in fact, that's what this tent needs, large doses of sunlight.' Carol's voice quivered. 'Thanks for your concern but I think my sunflower is … dead. Meaning it's beyond help.'

Scott dropped his eyes to the floor and smiled before looking back at her.

'You two are acting like you know each other, did I miss something?' Nikky asked.

'I can safely say I've never met this lady, but I have met people like her in my time. What can I say, Nikky, witches leave a bad taste in my mouth.' He reached out his hand to the dead sunflower and flicked it with his index finger. Nikky didn't notice his strange smile, but Carol did.

'Carol is very good at what she does, I can guarantee that. No need for insults!' Nikky smiled apologetically at Carol, who was still watching Scott. 'Perhaps you haven't been to the right fortune teller?' Nikky added, as she turned to Scott.

'Perhaps.' He smiled at her, then back to Carol.

Carol looked at Nikky with an artificial smile as she sat back down, gesturing for them to do the same. 'Shall we get started then?'

They sat opposite Carol, with the teddy bear between them.

'Let me go first Scott, I'm dying to see what my future holds.' Nikky sat forward with her palms facing upwards on the table. Scott also moved closer, his eyes not leaving Carol's.

Nervously, Carol tried to sit back, causing the black candle to topple from the table.

Without taking his eyes from hers, Scott's hand shot out, catching the candle before it fell, with the flame still alight. He placed it back on the table.

'Careful, you don't want to play with fire, Carol, you might get burnt.'

'Nice catch,' Nikky observed.

Carol shifted uneasily in her seat but reached out to take Nikky's hands in hers and stared into her palms.

'No "cross my palm with silver"?' Scott interrupted.

'What do you mean?' Nikky looked confused.

'In the old days it was customary for a fortune teller to ask the person getting the reading to cross their palm with silver, as a donation instead of payment.'

Carol hit back with a history lesson of her own. 'Actually, Scott, the individual getting the psychic reading had to literally make the religious sign of the cross with a coin, which was then placed on the fortune teller's palm. This made certain that the fortune teller was not connected with Satan, and the deceiver could not be present at the reading. There's nothing worse than deceit, Scott, wouldn't you agree? But to keep with ancient tradition, perhaps you'd like me to make the sign of the cross with you?' Carol ended, feeling courageous now.

'Wait, I remember.' Scott sat back into his chair. 'That's what happened last time I saw a fortune teller; it's coming back to me now. She vanished not long after that, never to be seen again, I guess my donation wasn't good enough?'

'Okay, can I just get my reading now? You two are freaking me out.' Nikky laughed. Carol reluctantly closed her eyes. Not watching Scott's every move bothered her. She didn't trust him, but he didn't mind that; the feeling was mutual. He observed everything. Every element of his surroundings, every hand movement she made. He hung on every word she said and was ready for anything.

'I see your past,' Carol intoned. 'You've had loss and pain. Your mother's loss hit you more than people think. You hide your tears, but they still fall. She says not to worry, her stars will guide you in darkness back to safety.'

Nikky opened her mouth at what she'd just heard. Scott rolled his eyes. As he'd expected, this was no genuine 'fortune teller'.

'I see your future and your destiny, I see love like no other, I see an unusually long life for you, I see a proud grandmother who doesn't worry because she knows you're safe. She's slightly jealous; I'm not sure why. I see happiness, but there will be more death in your family,' Carol concluded.

'My grandma?' Nikky interrupted.

Carol dropped Nikky's hands and opened her eyes at the same time. She gave Nikky a concerned look before glancing at Scott, who was losing interest by the second. Carol faked another smile then lied through her teeth.

'Yes, she is elderly but a while away from death yet, but don't forget, Nikky, we were born to die,' Carol added.

'Not all of us.' Scott said abruptly.

Carol looked at him with contempt. 'Indeed.'

Nikky didn't notice this exchange, still lost in thought about her grandmother. 'I know it's expected at her age but still, I want as much time as possible before that time comes.'

Scott turned to Nikky again. 'Believe me – make the most of it; *carpe diem,* as they say. Cherish every moment because it will never come again.' Scott spoke sincerely, more sincere than he had been since entering the tent.

'I intend to, life is precious,' Nikky agreed, sitting back in her seat. 'Your turn,' she gestured for Scott to put his hands on the table. to Carol's dismay.

'If you insist.' He sat forward placing his hands where Nikky's had been. He smiled again at Carol and shook his head as if in doubt. 'Okay Carol, make a believer out of me.' A cocky grin on his face.

She hesitated. Nikky watched in expectation to hear about Scott's past or, more importantly, his future. Carol readied herself and cautiously took his cold hands in hers. But she didn't just hold them, her hands clasped around his and locked in place like holding an electric cable, sending her into an unexpected trance. The candle next to them burst into a bright spherical light hovering above the wax that was now shrinking from the heat. Pools of black liquid expanded outwards onto the tablecloth. A cold breeze circled the tent shaking the canvas violently. Carol's eyes rolled back in her head exposing the white of her eyes. The vase containing the dead sunflower shattered, sending shards of glass in all directions.

Nikky screamed, covering her face with her hands. She pushed her chair backwards, distancing herself, and was now almost behind Scott. Scott was confused but also intrigued. This was a first for him as well. He switched from watching the flaming fireball back to Carol, fascinated to see what would happen next. Only now was he entertained. Flashes of intense imagery began to appear inside the crystal ball. Carol jolted in her chair as each new image revealed itself before Scott's eyes. Through her mind's eye she shared the visions with him, responding to each one with a look of terror. Silent tears streamed from her eyes. The visions varied from place and time; from centuries ago to almost present day. The back of horse-drawn carriages lit up by candlelight on cobblestone streets, when men wore top hats and carried canes. Bodies ripped apart in alleyways. A high-rise apartment block overlooking a city skyline at night where a lifeless body fell to the floor before an outstretched hand holding a blood-soaked heart. Sailors' bodies drained of blood and carelessly tossed over the side of a ship into the Mediterranean. A mouth overflowing with blood dripping onto the roof of a dwelling in Paris as church bells rang out; a female body left unrecognisable. A small village smoking in ruins on the foothills of a mountain, bodies strewn across the streets. Men, women and children, no discrimination. A never-ending thirst. Cruelty beyond belief.

For Carol, the final scene was more personal than the rest. Scott was on his knees, his lips bloody, surrounded by trees. A woman lay draped across his arms as he stared blankly into the night sky. She had blonde hair with pink ribbons, but her face was familiar. Carol knew her. Scott's head snapped back. He scanned his surroundings, as if being hunted or disturbed, setting his gaze on a figure who was pointing a gun in his direction. Three shots echoed through the forest.

In the tent, the smile had disappeared from Scott's face. A face smiled in darkness, almost demonic. Red eyes glaring from the crystal ball. Scott jumped to his feet, ripping his hands from Carol's grip and knocking his chair to the floor behind him. The fireball gave one final flash of light before the tent became dark and silent. Nikky opened her eyes. She fumbled inside her pocket for her phone and activated the torch. The light found Carol on the floor with her hands by her sides. Her head was slumped forward between her legs. A moment later, she spoke in a calm voice as if talking to herself. 'Stay away or we all die, stay away or we all die, the spell was cast, the spell has faded, the spell will be cast again.'

'Carol? Are you okay?'

Upon hearing her name, Carol began to scream uncontrollably, causing Nikky to jump and hold her hand to her mouth. A hand touched Nikky's shoulder causing her to jump again but it was Scott. She pointed the torch in his direction. He quickly reached out and deflected the light, aiming it back at Carol, who was now moaning from the floor behind the table.

'I think we should go.' He spoke loudly above the moans.

'But what about Carol?'

Scott pulled the canvas aside waiting for Nikky to leave ahead of him as she picked up the teddy bear. 'I'm sure she'll be fine, I think it's part of the show, you know, for dramatic emphasis.' Scott didn't even believe himself but hoped it would alleviate her concern. He dropped the canvas behind him muffling Carol's moans that continued as they headed back towards the coffee dock.

'I'm impressed, you don't get that kind of experience with just any fortune teller,' he remarked, hoping to make light of what they had just experienced.

'Do you think they were some kind of special effects?' Nikky mused.

'I've seen it before. But tell me, what did *you* see?' Scott queried.

'Not much and to tell the truth I'm glad I kept my eyes closed.'

'Didn't you tell me a while back that you don't scare easily?' he smiled, tongue in cheek.
She stopped walking. He smiled again and waited for her reaction to the bait, stopping just ahead of her.

'Hang on a second, Scott, I didn't expect anything like that to happen … whatever that was. And so much for your reading. I wanted to hear about your past and your future, all I'm left with is a blur, bits of glass in my hair and those horrible screams.'

Scott was relieved. She apparently hadn't shared the experience that he and Carol had simultaneously or see what they'd seen. 'Okay, so let me get this straight, I can scare you, but not too much, is that right?'

'Yes ... no ... well, maybe? I dunno, I like little surprises instead of being terrified, think you can manage that?'

Scott looked to the tent behind her. The smile had left his face. He took in a deep breath and exhaled slowly. 'How would you manage both at the same time?' he asked, seriously.

'What do you mean?' she said as they resumed walking.

'Some things are harder to say out loud than others.' Scott looked down at his feet.

'Everyone has skeletons in their closet, Scott.' Nikky was sympathetic.

'Literally,' Scott said under his breath, again looking back at the tent.

'What?'

'Nothing, don't mind me Nikky, I ramble sometimes.' But something was wrong. For the second time this evening, he got that rare warning sign. The vibrational hum in his chest was back. His usual response, caution and observation, were required again. Tonight was turning out to be more ... interesting than he'd expected. More games to play for personal entertainment. Nikky remained oblivious to his concerns and continued talking.

'Hey look, we're here to have some fun, right? So, let's do just that. And forget … whatever that was. Special effects.'

Scott nodded in agreement.

'What's all the commotion over there?' Nikky pointed towards the main gate, where a small crowd had gathered around a central figure.

## Chapter 15

Waving to the crowd, with an artificial smile and a solid handshake, Governor Patrick S. Cartwright couldn't resist free publicity and a photo opportunity with the public. After all, the fairground belonged to his family; it was a win-win scenario. They would post photos in *The Tallant Journal*, to be handed out at tomorrow's traffic lights, advertising the fairground, and the Governor himself. He mingled amongst the crowd with an air of authority, flanked by two tall men with SECURITY embroidered in gold on the back of their black T-shirts. Not surprisingly, they were also Cartwrights. It was a family affair, and everyone knew who ran this town.

Standing 6' 2", the Governor was fit for a man in his mid-forties. Now thinning on top, his fair hair was brushed to one side in an effort to disguise time catching up on him. He wore a lightly fitted grey suit ironed to perfection. On his right hand, an oversized silver ring adorned his ring finger with the letter 'C' engraved on it. As he strolled through the park, he handed out free tokens for the rides, stopping for the occasional selfie, reminding people to follow him on social media.

'Just another publicity stunt from the Governor, nothing new.' Scott answered Nikky's question with contempt.

'I'm guessing you don't like our Governor, Scott?' a smile escaped her lips.

'He's a Cartwright.'

'Yeah, but so is Dan?'

'Long story, Nikky, for another time, perhaps.'

'Dan and I've been friends for years, but hey, live and let live, I always say.'

'I wish I could do that.' Scott looked uneasy.

'Well, whatever's going on between you and the Cartwrights isn't gonna spoil our fun tonight, right?'

'Right.'

Something caught Nikky's attention over his shoulder. 'Please say you'll go in there with me!' She pointed for his eyes to follow hers to the Passage of Terror, the stereotypical haunted house attraction. A nervous line of teenagers waited their turn to see what horrors lay within. A member of staff dressed as the Grim Reaper patrolled the line, a plastic scythe in one hand, stopping to terrify anyone who reacted to him.

'Are you serious?' Scott laughed.

'Oh, come on! You're not scared, are you?'

He gave her a serious look for the question that followed. 'What if they've got clowns inside?'

'I'll be okay, I have my clown bodyguard to keep me safe.' She tapped his chest and smiled before heading for the house of horrors. He caught up when she reached the rear of the line, just in time for the Grim Reaper to break character and check they were wearing wristbands before admission. At the exit on the right, a wooden door flung open with a loud bang as it hit the guardrail. All eyes looked to the right. The previous group ran screaming through the exit. Some were hysterical, some played it down by laughing it off, trying to look brave.

'Are you sure you and the bear are up for this?' Scott was watching Nikky's reaction.

'Sure, why not? It can't be worse than getting our fortunes told!' They reached the limit for the next group to enter, with Scott and Nikky being last to go inside. The Grim Reaper pulled a chain across behind them before returning to frighten the next group who'd started to gather.

'No going back now, I guess,' Nikky said, holding the bear tightly under her arm. A coffin-shaped door slowly opened to reveal a ghoulish hooded figure that stood in silence, a flickering rusted lantern held at head height. He beckoned them inside. The group cautiously made its way into a small, dark room with an old-fashioned prison cell door to the left, a wrought-iron knocker in its centre. The door to the outside world slammed shut unexpectedly behind them, causing many to leap with giggling fright. All faces vanished as the room filled with blackness, the only light now came from the hooded ghoul's lantern. Nikky moved closer to Scott, almost standing right behind him for cover. Her head brushed against the back of his right shoulder, close enough to smell him. Scott smiled in the darkness, knowing she couldn't see, a difficulty he didn't share. She pulled his hand from his pocket and clasped it, while still using him as a human shield. The ghoul waited to see who would break the silence first. When someone up front started to whisper, he was cut short by the ghoul, who had been waiting for his cue.

'Welcome ... to the *House – of – Horror*!' he shouted in a deep, spooky voice. Some nervous laughter followed. 'For all those souls brave enough to continue, you must follow me through that door and into the deepest and darkest depths of your worst nightmares! I am your guide through hell ... only the bravest may enter, and there are no guarantees for your safe return!' The ghoul momentarily broke character, speaking rapidly in his normal voice.

'For all of those with a heart condition, nervous disposition or pregnant who haven't read the warning signs it is advised that you turn back now and claim a full refund, you must follow my lead at all times and there is strictly no running, you must continue forward and cannot return to the point of entry, you may not hit or touch any of the characters inside who will attempt to frighten you, mobile phones and photography of any kind is not permitted inside.'

With the rehearsed speech over, the ghoul quickly got back into character and resumed his spooky voice. 'Which one of you is brave enough to knock three times on the door of the damned so that we may proceed?' The girl closest to the door volunteered her boyfriend to do the honours. He gave into peer pressure, knowing that all eyes were on him. Taking hold of the knocker, he began to rap as instructed. As the knocker banged down for the third time, a hatch to the left slid open. A hand covered in fake blood reached out to grab the hand that knocked, causing him to pull back into the crowd. Scott felt Nikky's hand grip tighter. The door creaked as it began to open inwards. The group huddled together and pushed forward to see the next room. The floorboards creaked with the shuffle of feet as they followed the ghoul and his lantern.

'Stay near the light for protection! They fear the light!' the ghoul intoned. Being the last ones to leave, Nikky whispered into Scott's ear. 'Are you okay?'

'What do you mean? Did you think I was afraid?'

'No, it's just … your hand, Scott … it's so cold!'

# Chapter 16

Darkness again inside the next room. The theme had morphed into that of a creepy forest. Artificial branches and plastic leaves with vines entwined surrounded the walls. The sound of frogs croaking played on repeat from speakers disguised as rocks. A rickety wooden bridge in the centre of the room was held together with snap hooks and chains. Underneath, a dry-ice machine released white smoke, disguising a fake stream of water.

The bridge shook and creaked when the ghoul stopped halfway across to address the crowd. Further ahead, the pathway divided left and right, each leading to a doorway with a picture and inscription next to it.

On the bridge behind the crowd, Scott came to an abrupt halt, suddenly aware of a familiar smell; one he knew all too well. He tugged on Nikky's hand.

'Something's not right here,' he stated in a low voice, trying not to alert the crowd in front.

'It's okay Scott, I'll keep you safe,' Nikky winked.

He scanned their environment again. 'Just stay close to me, okay?'

'Sure thing,' Nikky smiled, thinking he was adding a little drama of his own.

'Have we lost anyone yet?' The ghoul suddenly spoke. . 'No? That's a pity... for all those souls still breathing, you now have a difficult choice to make. Behind me, hidden in the shadows, lie two doorways, neither of which I can enter. It's for you and you alone to decide which route to take and which is the lesser of two evils. On your right is the lair of the werewolves, and on your left, the crypt of the vampires. Those who survive will meet me on the other side, and those who do not survive … will still meet me on the other side!'

A shy mumble of laughter greeted this dire warning. The group slowly divided, with the majority taking the left path, leaving only three destined for lair of werewolves' lair.

'What'll it be, Nikky, werewolves or vampires?' Scott offered, curious to find the source of the smell.

'I suppose I'll go with werewolves, that okay with you?'

'Good choice, I prefer werewolves too.' From a fake branch above the bridge, an owl watched all who passed beneath. Scott stared at it for a moment, lost in thought. Mechanical and battery-operated or not, the glowing red eyes spooked him. The three girls who'd chosen the werewolf path had already gone, closing the door behind them. The ghoul didn't wait for them to leave before disappearing for a cigarette break through a hidden staff door behind the trees. Scott held the door open for Nikky and, with his other hand gripped in hers, they made their way through the door, letting it slam shut behind them.

A narrow corridor lay ahead. Forest scenes with jagged cliffs adorned the walls on either side; a thin line of cloud partially covered a full moon painted in glow-in --the dark paint. The sound of frogs croaking had been replaced with the distant howling of wolves The howling grew louder, and for Scott the familiar smell intensified. Nikky's hand gripped his tightly; she was genuinely nervous this time. Even with the smell as a distraction, Scott could hear her heart racing. Screams suddenly erupted from the next room at the end of the corridor. Sounds of night from a speaker system don't hold a candle to the unmistakable sound of distress from a real person in a state of panic. The trio of girls ahead ran through the hanging cloth doorway, ignoring the 'no turning back' rule.

'What do you think is in there?' Nikky said.

Scott turned around to face her, standing closer than he'd been all night. He placed his hands on her shoulders and looked into her eyes. Nikky wondered why, with all the chances they'd had to kiss, he would choose this one.

'Look into my eyes,' Scott intoned, emotionless. 'Don't be frightened, just stay right here till I get back.' Before he could take two steps towards the cloth door, Nikky spoke.

'Don't be afraid?! With you leaving me here by myself? The hell you are, I'm going with you!'

Scott couldn't hide his astonishment. 'What the … it didn't work?'

'What didn't work? Your plan to abandon me?'

'No, I'm just trying to protect you, that's all.' Best recovery he could come up with. they advanced into the next room, where Scott already knew something was very wrong. Nikky stumbled over a manikin lying on the floor, but Scott grabbed her before she could fall. Inside this room, plastic boulders covered the walls, giving focus to one large central rock. circled by the pathway. The ceiling was painted black and was covered with tiny lights that sparkled around a full moon, giving the impression of arriving at werewolf central. The cry of wolves was now constant, and the strange smell had reached its peak. A seven-foot-tall model of a werewolf stood upright on the central boulder, outstretched claws exposing a hairy muscular frame, as if celebrating the victory of a kill. The creature seemed to proudly display a human carcass that was propped against the rock below. But the picture didn't look right. Something was terribly wrong.

What was supposed to be a manikin of a human body sitting against the rock had been replaced; Nikky had tripped on that manikin entering the room. Instead, the disfigured body of a fairground worker now sat against the rock. A brown shirt was partly torn open, exposing its chest and abdomen. And the innocent worker and the werewolf had something in common. Someone had switched their heads. On top of the werewolf manikin was the decapitated head of the worker whose body, of a man in his mid-twenties, sat on the floor below. His half-opened eyes revealed bloodshot eyeballs with blood dripping from under his chin into the chest hair of the beast.

Below, the oversized head of the werewolf model was stuck on the lifeless corpse, its mouth was wide open as if frozen mid-roar. Below the corpse's ribcage, a deep laceration was cut into the abdomen, still partially hidden by the brown work shirt. Behind the boulder, another body lay face down, its legs sprawled to one side. Nikky gasped, her other hand still glued to Scott's. The teddy bear fell from under her arm and tumbled forward into a pool of dark blood. She reached for it before Scott put his arm on her shoulder. 'Leave it, I'll get you another one.' Scott rapidly scanned their surroundings, analysing blood spatter and wound types, and the entrances and exits into and out of the room. He was impressed by Nikky's air of calm as she spoke.

'Oh God, I can see why the others ran, it's so lifelike, isn't it?'

Scott shot Nikky a confused look, now realising why she hadn't freaked out. 'Sure, just … don't touch anything, okay?' He squatted next to the body. The rear side of the pin from a name badge could be seen folded back on the shirt. He turned it outwards and read, 'Jason Cartwright – Electrician'.

The marks that were cut deep into the unfortunate Jason's abdomen caught Scott's eye now, it looked like lettering of some sort, only the last three letters visible on the right side with the rest blocked by the tattered shirt.

'*TUS*'

Scott moved the blood-soaked shirt aside and read: '*REDITUS*'. 'Return'. He covered it back the way it was, stood up and returned to Nikky's side.

'I don't think you're supposed to touch the display, Scott?!'

'Yeah, I suppose I'm a true rebel at heart,' Scott replied, still scanning the scene as he made his way to the second body. It was another male worker in navy overalls. Although the body lay face down, its bald head was twisted backwards, staring up at the artificial stars. Without Nikky noticing, Scott touched the fresh blood gathered the corpse's bottom lip. He sniffed then grinned before checking the name badge.

'Joseph Taylor – Health & Safety'

Having seen enough, he returned to Nikky's side. 'Let's get outta here? I think I know a shortcut.' Before reaching the staff door near the bridge, he again scanned the room.

Almost undetectable, hidden high in the corner, the red light of a CCTV camera blinked in unison with the twinkling of the starlight. As they retraced their steps to the corridor, two staff members carrying walkie talkies approached, being led by one of the girls who'd run screaming earlier, still visibly upset. As they passed, one of the staff smiled and shook his head at Scott and Nikky: another wild goose chase by a crazy teenager on a sugar buzz. The girl stopped and pointed to the doorway, refusing to go any closer. Scott waited and watched. A walkie-talkie fell to the floor and bounced off the manikin, scattering the waist clip and battery.

'Oh my God …'

## Chapter 17

Outside the staff exit, Nikky looked at Scott. 'What the hell was that about?'

Scott answered without looking in her direction. 'We should go. I promise I'll tell you later, okay?' Nikky followed Scott around to the entrance to see security swarming from all directions. Those in line were told to disperse and evacuate the area as remaining staff members still in costume ran out through the entrance.

'What the hell is happening here?' Nikky stopped to check her phone. No new messages. Scott didn't answer but continued to scan the area for the rest of the group, spotting PJ's baseball cap at the rear of the crowd that had gathered to rubber-neck at the commotion. He also noticed the Governor approaching, escorted by his minders.

'The guys are over there,' Scott pointed and began to head towards them, hoping that she wouldn't ask again.

'Where did you guys go and what the hell's going on here?' PJ demanded.

'Long story with no pretty ending,' Scott replied, watching the Governor, who stood surrounded by his security team. An arm was placed on his shoulder and words were spoken into his ear as the Governor shook his head in disbelief. A photographer took more random snaps before security blocked his camera lens. This was not good

PR. Nikky went to join the girls, leaving Scott with PJ and the others. Dan Cartwright spoke up self-importantly.

'Something's not right here, guys, I'm gonna find out what's going on, you guys stay here.' He approached the Governor, waving his hand to get his attention as security stepped forward to stop him. A nod of approval allowed him to pass.

Scott spoke to PJ without taking his eyes from the Governor. 'The police are on their way.'

'How do you know?'

'Because I heard the Governor talking.'

'From this distance?' Losing interest he added, 'More importantly, how did things go with you and Nikky?'

'She seems nice.' Scott's focus was still on the Governor.

'That's it? "She seems nice"? That's all you got?'

'Things didn't go quite as planned, PJ, what with the murders.'

'The murders? What murders?'

'You'll find out soon enough.'

Dan Cartwright got no more than a few words from the Governor before being dismissed. The group gathered around, awaiting his report from the powers that be.

'Two bodies were found inside the House of Horror, that's all he knows right now; cops are on the way.'

PJ glared meaningfully at Scott, who pretended not to notice. Nikky looked between Cartwright and Scott before speaking.

'Dead bodies? Actual *dead bodies*?' she quizzed.

'That's all I got from him.'

Nikky moved closer to Scott. 'Scott, that werewolf display was ... just a display, right?' Her eyes were wide. Scott didn't reply, but from the look on his face she already knew the answer. Her hands raised to cover her mouth.

'Oh my God! Now I know why those girls ran screaming, Jesus, that was *real*?'

'Try not to think about it,' Scott replied, realising the futility of his attempt to comfort her.

'Think about what?' Cartwright butted in.

'We saw the bodies inside! They were so … mutilated! I thought they were part of the display.' Nikky's voice quivered.

'You've seen them? We gotta tell my uncle, maybe you can help?' Cartwright said, grabbing Nikky by the arm and pulling her towards to his uncle, with Scott following behind.

'Wait Dan, I –' Before she could finish, they were in front of the Governor.

'Uncle, this is my friend Nikky, she was inside and saw the bodies; maybe she can help.'

The Governor looked at her inquisitively. 'Did you see who they are? Did you see any faces, or name tags?'

'Scott saw more than I did, I was behind him. Anyway, I thought it was fake, just part of the display.' She pointed behind to Scott who stood silently watching the Governor.

The Governor seemed impatient. 'I didn't ask about –' He stopped mid-sentence and stared at the teenager standing behind her. The stare continued, for much longer than he'd intended. He began to twist the silver ring on his finger. Scott let a sly smile escape and calmly returned the stare.

'Hello Governor, to answer your question, I believe one name was Jason Cartwright, if that's any good to you; the other was Joseph Taylor.' Scott's demeanour didn't change, and the Governor didn't respond, but Dan Cartwright did.

'Jason Cartwright? That's my cousin! Holy crap, Jason is *dead*?'

Sirens could be heard in the distance.

'Uncle, maybe Scott has information that could help the police?' Dan said reluctantly. The Governor ignored his nephew, still locked in a staring match with Scott.

'Uncle?' No reply. 'Uncle'?

'No,' the Governor said emphatically, 'you should go home now and leave the police to do their job.' He finally broke the stare to look at Dan.

'But –'

'Go home, Daniel, leave this to the police, and you are to say nothing about this to anyone, is that clear?'

'Sure? But –'

'Now go!' The Governor barked his final order, then called one of his security team over. 'See that my nephew gets home, and I want confirmation the moment he crosses the threshold of his front door, is that understood?' He looked again at Scott. Tension was visible on Governor's face. What would he say to his brother and the rest of the family? What would he tell the press? How would this affect his image and the reputation of the fairground? Rivulets of sweat appeared on his forehead, forcing him to loosen his tie. Two gruesome murders in his town, one against his family. He already had a theory, which he couldn't share with the police. But somebody would pay for this.

He spoke to his security team. 'I need to take a break; I'll talk to the police when I get back.' Making his way under escort to the side of the House of Horror, he stopped outside the restroom and waited before giving another order. 'I need some space to breathe, guys, don't let anyone in behind me, I need a few minutes.' He went inside, closing the door behind him. Security blocked the door and waited.   The fairground was closing, and crowds flocked in droves toward the exit. A black 4x4 waited outside. Security pointed for Dan to get in.

'What about my friends, can I give them a ride too?' Cartwright posed the question to the lead security officer.

'That wasn't what the Governor ordered, we gotta get you home immediately.'

Cartwright shook his head and turned to face the others. 'Gotta go guys, see you tomorrow, I guess.' He looked around, noticing the group was one person short.

'Where's Scott?'

# Chapter 18

In the solitude of the restroom, Governor Cartwright gathered his thoughts. Three small, glazed windows high up flashed from red to blue, signalling a substantial police presence at the House of Horror outside. Inside, a single fluorescent light lit the white tiles that covered the floor, leaving the room in a constant state of shadow, even during the day. Five empty stalls ran along the left side, facing a line of washbasins. Above them, a mirror ran the whole length of the wall to the ceiling, making the room look bigger than it was.

He removed his suit jacket and hung it on a coat hanger next to the hand dryer. His white shirt was soaked with sweat. Facing the mirror, he cupped his palms and filled them with cold water to throw on his face. He repeated the ritual three times before leaning forward on his outstretched hands. Staring into the mirror, he murmured to himself.

'Jason, why Jason? Why did they kill a Cartwright? And here of all places?'

A voice answered from the empty room. 'It was a message.'

The startled Governor spun in shock to be confronted by the teenager he'd noticed earlier, standing at ease with his hands in the pockets of his leather jacket.

'SWEET JESUS!' The Governor bolted backwards and fell to the ground, banging his skull against the sink. Almost instantly, the door flew open, and two flashlights shone through the opening. One beam of light found the Governor on the floor, the other was focused on the back of a head that was turned away facing the far wall.

'Governor? All okay in here?'

The Governor caught his breath, relieved to recognise his security team. 'It's all right, I just lost my footing, I'm fine, but thanks; you can close the door.' The Governor pulled himself to his feet and brushed off his suit. He glanced at Scott. He turned again to face the mirror. The only reflection looking back was his own, the rest of the room was empty. Again, he looked back and forth, confirming what his eyes told him.

'Are we playing peek-a-boo? I do love that game.'

The Governor folded his arms and leant back against the sink. 'So, it's true, no reflection.'

'I've never needed one, but I'm told I'm handsome.'

'Another thing I can add to the dossier on you, Scott Maglace.'

'I'm flattered you know my full name.' Scott gave a half-smile.

'It's in a governor's best interest to know about any and every threat in his hometown. And I know a great deal about you, boy.' The Governor's fear was now replaced with his more usual smugness.

'I'm just an innocent 17-year-old kid living with his mom trying to keep the ... wolf ... from the door, if you get my drift.'

The Governor smiled and shook his head. 'Very brazen of you to kill a member of my family in a crowded fairground, you do realise that you're surrounded by Cartwrights, don't you?'

'First, do I look worried to you? You say you know a great deal about me, yet this is the first time we've ever spoken. You don't know me that well, Governor. You could call your entire family in here, even on a full moon, and I would still be the only one to walk out alive, or ... dead, whichever. And second, I didn't kill your nephew, or the other guy; I stumbled across their bodies.'

'Do you expect me to believe that, with your history?'

'I don't care what you believe, Governor, you can see for yourself. There's a CCTV camera in that room which I suggest you confiscate before the police get their hands on it. The answer rests there.'

'I'll examine the evidence in my own time, but why send a message to my family in that manner?'

'Plenty of people dislike your family, myself included. The motive is out there, but this was a message for me, not you.' Scott removed his hands from his pockets and folded them across his chest.

'Someone killed a member of my family and an innocent worker just to send a message to you? Tell me who did this and why?' The Governor's patience was wearing thin.

'It was a vampire. I encountered one earlier tonight, and as for why, read the message on the body, but brush up on your Latin first. Sending me a message and killing a Cartwright in the process was killing two birds with the one stone, but the message is my problem to deal with, not yours.'

'They'll pay for this attack on my family; there's nothing I despise more than vampires.'

'Then I guess we have something in common, Governor.' Scott moved as if to leave but stopped himself short for another question. 'I don't suppose you know anything about another hiker being attacked today?'

'Something came across my desk earlier, and once again you were the first suspect that came to mind.'

'I think your dossier needs an update, Governor, get with the times. I keep this town safe, especially during certain lunar events, if you get my meaning?'

'Funny, it wasn't always that way if I'm not mistaken.' The Governor smiled thinly in reply.

'Those days are long gone, and besides, you know what they say about people who live in glass houses.'

'There was no "lunar event", as you put it, yesterday or today.'

'Indeed, luckily for you, but I think I know who's behind all this and, as I said, it's my problem not yours, Governor.'

'You expect me to sit back and do nothing?'

'You can huff and puff all you want but know this: it's my axe to grind so don't get in my way. Goodnight, Governor.' Scott turned on his heel and walked out, leaving the Governor alone this time. He took out his phone and raised it to his ear.

'Contact the others, we need a family meeting ASAP. Yes … I've made contact.
What? Obviously I'm still alive, you idiot, just do it!'

# Chapter 19

Outside the fairground entrance the group had watched as Cartwright was escorted home by security under direct orders from the Governor, leaving PJ, Brad and Gary without their leader. The lights and music were turned off and the remaining crowd questioned the increasing police presence. Amber was pleased to see Nikky with no sign of Scott. Best friend or not, she didn't want to be upstaged by Nikky with the hot guy. Amber was dating the leader of the group, and she liked it that way.

'Where's your boyfriend, Nikky? Or is it too soon to call him that?' Amber hoped she was wrong in trying to make the idea sound like a joke.

'He's not my boyfriend, Amber, we've only just met.'

'My boyfriend had to leave under orders from the Governor, what's Scott's excuse?' Nikky took her phone from her pocket, hoping to see a text from the guy that didn't even have her number, adding to her frustration. 'Scott can do what he wants. And as much as I might like the job of being –' Nikky stopped. Scott was standing behind Amber, looking over her shoulder and listening to the conversation.

'Here's my excuse, Amber.'

Scott was holding a big pink teddy bear with a ribbon around its neck. He handed it to Nikky who was blushing, knowing he must have heard what she'd said.

'That's so sweet, thanks, Scott.'

'I thought the bear was blue?' Amber questioned.

'No doubt this is a different bear, am I right, Scott? I wish I could play darts like you; I'd love a lesson or two,' PJ interjected.

'Where's *your* teddy bear, Amber?' Scott fired a warning shot across the bow. Nikky looked at her phone, pretending she hadn't heard the remark.

Amber shook her head and narrowed her eyes. 'Bite me, Scott.'

Scott's smile spanned from ear to ear. 'Believe me when I say, if it was the old me you wouldn't have to ask.'

Bored of the insults being traded, Gary and Brad sloped off, saying nothing. PJ butted in again. 'What are you talking about? You wanna bite her? You might catch something!'

'Screw you PJ!' Amber shot back. 'At least I can get a date, even Rebecca Chambers won't touch you!'

PJ looked at his wristwatch and tapped it before his comeback. 'Amber, why don't you go; if you hurry you can catch the ten o'clock broom.'

'You know what? You're right.'

'About the broom?'

'Oh just shut up, PJ, I'm not wasting any more time on you losers tonight, we're outta here, you coming, Nikky? We can share a cab.'

Nikky contemplated two difficult options. Leave with her friends or stay with PJ and the mysterious guy who'd won the teddy bears. She turned to Scott and PJ.

'What are you two guys doing?'

'I guess we're gonna head back uptown?' PJ answered. Scott nodded, waiting for Nikky's response.

'I'm gonna hang on with Scott and PJ, I kinda owe him for the gifts so I'll see you girls tomorrow?' she said

Amber glanced at Scott, getting a bland smile for her trouble. 'Sure thing, call me, okay?' Amber's fake smile vanished as quickly as it had appeared, letting Nikky know she wasn't happy with her decision. More girl hugs were spread around with the words 'Call me'.

'I'll call you too, okay, Amber?' PJ threw in one more insult.

'Do you hear that PJ?' There was a brief silence. 'That's the wonderful sound of you not talking for once, and by the way, drop dead.' Amber turned with the girls and walked off, happy to get the last word.

When they were out of earshot, Scott was the first to speak. 'I don't think Amber likes me.'

'I don't think she even likes me right now, but I'll call her later and fix it,' Nikky replied.

'Screw her! She's just jealous of you hanging with Scott, she likes to be the centre of attention.' PJ insisted. Nikky looked at Scott.

'But I've only just met Scott here tonight. Why would she be jealous?'

'Because Scott's giving you way more attention than her.' PJ tipped the fingers of his left hand one by one as he went through some examples. 'Going off alone with you for starters, winning two teddy bears, the Passage of Terror with the "fake" murder scene.' He winked in amusement. 'Then choosing to stay with us rather than leave with her.'

'Okay, I get the message, PJ; you're making me feel bad about the whole thing. I'll text her. Speaking of which, Scott: I better get your number before I forget.' Nikky took out her phone, ready to save a new contact.

'Best of luck with that, Nikky, Scott here doesn't have a phone,' remarked PJ.

Nikky laughed, still waiting for Scott to call out his number. He said nothing.

'Nikky, I'm not kidding.' PJ shook his head and smiled at her.

'You don't have a mobile phone? What century are you from?' said Nikky, baffled.

'The fifteenth.' Scott didn't smile this time, but Nikky took his last sentence as a joke.

'So how am I supposed to contact you?'

'I guess I'll see you around, I don't live far from here. I'm sure I'll bump into you again; I'm at Trevor's a lot.'

'What's your address then, you weirdo?' PJ was straight to the point.

'Believe me, you don't wanna go there. Honestly, I'll be at Trevor's again soon, Gerry and I are old friends.'

'That moron who stands at the door? Isn't he a little old to be your friend, Scott?'

'We'd better start walking, PJ, Nikky has to be home by eleven.' Approaching the boundary wall of the cemetery, the top of his house came into view. Scott looked at his watch.

'I'd better flag down a cab for you guys, it's 10.45, Nikky won't make it back on time.'

'I spent the last of my cash in the park,' PJ commented through his teeth Scott flagged down a cab that seemed to be crawling past, looking for a fare. 'Relax, PJ, I have cash, just get Nikky home on time, okay?'

'I have money but aren't you coming too?' Nikky wasn't expecting to say goodbye so soon, with no phone number to contact him, this felt like the big goodbye.

'I live close by and should get home myself.' Scott stopped moving. The hum was back in his chest. He knew what this meant but the cab had pulled in next to them. PJ opened the rear door before turning to Scott with his fist held high, waiting for him to bump it. Scott looked confused. He held out his hand for an old-fashioned handshake.

'I was right, you are a weirdo, but I'll see ya again, Scott!' PJ shook Scott's hand and slid across the backseat of the cab, leaving space for Nikky. She stood at the door, looking at Scott.

'Oh, before I forget,' Scott said. He took twenty dollars from his pocket and tapped his knuckles on the driver's window. The window opened, the driver took the money without comment and closed it again. In those few brief seconds, Scott suddenly felt uneasy. He turned to Nikky.

'You know what, I think I'll join you guys for the ride, I'm sure my mom won't mind me being a little late tonight.'

Nikky's face lit up as she slid into the centre seat with Scott getting in next to her.

'Eastbrook Lodge estate, please,' PJ called out cheerfully, but got no reply. The driver turned on the meter and remained silent for the entire journey.

## Chapter 20

Eastbrook is one of the more popular housing developments in Tallant and the furthest away from Chequamegon-Nicolet National Forest. Its large, detached homes are spaciously landscaped, with large trees. PJ wasted no time pointing out Dan Cartwright's over-lavish house to Scott, opposite PJ's more moderate home across the street. The Cartwrights' house boasted a double garage with two new SUVs parked outside.

'Anywhere here will do fine, thanks; Nikky's a little further down.' PJ started to open the door before the car came to a complete stop. 'I'll catch you guys' tomorrow or whenever; Nikky I'll see you at school, take it easy.' He closed the cab door and banged twice on the roof before turning into his driveway. As the car moved off, Scott looked back to see him go through his front door. Three houses down, on the same side, the car stopped again on Nikky's instructions. She got out, followed by Scott. He stuck his head back into the open cab door.

'Could you hold on for me, please, I need a ride back. Just leave the meter running, I won't be long.' The cab driver watched as Scott trailed Nikky to her front door, holding her teddy bear. A motion sensor light lit up the driveway as she stopped just short of the entrance,, twisting anxiously to face Scott, not knowing what to expect. He glanced at his watch.

'I guess you just about made it, eleven o'clock on the nose.'

'Barely, but still good enough.'

'Is that Buster I hear barking?'

'Yeah, he's a good guard dog, goes nuts when someone comes near the house, he'll stop in a minute.' She paused. 'Wait, how did you know his name?'

'I guess it must have come up somewhere in conversation.' He kept a straight face, unable to tell her he heard her father mention his name earlier when she was dropped off. Lying was easy. He changed the topic. 'Here, I guess you'll want this.' He handed her the bear before returning his hands to their usual place in his pockets.

'Thanks again, and I mean for everything. It's been one weird night, with the … murders and stuff.'

'You took it pretty well.'

'Yeah. I meant to ask you how come *you* took it so well, Scott? You knew it was all real, unlike me.'

'Long story for another time, perhaps.'

'You're so mysterious, Scott, but you never answered my questions earlier, and now I'm about to go inside until we meet again, but I don't know when that will be seeing as I can't contact you … That is *so* weird, by the way.'

'Now I know where you live, though, right?'

'So, you might just drop by someday? Like maybe never, or maybe tomorrow? Or perhaps tomorrow? Did I mention tomorrow is good for me?' She knew she was babbling, feeling lost not being able to communicate by text.

'Possibly, you'll never know, I'll keep you guessing.'

Buster continued barking and jumping in the hallway behind the closed door, almost knocking an empty blue vase from the hall table.

'You know the way I mentioned that tomorrow is good, if you dropped by tomorrow, you could come in and we could hang out and stuff. I wanna get to know the real you!'

'I'm still a stranger, Nikky, don't invite a stranger into your home. I'd rather we hung out somewhere else.'

'That's why I wanna get to know you better, Scott, so you're not just this mysterious stranger!'

A shadow appeared behind the glass that surrounded the doorway before the door opened behind her.

'Nikky I thought I told you –' James Brennan stopped talking as he realised she had company, and glad it wasn't Cartwright. 'Oh, I thought you were with someone else … do you know what time it is?'

Nikky turned to face her father as Buster barked uncontrollably now that the door was wide open. The hair on his back stood on end, showing his teeth as he growled.

'Be quiet, Buster!' Nikky laughed. Scott made eye contact with Buster, who stopped barking and dropped onto his back legs. He whimpered, then disappeared back inside the house.

'Dad, this is one of my friends, Scott.'

Scott knew this man. He never forgot a face. Now things were finally starting to make sense. He looked at Nikky with a stab of pain and regret, as he suddenly understood her story about the death of her mother. Memories flooded his mind. He held out his hand to the ranger.

'It's nice to meet you, sir; that's a fine animal you have there.'

Nikky's eyes widened on hearing Scott speak with such courtesy. She liked the respect for her father. After all, he was the only parent she had left. The ranger shook Scott's hand while glancing at his daughter.

'Hello Scott, I take it the teddy bear is from you, then?'

'Got lucky, I guess.'

Brennan studied Scott's face for a moment, looking puzzled. 'Have we met before, Scott? Your face looks familiar.'

Scott paused before answering; to say they had met under unfortunate circumstances was an understatement of the highest degree. 'Not that I'm aware of, sir.'

Brennan looked again at his daughter. 'It's getting late, Nikky. Nice to meet you, Scott, thanks for seeing my little girl home.' He gave Scott a nod of approval before turning around and closing the door behind him.

'I'd better go inside, but I have two questions you never answered,' Nikky said.

'Shoot.'

"What was it that scared you and who called you their hero?' He leant forward and kissed her on the lips as a response. She closed her eyes, dropping the bear. She wanted to freeze time there and then. As far as she was concerned, this moment could last forever. But he turned and began to walk back to the waiting cab. She stood still, her eyes closed and lost in the moment. Then she shook her head and shouted after him.

'You never answered my questions, Scott!'

He stopped, tilted his head to the side and finally replied.

'Nothing on Earth terrifies me more than red eyes … monsters are real. And I've been called a hero by only one person; I didn't agree with it then, and I don't agree with it now.' He touched his bracelet before getting back in the car.

## Chapter 21

The first words from the cab driver were straight to the point. 'Where to?'

Scott stared out the window at the houses flying past, delaying his answer until it suited him. 'South.'

'I'll drive south, but I need to know where I'm going.'

'No you don't, just keep driving south, any way you want; I'll tell you when to stop.' Scott lay his head against the head rest behind him and, letting out a long deep breath, he closed his eyes.

'Something troubling you, buddy?' The cabby seemed to have found his voice.

'You could say that alright, I'm playing with fire again, and someone always gets burnt.' He opened his eyes again to check his surroundings then closed them again.

'You mean you or her?'

'Both … it will hurt her more than it hurts me, but my pain will never stop; hers will with time.'

'What's gonna get you both hurt?'

'The truth. The truth about me, my past, my demons, who I am and what I've done. I don't deserve someone like her, or anyone for that matter.'

'But you care about this girl, right?'

'I guess. I could fall in love with her tomorrow, but she reminds me of someone.'

It was ten minutes before the driver spoke again. 'You know we're leaving town, right?'

Scott sat up and looked out to see the 'Thanks for visiting Tallant!' road sign on his right. The road ahead was dark beneath the evergreens on either side, illuminated by the cab headlights. They were far enough from town now.

'Pull in here, this will do just fine.' Scott was staring into the forest.

'You wanna get out here? In the middle of nowhere? Isn't that dangerous, kid?' The driver stopped the meter and turned on the interior light.

'What should I do?'

'Go back to town for starters.'

'No, I mean about the girl.'

'Take a chance, what have you got to lose?'

'I don't know what to do yet, but she'll face other threats because of me.' Scott opened the window closest to him as he spoke.

'Like what?' the cabby looked at the empty road ahead.

'Well, pieces of shit like you for one.' Scott was still looking through the side window, not bothered in the slightest. He leaned across and opened the window furthest from him.

'Excuse me?' Anyone watching from outside would have seen the cabby turn his head to look back at his passenger. He seemed to say something before the car rocked violently. The windshield became a red beacon lit up by the interior light. The driver seat burst into flames, sending thick black smoke through the rear open windows, bound for the heavens. The back door opened. Scott stepped out. Blood ran down his hand, reaching his middle finger before dripping to the road like tears falling from a face with no remorse.

'Told you someone always gets burnt.'

**Chapter 22**

Nikky's usual response to her morning alarm was to hit the snooze button. But not this morning. Today, just before the tune began to play its loudest, she sat up, yawning, and hit cancel on the touch screen. She was happy and positive most days but didn't always wake up smiling. Something was different. She felt an optimistic flutter like butterflies in her stomach, a combination of excitement and energy.

'Nikky, you up?' Her father gave his usual weekday knock on her bedroom door, ensuring she was awake for school.

'Yeah, I'll be right down.' She opened her bedroom window and leaned out for a breath of fresh air. The large oak tree holding her brother's treehouse dominated her view to the side of the house, tethered by an empty clothesline wet with dew that glistened in the morning sun. Buster ran about below, stopping to investigate scents that caught his attention. Downstairs, Ranger James Brennan sat eating pancakes at the breakfast table with his back to the TV. His beige hat hung on the corner of his chair, matching his shirt above his faded green trousers, with his utility belt and sidearm hung opposite. Standing at 6'1" with the fitness level of a 25-year-old, no one would guess he was in his late forties. Sitting opposite him, his 14-year-old son Caden held a spoon over a bowl of cornflakes while he flicked through social media on his phone. The seat next to him held an open schoolbag and last night's unfinished homework, half of which still spread out on one side of the table.

'It's not like you to have the TV on first thing in the morning, big guy?' James spoke as he lifted a coffee cup to his lips for his first caffeine fix of the day.

'Just getting information about the murder last night at the fairground, Dad, it's all over social media.'

'At the fairground? That's the first I've heard about it.'

'That's because you're not on social media, Dad, and your phone is prehistoric.' Caden shook his head and continued shovelling cornflakes into his mouth, disapproving of his father's self-confessed technophobia. Nikky appeared, still smiling, and dropped her school bag to the floor before joining the other two at the table. She took her late mother's vacant seat and helped herself to the plate of pancakes that sat between her father's newspaper and Caden's homework.

'Nikky, you hear anything about these murders last night?' asked the ranger.

'Well good morning to you, too!' she replied, pouring syrup on her pancakes. 'But yeah, I did. Oh God, it was gruesome, Dad, inside the Passage of Terror, I thought it was part of the display.'

'You actually witnessed it first-hand? You don't seem that upset about it? And why didn't you tell me this last night, Nikky?' the ranger queried, wondering if this new boy was dominating her thoughts to the exclusion of everything else, including murder.

'Sorry, Dad, my mind was elsewhere; it was in the werewolves' lair. Scott knew it was real right away.'

'*Werewolves*? Was Dan Cartwright with you?'

'No, just me and Scott, why do you ask?'

'Nothing, so what happened next?'

'Scott got closer to it than I did, I could barely look. I only found out later that it was real. What time is grandma's train getting in?' Nikky changed the subject without realising.

'Three o'clock; that reminds me, Nikky, there's an old box with some of her old things in her room that should go into the attic, can you take care of it?'

'Why me?' She looked pointedly at Caden, who ignored the question.

'Because your brother feeds the dog.'

She rolled her eyes as Caden smiled without taking his eyes from his phone. James looked at his wristwatch before finishing his last drop of coffee. 'Okay people, ten minutes or I'll be late. Nikky, you can fill me in about the incident last night later, I'm just glad you're okay.' Monday through Friday, the ranger dropped the kids to school on his way to work, letting them to make their own way home later that same day. One perk of the job was free use of the pickup truck. Today's mission was to collect grandma from the train before Nikky and Caden got back from school. He took his utility belt from the back of the chair, locking it around his waist before leaving the room to gather his belongings.

  Caden was done with breakfast. He pushed his empty bowl away and chose his phone over having a conversation with his sister sitting next to him. Things hadn't been the same since their mother died; sibling communication was at an all-time low. Nikky stabbed her pancakes with her fork. She watched for his reaction, knowing he knew she wanted to talk. He didn't take the bait. Turning off the TV with the remote, he packed his homework into his school bag and left the room. Nikky sighed, having lost another opportunity to chat. A new message on her phone distracted her chain of thought. It was PJ.

  'Hey, how are ya? You get your goodnight kiss? ☺'

  'Hilarious, I'm good, you?'

*'Not great, had Mexican last night, my ass is like a Japanese flag ATM.'*

*'TMI, PJ!!!'*

*'Anyway, if you're interested we can try find out where the mystery dart champion lives?'*

*'Just how are we supposed to do that?'*

*'He said he lives near the cemetery, right?'*

*'That could be anywhere.'*

*'He also mentioned his house has a flat roof?'*

*'So?'*

*'So, I happen to know a flat-roofed house inside the cemetery with the letter M over the door. M as in Scott's last name?'*

*'I didn't get his last name :)'*

*'I'm shocked and stunned! You kissed the guy and don't know his last name?'*

*'Who says I kissed him? ;) And what if it's not his house?'*

*'Yeah. Then we wait to bump into him again at Trevor's, I guess.'*

*'Okay, what time? :)'*

**Chapter 23**

With the school run behind him, Ranger James Brennan and Buster pulled up at the US Parks Department on Main Street. After locking Buster in his kennel at the rear of the building, Brennan entered through the aluminium door that swung shut behind him, into the air-conditioned lobby where his receptionist, Ellen Coleman, sat behind her hatch, typing.

She looked up from the monitor and spoke as he was sliding open the hatch. 'Morning Jim, I left the reports about the recent animal attacks in the envelope on top of your desk, and there's a fresh pot of coffee brewing.'

'Thank you, Ellen, you truly are the heart of this operation; the good people of this little town are in debt to your years of professionalism and dedication.' He grinned sarcastically but Ellen was used to James Brennan and his good morning charms. Without taking her eyes from his, she picked up a stress ball and threw it at him, giving him barely enough time to pull the sliding window closed, taking the impact instead. He laughed and reopened it.

'Your aim needs to improve if you want to come on field trips and protect me from bear attacks.' He knocked on the wooden counter with the key to the pickup truck. 'I see they've started preparations for the centenary celebration this Saturday, the Town Hall is covered in bunting.'

'I believe they're planning a fireworks display, I promised my nephew I'd take him, should be fun.'

'Yeah, Caden mentioned that. Let's hope people stay in town and not venture into the forest for us to pick up the pieces when it's over. I'll be in my office – oh before I forget, I'll be picking up Beth from the train around 3 o'clock but that won't take long.'

'Sure thing, Jim, but there's one more thing: the volunteer search party for those missing kids came in empty-handed again last night, just thought you'd like to know.'

He nodded regretfully then headed to his office, passing the notice board that served as an endless reminder of the never-ending missing person reports in Tallant. Some he knew in his heart of hearts were not all down to random animal attacks, whatever the reports claimed. Knowing what he did felt like a constant dark cloud hanging over him. Even if he wanted to speak about what he knew, his family's safety came first. He opened the door to his office and threw his hat onto the desk before collapsing into the leather chair behind it, staring down at another envelope he didn't want to open, but knew he had to.

It was his job. Not to lie to the public, but to protect them with delicately gauged information, privy to only a select few in prominent positions in the town. A photo of his wife smiled back at him from his desk, taken in happier times; a constant reminder of how dangerous Tallant could be. He'd learned his lesson. He would never jeopardise his kids' safety after what had happened to his wife. He reluctantly tore open the sealed envelope, spilling its contents onto the desk.

A collection of pages officially headed 'Coroner's Office' and labelled private and confidential lay before him. Blank forms, files, colour photographs and reports awaited his signature for completion. The paperwork was fine, but the photographs were not. Some things once seen can't be unseen. Over the last fifteen years on the job, he'd seen things that would stay with him forever. Things that make a man rethink his place in the world. The same things that make you want to cherish every moment in those joyful periods because they will never come again.

Accidental deaths from exposure, bodies found months later after drowning incidents, traumatic injuries from rock climbing, and suicides. James could never get over how far people go to end their own lives, and at this point he'd just about seen them all. All terrible in their own right, but the ones that stood out for him were the 'animal attacks'. The photos on his desk would give the impression of a scenic landscape if one didn't know any better. A closer look would reveal the finer details. Body parts no longer attached. Blood splashes on tree bark with human entrails still connected to a body that led a path of blood ten feet from the victim. No animal could do this, and both the ranger and coroner knew it.

He sat back in his chair, tapping his pen on the desk. This incident had occurred two days ago. Standing up, he inspected a calendar of city skylines on his personal noticeboard. Every month had one date circled in red marker next to an exclamation mark. Full moon. He examined the date on the calendar, comparing it to the incident on his desk.

'The last full moon was weeks ago … The next one is September 30th, followed by another on October 31st,' he said to himself. Halloween, how fitting. Sitting down, he flicked through the coroner's notes again. Time of death estimated at approximately two days ago due to decomposition with minimal insect and animal scavenging post-mortem.

'It doesn't add up,' he muttered. He picked up his phone and punched a key. It rang only once before a voice answered.

'I hope you're not calling to compliment me again.'

'Ellen, I need you to make me an appointment ASAP, please.'

Hearing the seriousness in his voice, Ellen dropped the usual banter and changed her tone. 'Of course, Jim, where exactly?'

'The Governor's office.'

**Chapter 24**

From the moment she turned in her driveway, Nikky knew they had a visitor. Visible through the glass that surrounded the front door, a fresh bunch of sunflowers filled the blue vase on the hallway table, signalling that Grandma had arrived. She brought an atmosphere of home, reminding Nikky of when her mother had been alive, with beds made and windows sparkling. Nikky's mother always made room for Grandma's sunflowers, knowing that she never came without them. Nikky grinned, knowing that her father had come home via the Enchanted Florists.

Before she could use her front-door key, the door opened from inside, revealing the familiar face she had not seen for six months. Nikky ran into her outstretched arms.

'Welcome home, Grandma.'

'You get prettier every time I see you.' Beth Pursch stepped back and cupped Nikky's face in her hands to admire her granddaughter's beauty. 'More and more like your mother with each passing day.' Nikky nodded in sad appreciation. After all, her grandmother had lost her only daughter. It was a pain they both shared, but only one of many things they had in common. She paused to examine her grandmother. Beth's favourite colour was blue, always was and always would be. There's only so many blue scarves, dresses or coats one can buy for a senior citizen, leaving Nikky and her mother little choice other than a blue vase for Christmas one year, which sat now on the hall table.

Her colour choice for today's summer blouse was predictable. Aged 82, with a walking stick strapped to her wrist allowing her to use both hands should the need arise, Beth still got about unassisted for her daily tasks. A nest of white hair satin a bun on top of her head; her days of caring about dying her hair were long gone. In her early twenties, she'd moved from Tallant to the suburbs of Green Bay, where she and her husband settled down and started a family. Before Nikky was born, her mother returned to Tallant with her then boyfriend James Brennan, finding new roots in the town her mother had once called home. Beth remained in Green Bay with her husband, her visits becoming more regular after his death. But the loneliness and constant invitations to come back to live in Tallant were not enough to make her return.

'How about a cup of tea and a chat? We have lots of gossip to catch up on!' Beth said, wrapping her arm around Nikky like her mother used to do, and leading her to the kitchen where a tea tray sat waiting on the counter. They stepped into the afternoon sun of the patio, Nikky checking first that the tea was brewed before she picked up the tray with its old-fashioned teapot. 'We only spoke two weeks ago on the phone, Grandma; it hasn't been that long,' Nikky laughed, sitting to face the garden, and placing her phone on the table in front of her.

'Believe me, two weeks is a long time when you live alone, with your only entertainment being a get-together with some old folks in the nearest retirement home!' Beth sat across from her granddaughter, propping a cushion behind her lower back for support. 'I'm not as young as I used to be.' Her voice was now withered with age, but to Nikky it felt comforting and familiar, and much nicer to hear in person than over the phone.

'So, how was your journey?' Nikky asked as she took a sip of tea.

'I met a nice couple on the train, the chatting helped make the journey less tedious.' Beth clasped her hands together across her lap, allowing her tea to cool before taking a sip.

'I see you went via the Enchanted Florist?'

'Yes indeed, it was a delight to see Carol again. I didn't have to ask; she knew what I wanted as soon as she saw my face at the door!'

'How is she doing? I was worried about her after last night.' Nikky looked concerned.

'Last night?' Grandma took her first sip from the teacup.

'Yes, she gave us – me and a friend – a palm reading at the fairground, it was … a bit weird.'

'She never mentioned that, although she had quite a few customers, so it wasn't the best time to chat.'

'I'm glad to hear it. She's such a nice person,' Nikky added, hoping to deflect any questions about last night. Her tactic worked, as Beth's thoughts moved on.

'It's important to keep a fresh batch of sunflowers in the house, Nikky, I wish you would keep that vase full when I'm not around,' Beth said in a serious tone.

'What is it with you and sunflowers?'

'I promise to tell you someday, until then do your grandmother a favour and keep it full, think you can do that?' Nikky nodded and returned the smile.

'If it keeps you happy, Grandma, sure, I'll try persuade dad to cough up the money!'

'Anyway, tell me about you. I want to know how you've been and what have you've been up to. Any boys on the scene?' Beth winked. Nikky blushed, biting her bottom lip through a smile that was becoming more difficult to conceal. Her grandmother waved a wrinkled index finger.

'Aha! The smile that cannot lie! You can't fool me!'

Nikky hesitated before answering. 'Well … there's this one boy I've met …'

'Come on, don't keep me in the dark, tell me all about him!' Beth sat forward eagerly. Nikky considered her words before replying.

'He's ... so... well ... brave and mysterious is my best way of putting it, I guess.'

'And handsome?' Beth looked sideways across the table. Nikky said nothing, a smile and nod was enough.

'So where is this boy from?' Beth probed.

'Actually, I'm not really sure.'

'Has your father met him yet? He's a good judge of character.' The topic now had her grandmother's undivided attention.

'Yes, he met him last night, says he's nice and polite; I think he's just happy I'm not dating Dan Cartwright, to be honest.'

'I agree with your father, dear.' Beth didn't hesitate with her reply. Nikky laughed. 'But you don't really know Dan, Grandma.'

'I know his family and that's enough, believe me, you need to heed your father's advice.'

'Sure, but we're just friends, there's nothing to worry about.'

'If you say so, my dear, my only concern is your safety. So you don't know anything else about this mystery man?'

'Well, he's not a Cartwright if that puts your mind at ease.'

'Whoever he is, he's a lucky boy. I'd like to meet him, perhaps I'll get the chance while I'm here.'

'I'm sure you will, if things go to plan, that is. Oh, Dad said I'm to put the box of your old stuff in the attic. The box in your bedroom? I'm sorry I forgot to do it earlier.'

'No that's better, dear, there's something inside I want to give you.'

'You being here is all the gift I need, Grandma, you know that by now!' Nikky reached over and touched her hand on the table.

'You're at that age now and I think you should have it. If anything, it will keep you safe. That old box is full of memories from my youth, I must show you sometime. Life goes by so fast … *carpe diem*, as they say.'

'I've heard that before, what does it mean?'
'It means seize the day, cherish every moment, because it will never come again.' Beth sat back in her chair, her mind full of vivid memories, accepting difficult decisions that seemed a lifetime ago. Thoughts arrived faster than the dark clouds that began to gather above. Evening was approaching. Everything happens for a reason, she told herself; her daughter and Nikky were proof of that. No regrets. Nikky's phone vibrated on the table, rattling the

empty teacups. She sat forward to inspect the screen. A message from PJ. She already knew what it said without having to read it. Beth pointed at Nikky's phone.

'That must be Mr Mysterious now?'

'No, just a friend I'm meeting later.' She dismissed PJ's message with a wave of her hand.

'It's okay, dear, if you have to go, don't let me keep you. I'll be here for the next few weeks;, we have plenty of time to chat.' Beth stood up with the aid of her walking stick to bring in the tea tray.

'I've got this, Grandma, honest, you take a seat and relax.'

Beth put her wrinkled hand softly on her granddaughter's shoulder, still taken aback by her beauty and resemblance to her own daughter.

'Go see your friends, time is precious, and these are the best years of your life. Besides, I'm have an errand of my own.'

'Are you sure, Grandma because that can wait?'

'Absolutely sure, now go enjoy your day, I'll be here when you get back.'

Nikky stood and gave her another hug before turning to leave, carrying the tray. After she'd disappeared inside, Beth called out to her again.

'Try be back before nightfall, it's not safe in Tallant after dark!' But her words of warning echoed back to her from an empty room.

# Chapter 25

Leaving her driveway, Nikky turned left and headed towards the estate entrance, where the homes of Dan and PJ stood facing one another. The differences between the two houses were not subtle, PJ's being one of the smaller houses in Eastbrook Lodge and looking more run down than the lavish Cartwrights' house across the street.

Even the Brennans' four-bedroom home looked average compared to Dan's trophy house. None of the Cartwrights in town were on the lower end of the pay spectrum, Dan's father included. Being a lawyer with his own law firm made sure of that. And having an uncle as Governor made sure that every legal deed and lawsuit in Tallant came across his father's desk. It was game set and match for the Cartwrights' influence in Tallant.

The Cartwrights' front door was opening as she approached. She assumed it was opening for her until PJ was ejected, with the door slamming briefly shut behind him before opening again to reveal Dan, who threw PJ's bag after him and slammed the door a second time.

Nikky smiled and shook her head. 'What have you done now, PJ?'

'Jeez! It doesn't take much to piss some people off these days,' PJ grumbled as he picked his bag up from the ground.

'Aren't you gonna tell me? Or knowing you, do I really wanna know?'

'All I said was that his mom was killing it eating that banana. No big deal.'

Nikky couldn't contain her laughter. 'Yep! I was right, could have done without hearing that.'

'It's how I roll, Nikky, you know me.' PJ grinned in her direction as they exited onto the footpath. PJ turned right with Nikky following, heading towards town.

'Wait, where exactly are we going?'

'You wanna know where our mutual friend lives, don't you?'

'His name is Scott, PJ, and yes of course, but I don't know how you're so sure which house is his?'

'You're lecturing me about his first name, and you didn't even know his last name?'

'Okay so I don't know his surname, big deal, my mind was elsewhere last night. I'm sure you're gonna tell me now, anyway.'

'Oh, I'll bet your mind certainly was elsewhere last night.' He gave her a sly wink.

'Grow up. What's his last name so I can search social media?'

'Already tried that, I guess he wasn't lying. No sign of him anywhere at all, it's like the guy doesn't exist.'

'That's just so weird ... especially the having no phone part.'

'Exactly, and you didn't see what I saw at the fairground dart stall, either.'

'Why, what did you see?' Nikky was intrigued.

'Oh, just something very interesting; nothing I wanna share until I find out more.'

'So his last name, PJ, what is it?'

'Maglace.'

Nikky pondered the name. Unusual as it was, it had a nice ring to it.

'Yep, and I know just where to start looking. He told me he lived in a house with a flat roof near the cemetery, okay?'

'I'm listening.' She pretended she was only half interested because it was PJ, but secretly she was all ears.

'As I said last night, there's a flat-roofed house just inside the cemetery wall, and this flat-roofed house has the letter "M" carved above the doorway. Do you follow me?'

'Yes, I follow you.'

'Well stop following me or I'll have you arrested!'

She studied him in annoyance.

'Anyway, that's our second port of call, there's somewhere else I wanna check out on the way.'

'Trevor's?'

'No, there's something I wanna check out before it gets dark, at the pedestrian entrance off Trail Street.' PJ spoke like he meant business.

'What exactly, PJ?' Nikky was cautious. Knowing PJ as she did, the reason could be anything under the sun. How could she forget the humiliation of being led into a sex shop in town, with PJ asking the store clerk about the different toys on sale. The lady that worked there spoke to them as a couple, playing right into his hands. Apparently, the store did not do demonstrations, to PJ's disappointment. That was bad enough, but what made Nikky want to die from embarrassment was PJ telling the clerk before they left that Nikky was his sister. A lesson well learned. PJ could put anyone's patience to the test and often did.

'I had some sort of memory loss or blackout at the bench near the fountain last night just before Scott showed up. There's something there I want to check out'

\*\*\*

Dusk had set in by the time they were passing Trevor's Diner, the inside of the restaurant was now brighter than outside, making it easy for Nikky to check for Scott through the window without having to enter. PJ didn't slow his pace after he saw Gerry at the door. He'd had enough confrontation for today.

Nikky was disappointed after her scan of the interior revealed only the faces of strangers. Part of her had really hoped to see Scott sitting alone somewhere at the back, waiting for her. Breaking into a short sprint, she caught up with PJ near the entrance to the forest trails parking area.

'PJ! Can you slow down, please?'

'No can do, Mrs Maglace, I wanna get to that bench with the little light we have left. Look, it's still open, we're good.' He pointed to the small pedestrian gate with the bend in the bars his friends had passed through the night before. Mr Coventry hadn't started his lock-up rounds yet so there was still time to enter the normal way, instead of embarrassing himself in front of Nikky.

'Isn't it getting a little late to be going in here? I mean, it is a graveyard, PJ, and you're not even certain where Scott lives. Who the hell would live in a graveyard, anyway?'

'Trust me, I have to get to the bottom of this.'

With one hand on the gate, Nikky turned to look back at Trail Street and hesitated for a moment. Pushing her better judgement aside, she went through the gate and broke into a jog to catch up with PJ, who had paused next to the water fountain, baffled, as he looked around for answers to last night's mystery.

'Where's it gone?' The remains of the broken bench had been removed. Two small pieces of metal remained, showing where it had been bolted to the ground. Even the fountain had been cleared of floating debris. The entire area had been cleaned up, leaving no evidence or clues to what happened.

'What's gone? The bench? Maybe it's getting repaired? Honestly, I don't see the big deal here.'

'No, you don't understand! I was here last night with the guys and this bench was in perfect condition, then I had a blackout and then, hey presto, it was smashed to bits, with pieces scattered everywhere.'

'How come you never mentioned this till now? What do you think happened?'

'I don't know!' PJ squatted down and grabbed a handful of gravel, before letting it slip through his open fingers. 'I can't remember much after that, except … Scott … yeah, Scott appeared around then, and we left for the fair. My mind's a total blank, Nikky, it's freaking me out.'

'Sshh, wait a sec, PJ, do you hear that?' Nikky whispered. PJ stood up and they faced the direction of the sound.

It was the unmistakable crunch of footsteps in gravel, and it was getting louder.

# Chapter 26

'I'm locking the northern gate, folks, if you want to leave, I suggest you do it now.' Mr Coventry walked with a limp from a previous hip replacement and slowed on his approach as he addressed the two teenagers at the fountain.

PJ was relieved to see the groundskeeper simply going about his usual nightly lock-up. For some reason, he felt afraid at this location, and he couldn't explain why. He leaned in close to Nikky's ear so that only she could hear.

'How would you like to feel the way he looks?'

Nikky responded with a subtle thump to his side, causing him to respond more appropriately. 'We're okay, thanks, we'll go out through the main exit ... oh, do you know what happened to the bench that was here yesterday?'

Mr Coventry raised his hands to his hips, jingling a large set of keys looped around one of his fingers, using the opportunity to get his breath back. His age showed through a wrinkled unshaven face, a head of white hair hidden under an old-fashioned tweed cap. He wore a green waistcoat over black shirt and black trousers that had seen better days. The green stains on both knees matched those on his hands from years of gardening and the upkeep of the cemetery.

'I've no clue, all I know is I'm the one who had to clear it up. Took me over an hour to get the metal pegs out of the ground just to stop people from tripping over them. And let me guess, I don't suppose you know anything about it either, hmm?' He looked at PJ suspiciously and pulled a handkerchief from his waistcoat pocket to dab the sweat behind his.

PJ went on the offensive. 'Hey, just a minute there, you cranky old –' Nikky jumped in mid-sentence, squeezing PJ's shoulder.

'What my impulsive friend here means is that he was curious about what could have broken a bench like that, leaving such a horrible mess for you to clean up, sir.'

Mr Coventry glared at PJ before answering the polite girl. 'I'm not sure, miss, but this here bench was made of oak which doesn't break easy, only for the fact that I locked the gates last night I would have said a car hit it. That's all I can tell you. Now, if you'll excuse me, I've got to lock up, and I wouldn't stay in here after dark if I were you.' He nodded and started to walk towards the gate.

'Just one more question, sir, if I may?' Nikky interrupted. Mr Coventry stalled again, the momentum jingling his keys. 'Do you know who lives in the flat roof house near the main gate? We're looking for a guy called Scott, and we're not sure where he lives but we think he lives in there?' she finished in a hopeful voice.

Mr Coventry stood still this time. Even his keys were frozen. He gave a concerned glance at Nikky, then switched his eyes to PJ without moving his head. He seemed to contemplate his answer.

'Closest exit is this way; I'll lock the gate behind you.'

'Please, he's our friend, do you know anyone around here with that name?'

'Who told you he was your friend?'

'He did, and Nikky here has the hots for him,' PJ chimed in.

'Take it from me, stay away from that house, it's private property and the residents don't like to be disturbed.'

'Does he live there or doesn't he? What's with all the secrecy? Jeez!' PJ was growing impatient with the brush-off.

'Good evening, miss.' Mr. Coventry tipped his hat to Nikky, ignoring PJ entirely now. The two were alone again.

'Well?'

'Well what, PJ?'

'He didn't say no.' He grinned, raising his eyebrows up and down.

'But it's almost pitch dark, and the gates will be closing; let's leave it till tomorrow.'

'Exactly, so we'd better get a move on, follow me.'

## Chapter 27

PJ was more determined than ever. Being told not to do something was always a challenge. He took off towards the main gate with Nikky in tow.

'So, what do you think happened to your precious bench, then?' she jested.

PJ stopped again. 'Hmm … memory loss? Unexplained circumstances? Missing time? I think I got it!'

'I'm afraid to ask,' Nikky rolled her eyes in advance of the spectacular theory coming her way.

'I've been abducted by aliens! It all matches up! Hey, don't laugh! I'm all brushed up on that stuff, man. I listen to Richard Syrett, *Conspiracy Unlimited* is my favourite podcast. And I have O negative blood, so I match the criteria.'

'The criteria? Okay, whatever, then we'd better get moving in case they come back for you,' Nikky laughed, tongue in cheek. Hurting his feelings didn't come into the equation; after all, this was PJ.

'Non-believers,' PJ whispered to himself.

By the time they arrived at the house, darkness had fallen. The only window to the left of the door was covered from the inside with a blackout blind. Nikky and PJ stood next to a broken lantern that hung by the door and whispered, unsure what to do next.

'Just remembered, last night I told Scott this place looked like something from *The Munsters*.'

'Do you ever not put your foot in it, PJ?'

'How the hell was I supposed to know it really is like something from *The Munsters*?' PJ shrugged.

'What now?'

'I guess we knock?' Before she could respond he thumped the door with his fist. They looked at each other and waited. No response. The house remained as silent as the graveyard behind them.

'Okay, we tried, can we go now?' said Nikky, folding her arms.

'Don't you wanna see who lives here, Nikky?' PJ was still whispering as he twisted the doorknob before Nikky could object.

'What are you doing, PJ, no, wait!' she hissed. It was too late. The aged wooden door opened inwards with a creak. 'Really, PJ? So we're breaking and entering now?' Nikky was on edge knowing she was now an accomplice to a crime.

PJ whispered back, 'I didn't break anything, only entered … besides, it looks derelict, and we just happen to be looking around for … you know, a place to make out.'

'In your dreams, PJ.'

'Hey, that's my story if the police arrive so make it convincing.' He gave her a wink.

Nervously, Nikky looked left and right, double-checking that nobody was watching. Her feelings for a boy she'd just met paired with PJ's curiosity could land them both in a lot of trouble. PJ placed one of his Converse against the bottom of the door and pushed until it was fully opened. Nikky's heart raced. A tiny, dark room awaited them.

'Hello, Scott? You there?' PJ pulled Nikky inside and closed the door quietly. The cold, musty air gave the feeling of being in a museum or wine cellar minus exhibits or wine. They each thought of lighting up their phones at the same time.

'Now what, PJ?' Nikky whispered. He didn't answer but pointed to another door that opened off this tiny claustrophobic room and gestured for her to follow. He pressed down the door handle and pushed it inwards, pointing the flashlight from his phone through the crack as it widened. 'Scott?' he whispered. A grandfather clock was ticking away the seconds somewhere, breaking the silence. Two brown leather chairs sat facing a stone fireplace, separated by a coffee table that held a small lamp that barely lit the room. PJ looked over his left shoulder at Nikky.

'Nice cheerful place, I wonder what time they bring the mummies out?'

'Would you please stop it?' she whispered back angrily.

'Maybe my *Munsters* joke wasn't quite right.'

'What?' she hissed, pointing the light from her phone around the room for a better view.

'I'm thinking more along the lines of the Addams family now.'

'This is not the time, PJ, anyway I don't think he'd live in a place like this … can we please go now?'

'Hold on, sister, we've come this far, haven't we? Let's check this place out.' He pulled away from Nikky and edged further into the room, tiptoeing around the chairs towards a closed door to the right of the fireplace. He placed his hand on the door handle and looked at Nikky before shining his light where the crack in the door was about to open.

A voice spoke from the darkness behind them. 'Boy oh boy, did you choose the wrong house to break into.'

They jumped simultaneously, turning their phones in the sound's direction.

'We don't want any trouble, ma'am, we're sorry, please don't call the cops!' PJ attempted to play the innocent teen approach. A woman in her mid-thirties stood facing them, arms folded across her chest.

'The police?' she grinned. 'Even the police can't help you now.'

Nikky held an index finger in front of PJ's face, advising him to stay quiet while she explained more politely. 'I'm terribly sorry, ma'am, but we're looking for our friend, we thought he lived here but ... we honestly didn't mean to trespass, we'll be on our way now.'

'I'm afraid you're not going anywhere, my dear.' The peculiar smile intensified as the woman unfolded her arms and ran an index finger along the top of the leather through the dust before examining it.

'You can't keep us here, we're leaving,' PJ said. He moved to pass behind her but was grabbed by his clothing a chest level. She picked him up with astonishing ease and threw him past Nikky against the closed door in the corner behind. He hit the door with a thud and slid to the ground, his backpack taking most of the impact. He sat staring up in shock with his hand to the back of his head as Nikky rushed to his aid, squatting down next to him.

'Jesus, what the hell was that? Nikky, we need to get outta here, and I mean right now. Scott can wait.' Nikky helped him to his feet.

'Wait, what about Scott?' the stranger asked, a look of intrigue replacing her smile.

'What's it to you, psycho! She's his girlfriend, we tried to tell you earlier. We thought he lived here, obviously we got that completely wrong,' shouted PJ. Nikky shot him a warning look and shook her head. The stranger moved closer.

'You know my son?'

'Son? You're Scott's *mom*?' PJ turned his head to Nikky and spoke from the side of his mouth. 'Scott never said his mom was a hotty.' Nikky responded with a thump.

'Did you say that you were Scott's friends?' the stranger persisted. Nikky answered cautiously after that bizarre show of strength. 'Yes … we are.'

The woman stopped in front of Nikky, examining her facial features. 'Aha, I see it now. I can see why he's taken an interest in you.' Her grin became a smile, suddenly pleasant and welcoming. She held out her hand for Nikky to shake.

'I'm Scott's mom, but you can call me Amdis.'

# Chapter 28

Across town next door to Trevor's Diner, Carol was beginning her routine evening lock-up of the Enchanted Florist. After the last customer left, she flipped the sign from open to closed, locked the door, and switched off the lights, then walked back through the artificial jungle of greenery and flowers to the serving area. She removed her green apron, exposing a black polo neck jumper and matching skirt and draped it across the worktop over a large scissors and plastic wrap. Still exhausted and drained from the previous night in the fortune teller's tent, she closed her eyes.

The peaceful moment was interrupted. Behind her, the bell rang, announcing a new customer with the sound of the door opening and closing.

'I thought I just locked …?' She spun around to find the shop empty and silent. Shaking her head, she opened the door and peered left and right, but the street was empty. Stepping back in, she turned the lock a second time, this time testing it by pulling on the door frame. Satisfied it was now locked, she turned to return to the shop counter.

After taking a few steps, she noticed something on her right which stopped her dead in her tracks. Today's new sunflowers were now standing lifeless and withered in their tall glass vases. She knew she was being watched.

And she also knew that only one thing can cause a sunflower to instantly wither and die.

Slowly she scanned the interior of the shop. Beads of sweat gathered on her forehead. She glanced over to the serving counter, remembering the large scissors under her apron. Counting to three inside her head, she bolted forward, diving towards the countertop. Reaching underneath the apron she grabbed the scissors and turned around to face the shop floor, holding the blades high in front of her.

Nothing. The shop remained still. From behind her, a voice spoke.

'Shame about your sunflowers.'

Carol spun around, the blades shaking in her hand.

'I think we need to have a little chat, Carol.'

Carol's voice quivered in real fear. 'What do you want with me? You're not welcome here, leave! Before I cast you out.'

Scott stood with his hands outstretched and resting on the countertop. His reaction to her threat was a simple smile.

'I think we both know that scissors won't harm me, did you not pay attention in Witchcraft 101?'

She knew he was right, but maybe she could slow him down enough to escape. He wouldn't dare follow her next door. Too many people in Trevor's at this hour. In a daring outburst of adrenaline, she jumped forward and jabbed the blades towards his chest. Scott slapped the scissors aside, sending it flying from her grip to hit the wall. She stared in disbelief at his reaction speed, forgetting how he'd caught the falling candle the previous night.

'I said it won't harm me, but I like this jacket, Carol, be a shame if it got sliced.'

'Why are you here, demon, what do you want from me?' A single tear rolled down her face. Scott walked around the counter, causing her to take a few awkward steps backwards while maintaining eye contact. He jumped lightly up to sit on the countertop, with his hands by his sides.

'I want some answers about what happened last night. I know I could enthral you against your will but I'm giving you the benefit of the doubt.' His smile was gone now, and he sounded sincere.

Carol folded her jellylike arms trying to stop them shaking. 'I saw what you are, you're a monster.'

'You seen my past not my present, something I'm not proud of but then again, we all have skeletons in our closets, would I be right?'

'I don't know what you're talking about.'

'I think you do. You come from a witches' coven that aligns itself with vampires to perform human sacrifices, so don't play the innocent palm reader with me.'

Carol dropped her gaze down to her feet with a feeling of guilt. 'If you know so much about me, then you should also know that I left the Grand Corinthian coven in Green Bay years ago.'

'True, but you still practise witchcraft in Tallant and no doubt keep in touch with your old coven friends. But I'm here to find out what you meant last night in your trance. You said a spell was cast, and it faded, but will be cast again.'

'You don't know who or what you are, do you?' She shook her head from side to side, almost with pity.

'You might help fill in a few blanks. I'll be honest: I was expecting another money-grabbing charlatan.'

'I can't tell you anything here, I feel as if the walls have ears,' Carol replied after a short pause.

'Name the place, I've got all night.'

'My place isn't far; if I feel more relaxed, I'll be more inclined to tell you what you want to know.'

Scott smiled and shook his head. 'So you can refuse to invite me in and I'll be surrounded by all the witchy tools at your disposal? And here I thought we were making progress.'

Realising her plan was now wasted, she spoke abruptly and out of character. 'What's the point? You'll kill me tonight no matter what I say.'

'I'm not here to kill you, Carol. If I wanted you dead, you'd already be dead.'

'Who's to say you won't kill me after I talk?'

'I give you my word that I won't harm you, how's that?'

'I will never trust a vampire.'

'I wouldn't trust one either, but I'm different, as you know; you've seen through my mind's eye, remember?'

'I've seen your dark side. Tell me, how would Nikky feel about you murdering her mother?'

Scott's cocky demeanour vanished. He was in front of her with such speed that the leaves of surrounding flowers moved in unison. With little time to react, Carol jumped as he placed his right hand on the side of her face. Her breathing became rapid, and her eyes switched from left to right. She pulled away, taking a step towards the door. He held his hand in mid-air for a moment before dropping it back to his side. She raised a hand to her open mouth in shock. 'Oh my God, that was intense.'

After showing her the inside of his mind, he spoke while she gathered her thoughts. 'Do I have any intention of harming you, Carol?'

She hesitated for a moment before side-stepping his question. 'I don't know, but I know we shouldn't stay here;

I suppose if you're going to kill me, it won't matter where we go.'

Scott jumped down from the counter. 'Good point, you'll just have to take a leap of faith. I know a place we can talk.' He moved to the door, keeping eye contact until he passed her, then stopped with his hand on the door handle. 'Ready?'

Realising she had no other option, she reached behind the counter, grabbed her coat and bag then made her way outside, locking the door behind her. She gestured sarcastically for him to lead. 'After you.' After a gentlemanly bow of his head, he led her down Fourth Avenue towards Trail Street and the forest. He turned right before the car park and made his way along the hiking track, stopping below the pine trees that led into the void.

'Follow me.'

'Seriously? You don't expect me to follow you into the forest in a town with a population of werewolves, do you?'

Scott stopped to face her; his eyebrows raised. 'Who will harm you in the spooky forest when you're with me?'

'I feel so much better, now the only person I need to worry about is you.'

'We've had this discussion already, let's go.' Scott turned and continued along his route. For a moment, Carol was alone. She glanced at the car park to her left and pondered the possibility of making it to a car for help. With a quick look in Scott's direction, she turned with a burst of adrenaline to bolt toward the closest car she could see. She ran straight into Scott's chest. He stood with his arms folded, blocking her path. She'd forgotten about his unnatural speed.

'How many times must I demonstrate? After you this time.' He pointed his hand at the forest. Accepting there was no escape, she made her way beneath the branches into the wilderness. No more than a few feet in, she succumbed to the blackness and stopped.

'I can't see a thing.'

Scott's spoke from the darkness, startling her. 'I can see perfectly.'

'Yeah well, I'm not a vampire.' He was becoming impatient. 'I'm going to carry you, hold on.'

'What!? You're not going to c–' Before she could finish her sentence, he scooped her up in his arms and they vanished.

## Chapter 29

They came to a stop deep within the forest a moment later.

'Do not do that! Never do that again! Where the hell are we?' Carol shouted.

'Relax, it would have taken hours for you to get here, I just helped you a little. We're about two miles from town in the forest.'

As her eyes adjusted, she took in her surroundings but was utterly disorientated and had no idea what direction they'd come from. They were standing in a circular clearing of trees. The stars were now visible overhead and enough moonlight to make out basic features in the immediate vicinity. Three large boulders circled them, with smaller ones scattered around at ground level on a carpet of pine needles and dead foliage. At the centre, a log used as a seat was beside the scorched remains of a campfire.

'Why did you bring me here?' asked Carol.

'Hold on a second.' Scott leapt onto the highest boulder, which stood about fifteen feet in the air, and stood, casting a shadow in the moonlight. Silently, he turned his head from left to right and waited.

'What are you doing now?' She dropped her bag beside her, hitting the ground with a thump.

'Listening. It's okay we're safe, there's nobody within a mile of us.' Scott dropped to one of the lower boulders closer to the centre. He sat down crossing his legs and watched as Carol approached the campfire. She dropped to her knees and waved her hand over it, muttering. Fire instantly ignited with an orange glow of flickering light, sending a spiral of smoke skywards. Scott didn't move but watched her closely.

'Neat trick.'

'At least now I can see you.' She sat down on the moss-covered log and looked at Scott sitting above her.

'So? I'm not getting any younger Carol, or … older for that matter. Tell me what you know.'

Realising she still had no choice, Carol began. 'It's vitally important that you're not cursed with another spell, that's why I'm helping you … also because I'm terrified of you.'

Scott held up a finger. 'Wait, go back, what do you mean *another* spell?'

'Don't you know the werewolf legend?'

'In part; I know of the werewolves in Tallant, but only some of their family history.' He was intrigued to discover that this witch had more information than he did, even after hundreds of years of existence. He mainly understood that vampires and werewolves somehow knew when they were in each other's presence. Like two magnets repelling.

'To make you understand, I must go back to the start and tell you how the legend began.'

'I'm all ears.'

Carol took a deep breath and exhaled.

'Centuries ago, a rich nobleman in a central European village was plagued by a pack of wolves attacking the local livestock. After exhausting all options, a meeting led to the desperate consideration of approaching a coven of witches, who lived on the outskirts of the town in the forest. The witches agreed to help the nobleman, but only if he would offer them a plot of land in his village. He agreed and they placed a protection spell on the village to keep the wolves at bay. As time passed without incident, his livestock flourished. The spell had proven its worth.

'Am I boring you, Scott?'

'Continue.'

'Before winter arrived, the witches approached the nobleman to receive payment. He laughed and told them their ungodly ways weren't welcome in his village. When they insisted, he removed a silver ring from his finger with his family's insignia inscribed upon it and threw it at them. Little did he realise that giving a personal belonging to a witch was asking for trouble. That item could curse not only its previous owner, but his entire bloodline.

'The witches took the ring and warned him that even though the wolves from outside the town boundaries would never return, his town would not be safe from the wolves within. He laughed again then banished them, never to return. With this ring, the witches performed a binding spell, cursing the nobleman and his descendants for generations to come.

'That's a lovely story but what's it got to do with me? I'm a vampire not a wolf.'

'I'm getting to that if you'll have some patience, I'm sure you know what happened next.'

'They turned into werewolves and ate the town? Go on, I'm listening.'

'Something like that yes. The nobleman's name was Cartwright. Sound familiar?'

'Continue.'

'From that time on, he and his descendants hunted all who called themselves witches. He collaborated with the Church to have suspects rounded up and burnt alive at the stake. They brought their feud across the Atlantic when they moved here in the last century.'

'Tell me again what this has to do with me? I bore easily, Carol.' Scott lay back on the boulder, resting on his elbows.

'Patience! As you know, vampires have been around since the dawn of time, and were once mortal enemies of those versed in the art of witchcraft. But vampires discovered that the bite of a werewolf was fatal to them; that along with sunlight and a good old stake through the heart.' She pointed at Scott's chest causing him to roll his eyes in annoyance.

'The number of practising witches began to dwindle from being hunted and persecuted by the Cartwright bloodline over the centuries. The opportunity for vampires to eliminate an enemy that could kill them was too good to miss. So the age-old feud between vampires and witches was put aside to stamp out a common foe. An alliance that has crossed continents and time to survive to this day.'

Scott sat forward again before replying. 'I know of some deals still in place. Your kind give daylight rings to vampires, allowing them to tolerate sunlight in exchange for victims to be used in human sacrifice. Not here in Tallant because I won't allow it, but not far from here, as I'm sure you know.'

'Yes, that's also true, it's why I'm back living here, to escape the atrocities.' She looked down into the glowing embers at her feet.

'Under the watchful eye of the Cartwrights?

'Why do you think I wanted to leave the store earlier? They have eyes everywhere. No doubt they were involved in the anonymous tip-off to police in Green Bay when those hostages were discovered.'

'Back to the story: what happened with the alliance?'

'I was just about to get to that part. Vampire ancients assisted the witches with a new unstoppable plan, two of the most ruthless vampires ever to have existed were chosen, and a spell was cast upon them. They continued killing and maiming innocents until the enchantment caused something unheard of in the history of vampirism. A vampire became pregnant.'

Scott stood up. This was what he'd been waiting for. 'Amdis …?'

'Yes, Scott, your mother. The spell created you.'

'To kill werewolves?'

'In theory, that was the plan. Vampires are hybrids, half human, half demon, created by a human ingesting a vampire's blood then dying with the demon's blood in their system. A human host is needed. But the ancients wanted to create a pureblood vampire with abilities enabling it to overcome methods that would kill an average vampire.

'A pureblood not affected by sunlight, impervious to the bite of the wolf and possessing other talents that I'm sure you keep close to your heart. Once that vampire was born, another spell was cast in a ritual that caused his blood lust to be unquenchable compared to that of other vampires.

The only problem was that the spell worked too well. He killed werewolves, yes, but his thirst for blood ran so deep that he began to attack his own kind along with the witches who had helped create him. He took out his uncontrollable rage on all who crossed his bloody path of destruction.'

Scott slumped back to a squatting position, his head and shoulders hung low. 'Why did I stop ageing as a teenager?' This time he didn't look at Carol.

'I'm not sure but I can hazard a guess. Something was probably triggered in the spell when you first killed one of your own kind hundreds of years ago.'

Scott nodded. 'Sounds about right. "As the bonfires of knowledge grow brighter, the more the darkness is revealed to our startled eyes." He shook his head. The more he learned, the more he wished he hadn't. Carol almost felt sorry for him until she remembered she was there against her will.

'Can you explain to me why I'm the way I am now? I haven't taken a human life for over seventy years.' He looked up to the stars for a moment, then closed his eyes while keeping his head tilted towards the heavens. 'I can only guess the spell began to weaken over time. Some other factors may also have helped.'

He remembered when he had stopped feeling the urge to kill humans, and how he became the way he was now. But that was nothing he'd be willing to share. Not with her, anyway. He spoke in defiance this time.

'For centuries the ancients wanted me to help rid the world of werewolves, but I refused. Instead, I kill every vampire that crosses my path as a message that I'm not going anywhere. That's why they stay in the mountains, hidden in the Great Hall with their numbers dwindling. I know what I've done in the past and that's my burden to bear. The vampires want the Cartwrights gone, leaving the way clear for them to return from the mountains, but I won't let that happen. Vampires are more of a threat than werewolves to Tallant. I can't make amends, but I keep this town safe from all of them – vampires, witches, werewolves. I patrol the forest every full moon on the lookout for those. I know they have their own methods in place for when the full moon occurs, but I don't trust them.'

'There is something else you need to know, Scott. You say you protect this town, but can you protect it from yourself?'

'What do you mean?'

'Last night I saw your past – but I also got a glimpse of your future, the spell will be cast again.'

'How can I stop it?'

'If the ancients can't have you on their side, they will let you tear the town apart all by yourself.'

Scott scowled in her direction. 'Wait, they can't perform the spell alone, they need the help of ... a witch?' He glared at her suspiciously.

Carol stood up nervously. 'Now just wait a minute, Scott! I'm trying to help you; having that spell cast again is the last thing I want to happen. I've seen your past, remember? I know what you once were. If anyone will cast the spell it'll be the witches in Green Bay. But even they don't realise the hornet's nest they'd be stirring up.'

'And just why should I trus–' Scott stopped short. His head snapped upright. Without moving a muscle, he looked to his left into the darkness. Carol continued, hardly noticing that he had stopped talking.

'Why should you trust me? Because I don't want to die or see this town disappear, that's why! Have I not given you enough reasons why I –' Carol stopped talking. The teenager who had been feet away, high on the boulder, stood in front of her. Now close enough for her to smell his cologne, he stared into her eyes with a peculiarly uncomfortable look on his face. Carol screamed, 'No! Scott, wait! Please don't!'

He turned his head to his right and looked at the ground behind him before looking back at Carol's shocked face. She watched as he did an about turn towards the campfire, staring beyond the rising sparks into the darkness. Her mouth fell open when she saw the handle of a knife sticking out four inches from the centre of Scott's back. She now realised why he had appeared in front of her like that. And, more terrifyingly, she knew that they were no longer alone.

## Chapter 30

'Would you mind doing the honours, Carol?' Scott spoke knowing someone was listening.

'Are you okay?' she stepped towards him.

'I'm fine, just do it.'

She grabbed the handle and slowly pulled the five-inch blade from between his shoulder blades through his leather jacket. Scott turned to inspect the blade covered in his blood. Carol looked over his shoulder behind him.

'Did a werewolf just try to kill me?' Scott spoke that so the surrounding forest could hear him. 'No ... I've seen this before. That's the blade of an ancient vampire. Draven, if I'm not mistaken?'

Hands began to clap before a figure appeared and approached the campfire. 'Bravo, Scott, I must say, bravo ... how did you know? Another of your talents, I'm sure.'

Carol moved close behind Scott to shield herself from the ancient vampire.

'How long has it been, Scott? Give or take two hundred years?' Draven stopped short of the fire, holding his hands above the flames as if trying to heat his lifeless body.

'Not long enough, Draven.'

To Carol, this was a clash of the titans. Throughout the ages few had witnessed a face-off between an ancient and the pureblood. The older a vampire was, the stronger it became. And they don't come much stronger than the ancients. Scott was nowhere near as old as Draven but was the only pureblood vampire in existence. One created through witchcraft.

Draven dominated Scott in height. He wore a brown leather hooded robe that parted at the front with a high collar standing at the back of his neck. Underneath, he wore a faded gold tunic with black leather trousers and grey boots. A metallic belt hung around his waist with an empty scabbard to house the blade now in Carol's hands. He pulled back the pointed hood of his robe, exposing a grey wrinkled face with long jet-black hair. A lone blue vein ran from his right temple down his neck.

'Killing your allies now, Draven? I thought you liked witches?' Scott spoke across the fire.

'This witch is a traitor to her own kind and won't be missed by anyone.'

'I gave her my word that she'll be safe with me. I won't let harm come to her, especially from you.'

Draven smiled and folded his arms across his chest. 'And just how do you think you can stop me, boy?'

'The same way I stopped your friends last night. It didn't end well for them, or haven't you heard yet?'

Draven's smile vanished. 'Any vampire that kills one of their own kind must answer for their crimes before the ancients.'

'Oh stop it, no more bullshit. I've been killing vampires for centuries. You're pretending it didn't happen because you're afraid to face me.'

'We do not fear you, boy, rest assured of that.'

Carol spoke now, causing Scott to turn his head, while not taking his eyes from Draven. 'This looks like an age-old personal matter, Scott, I should go; I'll find my way back and leave you two alone.' She took two hesitant steps backwards before Scott spoke, still looking at Draven.

'If you leave my sight, he'll kill you. Trust me, stay with me a little longer and I'll get you home.'

'Tell me, witch, who says I won't kill you in front of your protector?' Draven grinned.

'Don't worry about Draven, Carol, he'll think twice before he tries anything. He knows what I'm capable of first-hand, isn't that right, Draven? Or have you forgotten?' Scott grinned back.

The grin on Draven's face dissipated. 'I'm older and stronger now than when we had our last "disagreement", boy, and you're not the vampire you once were. You haven't fed on human blood for decades; animal blood has made you weak.'

'Keeping tabs, are we? Perhaps you would like to test that theory?' Scott knelt down at the campfire while speaking. He removed the silver bracket from his wrist and placed it in an inside jacket pocket. With his blue eyes still locked on Draven's, he held his right arm above the flames. Slowly, he began to lower his hand, causing his skin to redden as it blistered. Carol raised both hands to her mouth and turned away in horror. The sleeve of his leather jacket started to smoulder. A strong smell of burning leather and flesh filled the area. Blisters formed and popped the entire length of his arm with a sizzling sound. He turned his hand over, making sure both sides were engulfed within the fire. Within minutes, his arm was charcoal black and almost burned to the bone. Scott's facial expression didn't change as he glared at the ancient.

Scott stood up, his arm still blazing. He turned his gaze from Draven and onto his arm, watching as a remaining piece of leather sleeve melted and fell to the ground. The flame subsided as the charred remains of his arm began to change. The blackened flesh slowly turned back to the red and blistered skin it was before its exposure to the fire. Scott began to move his fingers. Within a minute his arm had healed, with no trace of scaring.

'You ... you belong with your own kind, Scott, and should take your place among the ancients. That's why I came here personally. Be thankful I didn't desecrate your grave to get your attention,' Draven said, trying to hide his amazement.

Scott noticed the change in his tone. He placed his bracelet back on his now bare right wrist. 'I got your message in the fairground last night. Latin, nice touch, but attacking the innocent people with me was not a good idea.'

Carol turned back to face them, relieved, if baffled, to see Scott's sleeveless arm back to normal.

'Amdis hasn't helped our cause,' Draven said. 'She still can't persuade you to return to your own kind.'

'Amdis is torn between her loyalty to her own kind and a son who refuses to cooperate with her beliefs. Someday she must choose where her loyalties lie. But what puzzles me is why you approach me now, Draven? After all these years?'

Draven nodded towards Carol. 'Things are changing, Scott; I can't explain right now but your own kind needs you more than ever.'

'"Scott"? Wasn't it "boy" a moment ago? You know my decision, so stay away from me, my friends, and Tallant itself. Take this as a personal threat, Draven. Keep your minions in the mountains away from town because I'll kill them on sight. Now if you'll excuse me, there's somewhere else I have to be tonight, thanks to you. Have a nice night.' Scott took the dagger from Carol's hand and threw it to Draven, who caught it mid-air before placing it back in the scabbard on his hip. Carol picked up her bag, looked at Scott and nodded. A second later Scott disappeared from where he stood then reappeared in front of Carol, before they both vanished in a blur.

Back in Tallant at Carol's apartment building, Scott watched as she unlocked the door to the lobby. Once inside, she turned to face him. 'A few questions, Scott: how did you know Draven was there in the first place?'

'Just one of my "talents", as Draven put it earlier.'

'What did he mean when he said he hadn't desecrated your grave?'

Scott hesitated, wondering if she already knew too much. 'A vampire instantly knows if someone has tampered with his grave, it's like a sixth sense. It's a good way to get a vampire's attention. Even though I didn't die to become a vampire, one mausoleum in the cemetery was my burial place ... a place I remained buried for years as self-punishment for what I'd done, before someone woke me over seventy years ago.'

'You also mentioned that he knows what you're capable of? What did he mean?'

Scott turned and began to walk away. 'Gotta go, have to tie up a loose end before it unravels.'

'Scott, please tell me: am I in danger?'

He stopped and looked back over his shoulder. 'The vampire I killed when I was seventeen was an ancient. He was Draven's brother.'

'Wait, you've already killed an ancient? I was terrified for our lives back there, not sure if you could protect me, and you'd already killed one?'

But he was gone.

***

In the forest clearing beneath the stars, Draven stood alone by the flickering light of the campfire and smiled. Removing the dagger from his hip he stared again at the blood stain before vanishing into the darkness from which he came. He'd achieved exactly what he needed.

## Chapter 31

Tyres screeched in an empty parking lot on the east side of town as three black SUVs with tinted windows came to a halt outside a high-tech medical facility. The doors on the three vehicles opened simultaneously and a group of men dressed in black exited to stand around a man who stood waiting, facing the laboratory. He pointed a black, leather-clad finger at the red light from an infrared camera mounted on the top of the building, which was aimed in their direction.

'Let's get the hard drive.' Governor Patrick Cartwright watched as one of his team inserted a security card to the receiver on the doorway, causing the automatic doors to slide open with a hiss. The twenty-second delay to enter a six-digit code inside the main door was no obstacle as all team members had security-override access. Six beeps from the keypad later and the lead man spoke. 'Clear, sir.'

Apart from the hum of a vending machine in the reception area, the building was pitch-black and silent. The team proceeded inside with flashlight beams jumping from wall to wall, lighting the path past the reception area and down a flight of stairs to an underground corridor. The

Governor stopped outside a set of double doors with frosted windows, labelled 'Autopsy Room 1'. The strong smell of formaldehyde indicated what the room contained. To the left of the door, a clipboard with a single piece of paper hung on the wall, identifying the room's current occupants.

The Governor removed it and read. Six autopsy tables were listed. The first three were blank. The last three had names filled in.

*Table 4 – John Doe – Deceased*
*Table 5 – Jason Cartwright – Deceased*
*Table 6 – Joseph Taylor – Deceased*

Satisfied, he placed it back on the wall and turned to face the men. 'This is it, everyone ready?' Nine men nodded, psyched for what lay ahead.

'Proceed.' The Governor held back as two men opened the double doors, allowing the others to advance into darkness. This larger, windowless room held a small office on the immediate left separated by Perspex from a large floor space with six stainless-steel tables. The white tiled floor had random plugholes throughout to allow drainage after certain procedures with scalpels and bone saws. At the back wall, two porcelain sinks stood next to a table with a weighing scales and various medical instruments on trays. Flashlights scanning the room came to a stop pointing at the same location. Three of the six tables near the far wall were covered in plastic sheeting exposing wax-coloured feet with an identification tag tied around the big toe of each foot. This was not where the flashlights came to a stop. Bodies on tables were to be expected here.

It was the lone figure sitting with his back to the men on an empty autopsy table that was unexpected. The team stopped advancing into the room. The figure circled in light didn't turn around to witness the intrusion. In response to a nod from the Governor, one of his team flipped the light switch. Fluorescent lights flickered on, reflecting light from every stainless-steel surface. The figure with his back to the men broke the silence. 'I preferred it dark.' The Governor approached slowly, followed closely by his men. He had recognised the person sitting on the autopsy table. 'What the hell are you doing here?' he said angrily, folding his arms with gloved hands.

Scott was eating a bag of popcorn from the vending machine as he looked up. 'Same reason you're here I guess, great minds, eh?' He winked before taking another handful of popcorn, not concerned about being surrounded. 'So, I'm guessing you've seen the CCTV footage, Governor?'

'That's why we're here, but how did you know?'

'I knew the blood on your unfortunate relative's lips wasn't his own, he was force fed a vampires blood.'

'We'll take care of this, like we've done many times in the past. Your help is not required.'

'I wouldn't bet on that, Governor.'

'You can leave now.'

'Not a good idea, think I'll stay and watch if that's okay, to make sure it's done right.'

'I didn't realise there was a humane way to do this,' the Governor laughed grimly.

'There's something else you should know,' Scott added.

'We don't need advice from you or your –' The laughter stopped as the sheet covering the middle body moved. Scott spoke again. 'Yes, that's the one. The one on the left is the John Doe from the forest, and I believe you're related to the one on the right?'

One of the Governor's team inspected the tag on the body lying on the table to the right.

*Jason Cartwright – Deceased.*

He nodded to the Governor as the others moved forward around their dead relative.

The toes on the body lying on the middle table began to twitch.

'Almost there.' Scott crunched more popcorn.

The Governor nodded. His men surrounded the naked body of Joseph Taylor, three either side. The one nearest the head removed the plastic sheet. The head had been twisted back by the mortician to face the correct way, but the neck still looked badly deformed. The fingers on the right hand were next to move, twitching briefly then lying still. One of the team pulled a wooden stake and mallet from an inside pocket of his jacket and held them above Joseph Taylor's chest bone. The bones in the neck began to twist and reshape, with a sound like the cracking of knuckles. Scott inspected the body from where he sat, the vibrational hum starting up in his chest. He glanced at the Governor with a smile and raised his eyebrows.

'Showtime.' Joseph Taylor's eyes opened suddenly, revealing lifeless, black eyes that reflected the fluorescent light shining down from above. He remained still, staring emptily at the ceiling. Slowly, the pale wax- coloured skin covering his body turned grey, highlighting the blood vessels that ran near the surface of the skin. Every fingernail visibly lengthened, then every vein turned black, covering the grey body like a spider web from head to toe. The transformation was now complete.

Scott could almost taste the nervous energy of the men that surrounded him, noticing a quiver in the stake held above the cadaver's chest. All their hearts were racing in anticipation.

The man holding the stake in position looked at the Governor for instruction.

'Do it now,' the Governor said sharply.

Before he could plunge the stake into the breastbone, an ear-piercing scream followed by a deep growl escaped from the mouth of what was once Joseph Taylor, exposing two lengthened fangs in the top row of teeth. A grey hand shot upwards, grabbing hold of the trembling arm holding the stake. As the newly created vampire sat up, he pulled the man with the stake across the table and flung him over the body of Jason Cartwright. He hit the wall then landed on the floor, his eyes turning yellow with anger. Yellow eyes now surrounded the demon on the autopsy table as each member of the Cartwright family moved in close to kill their mortal enemy.

The former Joseph Taylor sprang up, grabbing two more Cartwrights and shoving them against the autopsy table of John Doe. The body and table overturned, crashing to the floor, and exposing the dismembered corpse from the forest. Scott looked at the Governor, who looked back at Scott.

'We've got this,' the Governor said, as his own eyes glowed yellow. Each Cartwright now held a stake and waited for an opportunity to plunge it into the vampire's chest. The former Joseph Taylor did an about-turn and grabbed hold of the autopsy table he'd been lying on a moment ago. He upended it, knocking three more Cartwrights to the floor below their dead relative. Scott continued eating his popcorn as the drama unfolded before him. The alpha of the pack took his turn now. Governor Cartwright jabbed his stake at the undead, but the vampire dodged then grabbed him by the throat and tried to sink his fangs into his neck.

The Governor landed two punches to the creature's head, forcing it to release its grip. Next, it grabbed the Governor and effortlessly tossed him to the wall behind, landing on the washbasin, which smashed to pieces as it hit the floor.

Scott spoke again across the carnage to the Governor struggling to get back to his feet. 'As I tried to tell you earlier, this guy was sired by an ancient, meaning he's stronger than the average vampire.' The vampire's focus suddenly changed from those attacking him to the one casually eating popcorn. With stakes held out in front, the remaining Cartwrights took a step back and watched. The former Joseph Taylor approached Scott slowly, as if unsure what to do.

Scott stopped chewing and returned the creatures' stare for a moment before emptying the remaining contents of the bag down his throat. He placed the empty packet on the table behind him before looking to the Governor again. 'My turn?'

Governor Cartwright's pride made him hesitate. The new vampire decided for him. In a split second, it ran screaming towards the Governor, again grabbing him by the throat and lifting him up against the wall. The

Governor's yellow eyes tried to focus on Scott. He could barely get a word out from his crushed windpipe. 'Yes!'

Scott picked a popcorn kernel from one of his teeth and inspected it. He vanished from the autopsy table and reappeared directly behind the undead creature. In one swift motion he plunged his hand into the vampire's back, grabbing its heart and shoving it through the chest cavity. The former Joseph Taylor staggered, dropping the Governor before staring at its own lifeless heart in Scott's hand, sticking through the front of its ribcage. The room was silent and still.

The newly formed vampire began to combust, bursting into flames and slowly dropping piece by flaming piece to the floor before turning to dust. With his blood-covered hand still holding the heart, Scott released his grip, letting it fall to the tiles between their feet. Scott said nothing but he stared into the Governor's eyes. A member of his team finally spoke.

'Are you okay, Governor?'

He brushed himself off before answering. 'I'll heal, I'm fine.' Scott leaned in close to the Governor and spoke in a whisper. 'You're welcome.' An instant later, one of the double doors flew open and Scott was gone. A scattering of paper pinned to a noticeboard fell to the floor in the breeze. The Governor stepped forward across broken pieces of porcelain and spoke to his family.

'You've all seen him, now you know what we're up against.'

# Chapter 32

'The Governor will see you now.' Secretary Millicent Cartwright placed the phone back on the desk in front of her. With a generous smile at Ranger James Brennan, she gestured at the closed double doors to the Governor's office. James took his hat from the seat next to him and nodded to the young Cartwright behind the desk. He straightened his shirt and polished his badge in an effort to look more presentable. Even though he and Governor Cartwright had known each other for years, James liked to keep things legitimate and professional where possible when dealing with the Cartwright family. Few in town knew the information that he was privy to. Information that made him feel uncomfortable. The chief of police and coroner also carried the burden of truth, but that topic would never come up in any conversation.

With a certain trepidation he knocked once before pressing down the brass door handle. Sitting behind an antique desk, Governor Patrick Cartwright was signing documents as the ranger entered. James noticed something unexpected: they were not alone. Sitting with arms folded on the front of the Governor's desk was the Governor's brother, lawyer Damien Cartwright.

'Jim, good to see you. Please, close the door and take a seat,' said the Governor, pointing to the two empty office chairs facing his desk. 'I believe you've met my brother on more than one occasion?' James took a seat and settled his hat on his lap. He reached to his belt and turned his radio to the off position.

'Yes, we've met.' He nodded and got the same in response. No handshake this time. Same as last time they'd met, if James remembered. Damien Cartwright only offered his hand in return for payment on legal matters. Governor Cartwright picked up the phone on his desk and pushed a button.

'Millicent: no interruptions.' Being a Cartwright, Millicent knew what those words meant. He placed the receiver back in its cradle.

'What can I do for you, Jim? Your secretary said it was urgent.'

The ranger looked at the Governor's brother before looking back across the desk.

'It's okay, you can speak,' the Governor said.

'If you say so. It's about the last animal attack, Governor.' James felt uncomfortable with this topic, hesitating slightly before the word 'animal'.

'Yes, I've heard. A lone hiker, wasn't it?'

'That's what myself and the coroner have agreed on. No family have registered a missing person's report yet,' James replied. Damien remained silent, switching his gaze between his shoes and the man in uniform sitting next to him.

'Good, let's hope it stays that way, shall we?' The Governor sat back in his chair, placing both hands on the desk.

'It's just … how can I put this, Governor?' James looked through the window behind the Governor's chair for a polite way to address the situation. 'Decomposition has given us a time of death, and, well … there was no full moon on the night the victim was killed, and it wasn't an animal attack.' Damien twisted his head around and looked his brother in the eye before retraining his stare on the ranger.

'Yes, Jim, but not every death in the forest is related to a full moon. As you know, we've taken steps to ensure precautions are in place on those nights. If I'm correct, there hasn't been a death in Tallant on a full moon in the past three years.'

'Yes, Governor I'm aware of that, but if it's not to do with the full moon … well, who or what else is capable?' queried the ranger. The phone on the desk between them rang with perfect timing to ease the awkwardness of the ranger's question. Annoyed at the distraction, the Governor picked up the receiver.

'I thought I said no interruptions?'

Millicent's voice could be heard on the other end. 'It's one of our own.'

'Alright, have him take a seat, this won't take long,' the Governor replied before jumping back into the conversation without skipping a beat. 'I want you to let this go, Jim, it's being rectified, but this incident had nothing to do with us. I can promise you that. Just stay vigilant and report anything out of the ordinary to the chief of police, or me, like always.'

'Understood but …'

Damien cut across him. 'But what, James?'

'These attacks are easily distinguished from regular animal attacks – if anyone was to examine –' Jim was cut off again.

'If the coroner, the park ranger and the chief of police agree it was an unfortunate incident with a bear, then that's what it was, understood?' said Damien in a condescending tone.

The ranger looked to the Governor for his input. He nodded.

'Understood.'

'Will there be anything else, Jim?' The Governor spoke in a casual tone to lighten the atmosphere.

'One other query, if I may. I know it's not my jurisdiction, this is really just personal curiosity, but were the bodies found at the fairground last night related to the forest incident?'

'We're looking into that matter but it's nothing for you to worry about; nothing will come back on you, Jim, you have my word on that.'

'Thank you for your time, Governor.' James Brennan stood up, gave a nod and put his hat on his head as he walked out the door. Dan Cartwright sat waiting in reception, glued to his phone. Back inside the office, the Governor was pouring two whiskeys from a wall cabinet before returning to his seat. His brother turned sideways, half facing the door with one knee resting on the desk.

'Are you sure you can trust that guy?' he asked, sniffing the contents of his glass.

'Yes, I'm sure. He learned how to keep his mouth shut the hardest way possible.'

'You mean his wife?'

The Governor sipped his drink. 'With regret, an unfortunate accident. Wrong place at the wrong time. Jim is aware what happened that night.'

'Snooping around the forest on a full moon after receiving a tip-off?' Damien stated.

'Jim told her nothing, I'm sure of that. Why would he send his wife on a suicide mission?'

'True, but while we're on the topic of the full moon, you know the next change is September 30th, right?'

'That, my dear brother, is why your 17-year-old son is waiting outside. His life is about to change, forever,' the Governor replied.

'I still remember when Father told us; I can't believe it's Dan's turn already,' Damien said.

'Think he can handle it?'

'It's not like he has a choice, is it? None of us do. But do we tell him about the pureblood?'

'No need to alarm him, he'll have enough on his plate after this meeting.' The Governor picked up the phone again and spoke. 'Lock the front door and send him in.'

\*\*\*

Across town, in the depths of the cemetery, a single flower was placed on the steps of a mausoleum in the morning sun. Hidden within a central maze of headstones and evergreens, a lone figure stood facing a rusted door, beneath a name chiselled in stone now covered in ivy. A moment later, the tomb was abandoned again to time.

\*\*\*

Inside the Governor's office, Dan Cartwright was puzzled. 'Dad? I didn't know you were gonna be here.'

'Take a seat, Daniel,' said the Governor. 'Son, this is going be hard to swallow, but it might explain some questions you've probably had about our family as you were growing up.'

Damien stood up and retrieved another glass from the cabinet, placing it on the desk in front of his son. The Governor poured three whiskeys this time. Dan stared in disbelief, looking from one to the other, suspecting a test.

'Dad – I'm underage!'

The Governor picked up his glass before speaking. 'Trust me, kid, you're gonna need it.'

# Chapter 33

Later that evening, Scott finished updating his journal before returning it to the shelf at the foot of his bed. Darkness had fallen but his intention to go out was to be thwarted by an unexpected confrontation. Amdis sat facing the unlit fireplace, waiting for Scott's bedroom door to open. She felt uncomfortable. They hadn't spoken for months, but recent developments had forced her hand. She could recall years between conversations after an argument in the past. This was expected between immortals. Personalities clashed and awkward moments passed, but some long-ago atrocities were unforgivable, for both of them. But even though this friction was unbearable, nobody knew Scott like Amdis.

Scott stepped into the living room where Amdis lay in wait, sitting as if relaxed with her hands clasped on her stomach. She stared. He stared back. Two emotionless faces waiting for the other to speak. Scott had more important places to be and he had no problem waiting another year if necessary. He started for the door behind her until she spoke.

'Two of your friends were here last night.' She spoke without moving, now staring into the fireplace.

Scott stopped without turning around. 'I don't have any friends, Amdis,' he said, pretending he didn't care. He waited to learn what had happened while he was with Carol.

'That's not what I was told, you've had friends before in this town.'

'That was a long time ago, they're all long dead and buried.' He looked up to the dark ceiling, lost in memories that were better forgotten.

'Not all, Scott, how is Gerry? Or should I ask about that touchy subject?'

'Leave it be, Amdis,' Scott exhaled.

'That girl, Nikky's her name, I believe?'

Scott turned his head to one side. 'What about her?'

'The rude boy with the baseball cap said she was your girlfriend, is that right? Because if she is, Scott, well, you know what happens.'

'She's not my girlfriend, but I trust they made it out alive?'

'Oh, now, why the concern if they're not your friends? I'm not stupid, Scott, I can see why you like her.'

Scott stormed around to face Amdis. 'I never said I liked her!' he shouted.

She looked at him with a warped sense of pride. 'There's my boy. Nice to know you're still in there, Scott. For a minute you reminded me of your father.' Realising his anger had gotten the better of him, he dropped his hand back to his side. His father was someone he preferred to forget. Every so often, Amdis liked to remind him of unpleasant memories that still cut like a knife. She pointed to the empty chair.

'Take a seat.'

He looked at the chair then back to her.

'I won't bite, Scott.'

'It's not me I worry about you biting,' he answered, reluctantly sitting down, and imitating her pose with his hands on his stomach.

'As if I would harm your friends! I was very polite once I realised they weren't trying to rob us.'

'Glad to hear it, but I'll find out their version of what happened later. By the way, who was your latest happy meal, while we're on the subject of biting?'

She grinned. 'Father O'Malley is such a nice man. And confession is good for the soul … I don't recall you ever going near a church, come to think of it.'

He hesitated. She may be his mother and know more than anyone else, but she didn't know everything about him. Especially his weakness.

'I'm not religious.'

Amdis thought for a moment. 'Rawcliffe, York, England: 1825. If memory serves, you slaughtered almost the entire town. The only survivors I found were hiding in the church.' Wheels were spinning inside her head.

'I told you, I'm not religious. I take it Father O'Malley is still breathing?' he shifted the subject.

She shook her head as if a thought had just disappeared before replying. 'Yes, of course. I enthralled him, stole his memory, and healed him good as new to keep you happy. The temptation to drink until his heart stopped then rip his throat out never goes away, but I'm sure nobody knows that more than you. I do so enjoy playing with the clergy.' She was trying to remind him of when he had been more ruthless than her. Again, he changed the topic.

'Just so you know, I encountered Draven last night. He spoke about your failure to lure me back to "take my place with our own kind".'

Amdis looked uncomfortable on hearing this name. They had unfinished business that spanned centuries. Draven made her nervous; she continued to exist only because Draven permitted it. Because of who she was. That, and Draven's fear of what the pureblood might do should he harm her. Scott hated her. But he tolerated and protected her. She was the only vampire he wouldn't kill. Even though her atrocities were nothing compared to his own, she was all he had left.

'They're desperate for your return, something is rattling them.' she stated in a serious tone.

'They could never control me. Nothing has changed.'

'But you've changed: there was a time when you would've left this town in pieces. In fact, you did once, remember?'

He grimaced. 'It wasn't a town like it is today. Besides, times have changed, the world is a smaller place. It's not as easy to get away with murder.'

'Scott, you could conquer the world if you put your mind to it.'

'Lucky for you I lack the motivation.'

'Why not return and lead as they wish?'

'Because I'm not obsessed with power like you. It means nothing to me. You only want to tag along for the ride, just like with my father. No amount of power can give me what I've always wanted.'

She bolted to her feet; her eyes turning black in rage. 'How dare you speak about your father that way! You've never had respect for your parents.'

Scott sat watching her. He'd witnessed her swiftness to anger before and had never felt intimidated by it. 'You've got that right, Amdis. Respect must be earned. And I'm nothing like him.'

'You're not even half the man he was,' she said viciously, her eyes still black.

Scott reacted to her words this time. He leapt from his chair, stopping a fraction away from her face and glared into her lifeless eyes. She observed his reaction with uncertainty. Her eyes slowly returned to their usual blue as her anger passed, to be replaced by regret. The light between the chairs flickered on and off. In that split second, when the room was dark, she noticed his eyes before the light returned. For a moment she got a glimpse of the demon she knew so well.

Scott spoke in the demonic voice she hadn't heard for a long time. 'My dear mother, I am the monster you created. I don't live in darkness; darkness lives in me. I struggle to control it. You became evil when the demon took over, destroying what was left of your humanity. I was born the demon, lost in darkness, longing for what you gave up so easily.'

He turned and made for the front door, grabbing a jacket, and slamming the door shut behind him. Amdis sat back down and smiled to herself. 'I do miss the old Scott, but after all this time, I think I know what strikes fear into the demon you try to control.'

A moment later, Amdis stood at the threshold of Scott's bedroom, leaning her shoulder against the door frame, staring at the antique bookshelf towering over the end of Scott's bed. His journals would answer her questions about his fear of religious symbolism.

# Chapter 34

'Nikky! Are you up yet?' With a breakfast bowl in hand and a mouth full of cornflakes, Caden shouted his sister's name from the hallway. 'Nikky! You're wanted at the door!'

Still half asleep, Nikky turned to one side and pulled her unicorn eye mask to her forehead as she reached for her phone to check the time. The screen came to life. Smiling back at her was a photo of her mom and dad. Seeing the time, she dropped her head in disappointment, planting her face into the bedsheet. Speaking to herself in a groggy voice, she rolled back and stared up at the ceiling, thumping her fist on the bedcovers.

'Damn it, PJ, 9.30 on a Saturday morning? Seriously?'

'Nikky!' Caden was impatient, missing valuable minutes of morning TV.

'Yeah, I'll be right down, chill!' she shouted back. She spoke to the empty room. 'Honestly, PJ, this better be worth it.' She sat up and stuck her feet into her unicorn slippers and pulled on a pink unicorn dressing gown. Storming down the stairs, tying a bow in front at her waist as she ran, she noticed Caden disappearing back to the TV, leaving the front door ajar. She grabbed it in frustration.

'PJ, what kind of –' She stopped short.

'Good morning, Miss Brennan.'

Scott stood in the morning sun, wearing designer sunglasses and a sheepish grin.

'Oh God, I assumed you were PJ.' She ripped off the eye mask and folded her arms.

'Is PJ used to getting the unicorn greeting? Or should I feel privileged?' Scott smiled, letting her embarrassment endure a moment longer. Mortified, she attempted a smile, knowing there was no escape.

'I wasn't expecting to see you here, that's all. You caught me off guard, as I'm sure you've guessed.'

'Thought never crossed my mind, I thought you always looked this way.'

She was relieved to see his humorous reaction, but she was also delighted to lay eyes on him again. 'Nah, only a select few get to see me in my unicorn form, consider yourself lucky. Guess my secret's out now.'

'Glad I qualified for the honour,' he replied. Buster popped his head around the bottom of the door to inspect the guest. He made eye contact with Scott then took off with a whimper.

'Guess it's only fair if I get to see your true form too,' she added, oblivious to the dog's behaviour

'Not sure that's a good idea, my identity doesn't go down well with most,' Scott joked, half serious.

'Oh it can't be that bad? Let me guess: I know you live in the cemetery, which is, well, different, so maybe you're a zombie or a goblin of sorts?' she winked.

'Nope, but why spoil the fun finding out?'

'Again, with the mystery. Come on, Scott, you owe me something now that you've seen me all in my unicorn glory.'

Scott dropped his gaze to the ground before looking into her blue eyes. He paused, unsmiling now, contemplating his decision.

'I'm a vampire.' He watched her reaction. He knew she wouldn't take him seriously, but he half hoped she would.

'That explains the cemetery anyway.'

Scott stayed silent, unsure of a suitable response.

'You wanna step in while I get ready? I'll be a few minutes then we can go downtown.' She gestured him in with her hand.

'No thanks, don't invite me in. I'll hang out here, it's a nice day.'

'Are you sure? My dad and grandma are out for the day so it's just Caden.'

'I'm good right here. You take your time.'

'Okay, but honestly, don't worry about coming inside if you want.'

'I want to check out your brother's treehouse,' he said, pointing to the large oak at the side of the house.

'Up to you. I'll grab breakfast to go to save time, won't be long.' With a wave of her hand, she closed the door, leaving Scott alone in the front garden. A few minutes later, dressed and ready for the day ahead, she opened her curtains and was surprised to see Scott in her brother's treehouse looking back at her. She stuck her head out the window, leaning on the windowsill with both hands. 'A room with a view?'

'The view just got better,' he replied.

She blushed. Downstairs, she heard Caden opening and closing the front door. A memory flashed inside her head. Grandma had borrowed Caden's key. She leant further out, attempting to get Caden's attention from the front garden.

'Caden!' she shouted.

Scott watched from the treehouse. 'Nikky, be careful! That windowsill is –'

Before he could finish, her hands slipped, sending her tumbling through the window before she found herself looking skywards from Scott's arms, staring up at him, unable to comprehend what happened.

'– wet.' Scott finished his sentence with less urgency.

'What the hell happened?'

'You slipped, are you okay?'

'Well yeah, I can see that, but –'

He set her feet first back to earth and placed his hand on her shoulder as she steadied herself. 'Okay, I fell out the window, so stupid, but you saved my life ... how did you ...?' Her heart was still racing.

'Guess I was in the right place at the right time. Are you sure you're okay? You seem confused.'

'I'm fine, but of course I'm confused, how on earth did you catch me like that? You were in Caden's treehouse when I fell?'

'Are you sure you didn't bang your head, if you can't remember properly?'

She looked at him sideways, suspiciously. 'Yes, I'm sure ... curiouser and curiouser. Regardless of how you did it, I guess I ... I owe you my life?'

He shrugged. 'Don't mention it. What were you trying to do, anyway?'

'Tell Caden to take the spare key, Grandma borrowed his.'

'Not really worth risking your life for.'

'Totally stupid move on my part. I suppose you're my hero now,' she grinned.

'Ready to go downtown?'

'Wait, just a sec.' She patted herself down before pulling her phone from her back pocket in relief. 'It's okay,

I'm ready, let's go.' As they were leaving the house, Scott noticed the withered sunflowers on the table inside the front door. He wondered if they were innocently placed there for decoration, or for another reason entirely. Only time would tell.

Nikky spoke first. 'How was your cab ride home the other night?'

'Oh that, the conversation was a little, uh, dead.'

Nikky nodded. 'Yeah, he wasn't the most talkative.'

'Should we call in for PJ?' Scott asked.

As much as she liked PJ, Nikky wanted to get some time alone with Scott. This was her chance. If things went well, she might bring up the homecoming dance on Halloween night.

'Nah, we'll catch up with the gang later in Trevor's, it's been arranged by group text. Pity you don't have a phone.'

'Phones and TV are just not my thing. I prefer music and movies ...' Scott decided now was as good a time as any to ask her something that had been on his mind. 'Nikky, I've been meaning to ask how you guys found out where I lived?'

'Actually, it was PJ who guessed from something you'd mentioned, he's quite intelligent even though you might not think it.'

'And what did my mother say or do?' Scott stopped walking and turned to face her, apprehensive.

'Well, to be honest, she thought we were prowlers until PJ mentioned your name. But boy is your mom strong, she threw PJ to the ground like he was nothing! I wouldn't want to get on her bad side.'

'She ... works out. What else happened?'

'Nothing much, she didn't say a lot after that. We asked her to tell you we called and left soon after.'

Scott was relieved. He hadn't been sure if Amdis had enthralled them before they left. 'Right. Okay, I've no plans for the day so what do you wanna do? I'm all yours.'

Nikky felt her stomach churn with excitement. 'Today's the centenary celebration, there's an exhibition at the Town Hall, wanna check it out? There'll be fireworks later tonight as well.'

Scott avoided too many buildings in Tallant because of a particular time in his life he wasn't proud of. A dark time that should remain buried with the people who had died in 'unexplained circumstances'. The clock tower, now housing the Town Hall, was the oldest building in Tallant. The last time he'd been inside those walls was with somebody else. Perhaps now was the day to paint over those memories with some new ones. What choice did he have? His memories were as immortal as he was.

'Sure, why not?'

***

In Trevor's Diner, Kayce flipped the closed sign to open position, preparing for the centenary celebrations. Next door at the Enchanted Florist, Carol rambled about with a garden hose, spraying flowerpots while glancing at the passers-by. After a night of little sleep, her head was littered with worries for her own wellbeing, and possibly the safety of the entire town.

Scott stood outside Trevor's for a moment, acknowledging Kayce with a nod as she turned on the TV. Another news bulletin, same as before. A missing person's report. More arrests made in connection to disappearances across the state. Nikky cupped her hands to her face against the window of the Enchanted Florist. The figure outside caught Carol's attention. Perhaps now was the time for a discreet warning for the granddaughter of her long-time friend. She dropped the hose to the ground and made for the door.

Nikky waved, seeing she had her attention. Her last encounter with Carol had left her concerned. That night in the fortune teller's tent was hard to forget. Seeing Scott apparently engrossed in a news story she felt certain he couldn't actually hear, she turned her head towards him as Carol unlocked the door, leaving the closed sign facing the street.

'Be right back.'

He nodded and resumed listening to the new developments in the story that intrigued him. Nikky stepped inside to greet a worried-looking Carol, who almost caught her with the door as she locked it behind her. 'Nikky, are you okay?'

Nikky was baffled. 'Am *I* okay? I was wondering the same about you after the other night.'

'I'm fine, don't worry about me, but there are some important things I need to tell you,' Carol said hurriedly, glancing over Nikky's shoulder as if afraid someone was watching.

'Is it about my grandma?'

'No, no, your grandmother's fine.'

Nikky couldn't help but notice how agitated Carol was. It looked like she hadn't slept in days. 'That's good, so what is it then?'

'It's just –'

Nikky cut in. 'Carol, did you know your sunflowers are dead?'

**Chapter 35**

Reluctantly, Carol looked at where Nikky was pointing, hoping she was wrong but fearfully knowing what it meant. She wasn't wrong. Each new batch of sunflowers standing upright in their temporary plastic vases was now withered and dead. No less than five minutes ago they had been full of life. Carol scanned the shop interior as she took off her gardening gloves. Seeing nothing, she felt a false sense of safety. She placed her hand on Nikky's shoulder and spoke quietly in her ear.

'Listen, this is important.' She pulled her in close, adding to Nikky's curiosity. 'It's about –' She paused suddenly. In slow motion, a figure in a black leather jacket and sunglasses approached the shop window, stopping inches away from the glass. Mirrored sunglasses or not, Carol knew he was staring directly at her. She froze and stared back. She knew he'd saved her life, but he had put her into that predicament in the first place, and, as he'd put it himself, never trust a vampire. No doubt he could hear every word she said on the other side of the window.

Nikky shook her head, widening her eyes in anticipation for whatever Carol was about to say. 'It's about ... what? ... Carol?'

Carols eyes were still glued to Scott. She jumped as Nikky said her name, forcing her eyes back in her direction. 'It's, um … the …' Knowing she was being closely observed by the very person she wanted to warn Nikky about, she managed to throw together a brief sentence almost rolled into one word. 'Uh, the celebration this evening, will you be at the opening of the time capsule at the town plaza? Everyone will be there.'

She faked a smile. Not even close to what she'd wanted to say. Nikky looked puzzled.

'What? Oh that, yeah I'll be there, won't you?' With all the drama and build-up, she had been expecting more. Carol began to nod before she replied.

'Wouldn't miss it, see you there.'

'I'll keep an eye out, oh and Carol, you might wanna water those sunflowers more in future!' Nikky went back outside next to Scott before Carol could reply. The bell on the door chimed as it opened and closed behind her.

'All set, you ready Scott?' she continued walking ahead. Scott paused with a subtle nod of approval through the window to Carol, who nodded back in a mutual understanding that Nikky would be kept safe. Trust me, but don't trust my kind. He knew that if he were in Carol's shoes, he wouldn't trust him either. But what choice did she have? They strolled on in silence. That first-date kind of silence. The nervousness of who gets to speak next, without seeming too eager. Scott had all the time in the world, but Nikky didn't, so she spoke.

'You said you've been in Tallant a long time, right?' she asked, with a slight turn of her head.

'You could say that but define a long time.' He matched her head turn with a nod towards her. She responded with a witty response of her own. 'Well how long is a piece of string?' as she looked back to Main Street. Sirens could be heard in the distance, getting closer.

'Depends who you ask, I suppose, but in my case, hundreds of years long.' He watched carefully for her reaction through his mirrored sunglasses. She answered tongue in cheek, playing along with his joke.

'So, you're hundreds of years old, living in Tallant all that time and I've only met you *now*?' At that moment, a fire truck roared past, grabbing their attention briefly before Scott turned his head again to answer.

'I've been here for most of that time. I've lived in other places, but here is where I call home now.' Tallant may be home, but some places in Tallant were still too painful to face. He dreaded the prospect of tonight's festivities. The Town Hall; the time capsule. They had no idea what had really happened on this night a hundred years ago, and Scott knew it was nothing to celebrate.

Nikky stopped and faced him. He mirrored her stance, waiting for her to say that he was crazy. 'I don't get you, Scott. You're a dark horse. I don't know what way to take you, to be honest. I never know if you're joking or being serious. I've never met anyone like you.'

Scott wasn't sure if this was a good or bad thing. 'Perhaps you won't like what you find, the swan before you might turn out to be a crow, or worse.'

'That's just what I mean, no other 17-year-old talks like that!'

He waited. She was not deterred but a confused expression appeared on her face. 'Mystery surrounds you, Scott, but that's one of the reasons I like you, I think.'

Scott removed his sunglasses, putting them in his inside jacket pocket, and squinted as his eyes adjusted to the sunlight. He stepped forward with his left hand on her side, putting his right hand gently to her face and staring deep into her eyes. Her eyes met his, anticipating another kiss. He spoke in a low tone.

'Tell me your deepest, darkest secrets.' He waited. Things were now looking like they should have. Perhaps the last time he tried to enthral her was a glitch.

She laughed. 'No Scott, I won't!'

Or perhaps not, he thought. She smiled and stepped back, leaving his hand in the air where her face had been. His eyes widened and a half-smile grew on his pale face. He was even more intrigued than the last time. 'That's why I like you.' He dropped his hand to his side.

'I don't get it.' But she was still happy to hear him say it.

'Because I can't control you, Nikky.'

'That's it? Weird. Who would let you control them, anyway?'

'The fact that you're ridiculously beautiful might have something more to do with it,' he smiled. A disturbance ahead snapped them back to reality and the moment was lost. A large crowd had gathered past the movie theatre, blocking the path and part of the road where the fire truck had parked with red strobe lights flashing. One of the Manor apartments was on fire.

\*\*\*

Evacuation was in progress as smoke plumes billowed from a third-floor balcony. The fire alarm blared inside, getting louder each time the ground-floor entrance opened as people fled the burning building. Adrenaline-fuelled firefighters scrambled at ground level. One connected a hydrant to feed the pump at the rear end of the truck, calling on the crowd to stand back. Others pointed a hose, spraying water up to the balcony and into the open door behind it where flames raged out of control. The last of the occupants had been evacuated. 'All persons accounted for' rang out over the firefighters' radio comms. The officer at the scene spoke to the owner of the apartment. A woman in her mid-thirties held the hand of her eight-year-old daughter.

'Are you positive there's nobody else inside, ma'am?'

'Yes, my other daughter's with my husband, they went to the store, I just talked to him on the phone.'

The fire officer spoke into the radio clipped to his chest. 'Confirmed, all persons accounted for, hit it from the outside, guys, not worth the risk sending men into this death trap, prepare to make down a ladder.'

Scott and Nikky stopped outside the movie theatre and watched from a safe distance. Brakes screeched as a car ground to a halt in front of the theatre. The driver jumped out and bolted towards the apartment building, only to be stopped by the firefighters. The officer in charge noticed the commotion and approached the hysterical man.

'My daughter is inside! That's my apartment! She's inside! Get out of my way!' His wife ran to him, still clutching their daughter's hand. She screamed above the noise of pumping water.

'Where's Millie? You said she was with you!' He turned, relieved to see his wife and one of his daughters.

'No, I thought you said she was with you! She must be still inside!'

Scott watched and listened from a distance, able to hear word for word what was said. The fire officer shouted into his radio. 'We need a breathing apparatus crew under air immediately! New information, persons reported! I repeat, persons reported! Get the ladder back up there stat!' 'Look!' One of the crowd pointed at the third-floor balcony in horror at the sight of a little girl appearing through the smoke on her knees. She dropped in front of the railings, gasping for breath. Nikky turned her head. 'Oh my God, Scott, there's a little girl still up there!' Another fire truck arrived as police cordoned off the street and footpath. Onlookers watched in fascinated horror while some filmed the inferno on their mobile phones.

Two breathing-apparatus crew members entered the building downstairs, for the arduous task of rescuing the child from the inside, as another crew prepared a ladder to the outside. The girl reached out with outstretched arms to the onlookers, dropping the teddy bear she had been clutching, which landed at the feet of the firefighters who were pointing the water jet into the smoke-filled doorway behind her.

Tears were running down Nikky's face. 'Please let them get to her in time.' She turned around to Scott, but her eyes met the faces of strangers behind her, staring in disbelief at the fire.

Scott was nowhere to be seen.

**Chapter 36**

The little girl sat coughing and crying at the edge of the balcony, her feet dangling through the bars. She reached out with both hands towards her parents below, grasping nothing but smoke. An explosion behind her sent a large plume forward to engulf the entire balcony. Her parents watched in horror as their daughter vanished in the smoke. Flames continued to lick through the top of the door, pulsating back and forth as the wind shifted again, clearing the balcony of smoke momentarily. Onlookers below held their breath in anticipation of seeing the girl sitting where she had been a few seconds ago.

She was gone.

Her mother screamed. Simultaneously the crowd gasped. The officer in charger shouted into his radio again. 'OIC to BA crew come in, do you have the girl, over.' At that moment, two firefighters wearing breathing apparatus burst through the smoke and flames onto the balcony. One of them spoke into his chest radio as his partner threw up his hands in confusion.

'BA team alpha to entry control officer, we don't have her, the balcony is clear, continuing our search of the interior, over.'

'Understood team alpha, but I don't understand? She was right there twenty seconds ago?'

The child's mother dropped to her knees. She rocked back and forth screaming uncontrollably as she held her other daughter. The father stood motionless, staring up at the balcony. Tears rolled down his face. Paramedics began to lead the distraught parents to an ambulance to treat them for shock. As the mother was being led away, she thought that her mind was playing tricks. She thought she'd seen something over the shoulder of a medic in the grass to the side of the apartment building. She wasn't seeing things. Her daughter smiled and waved to the balcony.

Her mother broke free from the medic and ran to embrace her daughter, crying tears of joy, her father running to join them. The fire officer in charge looked on, utterly perplexed.

'BA team alpha to control, we've searched the entire apartment and found no sign of the girl, over.'

'OIC to alpha, it's okay, the girl is down here somehow. Cancel the search and continue firefighting, over.'

'Down there? How? Nothing could survive in here without breathing apparatus and she definitely didn't pass us!'

'I'm as confused as you are, alpha; as I said, continue firefighting and we'll count this as a rescue, over.'

'Understood, alpha out.'

Assuming the firefighters had rescued the child, the crowd cheered. Nikky turned again to look for Scott, only to bump into his chest and stumble backwards. 'You're back, I thought you'd gone?'

'Yeah, I, eh, thought I heard someone calling me; false alarm.'

'It looks like the little girl's gonna be okay. Phew. A happy ending after all.'

'Just like in the movies,' Scott said, relieved she didn't ask any follow-up questions about his disappearance.

'Except in the movies they share a kiss when the nightmare is over.' She moved closer, grabbed hold of his leather jacket, and kissed him. Her heart was doing somersaults; he could hear each and every one of them. 'We must have been closer to the fire than I realised, Scott, you reek of smoke.'

He thought for a moment before answering. 'Yeah, but it was worth the risk for the kiss afterwards.' She grinned. Now was the time to take him by the hand without feeling awkward. As she led him past the back of the ambulance to continue their journey to the Town Hall, a voice shouted in their direction. The voice of a little girl. Millie's arm was outstretched and pointing right at them.

'Him, him there! That's the one, Mom! He's the one who saved me!' Her parents looked on in confusion. She pulled the oxygen mask from her face and ran to hug the stranger in the leather jacket. Scott dropped to one knee and awkwardly returned her hug. She stopped and took a step back to look at him.

'Thank you,' she said softly, then turned and skipped back to her sister. Nikky took Scott's hand again and squeezed it tightly.

'What was that about?'

Scott shrugged. 'I guess her mind is in overdrive with the adrenaline from such a traumatic experience, poor kid.'

'Curiouser and curiouser, Scott.' Nikky looked at him again but said nothing else. As they continued walking, Scott looked back over his shoulder at Millie. He winked at her before putting his mirrored sunglasses back on.

## Chapter 37

They say that time flies when you're having fun. Whoever said that wasn't an immortal. What they don't say is how fast it flies when you spend an entire day with someone who mirrors your feelings right back at you. That special time in your life that's like no other. A time when you walk on clouds. When a certain someone is the first and last thing on your mind when you wake in the morning and close your eyes at night.

When you're immortal, that time gets your undivided attention. Being eternally here in the moment. Being a vampire is the very definition of mindfulness teachings. When time is not an issue, when the clock doesn't exist to hinder your plans, each unforgettable moment can last an eternity.

For you.

The eternal truth is realised. You may last forever, but with the memories and heightened emotions of times that ended long ago for other people. Living in the past, but not really being alive. Loving without a heartbeat. Terrified to let go and yet terrifying to others. Immortality to some might seem like a gift. But, just like everything, once you're on the inside looking out, things can seem very different. Remembering every second of every moment. One man's gift is another monster's curse.

The only thing wrong with immortality is that it tends to go on forever.

***

Walking hand in hand, lost in happy chitchat and the occasional discreet kiss, the evening crept up on them. Scott's sunglasses had been removed hours ago, and as the sun set he could feel his strength grow stronger. They sat on a bench in the town plaza across from the obelisk memorial. He'd managed to avoid the Town Hall up to now. The clock tower above it said eight o'clock, and a crowd had begun to gather around a small podium next to a rusted chest, partly covered in dried soil and sealed with an old-fashioned lock and bolt. To the right of the stage was a square of disturbed earth and a stone slab, marking where the box had lain buried for the previous hundred years. It was still locked. Scott thought it should remain that way.

Chains of lights hoisted up high now lit the sky like giant stars close enough to touch. The scent of popcorn and cotton candy wafted through the air surrounding the townsfolk, who sat in circles on the grass and congregated in groups waiting for the Governor's arrival. Children spelled out their name in the air with sparklers. Even the schools were closed from Monday through Wednesday next week, making the weekend celebrations last even longer. The town festivities were for everyone, especially the kids, but the Woodland Surge Rave in the forest on Monday night was for younger people only. It was officially unofficial, organised underground through chat groups and social media with its exact location not divulged until the day itself to prevent the authorities from pulling the plug.

'Eight pm, it's almost time for the grand opening, you wanna visit the Town Hall while we still have time?'

Scott dragged his eyes to the clock that was still difficult for him to look at. It rested on four pillars with a viewing platform beneath, giving a compass view across the entire town. At one time it was the tallest building in Tallant, with a view that stretched for miles in every direction over the surrounding forestry and northern mountains. The present-day scenery wasn't so glorious. Now dwarfed by stone buildings and modern architecture, it was no wonder the access hatch to the tower had remained rusted shut for the past few decades. Nobody needed to go up there for the view these days.

Scott nodded slowly without speaking, not taking his eyes from the tower. As they stood, Nikky released his hand to check her phone for new notifications, pretending she didn't notice Scott squeeze the bracelet on his right wrist. She knew it deeply represented something from his past, but what exactly? Now wasn't the time to be the jealous girlfriend, if she could even call herself that.

'Are you alright? You seem distracted.'

'I'm fine, it's just I haven't been in the Town Hall for a long time.'

'Good or bad memories?' she pushed a little further.

'Both.' He put his hands into his pockets in his usual fashion before responding again. 'But I want to make some new ones now, if that's okay with you.' She leaned in close linking his arm with a nod of approval and a flutter of butterflies in her stomach. Townsfolk entered and exited the double doors held open above the steps from street level to the large wooden porch reception area. American flags hung either side mounted high on the walls and the sound of classical music drifted out from within. Inside, people helped themselves to sandwiches and coffee from a side table. A central staircase led to a balcony where people chatted while looking down at the masses. Some posed for selfies, and some came for the free food and drink, others walked along the rear wall, pointing, and discussing the town's history made into a timeline display. Old photos, clothing, parchments, the names of the original town settlers and old tools and weapons lined the walls, giving a glimpse of times long gone but not forgotten.

One piece in particular stood out. A crowd had gathered around a black-and-white photograph that was cracked and aged, with one corner missing hung framed next to a larger version of itself in a central position. This bigger copy was blown up and repaired with modern computer software, with an added paragraph of text printed underneath. It was an image captured precisely this day one hundred years ago, at the burial of the time capsule that sat outside in the plaza waiting to be opened. In the photo, around thirty townsfolk, mostly men, were gathered in a group, with the clock tower visible in the background. Some of the men stood resting their arms on shovels, some wore top hats, some rested their thumbs inside front waistcoat pockets, while others squatted to allow people behind to take part in the excitement of having their picture taken. A freshly dug hole in the ground in front of them held a shiny new treasure chest waiting to be covered with soil, not to see the light of day for a hundred years. A St Bernard dog stood front and centre, its gaze fixed on a face in the crowd on the far right of the photograph. A boy in his late teens who was also fascinated by this new image-capturing device seemed to be the only person present who was not smiling at this historical event.

The text underneath read:

*This photograph was developed days after being found at the site of the most mysterious event in the history of Tallant, on September 27th, 1919. All persons pictured above died in horrific circumstances that remain unexplained to this day. Historians believe that not long after the time capsule was buried, a wild animal attack occurred in the town, leaving nobody alive to tell the tale. Some dispute this, due to the fact that all firearms found at the scene afterwards were still fully loaded.*

*A memorial obelisk now stands upon the site in dedication to those who died. Experts believe the time capsule may contain clues as to what happened on that fateful day. The mystery remains intact until that box is opened 100 years from now.*

Nikky scanned the enlarged print over the shoulders of two spectators standing in front of her. When they moved on, she moved forward to read the text, followed by Scott, who also seemed intrigued. The display was new; nothing like this existed the last time he'd set foot inside. He read the inscription, focused on the photo one last time and turned his back to the wall, looking down at his feet.

He knew this was a bad idea. He should never have come here. Unwanted memories came rushing back like a flurry of slaps to the face, forcing him to face the reality of what had happened that day. Scott raised his head and scanned the room as if to check if anyone could possibly notice the look of guilt on his face.

Nothing. Life went on.

None of these people had existed one hundred years ago, nor did they really care about what had happened. These days it was little more than an oddity in the town's history that gets mentioned in history class, or the occasional ghost story told by seniors to scare kids at Halloween. But not to Scott. To his knowledge, there was only one other individual present that day who still existed. His unwanted thoughts were interrupted by Nikky, who turned to join him facing the room, which was now starting to empty to witness the opening at the obelisk.

'Curiouser and curiouser, as Alice put it.' She linked his arm and hugged into his right shoulder while looking up at him, smiling. 'What say you, Scott? You're being very quiet?'

Turning his head towards her, he opened his mouth to speak, but no words escaped. He stared blankly into her eyes, hoping his pain wasn't showing. She moved in front of him, grabbing his jacket with both hands. 'Hey, are you okay, what's wrong?'

Again, no words left his open mouth. He turned his head to the right, looking down behind him, and tried to speak again. 'I ... ah ...' At that moment, further along the display to his left, a young boy threw a question to his father, pointing at a rusted axe head with a broken handle mounted horizontally on the wall.

'Dad, was that a weapon or was it just for chopping wood like your one?' Before the father could answer, Scott turned, glad for an excuse to escape the awkwardness of Nikky's question. He reached out to touch the wooden handle but stopped short. He answered the boy without turning to face him.

'It was a tool for chopping wood, like today, but ... on that day, it was used as a weapon, to no avail ... unfortunately.' He stared blankly.

'How do you know?' The kid looked sceptical.

Scott placed his hands in their usual position inside his pockets. He turned his head to look directly at the kid, realising that another escape clause was needed.

'Lucky guess?'

The kid looked at his dad then back to the stranger who seemed to know everything.    'Sure, whatever, mister.' The kid rolled his eyes before moving on towards the door, leaving Scott and Nikky standing by the wall. The room was emptying fast. A caretaker pulled the plug on the background music then grabbed some used paper cups left on a nearby table before heading for the door himself. Scott returned his gaze to the axe. This time he made a conscious decision to interact with it. Pulling his hands from his pockets, he reached up and gently placed his right hand onto the rusted metal head, knowing what to expect. Touching it was like closing a circuit.

*It was night. Torches blazed, lighting the surrounding area. It felt as real as today. But this was more than a flashback. This was reliving the moment in full high definition. The adrenaline, the smells, the arrogance, the lack of remorse. Witnessing all that had happened in real time, the only difference being that this time, he couldn't change the outcome. All he could do was watch. He was powerless to intervene.*

*The rusted axe head was now black; the handle, back to its full length, was swinging violently towards him. He rapidly dodged left then right as the man who swung it desperately tried to butcher the threat before him, his eyes showing desperation and fear. His blood-soaked clothing, once white, had been ripped in the struggle to protect his wife, who was standing behind him. She hunched down low, screaming at a lifeless body in her arms.*

*They were all that were left alive. Bodies surrounded them. But someone else was also present. Although also dead, she was still standing. Her back was turned to Scott while she fed from the neck of a peasant before dropping her lifeless victim to the ground.*

*Scott took a step forward towards the desperate father, his grin dripping with blood. Eyes alive with cruelty, he opened his arms wide in a gesture of fair play, allowing his prey the chance to strike a blow with his axe.*

*It was an offer the man could not refuse. Everything he cherished was at stake. He threw all of his might into this one last chance and swung. The axe embedded itself into the centre of his attacker's chest with a thump as deep as the handle would allow. The smile disappeared from Scott's face as he steadied himself from the impact by repositioning his feet.*

*He looked down to admire the damage, then turned to face his attacker, who had taken a step back, desperately hoping it was enough to drop him. Scott grabbed the handle and pulled it downwards, ripping the bloodied axe head out of his flesh. The man watched in disbelief as the gaping chest wound began to close, leaving only a trail of blood. Holding the blood-covered weapon up high in both hands, Scott snapped the handle like a twig before throwing at the boots of the innocent father.*

*And now it was his turn. Scott began to move towards him.*

Instantly regretting his decision to revisit this piece of history, he pulled his hand away from the artefact, exhaling deeply. He knew what had happened next. No reminder was necessary. Lost in the moment, he gathered his bearings and realised he was back in the present. And he suddenly remembered he was not alone; he turned his head to look at Nikky. She was staring at him in horror and confusion. Scott dropped his gaze, only now noticing that her hand had discreetly interlocked with his during his flashback. She had somehow relived the memory with him, in all its gruesome glory.

# Chapter 38

'What the hell was that?'

Scott stared blankly at Nikky , desperately searching for an answer he hadn't been prepared to give. Exactly how much had she seen? He could usually handle this, but he had just remembered that Nikky couldn't be enthralled, because of the way he felt for her. Leaving aside that ongoing mystery, there seemed to be no escape right now. His stomach churned as internal panic set in.

She can't find out. Not yet.

He mentally replayed what just happened. Slight relief. The vision had been through his eyes, so that meant she couldn't have seen his face. But what about *her*? The other one who was with him. She'd had her back to him, feeding. An idea sprang to mind – but would it work? He decided to run with it. 'Wow! Did you just see something spooky, too?'

'Yeah, it was like something from the past in crazy detail? But it was terrifying, there were lots of dead people and, oh God, Scott, I think … it looked like it happened right outside here.'

'This is beyond weird … has that ever happened to you before?' He played dumb.

'Never, do you think we've just seen what really happened here, somehow? But how?' She looked around the empty room in total confusion, at a loss for words. Scott copied her movements, looking lost in thought before answering.

'This place is pretty old, I've read stories before about timelines crossing over and people seeing weird things from other times, especially if places are haunted …'

She gave him a sarcastic look. 'You believe in ghosts?'

'Let's just say I'm open to the possibility. Anyway, we –' He stopped mid-sentence and snapped his head towards the entrance, eyes narrowing. A vibrational hum inside his chest took his attention. A vampire was nearby.

Nikky noticed his alarm. 'What's wrong?' She looked towards the door, saw nothing, then looked back at him.

'Things are feeling a bit weird in here, I think it's time we left.' Before she could reply, he took her hand and made for the door. She would be lying if she'd said she wanted to stay there a second longer. The hair standing up on the back of her neck agreed. With a shock, she realised that she was only starting to notice how many bizarre and unusual things seemed to happen around Scott.

Outside, the crowd had moved to the podium near the obelisk. The Governor had arrived in his usual fashion and was standing in front of a microphone next to the locked time capsule, addressing the gathering. Scott tried to rush Nikky through the crowd, towards the obelisk, while scanning the vicinity for danger.

'Wait, Scott, hold on, what's the rush?'

'I just don't wanna miss the opening, we've waited all day.'

Five rows of senior citizens sat facing the front of the podium as photographers snapped pictures for posterity. The remaining plaza and area surrounding the water fountain was taken up by people standing behind. Scott came to a sudden stop by the group near the fountain. Governor Cartwright stood behind the microphone holding a red bolt cutter in one hand as he spoke. He noticed their sudden movement through the crowd and paused,, locking eyes with Scott. Nikky looked back and forth between them, curious as to how they knew each other. A few seconds later, the speech continued.

Nikky tugged at Scott's arm. 'Isn't that your mom over there?' Scott looked to where she was pointing. Sure enough, Amdis was approaching through the sea of guests. Scott's relief that the vampire was only his mother was not visible over his anger at her arrival. He couldn't remember the last time she had been seen in public with him. At least now he knew the reason for the sensation in his chest.

All eyes except Scott's were fixed on the makeshift stage. He glared at his mother from the moment they'd seen each other until she'd stopped next to them. She'd noticed Nikky holding Scott's hand. Multiple scenarios ran through his head. How would this play out in front of Nikky?

Amdis spoke first. 'Well fancy seeing you two here, nice to see you again, Nikky isn't it?'

Nikky smiled with a slight wave of her free hand, expecting Scott to respond. He didn't. He glared silently at Amdis.

Amdis spoke again. 'Never in a hundred years would I have expected this many people today, eh Scott?'

Nikky waited in awkward silence, expecting a reply from Scott. She looked at him before looking back to Amdis. 'Yeah, great turn-out, I suppose it's to do with –'

Scott cut her off abruptly mid-sentence. 'What are you doing here, Amdis?' Emotionless.
Nikky turned her gaze to Scott in utter confusion. Why was he calling his mother by her first name and, more importantly, what was with the tone?

Amdis smiled back then glanced at Nikky before looking back at him. 'Come on, Scott, no need to be grumpy, don't you remember the fun we had the last time we stood here amongst a similar crowd?'

Scott remembered every detail. Unfortunately. He remained silent. She spoke again.

'We both promised to witness the grand opening knowing full well that another crowd would have gathered.' She pointed to the obelisk. He knew what she meant. She wanted a repeat of the massacre from a hundred years ago, after the chest was sealed. Back then, he'd said he'd attend, that no matter where they were in the world, they would return together for that. They promised a similar opening to the closing. But that was then, times were different now. So was Scott. He remained silent but if looks could kill, she'd be dead if she wasn't already. Their conversation was one-sided so far, but she continued, trying for a reaction of any sort.

'You do remember what's inside that chest, Scott?'

Of course he remembered, and Amdis knew it. He looked at the chest on the stage and then at Nikky's confused face next to him.

'Well, I've come to collect,' Amdis remarked. Nikky watched Scott clench his teeth. He turned to walk away before snapping his head one last time in his mother's direction.

'Don't do anything you might regret, Amdis, things are not like they were before, and trust me, there will be consequences.'

She folded her arms and turned to watch the stage as they walked away hand in hand. 'Yes, I know. Unfortunately,' she uttered to herself.

Scott started to walk away from the crowd, towards the cemetery, at a faster pace than she was used to. 'Scott, wait, where are we going? What about the opening? What was all that about?'

He said nothing and continued walking. Outside the cemetery gates, she stopped and pulled her hand from his, this time meaning business. 'Scott, just wait a damn minute, are you going to blank me now like your mom? What the hell is going on? We're missing the opening and why are we here anyway? Are you just going home? Is that it?'

He looked up into the night sky with his hands in his pockets and exhaled deeply. He turned to face her as if it caused him pain.

'It's just … I'm not good to be around sometimes, Nikky, bad things follow me. You're probably better off without me, trust me.' Every word caused him agony. He opened the small interior gate, stepped inside and slammed it shut behind him, vanishing into the darkness leaving her standing alone as cars passed on the street behind her. Nikky stood dumbstruck. This was not how she'd envisioned this perfect day ending. She wasn't leaving it like this. No way. She stepped inside the gate.

**Chapter 39**

Inside the cemetery, Nikky made her way to the flat roof, this time knowing for sure it was where he lived. In a temper, she knocked and waited. No answer. She spoke to herself in frustration. 'Great. Now what?' Behind her in the dark the sound of footsteps came close then faded away into the central maze of the cemetery. Against her better judgement, she rushed into the blackness. 'Scott? Wait up!'

She hurried along the gravel path, only stopping to listen for a direction change to the footsteps ahead. This was her first time venturing so far into the cemetery. She was now entering the oldest section with its central patch of forestry surrounding the mausoleums. The footsteps led her onwards. Even if she wanted to go back, she wouldn't easily find her way out now. Not by herself. She continued, knowing Scott was somewhere ahead. She spoke again to herself.

'Great work, Nikky, it's pitch black and you're alone in a graveyard at night, what were you thinking?' The footsteps ahead stopped. So did Nikky.

Dim light from the moon emerging from behind the clouds lit the area enough to make out her surroundings. Within the evergreens, a wide pathway was lined both sides with tombs facing one another. In all its creepiness, there was something picturesque about the setting. And so quiet you could almost hear the stars twinkling above.

She jumped. Her phone had beeped. A message from her dad.

*'When will you be home? There's someone here waiting to see you.'*

With both hands she typed a quick reply. *'Won't be much longer, leaving shortly, see you soon! xx'*

*'Don't delay.'* Her father's reply was straight to the point. Tech was not his thing. She put her phone back in her pocket, leaving the scene dark. She spoke to herself again. 'Oh my God, Nikky, could you be any more stupid?' Pulling the phone out again, she turned on the flashlight and pointed it ahead of her. 'Scott, you there?'

No reply.

Just ahead on her right, one tomb stood out from the others. It was made of granite with a pitched roof. Two large pillars stood either side of a set of double metal doors that were three steep stone steps up from ground level. These were usually sealed shut with a rusted padlock. But this mausoleum was different. It was in perfect condition. She shone her flashlight around, comparing it to the others. She was right. All the others had broken stonework or were missing the pinnacle crucifix above the doorways. Some were partially standing; others lay smashed, sinking into the grass.

She looked back at the undamaged mausoleum. Letters engraved above the doorway were partly hidden by overgrowth. She moved closer, making her way up the three steps up to the door. With her right hand holding her phone for light, she reached up with her left and began pulling at the branches and creepers covering the name. Uncovering the last three letters, she stood back.

'*ACE*'

She examined her discovery, lost in thought, until something unexpectedly moved on the apex of the roof just above the name she had started to expose. Impulsively, she raised her flashlight higher. A pale face stared down. She screamed and jumped, losing her balance, and falling backwards down the steps behind her, dropping her phone in the process. Expecting a hard fall to the ground, she was surprised by a soft landing.

She was lying in Scott's arms. She glanced back to the roof of the tomb and saw nobody where there had been a moment ago. Getting back to her feet and her senses, she hit his leather jacket with her fist.

'Damn it, Scott! Where the hell have you been? What were you doing up there and why didn't you answer when I called you?' She was angry, but relieved she was no longer alone.

'I needed some me time and this is where I go to be alone.'

'Jesus, Scott! Most people go to the beach or a cafe to read a book, but you come here? Seriously? And why did you take off like that in the middle of the speeches?'

He held up his hand. 'Just a sec, did you say you followed me here?'

She shook her head, still furious. 'Yes! Why didn't you answer me when I called you? Why did you take off like that?'

'Nikky, I just got here, you didn't follow me, I guarantee it.' He walked past her and stared into the darkness.

'But I don't understand? Wasn't that you on the roof of the tomb just now?'

He turned back to face her. 'Yes, that was me, but I'd just arrived.' He placed his hand on her shoulder. 'You said you followed me?'

'Well, yes, I could hear your footsteps, wasn't that you?' She looked around nervously, moving her eyes from side to side.

'No.'

'Who the hell was I following in the dark then?'

He looked at her like she was crazy, his lips pursed.

'This is the weirdest day ev–'

Scott put his finger over her lips. 'Shhh, be quiet for a minute.' Usually, she'd slap away anyone's hand if they did that, but that would be under normal circumstances. She was realising that she'd followed a complete stranger into a cemetery at night. Scott turned his head slightly to the ground behind him to his left, then to his right, before staring back into Nikky's eyes and removing his finger.

'A homeless person is sleeping on a bench just inside the north wall and some teenagers are camping in the forest just outside the south wall; other than that, the cemetery is empty.'

She picked up her phone and checked the screen, shaking her head as she glanced between him and the phone. 'Empty apart from the dead.'

'Well, the ones that don't still move, anyway.'

'What's that supposed to mean?'

He smiled, shaking his head. 'Nothing.'

'Wait, if that was you up there, which by the way is weird enough in itself, Scott, how did you manage to catch me like that when I fell?'

He walked up close, put his hands on her hips and stared deep into her eyes. Enthralling her was out of the question but this was the next best thing. He spoke softly, mere inches from her face. 'I, too, fell today, Nikky, and that's what scares me.'

She put her arms over his shoulders and linked them behind his neck, not losing eye contact.

'I only realised it when I saw my mother earlier: I'd risk everything to protect you, and that's not good.'

'I don't understand, why's that not good?'

He glanced at the tomb with his name on it before answering. 'I struggle to fight the demon inside, but if you control me, my eye's off the ball and my mind's not in the game.'

'What are you talking about, Scott?'

'I can't enthral you, but you don't realise the power you have over me, and it's dangerous, believe me.'

'Don't be so dramatic, Scott! And I'm not scared.'

'You should be.' He looked up towards the heavens and sighed heavily. Was he really going to do this all over again? 'Just, you have to promise me something, okay?'

'What's that?'

'This is going to sound totally weird but bear with me.'

'Scott, I've learned by now that being with you is beyond weird but go ahead.'

'It you ever see red eyes, at any time, promise me you'll run as fast as you can, preferably towards a church.'

She gave a twisted grin. 'I'm not even gonna ask what that's about, but yeah, sure, I'll keep it in mind if it makes you happy.' She put her hand on side of his face and pulled him close. As her lips touched his, fireworks exploded overhead, lighting up the night sky. The centenary celebration was in full swing, but nothing could distract them right now. She turned to face the direction of the town to watch the display that illuminated their faces.

'Scott, how exactly did you catch me twice today, what the hell happened at the Town Hall and how could you possibly know about who and where people are inside the cemetery right this second?' A suspicious tone now in her voice.

'You put it best earlier, weird things happen around me, but someday you'll understand why, I promise.'

'Why someday and not now?'

'Because I'm afraid that when someday comes, it'll be my last one with you.'

'What could possibly make you think that?'

'Because I don't think you could handle the real me.'

'You're not a monster, Scott.'

'The monster is on vacation, but all vacations have to end. Just remember, Nikky, even a white rose casts a dark shadow.'

'Can you ever speak in plain English? Whatever deep, dark secrets you have to hide and deal with I can understand, I have issues too. I lost my mom, remember?'

He raised his head and closed his eyes silently, shaking his head without her noticing. Of all the things to say, she had to mention her mother. It was like a dagger through his heart, or more like three bullet holes in his back. He needed to change the subject, for both their sakes.

'I've got something for you.' He held out his hand. A silver chain dangled in mid-air, sparkling in flashes of light from the fireworks. At the end of it was a small silver angel, kneeling and praying with open wings. She opened her eyes wide in appreciation.

'It's beautiful!' She pulled her hair back as he placed it around her neck.

'Just remember when you look at this, no matter what happens in the future or where we both end up, that right now at this time and place when I gave this to you, you were mine and I was yours, and nobody can take that from us, even if we go our separate ways.'

'You sure know the right words to say just at the right moment, Scott. Did I ever mention how weird you are?'

They stood cheek to cheek observing the colourful sky as the fireworks came to an end with distant cheers and applause. They stared at the heavens together for what seemed like an eternity.

'"And all I ask is a tall ship and a star to steer her by",' Scott quoted.

'Don't think I know that song?'

He answered awkwardly. 'Actually, it's from a poem.'

'My bad.'

'Do you know how to find the North Star?'

'No but I'm guessing you're going to show me?'

He pointed above. "You see the Big Dipper right there?'

'Yeah, everyone knows that one.'

'Well, if you follow the last two stars at the end in a straight line, they point to the North Star … just in case you ever got lost at sea.'

'I thought it was supposed to be brighter than that?'

'People generally mistake the planet Venus as the brightest star in the night sky.'

'How do you know this stuff?'

'I've stared in awe at the heavens for centuries, the stars fascinate me. A wise man once said, we're all in the gutter, but some of us are looking at the stars.'

'Centuries? Sure you did, Scott … anyway, who said that?'

'Oscar Wilde. I met him once, backstage after a play in London.'

'Really? You get a selfie?' She pretended she knew what he was talking about but wasn't fooling anyone.

'Em, no, not that time but he told me to be myself because everyone else is taken; it made me rethink my position, so I let him off easy. He was a pompous ass if ever I've known one.'

'I see. Well, that's all very romantic but it's getting late, I've to be home soon.'

'Sure, just one more minute before this moment is lost to time.'

She smiled. 'We have an eternity of moments to come, Scott.'

There was no smile on his face now. 'Indeed.'

# Chapter 40

Eastbrook Lodge was quiet at night. It was not the kind of place that engaged in or tolerated loud or antisocial behaviour. A police presence was out of the ordinary and a rare occurrence. But tonight, an empty police cruiser was parked outside the fourth house on the right, three down from PJ's.

Walking hand in hand towards Nikky's house, Scott stopped without warning.

'What's wrong, Scott, why are you stopping?'

'Just got one of those feelings.' A vibration in his chest.

'Like someone walking on your grave?'

Nice choice of words, he thought. 'Something like that. What's with the police car at your place?'

'Not sure, but my dad mentioned earlier about somebody being there to see me. Must be about the fairground incident … let's find out.' She led him at a brisk jog to the front door. Scott took note of the dead sunflowers still rotting in the vase. Nikky pulled out her key and opened the door, leaving Scott outside. Through the doorway at the other end of the hall, Scott made eye contact with a uniformed police officer speaking with Ranger James Brennan, who was also still in uniform, minus his sidearm.

He called in Nikky's direction after a mouthful of coffee. 'Ah Nikky, you're home, Officer Stanford would like a quick word.'

Nikky turned to face Scott, who was still locked into a staring contest with the officer. She leaned against the door frame, feeling awkward at having to say goodbye in front of an audience.

'I guess I'll catch you tomorrow? I know you've no phone so maybe we could –'

'Invite me in,' Scott interrupted, still staring at Stanford, whose attention was now on Buster barking out back.

'What?' She looked puzzled at the spontaneous request. He turned to her in all seriousness.

'You have to invite me inside.'

Knowing now how unpredictable Scott was, she assumed he was playing another game, or perhaps a string of riddles the way he usually speaks. She smiled.

'You told me never to invite strangers into my home, remember? And that included you, Mr Maglace.' She winked and poked his leather jacket, leaving a dent. He didn't return the smile. 'What's it worth?' she asked, hoping for a kiss. Over her shoulder, Scott watched as Stanford made his way down the hall towards them. Now out of time, Scott acted on impulse.

'Mr Brennan?' he shouted. Nikky was dumbfounded. That was the last thing she'd expected. 'Mr Brennan, perhaps I could help with the officer's investigation?' The cop stopped walking halfway and turned to face the ranger, still holding his coffee cup.

'That's not a bad idea, Scott, I forgot you were with Nikky when it all unfolded.' Another sip of coffee.

'Perhaps you could invite me in, sir, and I could assist?'

The cop looked at Scott and tried to hide a smile at his concern. Nikky's jaw almost hit the floor, her arms folded.

'Of course, come inside, Scott, maybe you can jog each other's memories of what happened that night.'

Scott's face instantly relaxed. He returned the cop's smile. Nikky pushed the door open wide and gestured for him to enter with one arm outstretched, her mouth still open wide. Stanford went back to the kitchen. Scott stepped inside, kissing Nikky on the cheek as he passed.

'What is going on with you?' She shook her head as she grabbed the dead sunflowers from the hall table, next to the photo of her mother.

'I'll explain another time, Nikky.'

'Why am I not surprised?'

'Who's upstairs?'

'Caden is probably in his room playing video games, why?'

'No ... there's somebody else?'

'Oh, must be my grandma – wait, how did you know?' He didn't answer. Just raised one eyebrow. 'Never mind, forget I asked.'

He followed her to the kitchen, where she dumped the flowers in the rubbish bin. The uniformed conversation stopped, and the two teenagers were now the centre of attention.

'Perhaps we could use your study for some privacy during the witness statements, Jim?' Stanford said, as he pulled a small notepad from his breast pocket.

'Of course, go right ahead, any promising leads yet?'

'Nothing I can go into right now. Nikky? Would you like to go first?' He gestured towards the double pine doors at the far wall with his free hand.

Scott butted in abruptly. 'If I may, Officer, could I go first? It's just, my mother's expecting me home soon and I don't wanna get grounded a second time this week.'

Officer Stanford shifted his gaze to the ranger then back to the cheeky teen. Nikky looked at Scott and silently mouthed the words 'What are you doing?' Scott responded with a wink and began walking to the study. He wasn't taking no for an answer. He opened one of the double doors and stepped inside.

An ornate wooden desk holding a green lamp and some paperwork sat at the other end of the room overlooking the rear patio from a large conservatory door. Behind the desk, a black rotating chair with a leather finish lay empty, facing the spacious room. A bookcase stood against the left wall opposite a smaller, glass-fronted cupboard. Next to it, a novel and a folded pair of reading glasses lay on a brown leather armchair. A small chandelier hung from the centre of the ceiling spreading bizarre light patterns across the furniture.

The cop shook his black notebook at Nikky. 'This won't take long, miss; I'll get to you shortly.' He followed Scott into the study and began to close the door as Buster continued barking. Scott started to speak loudly so that Nikky and her father could hear from the next room before the door shut.

'Officer, sir, I hope I can help you with your investig–' Click. Time was up.

As the door closed fully and Stanford took his hand from the handle, Scott flew at him. He grabbed him by the throat and ran sideways up the rear wall, slamming the back of the cop's head into the ceiling. The notepad and pen bounced off the floor. Scott stood with two feet on the side wall defying gravity with his arm outstretched, pinning the cop's body to the ceiling. His fingernails had lengthened and dug into the officer's neck, drawing blood. The flailing cop grabbed hold of the arm that held him in place, fighting to loosen the tightening grip as he slowly suffocated.

Scott spoke. But not in his usual voice. A deep demonic sound emanated from his vocal cords. The lights of the chandelier flickered.

'What are you doing here? Has Draven not learned by now that I'm not going anywhere?'

'H-h-how did you know I was –'

Scott finished the sentence for him, his fangs now making an appearance. 'A vampire? That's none of your concern. Tell me why you're here.' He released his grip slightly, allowing Stanford to speak as his bloodied neck began to heal. The cop smiled through the chokehold. 'As if I'd tell you. My loyalties are to my own kind, unlike yours.'

'I can force you to speak whether you like it or not.'

Stanford tried to laugh, forcing a bubble of spit from his lips. 'You can't enthral a vampire, that's impossible.'

'Guess again.' Scott stared into his eyes. The cop's expression changed. He became limp, dropping his hand from the arm that held him in place. The cocky smile was replaced by a blank stare.

'Now, why are you here?'

'Draven knows the girl is important to you.'

'Who informed him?'

'I don't know.'

'Was it the witch?'

'I don't know.'

'What is Draven planning?'

'He intends to use Amdis as your Achilles heel.'

Scott was taken off guard, his fangs disappeared, and his voice returned to normal. 'Amdis?' The cop couldn't be lying, he was enthralled. He remained still, staring blankly at the floor over Scott's shoulder.

'You're going to report everything back to me from now on; Draven is to not to know about this; and you'll continue with his plan like this never happened, do you understand?'

'I understand.'

'Another thing, those kids who went missing, who's behind it and where can I find them?'

'Witches, Green Bay.'

'Such a pity I don't kill humans anymore.' Scott snapped his head towards the double doors below. Someone was approaching. He quickly shot the cop another look. 'Here's what you're gonna do.'

\*\*\*

In the next room, Nikky thought she heard a muffled thud in the silence between Buster's barking. She glanced at her father, who was flicking through today's paper.

'Did you hear something?' Before he could answer, she made her way to the double doors, pulling the left one open. In the study, Officer Stanford ignored the opening of the door and continued jotting notes, nodding to Scott, who sat in the leather armchair.

'And that's pretty much how it happened, Officer, we left soon after.'

Stanford tapped his pen on the notepad twice before flipping it onto itself and tucking it back into his shirt pocket. 'Okay, that's good enough, I'll add the information to my report.'

Nikky addressed them both. 'Everything okay in here? I thought I heard something.' Scott sat silently.

'Of course, miss, and I won't need your statement right now, your friend here has given enough. I'm needed back at the station, if you'll excuse me.' With that, he left the study and passed the ranger without saying another word. The ranger stood up, folded his paper and followed him to the hall, passing Nikky's grandmother coming down the stairs in her dressing gown balancing an empty teapot on a saucer. Brennan said, 'Ben, you let me know if you need anything else, you hear?' but the cop didn't reply as he left the house. Nikky had followed her father to the front door and now saw Beth.

'Hi Grandma, good to see you up and about. I guess now is a good time to introduce you to that friend I told you about?'

'Ah yes, I've been dying to meet this young man since you mentioned him, where is he?'

Scott smiled at Nikky from the leather chair. Time for the *meet the parents or grandparents* bit, he thought. Nikky gestured him into the kitchen. 'Grandma, this is my friend, Scott.' The empty teapot and saucer in the old lady's hands fell to the floor where they shattered, sending shards of china in all directions. Her grandmother's mouth fell open as she stared across the room in disbelief. Nikky and her father rushed to assist, bending down to pick up the pieces spread across the floor.

'Are you okay, Grandma? What's the matter?'

Beth didn't reply. She was watching Scott closely, studying him, like he was about to commit a crime. The smile of politeness had left his face. His hands returned to his pockets.

Somehow, she knew.

**Chapter 41**

It was Sunday and late in the afternoon the following dull and overcast day. Outside 1 Eastbrook Lodge, Amber Sheridan waited patiently. She'd rung the doorbell five minutes ago and there was still no answer. She pulled her phone from her back pocket and dialled. Dan Cartwright's photo popped up on screen and she punched the call button. A groggy voice answered.

'Yeah.'

'You do know I've been standing outside the last five minutes, right?'

'Just a sec.' Call ended. While waiting, she flicked through the group chat messages for the latest. Earlier she had posted to the gang about meeting in the diner at three o'clock. A flurry of replies popped up in approval. Being the ringleader of the girls and the alpha male's boyfriend, she expected nothing less. But one name was missing from the replies. She clicked on it and sent a message.

*'Nikky, you coming later?'* Delivered and read. She waited. A moment later Nikky replied.

*'I saw the group chat; guess I'll be there too, I just have no way of contacting Scott to let him know.'* Amber rolled her eyes. She knew she was dating Cartwright but

that didn't matter. She couldn't date Scott even if she wanted to. Not only because she was Dan's girl, but because Scott showed no interest, and she craved attention. If she couldn't have the hot guy, she didn't want anyone else to have him either, let alone Nikky. Being notified that she couldn't invite Scott today was an added bonus.

*'Yeah that's a pity, I'll let ya know when we're leaving, you can come down with us xx.'*

Dan Cartwright opened the front door, half dressed, with a sleepy, unimpressed look on his face as Amber stepped inside. 'Jeez, you were in bed until this hour?'

'Why? What time is it anyway?'

'After two, what happened? You look terrible.'

'Aw just personal crap, had a meeting with my dad and uncle that didn't go too well.' He closed the door and scratched his head, yawning.

'What sort of meeting?' she queried.

'Family stuff, not sure if I'm buyin' it, though, think they're yankin' my chain.'

'What kinda family stuff?'

'Jesus, Amber! What's with the hundred and one questions? Seriously? Family stuff as in private family stuff so just leave it at that, okay?'

She held up her palms in defence. 'Okay, okay, a little touchy today, aren't we?'

'It's been a crappy few days, I'm not in the best of moods right now, alright?'

'Sure whatever, you wanna get cleaned up? We're meeting the gang shortly.'

No reply, just an apologetic nod. She kissed him on the cheek, trying to play on his better side.

***

Gerry watched as a gang of youths approached Trevor's Diner from the direction of Main Street. Another bunch of snotty-nosed brats ready to cause trouble, he thought. Today was a busy day, with most tables now occupied. He had been preparing his speech for the terms of their admittance in his head, but after noticing PJ's familiar face at the rear, their chances had reduced significantly.

PJ tried to hide behind Nikky's shoulder as they got close to the entrance. Gerry smiled and started shaking his head. Definitely no admittance today for this crowd. The last thing he wanted was a cheeky brat like PJ, meaning the gang would suffer the same fate. They stopped at the door with Cartwright and Amber at the front while Brad and Gary stood behind with Gwen; Charlotte and Nikky disguising PJ at the rear. Instinctively, Nikky checked her phone again. No new notifications. And there wasn't going to be, either. Cartwright and his ego decided to saunter in, but Gerry held out his hand.

'Not today, folks, we're crazy busy and you haven't a hope in hell getting in with him.' He pointed to PJ, who was pretending to be distracted behind the group. Nikky almost felt pleased. Maybe now she could swing by the town plaza and accidentally bump into Scott somewhere. If not, perhaps she could drop into the cemetery, but that might seem a little too eager. Damn it. Why doesn't he have a phone?

Cartwright was disgusted. 'This is ridiculous! Do you know who I am?' He stuck his index finger into his own chest. Gerry studied him, looking concerned.

'Oh wait I'm sorry, ain't you the Governor's nephew?' he exclaimed, raising his hand to the door handle as if preparing to open it. Cartwright beamed. This was exactly what he wanted to hear, especially in front of the gang.

'Yeah, that's right.'

'Yep, thought so. You're still not getting in.' Gerry dropped his arm back to his side. Cartwright almost burst a blood vessel, while PJ burst into laughter. As much as he hated Gerry, he loved to see Cartwright taken down a peg or two. The diner door opened from within, wafting music from the jukebox as Cartwright continued to argue his case. Without looking, Gerry moved to one side, to allow the customers exit while remaining focused on the group. But nobody exited. Charlotte tapped Nikky on her shoulder, interrupting her daydream state. She turned to see what she wanted. Charlotte said nothing but smiled and pointed into the doorway.

Scott was holding the door open. Nikky's face lit up. Scott gave Gerry a polite nod and got one in return. Gerry stood aside, allowing them all to enter, with an extra-long stare for PJ taking up the rear. Cartwright's eyes held Scott's until the last minute as he passed him leading the group inside, but Scott's eyes were squarely fixed on Nikky. PJ gave Gerry a silent nod of appreciation as he passed, getting no response before poking Scott in the stomach. 'God help any intruders who break into your house and come across your mom.'

Scott moved his gaze from Nikky to PJ. 'I'll second that!' Nikky was last in before Scott released the door, letting it swing shut. She leaned in close and kissed him on the lips. Amber glanced back jealously to witness the embrace.

'Hello stranger,' Nikky remarked.

'Fancy seeing you here.'

'Scott, we've got to get you a phone, I don't know how you survive without one.'

'Maybe someday I'll get one to keep you happy.' He took her hand and led her through the diner to the rear, where the others had joined up two tables that had become free. Cartwright sat in the centre facing the front door with Amber next to him, the girls on her side and the guys on his. Scott, Nikky and PJ sat opposite. Kayce approached with notepad in hand, giving Scott a wink. It was sodas all around.

She looked at Scott last. 'The usual, Scott?'

'Sure thing, thanks Kayce.'

'Aren't we the popular one,' Nikky commented in jest. Amber glared across the aluminium table at the happy couple in disgust, failing to hide her contempt. Silence ensued for a moment. Cartwright was scowling at Scott, as Amber stared at Nikky. He had his reasons and she had hers. Both trying to hide their true feelings, unable to express them to anyone. Cartwright's underlying hatred for Scott. Where did it come from? He knew it was more than just jealousy. It was almost as if he was pre-programmed to hate Scott from the moment he laid eyes on him.

PJ broke the silence, grinning from ear to ear. 'So, guess who's the DJ for homecoming next month and for Woodland Surge tomorrow night?'

Amber responded with her usual sarcasm when addressing PJ. 'If it's you, PJ, I'm glad I can't make it tomorrow, even though Dan asked me to go.' She flicked through the menu, seemingly uninterested in PJ's reply. But her words made Scott's ears prick up.

'Amber, you're lucky I don't have enough middle fingers to show you how I feel.' PJ couldn't help himself as usual. Nikky strained the muscles in her face trying to hide a grin. Eye rolls and sarcasm from Charlotte and Gwen in sympathy with Amber.

'And as for homecoming, it lands on Halloween night so you should feel right at home with all the freaks, no need to dress up, PJ, just go as you are, nobody could tell the difference anyway,' Amber fired back.

Scott spoke to Cartwright for the first time since they'd all sat down. 'Wait a sec, you're going to Woodland Surge?' Nikky chimed in.

'Aren't you coming?'

Scott appeared uneasy for a moment, contemplating his response. 'Actually, no, I can't make it tomorrow, sorry.' Short and sweet. He didn't elaborate, catching Nikky off guard with an answer she wasn't expecting. The first major group outing and her new boyfriend wouldn't be there. She knew it was too soon in the relationship to complain but the look of disappointment on her face was hard to hide.

'Oh, that's ... such a pity, I was looking forward to spending more time with you.' She waited to hear some kind of excuse. Nothing. Cartwright threw some sarcasm.

'So sorry you can't make it, Scott, but what's it to you if I go or not?'

Scott looked around the many faces who all watched patiently for his response to the comment. 'It's just the night that's in it, I thought you might be, ah, preoccupied?'

Cartwright had no idea what Scott was talking about. His father and uncle had decided to leave out the part about Scott until the time was right. No need to alarm him about possible threats to the family until he had his 'condition' under control. As far as he was concerned, they were telling tall tales about a family legend with no real basis, possibly to scare him into a state of humility. Besides, how could Scott know anything about the Cartwright family or the upcoming full moon? Dan brushed his family secrets to one side.

'Nope, I'll be there. Nikky you come with me, I guess somebody needs to help teach PJ how to do his job.'

'You're too kind, Dan, I'll try not to disappoint you.' PJ began winding an imaginary fishing rod with his right hand, slowly extending the middle finger on his left.

Nikky hesitated in asking Scott another question, wondering should she leave it until they were alone. After all, everything he'd said to her last night was still fresh in her mind. What did she have to lose? She took hold of his hand under the table.

'What about homecoming next month?' Decision made impulsively. Now to wait and see if he'd let her go without him to the biggest night of the year outside prom. Woodland Surge was one thing, but missing homecoming? Unforgivable in the eyes of any teenager. All eyes were on Scott again. No pressure. Amber crossed her fingers under the table, praying for the outcome she wanted.

Tumbleweed.

Kayce arrived, all smiles, with a tray of drinks and broke the awkward silence; she winked at Scott again before leaving to clean the table next to them.

The silence continued.

Scott turned his head sideways, now looking directly at Nikky. 'It's the first I've heard of it but I suppose you better count me in.'

Nikky beamed, much to Amber's disgust, before turning to PJ. 'What about you, PJ, you got a date for homecoming?'

PJ turned his cap backwards. 'I'll be busy playing music, but I suppose I could ask Rebecca Chambers, again, but this time I'm positive she'll say yes.' There was muffled chuckling around the group. Random conversations began now that the important questions had been posed and answered. A news bulletin played silently on the TV behind the counter. More about the missing persons. Nikky didn't notice that it had Scott's full attention. But Cartwright did.

When the bulletin was over, Scott whispered into Nikky's ear. 'Was everything okay with your grandma last night? She seemed a little, disturbed?'

'Yeah, we took her to the front room to relax and made her a cup of her favourite tea. I'm starting to think she may need round-the-clock care … probably best you left when you did, I know she'd prefer you to meet her at her best.'

Scott nodded but had one burning question that needed answering. 'Did she mention anything to you, anything at all?' At this stage he assumed that if her grandmother had told her what he suspected, things would be very different right now. But would she say it in front of the group?

'Hang on, actually, she did say one other thing.'

He nodded but didn't look at her this time, just kept his eyes on the table in front, waiting for the inevitable.

'She said she really wants to talk to you. Kinda strange but I guess it's better than a rejection, right?'

***

Later that same evening, about one hundred miles southeast of Tallant in Green Bay, Wisconsin, darkness had fallen. Six hooded members of what remained of the Grand Corinthian Coven congregated around a sacrificial altar inside a dimly lit basement. They chanted in unison.

A grimoire lay with its pages open, surrounded by candles, revealing scripture and diagrams from a history better left forgotten.

Before it, within a pentagram symbol etched onto the floor in red, a lifeless stag lay with its eyes still open, staring blankly into the abyss since the essence of life had left its body. One antler had broken in its struggle to escape, leaving its head looking unbalanced. But even in death this beast looked majestic. The ritual was almost complete. The chanting stopped. The circle parted, leaving space for a lone figure in a brown cloak to enter and approach the altar, with outstretched arm. It was time.

The dagger of an ancient vampire stained with unique blood was placed upon the open grimoire, instantly igniting the red pentagram symbol into flames. But the stag didn't burn. When the circle of flames ran its course, like a line of gasoline spreading, the majestic beast that lay dead a moment ago opened its eyes. It struggled to its feet, pulling itself upright on all fours to face the altar. Draven picked up his blade from the grimoire and stepped down between the hooded figures. Approaching the animal, he held out his blood-stained blade, running it sideways across the stag's face. The black lifeless eyes momentarily glowed red. He placed the blade back in the scabbard on his hip and spoke only two words.

'Find him.'

# Chapter 42

Governor Patrick Cartwright sat behind his desk with his eyes closed against the morning sun. He had a lot on his mind. Witches and their connection to several missing persons. Family members killed by vampires at the fairground, and now, for the first time, a vampire that had previously been a recluse was seemingly becoming involved in local vampire affairs. Not to mention this vampire was now regularly in the company of his nephew, who knew nothing of the danger he could pose.

But right now, the pressing issue was tonight's lunar event. This was the day before the night of the change. Even if the calendar didn't remind him, he and all male Cartwrights of age would know by the way they felt: a change was coming. Apprehension, agitation and a shorter temper were the usual signs. His secretary sitting outside, Millicent, had been warned of no interruptions under any circumstances. Being a Cartwright, she knew why. She also knew that when the Governor said no interruptions, he meant no interruptions with no exceptions. On this day each month his schedule was kept clear intentionally. His phone was switched off and all calls to his direct phoneline were diverted to her.

This was calm before the storm. He closed his eyes and clasped his hands together, trying to enjoy some serenity while he could. A moment later, the phone on the desk behind him began to ring. He jumped and furiously turned around to snatch the phone from its receiver.

'Governor, there's someone here to see you.'

'Millicent what part of do not disturb do you not understand? You know what day today is don't you?' he said sharply.

She paused. 'Monday?' she replied. Another pause. 'Anyway, he says he has an appointment.'

'What!? How can he have an appointment for today when you didn't give him one in the first place?' he shouted down the phone.

Another pause.

'Temper, temper, Governor, he has an appointment because I just made one for him.'

'Millicent, what in the hell is wrong with you?' he yelled.

Another pause. 'Anyway, you're probably sitting back with your feet up scratching your hairy dog's ass anyway, so I took it upon myself to pencil him in for right now.' She spoke in her usual professional manner. The Governor was irate. He slammed the phone down and stood up, forcing his chair back against the window, and scrambled his way to the door to deal with his incompetent secretary. Fuming, he pulled one of the double doors open with such force that a framed picture of the mountains of Tallant on his wall fell and shattered into pieces.

Stepping into the reception area, he saw someone sitting on his secretary's desk. Millicent Cartwright sat silently staring at Scott, still holding the phone to her ear. The Governor ground his teeth in rage. Scott addressed the Governor's secretary with a grin.

'You can put the phone down now, Millicent.' She placed the phone onto its receiver and stared instead at her computer screen.

'I should have known,' the Governor hissed. Hearing his voice unexpectedly, Millicent jumped to her feet like she had just been woken up.

'Governor, is everything okay?'

He looked at Scott with contempt before replying in a more relaxed tone.

'Yes, Millicent. You've been enthralled. It's not your fault. I'll be inside with our "guest".' He gestured at the door for Scott to follow him back to his office.

'But Governor, I thought you said no visitors today?' she muttered, to his back. Scott stood up.

'Nice talking to you, Millicent,' he smiled, before giving her a wink and following the Governor. She scowled in disgust as she realised what had just happened. Inside the office, Governor Cartwright dropped back into his chair and threw his feet up on the desk. He clasped his hands across his chest and glared at Scott, who was standing silently with his hands in his pockets.

'Usually I'd offer my visitors a seat, but in your case, you can stay standing.' Scott ignored this and came to perch sideways on the desk with one foot on the floor. Eventually the Governor spoke again.

'To what do I owe the displeasure?'

'Straight to the point, I like that. It's about your nephew.'

The Governor turned his head to one side before responding. 'What about him?'

'Tonight is his first change.'

'You don't think I know that? We've already given him the talk, not that it's any of your concern.'

'It becomes my concern if he decides not to heed your advice or instruction.'

'What are you talking about?'

'He's of the impression he'll be attending the Woodland Surge rave in the forest tonight.'

The Governor dropped his feet to the floor and sat up, his arms now resting on the desk. 'Who told you this?'

'He did, last night.'

The Governor thought for a moment. This was a stunt he knew his nephew could possibly try. 'Leave my nephew to me, I'll take care of it personally and make sure he's with the rest of us when the time comes.'

'I hope so because I won't be around tonight. I've another matter to attend to.'

The Governor sat silently for a moment as if contemplating a decision. All hatred aside, things had to be said for everyone's benefit. Perhaps now was the time.

'All matters relating to this town are vitally important to me, I'm sure you understand why.'

'I told you already, I keep this town safe,' Scott replied calmly.

'Then we both have the same agenda with different methods. Take a seat, Scott, and we'll talk.' He gestured towards the chair in front of his desk. Scott nodded toward the open blinds on the window, which the Governor twisted shut. Scott stood slowly, watching the Governor's every move before dropping into the chair without losing eye contact.

'Let's put our cards on the table, shall we?' The Governor stood up, took two glasses from the side cabinet, and began to pour whiskey into both, before sliding one across the table to his guest. Scott caught the glass and raised it in a toast before taking a sip, followed by a nod of approval.

'Giving alcohol to a minor is an offence, you know.'

The Governor ignored him. 'I'm sure you're aware of my family's history with witches?'

Scott swirled the whiskey in his glass, examining it before taking another sip. 'Yes, I've heard the legend about your bloodline; you want them all dead because of the curse.'

The Governor took a sip. 'That's one reason, the coven in Green Bay was raided because of a tip-off from this office, but it's only one of many. One coven falls and another replaces it. The missing persons' reports keep piling up as more innocent people are abducted by the vampires who assist the witches. Slowly but surely we're making a dent in their operation, that's why they want us out of the way.'

Scott stared across the desk, sincere now. 'It's starting to make sense to me now … the vampires are kept at bay in the mountains, knowing you run this town, rarely showing their faces. If you were out of the way, Tallant would be theirs for the taking and the witches get what they need for sacrificial purposes. You said before that you have a dossier on me, so tell me, what exactly do you know?' Scott waited, expecting the worst. Governor Cartwright looked uncomfortable, not wanting to reveal his fear to a potential threat. He sat back and folded his arms, hesitating.

'I know you're the pureblood, the one they created to destroy us. Before their plan backfired and you destroyed everything and everyone instead. Forgive me for being blunt, but you're the biggest risk to my kind.'

'And yet you've never approached me in all the years I've been here.'

'Keep your friends close, if you get my meaning? But I've never understood why you changed all of a sudden.'

Scott nodded in agreement, not exactly what the Governor was expecting. 'I understand why you'd be concerned, but I've helped keep this town safe for decades, from your kind should the need arise, and from mine. With only one mishap. Consider it a sort of penance for my actions. Not that it could ever heal what I've done in my past.'

'And what's stopping you from returning to your old habits? You said yourself, never trust a vampire.'

Scott placed his glass on the desk and leaned forward. 'You must know that the vampires have wanted me to return my loyalty to them for centuries, for reasons unknown – until now, that is.'

'But what's stopping you from returning to your old ways? Surely you miss the taste of human blood?'

Scott looked away. He did miss it. But he avoided every opportunity to feed from humans, for fear of losing control. 'I haven't fed on human blood for over seventy years. I was placed under a spell that wore off over time.

My actions were not entirely my fault, not that it's any excuse for what I've done.'

'A spell? I see. You have your own personal vendetta against the witches, like we do – and to my knowledge, there's only one witch living in Tallant these days.'

'Carol has no intentions of harming anyone in Tallant or anywhere else. She left Green Bay to escape her coven and make a better life here. She's innocent and not to be harmed.'

'How can you be so sure of this witch?' The Governor downed the last of the whiskey in one go.

'She's seen my past; she also knows a great deal about me. The last thing she'd want is a repeat of those days. She's already tried to warn someone close to me about the old me.'

The Governor nodded slowly. 'Jim's daughter? What are your intentions for her and what does she know?'

'Nothing yet, and I want it keep it that way as long as possible. My intentions are to keep her safe at all costs, from any and all threats.'

'Don't you think just being around you is dangerous enough?'

Scott bolted to his feet, slammed his hands down on the desk and leaned in close before grimacing in reply.

'Tell that to her mother.' He turned and towards the door before the Governor made one last statement to his back.

'One more thing I think you should know, Mr Maglace: you said you keep this town safe?'

Scott stopped and answered without turning his head. 'What about it?'

'One of those missing schoolgirls is from right here in Tallant, you protect this town from vampires and werewolves but do witches get a free pass?' A second later, his door was flung open, slamming against the wall. The Governor had stoked the fire enough for now.

Scott was gone.

**Chapter 43**

Darkness had fallen. A convoy of three black SUVs pulled up outside Damien Cartwright's residence in Eastbrook Lodge. Governor Patrick Cartwright along with two family members dressed in black approached the front door, knocking with his leather glove. A moment later, the door opened, and the group stepped inside. No words were needed. A subtle nod sufficed. It was time. The Governor stood focusing on his brother, waiting patiently for the newest member of the curse to join them.

Damien called out to upstairs.

'Daniel, it's time, son.' A moment passed. No reply. 'Daniel, we're waiting. Daniel?'

The Governor looked even more agitated than usual before barking at his brother. 'We haven't time for this, Damien.' Damien made his way up the stairs followed closely by the Governor. Outside his son's room he knocked on the door politely and waited. No answer.

'Daniel, we've talked ab–' Before Damien could finish, his brother forced open the bedroom door. The teenager's room was empty. The bay window was open, and a fresh smell of aftershave hung in the air. On the bed a crumpled piece of paper lay face down. Governor Cartwright picked it up to inspect the print on the back.

*'Woodland Surge Rave. Location will be revealed on social media.'*

The Governor looked at his brother with contempt before continuing to read out loud. 'Come celebrate the full moon with us, it's going to be … a howl.' He slapped the piece of paper against his younger brother's chest as he stormed past him. Damien began to panic as he tried to keep up with his brother thundering down the stairs.

'He, he mustn't have taken us seriously.'

The Governor turned and glared. 'You think?'

'Patrick, we have to find him, it's imperative!'

'Really? How exactly? With the risk of having twenty out of confinement tonight instead of one? Besides, we don't have time.'

'We just leave him out there alone?'

The Governor grabbed his younger brother by his jacket and shoved him up against the wall. 'I don't think it's him we have to worry about, do you?' He released his grip and stood back, pointing a finger into his brother's face. 'If there are any mutilated bodies reported tomorrow, I'll be holding you personally responsible, little brother.' He turned and made his way out to his SUV. The cold depths of the Town Hall basement awaited: all local Cartwright men spent one night per month locked up there, out of sight and harm of the general population who went about their business at ground level, oblivious to the danger beneath their feet.

***

At the same time across town, about two miles from the forest trail off Fourth Avenue, a steady flow of party goers walked together in groups towards a circular clearing of forestry surrounded by large boulders. Head torches and hand-lamp beams swayed from side to side in the distance back towards town. Multi-coloured head- and wristbands, body paint and hi-vis clothing glowed throughout the forest as the revellers approached the recently disclosed location. Tonight, the stars were replaced by strobe lighting, and the tranquillity of the forest disturbed by loud music. Two smiley-faced helium balloons floated either side of the trail to identify their destination.

Rucksacks and plastic bags filled with beer bottles and cans were scattered on the ground between large groups of youths shouting back and forth above the music. Some danced with hands in the air, while others made out in plain sight as an inflatable beach ball bounced above their heads, passed randomly from group to group. A cardboard sign was nailed to a tree pointing to a designated 'toilet area'. On a trail heading deeper into the forest, a generator hummed, feeding power to a makeshift DJ stage positioned on top of the central boulder from where the lights and music emanated. A large homemade white banner hung above, displaying the words 'WOODLAND SURGE' in red spray paint.

Behind the decks, PJ stood with a set of double headphones held to one ear in one hand, his other hand scrolling through his laptop preparing the next song to play. His serious demeanour looked out of place compared to his usual joking attitude. Meanwhile, Dan Cartwright and Nikky passed between the giant smiley faces and stopped inside the boundary behind the crowd to get their bearings. Nikky couldn't help but notice Dan seemed somewhat out of sorts, remaining quiet and agitated for most of the trip since leaving town.

'Okay, out with it, Dan,' she shouted above the music.

'What?' Cartwright looked back towards the town.

'What's up with you tonight, why do you keep looking behind us?'

Cartwright looked flustered. Again, he stepped aside to look further back down the line of party goers. Nikky clicked her fingers in front of his face to get his attention.

'Hello?'

Eventually he turned to face her, looking pissed for interrupting his chain of thought.

'What, Nikky?' he barked. She said nothing. Just shook her head at him again. He raised his hands up in a gesture of apology for his impatience. 'Okay, look, there's a guy in a dark hoodie back there and I think he's following us, okay?'

Nikky craned to look back down the line. 'Where? I don't see anyone?'

He pointed. 'Halfway back … wait, I can't see him now, but I swear he's been following us since we left town.'

'Dan, why would someone be following us here of all places? Maybe you're just being paranoid?' She over-exaggerated her words so that he could partially lipread over the background noise of the party. He leaned in close to her ear.

'It's just something my uncle said.'

'The Governor?'

'Yeah, he, well it's just.' He paused, looking for a way out. She raised her eyebrows in anticipation. 'Actually, it's nothing, forget it, I just wouldn't put it past him to have me followed.'

She shouted into his ear. "Why would your uncle have you followed, that doesn't make sense!'

He looked at her then back to the line. 'I suppose to see if I've been drinking, make sure I'm behaving.' He knew it wasn't exactly a good lie, but it would have to do.

It's not as if he could relay the scare tactics used by his uncle and father to keep him away from tonight's festivities. Desperation at its finest.

'Fair enough. I'm gonna go say hi to PJ, you comin'?'

Still preoccupied with the line, he kept his gaze towards town as he replied.

'Nah, you go, I'm gonna go find the other guys, I'll meet up with ya later.' She nodded and he disappeared into the crowd. As she made her way through the drunken masses, she stopped and looked back to the giant smiley faces where she'd been a moment ago. Cartwright was gone but, off to one side, something caught her eye.

A motionless figure in a black hoodie stood alone. His face was hidden, but he was eerily poised in her direction. Everyone was moving and dancing around him, making his still presence even more noticeable. Maybe Dan was right. Just then, a girl with rainbows painted on her cheeks bumped into her, knocking her to one side. A drunken salute as an apology and Nikky smiled back half-heartedly, before glancing back to the smiley faces. The hoodie was gone. Dan had made her paranoid, she thought. She shook her head and carried on towards the rear of the boulder where PJ was dishing out tunes, wearing his cap backwards. To her surprise, she recognised someone standing with arms folded watching PJ from below.

'Rebecca?' Nikky shouted.

She turned in response. 'Oh, hi Nikky, never thought I'd see you here?'

'I was just gonna say the same to you?'

Rebecca Chambers being a classic nerd and goody two shoes didn't generally frequent these types of get-togethers. Unless it was with her study group, she usually didn't socialise.

But on this occasion, she was clearly going all out, with a plastic smiley-face badge on the end of each of her usually plain pigtails. Big whoop.

'Well, this isn't really my style, but I'm head of the homecoming committee so I came to see how PJ's doing as DJ, what about you?' She unfolded her arms to push her black-rimmed glasses up.

'I'm here with friends, PJ being one of them, but "officially" I'm staying at Gwen's house for the night if you ask my dad.' She used her fingers as inverted commas. Rebecca watched PJ from behind a little longer and nodded to herself. She leaned in towards Nikky.

'He's not that bad, is he?'

Nikky smiled. 'Do you mean at playing music?'

'Of course, what else would I mean?' She looked shocked at Nikky's presumption.

'It's okay to like him the other way too, Rebecca.'

Rebecca blushed and paused. She wasn't used to talking about boys. 'He's younger than me, so it's out of the question anyway even if I was interested.'

'That's no big deal! I think he likes you, anyway.'

Rebecca's cheeks were rosy-red. She needed to change the subject. A topless drunk guy in shorts bolted past, holding his hand to his mouth ready to vomit.

'Who's this new boyfriend I've heard about? Gossip travels fast on social media, even if I'm not in the cool gang.'

Now it was Nikky's turn to be embarrassed. 'His name's Scott.'

'A hottie, I'm told.'

'He's my man of mystery in shining armour.'

Rebecca unexpectedly stopped and pointed to something happening over to her left at the forest edge. 'Isn't that Dan Cartwright over there? A little early to be that drunk, isn't it?' Nikky looked to where she was pointing. Cartwright had his arms hooked over Luke and Brad's shoulders as they dragged him from the crowd. They sat him down on a rock, but he looked like he was doubled over in pain. He slumped forward with his head resting in his hands and didn't move.

'Be right back.' But Rebecca's attention was now back on PJ. Nikky quickly made her way over to the others.

'What happened?' she shouted..

'Not sure, he collapsed right in front of us, so we carried him here for some air, what did he drink?' Brad offered.

'Nothing yet to my knowledge,' she shouted back. She put her hand on his shoulder and knelt to try and see his face. 'Dan, what happened? Are you okay?' He lifted his head and yelled at Brad and Luke, turning his head from one to the other.

'What do you two want? Get the hell away from me!' He felt unbearable pain and didn't know why. But he didn't need the embarrassment of everyone seeing him in his moment of weakness. Luke and Brad stood up and looked at each other.

'Now!'

Shaking their heads in disbelief, they turned and vanished back into the sea of people surrounding the bonfire. Nikky slowly pulled his hands from his face and looked him in the eyes.

'Dan, what's going on? You can tell me, it's okay; what did you take?'

He was breathing rapidly now and perspiring. He shouted a response while holding his hands to his ears as if the music was causing him physical pain. 'I ... I ... I just don't feel right, I think something's really wrong with me, I ...' He stood up and stared into the sky. '... I have to get outta here.' He turned towards the open forest behind him and fell face first over the rock he had been sitting on. He pulled himself back to his feet with the help of a nearby tree and bolted into the brush.

'Dan, wait! Where are you going?'

He was gone, quickly smothered in darkness and out of sight. Nobody but Nikky knew he was gone, and nobody cared.

## Chapter 44

Nikky knew this was bad. She knew Dan wouldn't be able to find his way back. Too many times she'd heard reports from her father about experienced hikers getting lost in these woods, with bodies being recovered days or weeks later. The lights and noise of the rave would only travel so far into the thickness of the woods before being stopped in its tracks by Mother Nature. But what could she do? He had no chance of survival alone. Her own mother was proof of how dangerous Chequamegon-Nicolet National Forest was. She never made it back alive. A memory flashed before her eyes. Sitting alone in her father's 4x4 on a remote forest road. Jumping with terror as three gunshots rang out, echoing over the mountains in the distance.

She couldn't live with that on her conscience. Not again. Her mom didn't come back alive; she wouldn't let the same thing happen to Dan. Amber would do the same for Scott, right? She thought. Okay, maybe not, but she wasn't Amber. Redirecting her gaze to PJ in a panic, she could see that he was preoccupied trying to impress his audience. She scanned the people around her: Brad and Luke were nowhere to be seen, and Dan was getting further away by the second. Her mind was made up. It was now or never. Pulling her phone from her pocket and tapping on the torch, she took off through the same patch of branches where Cartwright had disappeared a moment earlier.

Back at the makeshift DJ table, PJ leaned underneath to grab a bottle of water and for a quick check on the power cables below. Rebecca still stood with her arms folded, but this time gave him a nod of approval when they made eye contact. He held out his hand, gesturing for her to climb up and join him. From up here, she could see the entire clearing right back to the trail that led back to town, all lit up by the central bonfire and strobe lights. The music changing changed the reaction from the crowd. Most of them looked her way as PJ added his own mix into well-known tunes. Up here she felt important. Like she was helping. She had to admit, she was impressed. PJ slipped one ear from under the headphones and leaned towards her. 'You here on your own?' he shouted. The answer was yes, but she felt awkward admitting it.

'I was just talking to your friends a minute ago.' She pointed behind and to her left. But there was only a random couple making out and a guy throwing up against a tree. The others had gone.

***

Within the depths of the forest, Nikky was alone. She called out Dan's name several times to no avail. For the fifth time she dialled his number, hearing the faint sound of his phone guiding her in his general direction and further from the rave. She knew he was somewhere just ahead of her but why didn't he answer? The organised chaos of Woodland Surge was now quite a distance behind her. So much so that the music was now nothing more than a muffled vibration buried by evergreens.

She called out again. No reply. What the hell is he doing? she thought. At this point she not only wanted to see if Dan was okay, but also not to be alone in this wilderness any longer. She'd lost her bearings. How could she find the North Star again? She looked up to see the night sky in the thicket above. It was too dense. She needed a more open space.

'What the hell was I thinking?' she whispered to herself in the silence. She punched his number again. Success. The ringtone was closer now, seemingly just up ahead. The sound got louder as she approached but stopped again and went to his voicemail. The ground under foot was becoming solid. Finally: a clearing. Large rocks above dominated the opposite side of a fast-flowing river, overlooking the forest edge. She looked up again, able to see the night sky at last. She turned her torch off, reducing light pollution for a clear view of the heavens and the glory of the full moon.

One last try. She dialled the number again.

Jumping with fright as it rang loudly almost next to her, she turned to see Cartwright's phone lit up, lying on the ground partially covered by pine needles. But there was no sign of its owner. The screen showing Nikky's photo lit the area until his message minder kicked in again, leaving a green flashing light in the corner. Turning her torch back on, she waved it randomly around her position.

'Dan? You there? Dan?' Silence. The only sound was the running water rippling between rocks and crevices. On the opposite side of the river, up on the rock face, the silence was disturbed by a scattering of small rocks that fell into the river below. Nikky steadied herself, getting equal footing on the uneven ground, as she reluctantly pointed the torch to investigate. She instantly regretted her decision.

Towering above her, at over seven feet tall, what looked like a muscular form of wild bear stood upright, motionless, staring at the full moon. Yellow glowing eyes beamed into the heavens seemingly in awe at the splendour of the lunar surface. Arms with enlarged human-like hands and fingernails like claws hung low either side of the massive body. Nikky was paralysed with fear to the point where she could feel her own pulse beating in her ears like drums pounding. The terror froze every muscle of her body. Whatever this thing was, it hadn't seen her, yet. Trying not to breathe, and with no sudden movements, she slowly turned her light off and dropped her arms to her sides. Every ounce of her being screamed at her to flee, but one foot out of place on the smallest twig could attract its attention.

The silence was deafening. She waited. Maybe it would leave without ever setting eyes on her, she thought. Within a space of time that seemed like an eternity, a noise rang out behind her. She closed her eyes tightly, praying she was hearing things. But she wasn't. Cartwright's phone lit up the area beneath the trees, begging for attention. Nikky's picture appeared on its screen. She'd inadvertently pressed redial on her phone while trying to hide the light. The yellow eyes that were preoccupied with the moon a moment ago now had a new focus.

Prey.

Its ferocious eyes turned on her as it stepped forward, panting on the rock face before emitting a deafening roar, causing her to stumble and fall backwards onto the ground. Only one option remained.

Escape.

In complete panic, she began crawling rapidly on her knees before scrambling onto her feet. Raising her arms to protect her face from clusters of branches, she bolted as fast as she could back to where she thought she'd come from. All sense of direction was lost. Everything looked the same. Another roar pierced the surrounding woods. It had her scent. The heavy panting got closer. She didn't care now which direction was right, once she was heading away from the beast in pursuit. A tear escaped her eye and dropped from her face. Is this what happened to her mother? The yellow eyes were the only thing visible in the dark, and they had stopped moving. It was too late.

She knew she couldn't outrun her own scent, but she had to try. Stepping back slowly from the beast, she turned to make a break for it. After running five steps, she was blindly knocked back onto the forest floor. She'd run straight into something too soft to be a tree. Holding one hand up to protect her face, she tried to focus on the obstacle before her.

A figure in a dark hoodie stood staring down at her. She dimly realised that Cartwright was right, they had been followed. The stranger took two steps towards her, and she scrambled frantically backwards on her hands, digging her heels into the ground. This was too much. She screamed and sobbed uncontrollably. The figure kept coming. This was it, she thought. Killed by a beast or a psycho in a hoodie, alone in the forest, just like her mother.

She froze. The hoodie had stepped past her, stopping just beyond her to face the yellow eyes. She wiped her tears and watched as the hooded figure turned its head to where she lay. Under the hood, all she could see were red eyes. Another image flashed inside her head.

Something Scott had said. To her shock, the figure spoke, in a twisted, demonic voice.

'*Run.*'

# Chapter 45

Nikky didn't need an invitation to heed the advice from the hooded psycho. She made for the largest opening in the trees she could see, hoping to find her way as she went. If she was lucky enough to find another clearing, she could use the stars to find her way back to civilisation, using the method Scott taught her. As she ran for her life, another roar disrupted the silence behind her, but this one was different. Like the roar of a lion, it reverberated through the evergreens.

'Don't look back, don't look back,' she repeated as she dodged tree stumps and avoided branches, panting as she ran. . With red eyes piercing the darkness from under the hoodie, the stranger watched and waited while the two-legged beast with yellow eyes stopped to inspect his opponent. In a moment of defiance, it looked to the full moon, extending its arms wide, and cried out with a thunderous outburst, exposing razor-sharp teeth running the length of a projecting snout. Slowly and without any sign of fear, the figure raised his pale hands with their long fingernails to the sides of his head, pulling back the hood to let it rest on his shoulders.

Above the red eyes, a misshaped protruding brow stood out on an enlarged, wrinkled forehead. An open mouth exposed a set of four fangs, the upper ones longer in length than the ones below. The yellow-eyed beast suddenly charged, slashing the air with outstretched claws. When the time was right and the beast was within range, the dark figure performed a powerful back flip to kick the creature in its neck. The force sent it backwards through the air with a howl, causing the earth to shake as it made impact with the forest floor. A roar later, it leapt back to its feet, finding itself alone, its adversary seemingly vanished. The area was silent apart from its own panting. It scanned the vicinity, sniffing the air.

The dark figure flew at the beast from behind, grabbing its hair and ramming it face-first into the base of a tree. Toying with the creature, he bashed it against the tree again and again until its bloodied head hung lifeless and unresponsive. With incredible strength, he held the beast by the scruff of its neck and looked at it with contempt, before giving his own roar of domination. The beast was incapacitated.

Carelessly dropping it to the ground, he took two steps away from the bloodied mess, scanning the area in search of the girl. As he did so, the yellow eyes silently opened again. A claw pierced the dark figure's lower back, protruding through the front of his abdomen and lifting him from the ground. Simultaneously, the beast's mouth found the right side of his neck and shoulder, ripping and tearing both wound sites, decimating the pale flesh. He struggled and fell to the ground as the beast roared in defiance.

Pulling himself to his feet, the figure turned to face his opponent, holding his hand to the gaping wound on his neck that poured blood down his chest to join the hole in his stomach. Enough was enough. In a blur, he vanished from where he stood, appearing in an instant face to face with the werewolf. In one quick motion, he effortlessly snapped its neck, letting it fall to the ground without so much as a whimper. The dark figure had won. His wounds began to heal and close, leaving nothing but dried blood stains.

***

Rebecca Chambers went back to PJ at the rear of the boulders with two drinks in hand. A figure emerged from the trees behind, slamming into her back, knocking the bottles from her grip, and emptying them on the forest floor.

'Hey! Watch it!' she shouted as she turned to face the drunken idiot who'd just cost her ten bucks. Nikky stood with tears streaming down her face. 'Oh God! Are you okay? What happened?' Rebecca shouted. Nikky kept nervously glancing to the trees behind her. PJ looked down from the makeshift DJ stall and noticed the two girls chatting. Then they hugged. Cute, he thought. One of his best friends and the girl he had a crush on since first grade were getting along nicely. When the girl hugs ended, he noticed that something seemed to be wrong with Nikky. Rebecca was giving her another hug. What the hell's happened? he thought. He looked around. No sign of Cartwright or the others. With one hand on the decks, he gestured for Rebecca to return. Rebecca spoke to Nikky again then jumped back up onto the boulder.

'What the hell happened to her?' PJ shouted in her ear.

'Dan went into the forest, she followed him and got lost. I think she saw a bear or something, from what I can make out; she's freaking out, I've never seen her like this before.'

PJ looked down at Nikky, giving her a thumbs up. She stood with her arms folded, still glancing behind her every few seconds. 'A bear won't come anywhere near all this noise; you'd better get her home – can I call you later? Just to make sure she got home okay?' he replied.

Rebecca remembered something Nikky had said earlier. 'No, she can't go home tonight, her dad thinks she's staying with Amber. I'll take her home with me.'

'Okay, can you tell her I'll call tomorrow?'

'Sure, and it's a yes to calling me later … to discuss homecoming.'

PJ smiled. 'Of course,' he winked.

**Chapter 46**

Dan Cartwright lay naked on the forest floor, curled up in the foetal position. Groggily, he rolled over to inspect his surroundings. Where the hell was he? The fog in his mind slowly lifted as his memories returned. Holding his hand to his forehead did little to ease his thumping headache. But the legend about his family was starting to make sense.

He looked up to see a figure staring down at him, saying nothing. A moment of silence as two pairs of eyes met. 'I guess what my dad and uncle told me wasn't bullshit after all.' Dan held out his hand to the dark figure, asking to help him up from the ground. 'Yeah, you're a freak.' Scott pulled him to his feet. He steadied himself against a tree branch for a moment before responding.

'You're one to talk. If I'm a freak, then what the hell are you?'

Scott took a few paces back, picked up the hoodie he'd been wearing earlier, and tossed it to Cartwright. 'Put this on. I'm a vampire.'

'I don't believe in vampires.' He tied the hoodie around his waist, covering himself as best he could.

'You didn't believe in werewolves either but here we are. Try telling that to Nikky.'

'Oh shit, Nikky! Did she get away? Is she okay? Where is she?'

'Yes, yes, and back at the party last I saw her, no thanks to you.'

Dan looked down at the ground, a feeling of guilt building in the pit of his stomach. 'I would've ripped her to shreds, thank God you were there to stop me.'

Scott put his hands into his pockets before answering. 'God had nothing to do with it.'

'How did you know about me?'

'You're a Cartwright out on a full moon. A no-brainer, really, but next time go to ground with your family; that party back there would have been a massacre had I not stopped you.'

'I guess I should thank you.'

'Just get your ass home and do what your uncle told you at the next full moon.' Scott turned to leave. Dan took two steps towards him.

'Wait, please, I've a tonne of questions, Scott, I know we haven't seen eye to eye but things are starting to make sense now – Please – this is all new to me.'

Scott turned his head. 'What?'

'It's just, I know so little about us.'

'Your family will fill in the blanks; not my job.'

'Wait, just help me out here, please: what made me change back?'

Scott hesitated. 'I killed you in your werewolf form, so you reverted back a while later.'

'So, I can't die?'

'Of course you can die,' Scott laughed.

'How?'

'From personal experience I've found that ripping your head off does the trick.'

'You've ... killed werewolves before?'

'Your uncle will give you the low-down.'

'But I've healed?'

Scott turned to face him. 'All I did was break your neck. Now that you've had your first change, you'll heal faster in human form, too, along with a few other perks. Strength, hearing, sense of smell; eventually you'll have more control over the beast.'

'It's just so much to take in ... but I guess now I understand some of the things that've happened with my family throughout my life. But isn't a bite from a werewolf supposed to kill a vampire?'

'Usually, yes. But that's more for your uncle to tell you. That's why that vampire didn't kill you in the cemetery that night when you were alone.'

'That was a vampire? How did you know about that?'

'Little goes on in the cemetery without me knowing.'

'How do you know so much about my kind, anyway?'

'I knew your great-grandfather; he was a good man.'

'I don't even know his name ... how old are you, Scott?'

'Another time, perhaps.' Scott sprang twenty feet into the air and positioned himself on a large branch. Cartwright folded his arms across his bare chest.

'Impressive, so what else can you do?'

'You don't wanna find out. Heed my warning, Cartwright, the next full moon is homecoming night: you'd better be locked up with your family.'

'Amber's gonna be pissed but that's another story ... hey, does Nikky know about you?'

Scott looked up to the heavens. 'No, not yet. I'm delaying the inevitable ... I just want things to feel *normal* a little while longer.'

'She's dating a vampire and doesn't know it? Maybe if you started trusting those close to you, you might feel normal, as you put it, not having to keep secrets.'

'Cartwright, I don't care who you tell about your own predicament, but leave Nikky to me, the timing has to be right. Plus your ego was big enough before you found out you have certain abilities, I can only imagine the temptation will be too much for you not to try and impress your girlfriend.' Scott stood up on the branch then stepped forward and floated down to land in front of Cartwright.

'Neat,' Dan grinned.

Scott pointed to the ground behind Dan. 'Your phone's over there, text or call Nikky and tell her you're okay. Tell her it was a bear she'd seen, and just make up the rest, I don't really care.'

Cartwright nodded. Another moment of silence between the two. Scott turned to walk away taking three steps before stopping again with his back to Cartwright.

'His name was Joseph.'

Dan was confused. 'What?'

'Your great-grandfather.'

'Right.' Cartwright blinked and Scott was gone, leaving him alone with a thousand thoughts to dwell on.

## Chapter 47

The next day started bright and sunny. PJ was up and about earlier than he'd expected after the busy night before. Today was a good day, he thought; things were finally going the way he wanted them to go. An extra-long weekend meant more time off school and the DJ job for homecoming was, as he put it 'in the bag'. As was a date with Rebecca Chambers, following a text message exchange after Nikky had fallen asleep in her spare room last night. In his eyes, even the cemetery looked extra cheerful this morning as he made his way along the gravel pathway to Scott's house. Arriving at the flat roof he knocked on the door, turned his cap around backwards and waited.

No answer.

PJ went straight into an all-out assault with a cycle of knocks that turned to thumps interspersed with an occasional kick. 'Scott, you there?' he barked. No reply. Another kick. The door flew open inwards with Scott standing inside the small hallway in a black T-shirt, denim jeans and white socks, flabbergasted by PJ's lack of manners.

'Oh, you are there, I was just about to leave.'

Scott looked back into the living room area then back to PJ. 'You do realise that if you tried that trick at night, you'd be dead now?'

'What are you talkin' about, man? C'mon, grab your sneakers and let's go hang out, another day with no school.'

Scott shook his head in disbelief. 'Gimme a sec.' He disappeared back inside for a moment while PJ waited, throwing pebbles into an empty flowerpot to kill time. Twenty pebbles later, Scott emerged wearing his usual jacket, fixing the collar as he passed the threshold into the sun, prompting the instinctive reaction of putting on his sunglasses.

'What happened to your lantern?' PJ blurted out as he threw a stick of gum into his mouth.

Scott looked at the damaged light next to the doorway. 'Nothing ... what has you so happy today?' he replied, quickly changing the subject.

PJ stood with his arms wide, crucifixion-style, closed his eyes and looked up to the sky. 'Yours truly has scored the DJ job for homecoming.' He dropped his arms back to his sides as they walked toward the northern gate. 'And a date with Rebecca thrown in for good measure.'

'Good for you, still doesn't explain why you're here at this hour and where we're headed?'

PJ started pacing the gravel path backwards, facing Scott, relishing his moment of victory. 'Anywhere, I don't care, let's just hang out for a bit before you vanish with Nikky.' He beckoned him towards the bench that had miraculously fixed itself.

'Have you heard from Nikky today?' Scott asked.

'Not today, but late last night. She was pretty shaken up at Woodland Surge, said she'd seen a bear or something in the dark, but she's all good now and back home this morning, I assume.'

'She didn't go home last night?'

PJ offered Scott gum, which he refused with a wave of his hand. 'Nope, she stayed with Rebecca, my *potential* girlfriend, ya know.'

'How come?'

'Said something about her dad not letting her out when there's a full moon or something crazy, I wasn't paying attention to be honest; she pretended she was staying with Amber.'

'Good advice,' Scott muttered under his breath.

When they arrived at the bench, Scott sat stretching his legs out in front of him and crossed his feet. PJ sat on the back rest with his feet on the seat with his usual devil-may-care attitude. Something was bothering Scott and it wasn't PJ's behaviour. He was getting used to that. It was something Cartwright had said last night. In all his long years, perhaps this teenager's advice might actually work. Living a solitary 'life' for the most part and keeping secrets had taken its toll. Perhaps Dan was right? In the past he'd trusted a handful of people with his secret, and those were the best years of his existence. Albeit with the most painful memories.

Screw it. What did he have to lose? If sharing his secret didn't go as planned, he could always enthral them to forget, like he'd done to friends in the past whenever he'd been exposed. He turned his head to look at PJ, who'd begun playing some new music tracks on his phone, destroying the morning ambience. Nearby, Mr Coventry's morning routine was interrupted by the noise. With a pitchfork over his right shoulder, he went to investigate.

'PJ, do you remember the night of the fairground when I won the teddy bear for Nikky?' Scott asked. PJ stopped nodding his head to the music on hearing the question.

'I remember you doing the impossible, hitting those bullseyes without looking.' PJ stood up. 'Which, by the way, you told me you'd explain, and right now I'm all ears.'

Scott shrugged. Time for truth. 'Okay, ask me anything.'

'I just did! So how the hell did you do it? And don't tell me it was just luck again.' He pointed his finger at Scott.

'It wasn't luck. Okay, there's no other way of saying it so I'll just say it. I'm a vampire.' He watched PJ closely through his shades for the expected reaction. For a moment, PJ stared back, expressionless. Like a deer in the headlights.

'Aahhh, that explains everything. Now I get it. You're a vampire!' An over-exaggerated smile on his face. 'Scott?'

'Yeah?'

'Are you feeling okay? You want me to call someone? The men in the white coats will be here any second.'

Mr Coventry arrived with his usual limp and the jingling of keys. He was about to demand the music be turned off until he noticed Scott. PJ turned to see who'd joined them before rolling his eyes and muttering under his breath.

'Oh, this grumpy old fart again.'

Mr Coventry stuck his pitchfork into the gravel and leaned on the handle for support before wiping sweat from his brow. He looked at PJ. 'No respect for the dead?' Scott replied before PJ could respond with something disastrous.

'Ah Mr Coventry, I was just telling my friend here that I'm a vampire, but he doesn't believe me, any suggestions?'

PJ shook his head, wondering why Scott would want a random stranger to also think he was crazy. Mr Coventry looked Scott in the eye, then at PJ, then back to Scott before responding.

'Just one comes to mind.' Without giving either teenager a chance to reply, the groundskeeper raised his pitchfork and stabbed Scott through the centre of his chest, piercing his flesh with all four prongs, causing Scott to jolt backwards. PJ jumped, falling to the ground landing on the gravel path before shouting in astonishment.

'What, from the bottom of my heart, the fuck, have you done you crazy old bastard!'

With two hands, Mr Coventry pulled on the wooden handle, removing the metal forks from Scott's chest before placing it back into the ground where it had been a moment ago. Scott sat forward with his hands on his knees and looked up.

'Thanks for the warning, and you speak of respect for the dead?'

PJ was in shock at what he'd just witnessed. 'Scott?' he said in a panic.

'Yeah?'

PJ pushed forward onto his knees, suspiciously watching Mr Coventry's every move. With shaking hands, he picked up his phone and stopped the music. 'Are you okay? How are you talking to me?'

'I told you, I'm a vampire.' Scott looked at the groundskeeper again. 'Thanks for the *subtle* demonstration, Toddy.'

'Don't mention it, just don't try it on me as a demonstration next time.' Mr Coventry threw his pitchfork over his shoulder and limped away to continue his work, without giving the incident a second thought. PJ stared at Scott in amazement, almost missing the bench as he sat down next to him. He held out his hand to Scott's chest then stopped himself. Scott pulled up his shirt and turned to his friend, exposing his chiselled chest and abdomen, with no sign of injury.

'You can't kill what's already dead, my friend.'

PJ stood up to face him, again pointing his finger in disbelief. 'This, this is all staged, right? This is some kind of trick you're playing, and that lovely old man is in on it, right?'

'You called him an old fart a minute ago.'

'Yeah, that was before he turned psycho and impaled you; believe me, I won't ever mess with that guy.'

Scott shook his head. Perhaps another demonstration was needed after all. As PJ was looking at

Scott, he felt a double tap on his left shoulder. He flicked his head to investigate and jumped in fright to see Scott standing next to him.

'Jesus!' The bench was now empty. 'How did you … wait, wait, this is crazy shit, man.'

'I told you.'

'So that's how you won those teddy bears?'

'Yes.'

'And that's how you seem to hear the impossible?'

'Yes.'

'And you can't die?'

'All creatures can die.'

'So what? you mean like, a stake through the heart kinda thingy?'

'Something like that.'

'So, if I believed you that vampires are real, they're immortal, right? So how old *are* you? And remember you said you'd tell the truth.'

Scott thought for a moment. 'Six hundred and thirteen, this December I believe.'

'Holy shitsticks, this is insane! What year were you born?'

'1406.'

'Here?'

'No.'

'Transylvania?'

'No PJ, I'm not Vlad the Impaler, or Dracula, for that matter, and I'll slap you silly if you ask do I sparkle in sunlight.'

'What brought you here, then?' asked PJ.

'I travelled over the centuries until I finally returned to these shores, which the ancients call home.'

'This is insane.'

'Try being me.'

'Are there others like you, in town, I mean?'

'No other vampires in town except Amdis and me. Any who come into town, well, let's just say, they never leave. There *are* werewolves here, too, though.

'Oh shit! No wonder your mom could pick me up like she did!'

'Yeah, and you almost kicked down the door to wake her today.'

PJ swallowed. 'Wait back up, did you say ... werewolves? Here? In Tallant?'

'Yep, that bear Nikky claims she saw last night was none other than our old pal Dan Cartwright.'

'Right, the full moon.' He spun around holding both sides of his head like it was going to explode. 'Wait, what? *Cartwright*? Is a *werewolf*?'

'All male Cartwrights are.'

'This is way too much to take in.' PJ slumped onto the bench, desperately trying to process what he was hearing. Scott sat next to him, removed his sunglasses, and intervened for PJ's own good.

'Look into my eyes, my friend.'

PJ turned, looking overwhelmed.

'Accept all I've told you as truth and stop worrying about it.'

A moment later, PJ sat up like nothing had happened, back to his usual cocky self. 'How did you do that? You made it go away.'

'It's something vampires can do; we call it enthralling. We can make humans do our bidding, comes in handy, really.'

PJ stood up to face him again. 'Wait, so you're telling me you can make a person do … anything you want them to do?' He held his hands to the sides of his head mimicking an explosion inside his brain.

'Pretty much,' Scott nodded.

'Anybody?'

'Well, almost anybody … for some unknown reason I can't enthral Nikky. I've tried and it just doesn't seem to work on her. Very strange.'

'And all vamps can do this Jedi mind trick … thingy?' PJ waved his hand across the front of Scott's face, Obi Wan Kenobi-style.

'Yes. And all vampires have heightened senses and emotions. They're simply more alive than they should be, without a heartbeat. I can enthral other vampires and werewolves, but they can't do the same to me. I'm also the only vampire that can tolerate sunlight, and the only one with red eyes.'

'How come?'

'Because I'm, I'm different. I'm a pureblood *vamp*, as you put it.'

'What the hell does that mean?'

'It means I'm special.'

'Are there others like you?'

'No.'

'So, you're some kind of *super vamp*?'

'Something like that.'

'Okay, if you're a super vamp, what's your kryptonite?'

Scott smirked at him. 'Don't go there, PJ.'

'You won't tell me? What happens if you go bat-shit crazy and want to kill me?'

'Then you'd already be dead.'

PJ looked serious as he took a seat next to his friend. 'You've … killed people, haven't you?'

Scott just returned his stare, blankly.

'How many?'

'One was too many; let's leave it at that, shall we?'

'But don't you have to kill people to live? The whole blood-drinking thing?'

'Not necessarily, I feed on animals now. It's not perfect, but it keeps the blood lust at bay.'

'But the temptation is still there, right? To drink … human blood?'

'Correct. How can I best describe it … you know when you're holding your breath under water? It's okay at first because you can control it, then as it gets closer and closer to the time you must inhale, that need becomes incredibly urgent. Panic sets in when you begin to think you won't be able to, but when you take in air, the anxiety subsides. That, my friend, is what it's like to be a vampire and need blood. Blood is our oxygen.'

'So, If I bleed in front of you …'

Scott cut in abruptly. 'I wouldn't try it if I were you, my control can only go so far. I suggest we change the subject?'

'Okay, then do something to me.'

'What?'

'Enthral me, let me see if it really works?'

'I just did, to make you accept what I've been telling you.'

'No, I mean again, I wanna try and resist, go ahead, try me.' PJ knelt down on the gravel path.

'You can't resist. Stand up, you look like you're proposing.' PJ stood up. Scott looked at him for a moment and couldn't resist the urge to laugh. 'What am I supposed to do?'

'Anything, I'll resist, I'm very headstrong, you know.'

Scott smiled and shook his head. 'Okay, look into my eyes.' PJ was ready to defy, an excited grin on his face. 'Stop breathing.'

## Chapter 48

Scott slumped back down onto the bench behind him and watched PJ's facial expression change. His mouth opened and closed like a fish out of water. He grabbed his neck in panic as his oxygen supply drained from his last breath.

The only one smiling now was Scott. He stood up, placed his hand on PJ's shoulder and spoke to his friend who was changing colour before his eyes.

'PJ, I just remembered I think I left a pot on the boil; I'll be right back – you're okay here for a minute, aren't you? You said you could resist me, right?' PJ's look of panic intensified. He held out his hand to get Scott's attention but Scott vanished in a blur and sped toward the flat roof. A split second later, he reappeared. PJ's face was starting to turn blue.

Scott looked into his eyes again, still smiling. 'Breathe.'

PJ fell to his knees, panting rapidly, coughing and unable to speak. Eventually he got his breath back sufficiently to throw a sentence together. 'Damn it, Scott, I could have died!' He thumped Scott's jacket in retaliation, before raising his hands up in defence. 'Wait, shit, I, I didn't mean to hit you, please don't kill me!'

Scott laughed. 'Shut up and sit down, you moron.' Still out of breath, PJ pulled himself up and sat down heavily next to Scott.

'You know, PJ, I could actually feel the resistance there for a minute?'

Excitedly PJ turned towards him. 'Really!?'

Scott answered sarcastically, 'No.' PJ slumped down again, disappointed. 'In theory you could walk into a bank and enthral the clerk to hand over all the cash, so why aren't you living in a mansion?'

'I guess I lack enthusiasm. Priorities are different when you're immortal.'

PJ grinned. 'You could still do it for me, though?' Scott shook his head and smiled.

'Nice try.' A brief moment of silence was interrupted by PJ.

'Wait just a sec, my pale friend, you enthralled me before, didn't you? Right here at this bench? Something weird happened to me that night, didn't it?'

'I had no choice, I needed you to forget.'

'Spill it, now you can tell me what really happened the night I thought I was abducted by aliens.'

'A vampire was stalking you since you left the diner. But he didn't know I was stalking him first.'

'I could have been killed? What happened?'

Scott exhaled heavily. 'This will save me the effort.' He looked into PJ's eyes and said only one word. 'Remember.' PJ's jaw dropped as memory pierced his brain. Footsteps behind him in the gravel. Turning to face a hooded stranger alone in darkness. The cold hand that gripped his neck and effortlessly lifted him off the ground. The asphyxiation. The growl. A second growl coming from somewhere else. Wood smashing. A piece of bloodied timber bursting through the vampire's chest right before his eyes, causing him to be dropped to the ground. The hooded stranger bursting into flames. Scott standing before him, holding a broken piece of the bench, before turning his true face to PJ. He tossed the wood into the fountain before his face turned human again. Then he enthralled PJ to forget what he'd just witnessed.

'Oh crap! You saved my life!'

'Sure.' Scott didn't share PJ's excitement.

'He didn't know you were a vamp? But you knew he was one? How?'

'I'm not sure, but whenever another vampire is near, I have a sixth sense, like a vibration in my chest alerting me to their presence, even with Amdis.'

''Must be something to do with you being a super vamp?'

'Possibly.' Scott noticed something else seemed to be bothering PJ. 'Out with it, PJ, before I make you talk.'

PJ hesitated. 'Your face, it's ... terrifying when you're all, ah, vamped out.'

Scott nodded slowly. 'Consider yourself lucky. Not many get to see it, and if they do, they don't live to tell the tale.'

'Just to be clear, I'm safe with you, right?'

Scott smiled. 'Yes, PJ, you're safe.'

'I take it Nikky knows?'

'No, not yet, and I want it to stay that way.'

'Why don't you just tell her? I mean, I just found out my best friend is hundreds of years old, drinks animal blood, heals rapidly, has super speed, and has killed lots of people in the past, what could possibly go wrong with telling her?'

'Maybe because unlike you I can't enthral her to accept it if she panics, which ... she might.'

'Yeah, I see your point.'

'I want to remain normal in her eyes a little longer, before it's too late.'

'Normal?' PJ was confused. 'You don't wanna *be* a vampire, do you? I get it – after all those years, you've had enough.'

Scott paused a moment, thinking before he answered. 'I never asked for any of this, PJ, it wasn't my doing.'

PJ pulled out another stick of gum from his pocket, unwrapped it and threw it into his mouth, preparing for the long haul. 'So, tell me?'

'Tell you what?'

'Your life story?'

'You got six hundred years to kill? Actually, that was ... a poor choice of words, considering I've killed people for most of those six hundred.'

'Nope, but I got the rest of today. I'm shocked, man – vampires and werewolves *exist*? I've so many questions, but how about a summary for now?'

'Sure, ask away.'

'How did you become a vampire? Were you bitten by a vampire?'

'No, I'm the only vampire in existence that was actually born.'

PJ scratched his head. 'Vamps can have kids?'

'Actually, vampires can't reproduce, but they can sire other vampires.'

'You mean turn a human into a vamp, right?'

'Exactly.'

'Would you turn me if I asked?'

'Not a chance; this is a curse, PJ, not a blessing.'

'I said *if* I asked, Scott – how does it work, anyway?'

'I'm not turning you, PJ.'

'I know, I know, just tell me how you do it?'

'A human must drink vampire blood, then die within 24 hours while the blood is still in their system.'

'Then they come back as a vamp?'

'Yes.'

'Have you ... *"sired"* other vampires before?' PJ used air quotes.

'Unfortunately, yes. But because my blood is different, and more potent, it stays in a person's system for days afterwards, lengthening the time it takes them to turn.'

'Cool.'

'It's not cool. When I sire a vampire, they become more powerful than the average creature. They also have a special connection to me.'

'Meaning what exactly?'

'Meaning, if I'm in danger or need assistance, they sense it.'

'How many people did you turn and what happened to them?'

'That's a question for another day. Ask something else because I'm not going down that road.'

'Okay ... you've lived here a long time, right? Did you have any friends in town?'

'One other best friend *your* age long before you came along, and just like you, I confided in him.'

'What year was this? Is he still alive?'

'Yes, you've met him.'

'No way – who is it?'

'You don't like him very much.'

PJ threw his hands into the air. 'I don't like lots of people, Scott; who the hell did I replace as your BFF?'

'BFF?'

'Jeez, I forgot you're from medieval times, best friend forever?''

'Gerry from Trevor's'

'That ass of a manager? I'd have never guessed!'

Scott shrugged his shoulders. 'Neither would he.'

'You mean … Oh wow, you enthralled him to forget, didn't you?'

'I had to; he grew up.'

'Yeah, I guess.'

'This feels like the movie *Interview with a Vampire*, except, literally.'

'I avoid vampire movies. Was there really a movie about a vampire getting interviewed?'

'Yeah, some guy spends the day hearing the vampire's life story.'

'You want to know me, PJ? Truly know me and my life story?'

'Sure, we've all the time in the world, well, you do anyway. I'll probably die in sixty or seventy years. Carpe scrotum! Grab life by the balls, dude.'

Scott turned to PJ and now showed a face of serious intention. 'I can do better than any movie.' He slid sideways along the bench and placed his hand on the side of PJ's head before he could react.

Vision after vision flashed through PJ's mind. Vivid details full of emotion, and memories from the time Scott had been born to this very day. From his first kill as Amdis watched, screaming, to his first time feeding on human blood, leading to a never-ending thirst. A rapid barrage of violent interactions replaced each other one after another. An eternal life full of pain, suffering and relentless evil.

But somewhere within the chaotic mix of visions, a glimmer of light and hope. A rose stood in the desert. A single face emerged from darkness, inspiring a sense of belonging and happiness. Within the space of a minute, the roller coaster had ended. It was over. PJ stared into the sky in dazed disbelief. Eventually, he regained some sense of self and turned his head to Scott before speaking in a shy tone he was unaccustomed to hearing from his own mouth.

'Holy shit, Scott, the first vampire you killed was …?'

## Chapter 49

Later that same morning across town, an exhausted Nikky arrived home from her unexpected sleepover at Rebecca Chambers' house. She was greeted by the sight of a vase full of fresh sunflowers on the hall table next to a scribbled note.

'Hello? Anyone home?' She dropped her bag to the floor and picked up the piece of paper.

*Nikky,*

*Caden is with his friends, grandma's gone visiting.*

*Now would be a good time to put that box of her belongings into storage?*

*Love Dad xxx*

*PS: Feed Buster, he's staying home today.*

Short and sweet, but he did have a point, she thought. He'd been asking her to move that box for weeks and now was as good a time as any. Dropping her keys on the hall table, she ran up the stairs, taking two at a time. The door to the spare room where Grandma was staying was closed. She gave a polite knock just in case. She rarely entered this room. It used to be her parents' bedroom before her mother died, after which her father moved across to the adjacent bedroom. The double bed had been replaced by a single.

Most things changed over time, but one remained the same after all these years.

The smell.

Maybe it was the dust that caused her eyes to well up. Or perhaps the coincidence that her grandmother used the same perfume as her mother once did.

No. Now wasn't the time to be overtaken by emotion. Better to get the task at hand finished and resume her day of positivity. She scanned the room until a cardboard box under the nightstand caught her eye. She picked it up by the sides and the bottom fell out, leaving her holding the empty box as the contents crashed to the floor. She rolled her eyes in despair. Her plan for a rapid escape had backfired, leaving her sifting through piles of memorabilia. Old jewellery, trinkets, books turned yellow with age and memories of years past were scattered in a pile at her feet.

Resigned, she dropped to the floor and crossed her legs. She stared blankly into the pile for a moment before focusing on two photographs, resting on top of her grandmother's leather diary. The first was a photograph of her mother's wedding day. A white gown, a tuxedo and smiles outside the Priory church on Main Street. The second was a photo of her mother in hiking boots and green shorts standing next to a backpack somewhere in the forest, ready for a day of adventure.

Nikky smiled as a tear rolled down her cheek. She placed the photos back in the pile and thought about her own lucky escape in the forest last night. Her mother wasn't so lucky. Wiping away her tears, she noticed the corner of a black and white photograph sticking out between the pages of her grandmother's diary. A diary was a private place, she thought. A no-go area. Period. After all, how would she feel if someone went through her deeply personal thoughts? But within the viewable inch of the exposed picture, something stood out, calling for further investigation. A familiar-looking structure. Nikky glanced to the door, then back to the pile. She couldn't be blamed if the photo fell out when the box fell.

Yes, she'd seen that structure before, and she knew exactly where. In one swift movement, she pulled the photo in its entirety out from within the pages where it had rested, possibly for decades. For a second, she thought her mind was playing tricks. Her mouth fell open in total shock.

'Oh … my … *God*.'

**Chapter 50**

Darkness had fallen over Tallant later that same evening. At Nikky's front door, Scott observed the vase of sunflowers inside on the hall table wither and die as if filmed and sped up by a time-lapse camera. This was now gone beyond a coincidence, he thought. He rang the doorbell and waited with his hands back in his pockets. Buster charged the length of the hallway to investigate, only to whimper and perform a U-turn, sliding on all fours, when he saw who it was.

A minute later, a frail figure slowly made its way to the door and opened it.

A long pause.

Nikky's grandmother remained still, staring into Scott's blue eyes, then cut to the chase before he could speak.

'Hello Scott.' She paused again. He pulled his hands rapidly from his pockets. 'She's not here, before you ask.'

He nodded slowly before he replied. 'Do you know where she is?'

'No.'

Another pause. He glanced to the dead sunflowers then back to her face and was about to turn and leave until she spoke again.

'Can I talk to you for a moment?'

Reluctantly, he responded. 'Of course, ma'am.'

'Please come in.' She turned and made her way down the hall using her walking stick for balance. Scott stepped in and closed the door before following her into the ranger's study where he'd given his police statement previously. She opened the double doors and gestured for him to enter. He politely nodded and went in, noticing that the curtains were closed. Closing the door behind her, Beth made her way past the leather armchair to the desk in front of the window. Scott was surprised to see her lean against it rather than sit behind it on the chair. She rested her walking stick on the surface next to a small wooden box modelled as a miniature treasure chest before folding her arms.

The room was dimly lit, the only light was from the green desk lamp hidden behind the old lady, filling the room with shadows. Scott halted about six feet from where she sat, and waited. As did she. A staring contest. He had eternity; she looked like she had days.

She finally broke the silence. 'There's something I want you to see, Scott, come closer.' Intrigued, he stepped forward. She reached to her side and picked up the box. 'Come closer, take a look.' He moved closer to the box, staring at the wrinkled hands covering the top. She tilted the box towards him and in one swift movement pulled open the lid.

The chandelier overhead vibrated with the sudden roar from within Scott's chest as he soared backwards as if rammed by an invisible truck. His body slammed into the rear wall before he fell to the floor. Unexpectedly, Nikky's grandmother burst into laughter and reached inside the box to remove a silver crucifix and chain. Red eyes peered from the dark behind the armchair and a restless, demonic voice spoke angrily.

'You shouldn't have done that.'

She pulled her gaze from the crucifix and met the red eyes with a smile. 'Does this look familiar, Scott?'

Silence.

'Where, where did you find that?' His demon tone echoed throughout the room.

Unintimidated by this, she answered. 'Inside a crypt, many decades ago.'

'It's not your property to keep.'

She smiled again and wiped the crucifix gently with her hand. 'Actually, it is.' She paused. 'And you were the one who gave it to me.' She gently placed it back inside the box and closed the lid. Scott emerged from the darkness in vampire form and cautiously approached the smiling old lady. 'Very brave putting away my Achilles heel, but the sunflowers, the crucifix, the way you looked at me when I first met you – who are you?'

'You won't harm me, Scott.'

'Really? What makes you so sure?'

'You don't recognise me, do you? In all these long years you haven't aged a day since the last time I saw you.'

His red eyes stared deeply. She spoke again. 'We can easily to forgive a child who's afraid of the dark …'

His mouth fell open as his face began to take human form again. He finished her sentence for her.

'… the real tragedy of life is when men are afraid of the light … Beth?'

She slowly nodded. 'I'm glad to see you still wear the bracelet.'

'Is it … really you?'

She reached up and touched the side of his face. 'Go ahead, try to enthral me.'

He stared into her eyes. 'Who was the love of your life?'

She grinned. 'I don't need to be enthralled to answer that question, Scott.'

'I never thought I'd lay eyes upon you again, Beth.'

'That moment I saw you standing outside, looking like you did all those years ago, brought it all back to me. I felt seventeen again, like I never left Tallant.'

'You didn't have to leave.'

'I grew up and you stayed the same, but I never stopped loving you. Leaving town was the best thing I could do because the pain was just too much to bear.'

'Try being me, feeling emotions tenfold, every memory relived over and over for eternity; there's nowhere in town I can go without remembering the time we spent together.'

'I often relive those memories, too, but not the way you can, unfortunately.'

He sat down next to her on the desk. 'You changed everything about me, my life had purpose after I met you.'

'I still visit your mausoleum when I'm in town.'

'The flowers? They were from you, all these years?'

She nodded. 'It's my way of telling you I never forgot. How could I?'

'Beth, you were the best thing that ever happened to me.'

She turned to face him, holding out her hand. 'Scott, do an old lady a favour, help me remember? I want to feel young again, one last time.' He hesitated, knowing the journey would be painful. But she was special. He nodded and placed his hand over hers.

In a flash she was seventeen again, reliving the past like it was the present. From breaking and entering a crypt in broad daylight. Removing the lid from a stone casket that held a silver relic. A crucifix lay face down on a skeleton in ragged clothing. Screaming and being forced to the ground by her accomplice, who tried to remove her clothing as he thumped her face. Feeling the weight of his body lifting from her, before a pale figure sank his teeth into his neck.

From later that same day: the deal they made together, an agreement that he would feed on animal blood instead of human; chasing a deer through a forest across a road, colliding with a car on a stormy night. The nervousness of a first kiss outside the flat roof, pushing him against the wall, breaking a hanging lantern. Another kiss; being lifted as if by magic to the clock tower overlooking the town. Summer days at the lake over years that felt never-ending, like time frozen in a perfect world. Watching herself through Scott's eyes walking away, wiping tears as she aged and left town.

Scott removed his hand and the vivid flashback ended. She smiled silently with her eyes closed. He turned to look with sudden deep concern at the woman who had changed his life.

'You're ... you're dying?'

She nodded.

Scott looked down at his feet. If his heart could beat, it would be breaking right now.

'You must keep that to yourself, Scott, promise me, for old times' sake.'

'I ... promise.' Another pause.

'It was the hardest thing I ever had to do, leaving you behind.'

'Where did you go?'

'Green Bay. It took me a long time to move on, but eventually I met someone and started a family.'

'Something I could never give you.'

Her sad smile said it all. 'And then my daughter, God rest her soul, moved back to Tallant to start her own family.' Scott jumped off the desk and started to pace back and forth, searching for the right words. Guilt flooded his brain, paralysing his thoughts.

'Of course, I knew about Nikky's mother but ... it's only fitting into place now that she was your daughter.'

'You know about what happened to my daughter, don't you, Scott?'

He stopped pacing, snapping his head in her direction, a look of disgust on his face. She stood up and began to take steps towards him, holding out her hand.

'Please, Scott, show me what happened to my precious Lynn, I must know what you know, please show me.'

Scott pulled away. 'No! Beth, you can't, not this, please trust me, I can't!' He paused and shot a look at the door. 'Beth, someone's about to come in, we can't discuss this now.' The hall door opened and closed, and Buster barked an ecstatic greeting for someone. Beth whispered to Scott across the room at a level only he could hear.

'Please, you can never tell Nikky what you know about her mother.'

He nodded before there was a knock on the door. Beth shouted as best she could in her frail voice. 'Come in?' One of the double doors opened and Nikky entered. Beth noticed Scott's face lighting up.

Surprised to find Scott and her grandmother together, Nikky said, a little apprehensively, 'Oh – hi!'

'Hello my dear, welcome home,' Beth said.

'Nikky, hi, I called in earlier and your grandma asked me to … kill a spider she'd seen somewhere in here, a big one,' Scott added nervously. Nikky glanced at her grandmother who was now sitting back against the front of the desk for support.

'Must have been some spider, Grandma.'

Scott cut in, answering for her. 'Yes, it was, huge, right? Beth?'

Nikky turned to address Scott before responding. 'Scott, you don't understand – I meant it must have been some spider for my grandma to need assistance from a vampire to deal with it.' His jaw almost hit the floor as she pulled a photo from her back pocket and held it out in front of him. He stared at it in disbelief. He looked at Beth, who was smiling.

'You told her?'

'She found the photograph and had questions that I had to answer truthfully; she is my granddaughter after all, Scott.'

He examined Nikky's reaction for a few seconds before trying to speak. 'Nikky … I …' He was lost for words.

'It's okay, Scott, I didn't know what to say, either. Although, it did kinda make sense; you already told me, remember? At the fairground? But of course I thought you were joking and I forgot that you'd said it … and all the weird stuff that happened with Carol. So today I found out that creatures I thought were mythical are actually real. My boyfriend happens to be one of them, and, to top it off, he used to date my grandmother when she was my age. How many people get to say that in their lifetime?'

Beth picked up her walking stick from the desk along with the wooden box. 'I'll leave you two alone to talk, which I'm sure will be a very interesting conversation. But I will say this, Nikky, time is short so carpe diem. You must realise that you will age, and Scott will not, so enjoy every moment while you can. I'll be upstairs resting. Oh, and Nikky?'

'Yeah?'

'Hold on tight.' She closed the double doors behind her, leaving them alone in awkward silence.

'What did that mean?' said Nikky, sitting behind the desk in her father's chair. She leant back with her arms clasped across her chest, staring at Scott. 'Why is it so dark in here?' From where he stood, Scott raised his hand in the direction of the light switch, mimicking the pressing of a button in thin air. The light clicked on from a distance, illuminating the room. 'Okay that was impressive, you got me there; but what else can you do?'

Scott vanished from where he stood and instantly reappeared, sitting on the side of the desk with his arms folded. She jumped and laughed. He kissed her on the cheek.

'Let me show you.' He pulled open the curtains and opened the patio doors to the back garden. Taking her hand, he stepped outside, scooped her up in his arms in one fluid movement, looked to the heavens and vanished into the night sky.

**Chapter 51**

Having a vampire for a boyfriend has many perks. One downside, however, are the sleepless nights. Staying awake with him until the early hours of the morning before the sun rises, causing him to become weak and seek darkness indoors. For Nikky, days blended into nights and weeks in the blink of an eye. Unusual sleep patterns became the norm.

Waking at seven pm today, Nikky's first thoughts were the bizarre events of the past few weeks. The residue of recent memories was like the afterthoughts of a weird dream. Except she knew this wasn't a dream. This was her life now.

An hour later, the sun was gone as she approached Scott's house from the eastern gate, pondering the idea of Scott investing in a mobile phone. Random meetings, unless previously arranged, were starting to become ridiculous. Unexpectedly, a familiar figure was hurriedly closing the door behind her.

'Carol? I didn't expect to see you here?'

'Nikky? I …' Carol froze, lost for words. The witch nervously looked back to the door she just closed, then back to Nikky, realising that everything they said could be heard from inside. As Carol was making awkward small talk, she pulled her phone from her pocket and began to type, dodging Nikky's question about her presence at Scott's house.

'How's your grandmother? You know, I haven't spoken to her lately and there's so much to catch up on,' Carol said, as she was inputting text. Showing Nikky the screen of her phone, she raised her finger to her lips.

*'You're in danger, you don't know what you're getting yourself into, the fortune teller's tent, I've seen his past, he killed your mother.'*

Nikky's look of innocent confusion turned to one of horror. Could this really be true? The boyfriend she'd confided in all this time had a past that was mixed up with her own? Carol placed her hands on Nikky's shoulders and gave her a hug.

'Anyway, must be going.' She hurried off in the direction of the eastern gate. Nikky stared at the closed door in front of her. A few paces later, Carol stopped, thinking for a moment before turning back to Nikky.

'Nikky, one last thing before I go.'

Nikky dragged her eyes from the ground and glared at the witch.

'I ... I just want you to know that ... I'm sorry. For everything.' Without waiting for a reply, she took off again, leaving Nikky alone contemplating her next move.

Thoughts were racing around her head. She felt betrayed and gutted. He couldn't, could he? No, not Scott. Not the person she'd just spent another amazing night with, experiencing wonders she'd never thought possible. He couldn't possibly have killed *her mother*? Carol must be wrong. But why would Carol lie?

The front door creaked as it opened, pulling Nikky back to reality. A reality she no longer wanted to face. Her world was crashing down around her. A lone figure stood inside, silently watching her. Words escaped from the dark.

'He's not here.'

Amdis stood, arms folded, a lack of interest in her gaze. What was Carol doing meeting with Amdis? Did she also know about her mother? Nikky thought for a moment.

'That's probably a good thing right now, but can I speak with you for a moment, Amdis? I have a few questions if you don't mind.'

Amdis couldn't help but notice the tone in her voice. Something was bothering her deeply.

'What's it about?'

'About you and Scott being vampires.'

Amdis gave a sly smile. 'He finally told you.'

She nodded.

'Come inside.' Amdis stepped back and opened the door to the living room, still dimly lit by the single lamp between the armchairs. Again, Nikky was overwhelmed with racing thoughts. Was this a good idea after what Carol had just told her? Maybe everything Scott had ever said was a lie? Why should she believe or trust Amdis? Against her better judgement, she entered the house, determined to get answers to put her mind at ease. Ten minutes ago, everything was perfect. How quickly things can change.

Amdis closed the two doors behind them and sat down in the wrinkled armchair nearest Scott's bedroom door. She gestured for Nikky to sit opposite, which she did, cautiously. An eternity of silence. Nikky couldn't resist the urge to get the answers she needed any longer.

'Did Scott kill my mother?'

'Your mother? How the hell would I know?'

'Carol, well, she said she had a vision where she'd seen him killing my mother, and I need to know the truth.'

'Trust me, take everything that witch tells you with a pinch of salt; she just tried to warn me about something ridiculous supposed to happen soon, and how she's taken steps to prevent it.'

'But why would she lie to me?'

'I don't know, go ask Scott, I don't know anything about your mother.'

'But what if he's lying?'

A serious look now graced the vampire's face. 'I know Scott better than anyone. I've seen him at his worst and shared in the spoils. I've also seen the best he can be when his humanity takes over, to my dismay. It's true that Scott is very private. Only recently, I've discovered information about him that I never knew before. Right under my nose the whole time. But there's one thing I do know for certain, and it's that he doesn't lie, ever.'

'We talked for hours last night; he showed me memories from his past. Although I think I got the watered-down version. About the spell, about the ancients, and about killing Draven's brother, causing him to remain a teenager forever. Most of it was hard to watch, but some parts he kept hidden, only sharing flashes of a face. I asked him about it afterwards but all he said was that it was the first vampire he'd killed.'

Nikky now had Amdis's full attention. She sat up straight in her chair, eager to hear more. 'Did he mention anything else about Draven's brother?'

'No, he was reluctant to discuss that part with me. But why do you need me to find out about Scott? He's your son!'

'He hates me and blames me for what he did in the past. Most of the time Scott and I are like ships passing in the night, barely a word spoken between us; sometimes decades go by with nothing said.'

'But you said he never lies?'

'Correct. Scott tells the truth from within his humanity to ease his own suffering. But his alter ego in demon form tells the truth to cause suffering. Either way, the truth is spoken. If you want my advice, go ask him outright about your mother, but remember this, sometimes the truth we hear is not always the truth we want.'

'Amdis, please, tell me about him, and the parts of his past he refused to show me.'

Amdis grinned. 'I don't think you'd be able for it.'

Nikky stood up. 'Then show me, like Scott does.'

'You don't know what you're asking for.'

'I need to know the truth, please.' She held out her hand to Amdis. 'Show me.'

Amdis stood next to her. 'Prepare yourself.' She clasped her hands tightly around Nikky's, letting the journey into the past begin.

Nikky's eyes moved rapidly from side to side under closed eyelids, her face grimacing as each painful flashback became reality. They came hard and fast, hitting her like a tonne of bricks, each gruesome vision ending before the next took its place. For one minute of torment, Amdis continued to bombard her with information. Nikky pulled her hands away, dropping to her knees on the stone floor. She'd seen enough. She wiped the tears from her cheek before looking up.

'Draven's brother ...' Amdis nodded silently and Nikky continued.

'Draven's brother was ... Scott's father?'

## Chapter 52

Later that same night, Nikky lay on her bed, her arms behind her head, staring at the blank ceiling above, pondering all that she'd learned over the last few days, and what to do next. She fumbled with the silver angel on the chain around her neck. A playlist of sad songs from YouTube streamed from her phone through a pink Bluetooth speaker.

A few nights ago, everything was perfect. Her only concerns were upcoming exams at school and whether Scott liked her. Now her thoughts ran wild with the idea that her vampire boyfriend had killed her mother and the fact that he had killed his own father. She kicked off her sneakers, landing them on the floor with a thump, before crossing her feet and becoming lost in the music.

Two raps at her bedroom window caused her to bolt upright in alarm. Scott sat outside sideways on the windowsill. He smiled when they made eye contact through the glass but got no response for his troubles. An expressionless face looked back at him from the pink unicorn bedspread. It didn't take his six hundred years of life experience to notice that something was terribly wrong.

Reluctantly she crossed the room and opened the window, allowing him to step inside before closing it again. He watched for a moment. She said nothing, just stared at him.

'It's kinda chilly outside tonight.' He put his hands back into his jacket pockets and waited some more.

Nothing.

'Actually, I'm starting to think it's a bit chillier in here tonight. What's wrong? Are you okay?'

She spoke out loud to her smartphone. 'Okay, Google, stop playback.' The music stopped and the room was silent. She returned to her bed and sat on the side. He followed but decided to test the water some more before sitting next to her. She folded her arms and looked up at him in a no-nonsense fashion, before blurting out the question that had tormented her since reading Carol's message.

'There's no other way to ask you, Scott, so I'll just get straight to the point.' She paused. He waited. 'Did you kill my mother?'

He pulled his hands from his pockets and returned her gaze in astonishment. 'I … Nikky, I …'

She stood and picked up the framed photo from her bedside locker..

'Nikky …'

'This is her, Scott, now tell me, did you kill her that night in the forest?'

'I don't need to see her picture; I remember every detail. Who told you that, Nikky?'

'Remember the fortune teller's tent that night at the fairground? Carol saw deep into your memories just like you show me the past. She said she'd seen you holding my mother's body, with blood on your hands.' She wrapped her hands around the picture frame and hugged it into her chest tightly, waiting for an explanation.

Scott closed his eyes and shook his head. 'That witch.'

'She told me to stay away from you, that you're dangerous.'

'That's true, Nikky.'

'You have to tell me, Scott, did you do it?'

He looked deep into her eyes, unable to hide the sadness from his face. Without saying a word, he raised his hand with his palm facing her and waited.

'The truth, Scott?'

He nodded. Slowly and hesitantly, she raised her hand towards his and clasped it. Her eyes closed again as images flooded her thoughts Through his eyes, she saw a blonde woman draped across his arms, his hands covered in blood. She pulled away from him, instantly stopping the ghastly sight.

He spoke in sympathy. 'Please, you don't need to see this, Nikky.'

She wiped away a tear. 'Yes … I do.' She grabbed his hand again, only this time with purpose. More images entered her mind.

Beneath a full moon, Scott was feeding from the neck of a deer in the vast forest surrounding Tallant. He was interrupted by a scream echoing in the distance. He dropped the animal and vanished in a blur, only appearing too late to find a woman lying dead on the ground. He picked her up, attempting to give her his blood as a cure, when he heard someone approaching. He turned to see Nikky's father pointing a gun at him. Scott turned away to protect the victim. He fired three shots, each one finding its target deep in Scott's back.

As gently as he could in the time allowed, he gently placed the lifeless body on the ground and vanished into the darkness. He stopped to catch a scent in the air before snapping his head and homing in on a particular direction before taking off again to battle a werewolf in an encounter similar to the one Nikky had experienced. Grisly scenes of a savage battle ensued. As she watched Scott's hands tearing a head from its body, she pulled her hand back and ended the vision. She'd seen enough.

She covered her eyes and began to cry.

Scott stood for a moment with his hand still raised in front of him, before slowly returning it to his side. He walked to the window, resting his palms on the windowsill, and stared silently at Caden's treehouse, giving Nikky time to absorb what she'd just witnessed.

A few moments passed and he broke the silence 'I promised Beth I'd never share that with you, and now I've broken that promise.'

Nikky was wiping away the tears on her sleeve. 'She already knew?'

He didn't turn around. 'She knew something tragic had happened, but she also somehow knew that it wasn't me.' This time he turned to face her, hands back in his jacket pockets. 'I tried to save her, Nikky, if only I'd gotten there in time, things could have been different. After that night I chose to never again feed during a full moon. If it's any consolation, a Cartwright was buried not too long after.'

She continued to sit in silence.

'Nikky, do you remember that evening at the Town Hall, with the enlarged photograph of the townsfolk from a hundred years ago?'

'Sure. I certainly remember the weird vision I had.'

'When I touched the axe head it triggered that flashback in time that vampires are accustomed to; when you touched my hand you could experience my memories too.'

'That awful scene was a memory of what really happened?'

'Everyone in that photograph died that night, including the dog. I was concerned that you might recognise me standing in the front row; I think the vision distracted you.' He sighed. 'But at least I didn't kill anyone today.'

'You say that like it was a difficult task?'

Scott couldn't look her in the eye. She had seen first-hand the monster he had been, but still she took his cold hand in hers.

'Nothing can change the past, Scott. I'm sorry for doubting you but there's been a lot for me to take in lately. The truth is painful but I'm so glad you've shown me what really happened to my mother and, not to mention, incredibly relieved.'

'Truth always hurts.' His eyes dropped to the floor.

'Yes, it does, and while we're on the subject, earlier today I called to your house. You weren't home but Amdis was.' His eyes shot back up to meet hers. Nikky now looked uncomfortable. 'I, um, had, questions, Scott, and she showed me some … stuff from your past.'

He rolled his head back towards the ceiling and closed his eyes and exhaled deeply before responding. 'So now you know.'

'I know you can't help who you are. Nobody can, and from what I've seen, it's not your fault.'

'I never asked for *any* of this, Nikky, this was forced upon me by evil people with evil intentions. The person you see now is the real me, the *person* I want to be but never quite get to be, because everything is temporary. In my lifespan these little nuggets of happiness don't last long before I'm dragged back to reality. That's why I told you to cherish every moment because they will never come again. I lost Beth to time, and someday I will also lose you the same way.'

She took his hands in hers and smiled. 'We have right now in this moment, don't we?'

'Yes, we do, and years from now I will have vivid memories of this moment, like the ones I've shown you.' He held his hand to the side of her face. 'Remember, Nikky Brennan, at this moment, trapped forever in time, I am yours and you are mine, no matter what else happens in the future, where you might end up, or who you will be with when the time allows. Remember this, I will never forget you and this priceless time we spend together.'

She smiled and put her hand over his, against her face. 'Why did you break that promise you made with my grandma?'

His voice dropped to a whisper. 'Because I knew, since the moment I laid eyes on you, that I'd end up falling in love with you. I can't keep anything from you, and I can't enthral you. You show me the real you.'

'You're killing me here, Scott.'

He smiled and shook his head. 'Not a great choice of words, Nikky.'

She pulled him close to her by his leather jacket and kissed him passionately on the lips. Taking him by the hand, she lay down on the bed behind her, rested her head on her pillow and again pulled him towards her. He sat on the bed next to her and leaned down for another kiss. Mid-kiss, his eyes shot towards her bedroom door, which suddenly opened.

Nikky bolted upright. 'Dad! I … we ...' Nikky glanced down to see where Scott had been just a split second ago, but he was gone. She looked to the window, which was still closed, confused, but relieved that her father hadn't seen him on her bed. Looking back at her father, it was hard not to focus on the vampire who was now levitating just above the ranger's head with his back against the ceiling, looking down at her father from only inches above.

'Haven't you ever heard of knocking, Dad?'

'Sorry, hun, I thought you were out.'

'Well, here I am, not out like you thought.' She jumped from her bed and moved towards him, hoping he would leave before he noticed Scott defying gravity above his head. To her dismay, he stepped into the room.

'Nikky, I know we haven't had much time to talk lately with your grandmother being here and all but …'

She began to panic. 'That's okay, Dad, but … I'm just about to have an early night, totally exhausted, you know how it is; maybe tomorrow instead?' She faked a stretch and an over-exaggerated yawn. It didn't work. He moved towards her bed. If he sat down, it was game over; he couldn't miss Scott performing the impossible if he was facing the doorway.

Scott dropped silently behind the open door a split second before her father sat on her bed. She closed her eyes and blew through pursed lips in relief, then turned to resume operation *remove dad from my room.* The ranger patted the bed next to him, gesturing for her to sit and join him in conversation.

'Actually, Dad, I really wouldn't mind a hug right now, you know, like Mom used to give?'

He stood up and hugged his daughter. 'Are you sure you don't wanna chat for a bit?'

She nodded politely. 'Maybe tomorrow? I'm really tired, hope you don't mind?'

He shook his head in pride, seeing how much she'd grown. 'It's a deal, tomorrow then. Now, you get some rest.'

She kept one hand on the door as he left, making sure he didn't change his mind before closing it behind him.

Scott leant against the wall, grinning.

She shook her head and grimaced. 'That was too close for comfort.' Scott shrugged his shoulders like it was no big deal.

'If he caught me, I could just enthral him to forget, anyway.'

'*Now* you tell me?' She pulled him in close, looking into his blue eyes. She spoke again to her smartphone, which came to life on her bed.

'Okay, Google, play U2, "Song for Someone" on YouTube.'

A female voice replied, *'Playing music on YouTube.'*

Scott looked to the phone then back to Nikky's smiling face. 'Impressive.'

'Told ya, we need to get you a phone, it's the twenty-first century, Scott, you gotta move with the times.'

'It seems like only yesterday I saw my first telegram being sent; now you can do *that*.'

'You must have seen some incredible things over the years: tell me something beautiful.'

He moved closer and whispered into her ear. 'Nikky.'

Blushing, she draped her arms around his neck. 'Okay: what's your favourite song, Scott?'

'Why? Can your phone play that, too?'

She nodded. He thought for a second. 'That would have to be, let me see, it's been a while, yeah, a song called "Desert Rose" by Sting.'

'I wasn't expecting that!'

'You look shocked?'

'I was expecting Beethoven or something.'

He smiled. 'Just because I'm hundreds of years old doesn't mean I don't keep up with modern music.'

'I've never heard it before. Okay, Google, play Sting ...'

He cut in, stopping her mid-sentence. 'No, wait, is there a limit to what your phone can play; I mean, can it play classical music, too?'

'It's YouTube, it can play any song in history.'

'Perfect.'

'Why?'

He smirked. 'Tell me, Nikky, can you dance?'

'You mean ... hip hop?'

'I don't even know what that is. I meant like a waltz; ever done that?'

'To be honest, no.'

He held out his arms at shoulder height for her to mimic. She took his cold hands and looked down at her feet.

'Don't look down, just follow my lead, okay?'

'But I've never done this before, and we don't have the space to waltz here!'

'Let me worry about that, you just go with the flow, and keep looking into my eyes.'

'That won't be too difficult.' She winked playfully.

Scott spoke to her phone. 'Okay, Google, let me hear Antonin Dvorak, "Tempo di Valse", please.'

She laughed at his unusual politeness in addressing the Google assistant.

'Now just do what I do.'

The Bluetooth speaker again came to life, filling the room with a haunting melody. They began to waltz slowly, Nikky copying his every move, eyes locked on his without distraction. Back and forth they flowed across the room in unison to the music.

'You're quite good at this, you know?'

She didn't answer, trying to keep in step.

'Now let yourself go, don't worry about a thing, and follow my lead, okay?'

She nodded. The waltz continued across the room, but it didn't stop or change direction when they got to the far wall. A slight change in leg position and he led her waltzing up the wall and onto the ceiling, defying gravity. They danced around the light shade as if it was sharing the improvised dance floor with them.

She opened her mouth in amazement. To her, love was seeing the light inside someone who sees nothing but darkness. Only now, the necklace he'd given her made sense. Buried within the evil she'd seen deep inside his soul, if he had one, she knew that you could walk through hell, and still be an angel.

# Chapter 53

They say it's always darkest just before the dawn. But the glory of dawn doesn't last. In time, darkness must replace the sunlight to keep things in balance. It was the early hours of the morning in the forest, and the night still held control before the sun rose. It was quickly approaching, and Scott could smell it. After another night with Nikky, he had been driven back to the forest by hunger; an instinctive need to feed. He stopped and closed his eyes in silence. A moment later, he snapped his head to his left with eyes wide open, then vanished in a blur through the thicket.

Prey had been located.

Over a mile away, a stag with one broken antler sipped water from a stream, unaware of what was approaching rapidly from the dark. It stopped drinking and looked up, exhaling condensation in a burst before shaking its head. Something had startled it. Before it could bolt, Scott appeared behind it in full vampire form. Grabbing the stag under his snout with his other hand over his side, he sank his fangs into its neck, expecting the usual struggle of attempting to escape with its life.

But something was different. The majestic beast remained still, allowing him to drain its blood and life force willingly. Scott continued to feed, expecting the beast to collapse to its knees with weakness. But it didn't. As he fed, the creature began to decay rapidly in his arms. He stopped in confusion and watched in shock as the beast's hair receded, exposing flesh infested with churning maggots. Dropping the carcass to the ground he stood back in confusion. His face became human again, blood still dripping down his chin. He knew what was happening. He'd felt this way before, a long time ago. He looked to the heavens in panic.

'Draven!' he roared skyward. He held his hands to the sides of his head and dropped to his knees in sudden excruciating pain, which stopped as quickly as it had begun. He dropped his hands and stood up in one smooth motion. The panic on his face slowly became a smile as his eyes momentarily flashed red. He tilted his head from one shoulder to the other, cracking his neck before vanishing into the woods.

A few moments later, not far from that location, a car with three occupants returning to Tallant in the early hours travelled the winding road through the southern end of the forest. A sharp bend directed the headlights onto a dark figure standing still in the centre of the road. The car swerved, narrowly avoiding a collision. It stopped, facing the opposite way, headlights facing the stranger it had barely avoided hitting. The shaken trio gathered their thoughts before the male in the front passenger seat stepped out. The figure stood still, facing away.

The pissed-off male spoke as he approached, with a finger pointed at the stranger.

'Hey dickhead! Are you mentally ill or just plain stupid?'

Scott turned his head to the side, catching the guy in his periphery vision. When he was close enough, the man shoved Scott on the shoulder with the palm of his hand. Scott turned and sank his teeth into the left side of the man's neck. As he struggled, he tried to release a scream of pain that gurgled with a mixture of blood and air from a torn windpipe. Red eyes glanced back at the car over the shoulder of his victim as he fed. Two female voices screamed inside the vehicle. His first human casualty in years became weak and his legs began to give way. As he dropped to the ground, Scott pulled a pack of cigarettes from his victim's shirt pocket, letting the body fall to his feet. Scott moved his tongue from one fang to the other, tipping the points while relishing the taste he had missed so much.

His moment of tranquillity was interrupted by the car's engine coming to life. His face became human again. Instantly he appeared next to the driver's window, smashing his fist through the glass and, grabbing the starter key, bringing silence back to the roadway.

'Good morning, ladies.' They screamed and recoiled into the passenger seat before struggling with the door handle and tumbling out onto the road. One of them scuttled towards the dead man who lay face down. The other watched Scott in terror, keeping the car between them for safety. He leaped onto the roof causing her to fall backwards, landing on her back on the ground. Jumping down next to her, he looked into her eyes.

'Stand right here and don't move.' She obeyed his command without question, pulling herself to her feet. Scott approached the other woman who was hunched over the dead man, sobbing. Hearing him behind her, she reached into the pocket of her dead friend and pulled out a hunting knife covered in blood before standing to face her attacker. Seeing the blade in her shaking hand made him smile. He held his arms wide, inviting her to take her best shot.

It was her life or his. She plunged the knife deep into the centre of his chest. In floods of tears, she spoke aloud. 'I'm sorry.' She expected him to drop to the ground clutching his chest. It didn't happen. Instead, he looked deep into her eyes again and spoke.

'Remove the blade from my chest.'

Unable to refuse his commands, she took the blade in one hand and began to pull it towards her, watching his face through her tears for a reaction. She looked at the knife in disbelief before dropping it to the ground in disgust. Scott looked into the forest, able to hear something she could not. Again, he leaned close.

'Turn around, stand here, and don't move.' He walked back to the front of the car where the other girl waited against her will. Looking into her eyes he spoke. 'Sit up and enjoy the show with me.' He sat on the hood and tapped it for her to follow suit. Terrified, she copied his movements and sat next to him while he pulled out the cigarette pack from his pocket. He reached behind and forced his hand through the windscreen to press the cigarette lighter, then removed it to light his smoke. Casually blowing smoke from his first drag into the air through pursed lips, he offered his female companion one from the open pack. She refused with a disgusted shake of her head.

He looked at the girl sitting next to him. 'Sshh, hear that? That's the sound of your friends' demise.' The girl standing in the path began to scream. Headlights shone through the trees, winding their way in her direction, and just like her friend sitting behind, all she could do was watch. They both screamed now. The approaching car spun around the corner, unable to avoid the person standing in its path, with the body at her feet. One of the women's screams instantly stopped as the other's continued in horror. She was thrown onto the hood and through the windscreen, causing the car to swerve violently before rolling over onto its roof and into the ditch.

Scott smiled. 'Where have I seen this before? Oh yes, I remember, the last time I saw something like this was when I chased a deer in front of a car on a stormy night. In a moment of insanity and guilt, I saved a pregnant woman with my blood.' He exhaled deeply before continuing, like he was in conversation with an old friend, discussing old times. 'I won't feel guilty about what I'm about to do. The real me is back, but you don't have a clue what I'm talking about. You see that car upside down? Can you smell that? No, of course you can't. One of them is bleeding inside the wreck. I can hear his heartbeat fading.' He grinned. 'It's time to collect on that blood I donated years ago.'

He looked in his new friends' direction, but this time with glowing red eyes

## Chapter 54

As the sun began to rise over Tallant, Amdis arrived in a burst of speed at the front door of the flat roof, desperate to escape the sunlight. A familiar voice came from above. Scott stood on the rooftop, staring down with his hands in his jacket pockets.

'Hello, Mother.'

She stepped back, surprised. Scott exhaled deeply, took in a deep breath, looked to the sky, and spoke again. 'Ahh, as the sun rises in the east to open and illuminate the glorious day; cutting it close, aren't we, Mother?'

'Scott? Are you, yourself?' Running out of time, she looked to the trees behind her.

'What? No hug?' he laughed.

Now she knew. He was different. She half-smiled, stopping herself short. She was glad in one way, but deep down she knew, more than anyone, what this meant.

'Better go inside, Mother, before I'm talking to a pile of ash.' He jumped to the ground next to her, grabbed the broken lantern, ripped it from the wall and threw it far into the trees. She quickly opened the door and entered. Standing just inside where it was dark, with the door open, she watched him squint as the rays of light hit his face. He reached into his pocket and pulled out his shades.

'But we can catch up later. I'll be visiting some old friends to visit today while you're sleeping, so gather your strength, you'll need it for what I've got planned.' He smiled and turned towards the northern gate, whistling 'Ding dong, the witch is dead' as he walked away. She closed the door and leant against it in the dark. There was only one thing that she could do. What choice did she have?

***

It was nine am. At the Enchanted Florist, Carol flipped the wooden door sign from the closed to open position, before going behind the counter and putting on her green apron. The guilt of what she was preparing to do preyed heavily on her mind. Anguish was clearly visible on her face. How could she face her friend of all these years after what she'd done? Beth would never forgive her. But she would never find out. Amdis wouldn't listen, so Carol had no choice. She knew what was coming and what had to be done.

As she was checking her phone for messages, something in her peripheral vision caught her eye. Without moving her head, her gaze was directed to a sunflower in a vase on the countertop that had just began to wither. Her head snapped up in the direction of the door.

Nothing.

She walked to the door, opened it and looked up and down outside. No sign of anyone. As it was daytime, she knew there was only one vampire that could be nearby. Walking back to the counter, the door chime rang out. She turned to look again at the still closed door. Strange, she thought. This time her about-turn bumped her directly into Scott's chest, causing her to recoil backwards. She held a finger in the air in defiance.

'Seriously, Scott, you have to stop doing that, you're freaking me out! Not to mention costing me a fortune in sunflowers.'

He placed one hand on his hip, and with his other flicked an imaginary length of hair off his shoulder.

'Witch, please, I'm creepin' it real here.'

Carol looked confused.

'Did that not work? I was gonna save it for Nikky, I'm trying to be cool with today's lingo. Guess it needs some work.' He stepped past her and switched the open sign back to the closed position.

'What are you doing? I'm opening up for the day.'

'I'm afraid you're about to be closed, permanently.' When he turned in her direction, the evil grin on his face was overshadowed by his red eyes, which glowed intently at her. Carol's mouth fell open.

'Oh no … they got to you …' Her voice quivered. 'Scott, listen to me, I know this isn't your fault, but you can't let them win, I can help you if you give me the chance; please, Scott.'

The smile vanished from his face. 'Wait, you can help me?'

'Yes.' She nodded, starting to think that she was making progress.

'And you can reverse the spell?'

'Yes; if you work with me, Scott, I know what can cure you.'

The evil grin returned. 'And that, Carol, is exactly why I'm here to kill you.'

She slowly edged backwards with tiny steps. 'If you kill me, it means Draven is winning, can't you see that?'

He laughed.

'He turned you to rid Tallant of werewolves so that he can take back power: you're playing right into his hands.'

'Draven and his witches will get what's coming to them soon enough. I'll thank him just before I kill him, like I did my own father. They wanted a monster, so I'll give them one.' He held his arms out wide. 'Everyone loses; nobody wins but me.'

Foolishly she moved towards him in another attempt to reason. She took something from her pocket and held it out in his direction. 'Amdis didn't believe me when I said this day would come, so I already put a plan in motion, Scott; I took steps, horrible steps, that had to be taken. I've seen the devastation in your past, you have to be stopped no matter what.' Sitting on her palm was a small piece of tattered cloth, bound with a thin leather string. Burned into the cloth was a symbol he'd seen before. On her tent at the fairground. The triquetra, signifying the ever-turning cycle of life, death, and rebirth.

'A hex bag? Please don't tell me you think that'll work on me.'

'This is one of two, and the other wasn't meant for you.'

He shook his head, looking at the floor. 'You are losing my interest, Carol, and that's very dangerous. For you.'

'Scott, please, you can still do the right thing.'

'Oh, I know right from wrong – wrong is the fun one.'

His face changed before her eyes.

It was the last thing she would ever see.

## Chapter 55

Next door in Trevor's, Kayce placed an early breakfast plate on the table in front of Gerry, who sat at a rear table out of view from the window. The diner was closed to the public until 10 o'clock and it was their routine to enjoy a free meal and hot coffee before the busy day ahead. Their conversation was interrupted by an unexpected knock on the glass. Gerry finished his sip of coffee before shouting over Kayce's shoulder.

'Can't you read? We're closed until ten, come back later.' He shook his head in annoyance.

Another knock.

'Sit, finish your food; I'm finished anyway.' Kayce was already standing as she spoke. En route to the door, she reached behind the counter and picked up the TV remote and pointed it high to turn on the TV to the usual news channel. A familiar face came into view: Scott stood outside, wearing shades, with his hands in his pockets. Kayce unlocked the door with a smile.

'We're not officially open yet, Scott, but Gerry's down back if you wanna join him.'

As he passed her, Scott removed his shades and she noticed that his grin looked a little strange. Locking the door again, she followed him until he stopped unexpectedly, causing her to bump into his back. He turned and looked into her eyes, infringing on her personal space, and pointed at the deep fat fryer behind the counter.

'Turn that thing on, then be quiet and don't move.'

Unable to refuse, she reached behind the counter and twisted a red knob, starting the heating process of the newly filled fryer. When that was done, she stood perfectly still, and silently watched Scott walk to the jukebox. He inserted a coin, selected a song, Somebody that I used to know by Gotye, and danced to the back of the diner, where he sat down facing Gerry.

'Scott, what has you here so bright and early?' Gerry quizzed, as he wondered why Kayce was acting like a mannequin. The teenager helped himself to the fresh pot of coffee, pouring it into Kayce's empty cup, before taking a mouthful. He picked up a slice of toast from Gerry's plate and took a bite, staring at him across the table. This was a side to Scott that Gerry wasn't used to. This was definitely not the usual quiet, mannerly teen who had respect for his elders. Scott shook his head and placed the cup back on the table, swallowing the last of the toast.

'Had to get the awful taste of witch out of my mouth.' He leaned back, making himself comfortable, putting his feet on the seat next to Gerry under the table.

'Scott, what's gotten into you?'

'I'll get straight to the point, Gerry: 1970 is what's gotten into me.'

Gerry looked baffled. 'What about it?'

'You wanted me to turn you.'

'Turn me? What the hell are you talking about, kid? You weren't even born in 1970.'

Scott sighed loudly and rolled his eyes in annoyance. 'I forgot: I've enthralled you to forget.' He leaned across the table and spoke into Gerry's eyes. 'Remember everything.' Gerry's eyes swivelled rapidly from left to right, before he jumped to his feet, knocking the pot of coffee onto the floor.

Scott quickly pulled his feet back to avoid the spillage. 'Hey! That was a perfectly good pot of coffee, you moron!' Ten years of memories, of summer adventures and mischief, deep conversations by the lake, campfires by a large boulder in the forest, soaring above the treetops at night, and a friendship like no now flooded Gerry's memory. He stood in silence for a moment.

'Scott – why did you make me forget such a huge part of my life?'

'For the record, *I* didn't make you forget, the *other* me did.'

'The other you? You mean, you're ... you're evil again? Like the old you that you once told me about?'

Scott opened his arms, smiled, and faked a bow in appreciation of how quickly the penny had dropped. Gerry's eyes shot to Kayce who was still watching in silence.

'Kayce, you need to leave *right now.*'

'Relax, Gerry, she's been enthralled, she's powerless; now, sit and talk.' Reluctantly, Gerry resumed his seat 'I remember confiding in you, Gerry, I told you everything, shared nearly all my secrets, but there's one thing I kept hidden from you.'

'I'm not interested.'

'Really? Well, then, I'll end the suspense and tell you, shall I? I told you about the stormy night you were born, and how I saved your mother's life – what I didn't tell you is that the crash was my fault. I chased that deer in front of your parent's car, killing your father. I couldn't tell you that before, but now I don't give a shit.'

The revelations hit Gerry like a tonne of bricks. He looked like a broken man. Scott lapped up his reaction for his personal amusement.

'What do you want?'

'I'm here to give you what you've always wanted, remember?'

Gerry answered with hatred in his voice. 'I remember, I remember asking every day to make me like you, so we could be pals forever, but you refused, time and time again. Telling me it was a curse, telling me it was a waking nightmare that never ends, but I still wanted it.'

'Well, it's your lucky day because I'm here to deliver! I know you're not a teenager anymore but hey, I can't work miracles, now can I?'

'Why now? Whatever's going on here is obviously about you, not me.'

'True, Gerry, but honestly, I need allies. I know I'm already awesome but, ya know, just in case.'

'I'm much wiser now than when I was seventeen, Scott, you can go do your own dirty work.'

Scott turned Gerry's coffee cup upright. Next, he picked up the breadknife and proceeded to slice it into his own hand, until blood ran from the wound. Closing his fist tightly, he held it above the cup, letting his blood drip into the small amount of coffee left in the bottom. Instinctively, Gerry pushed the cup away as the wound on Scott's hand healed.

'Drink.'

Gerry folded his arms in defiance, shaking his head.

'Drink, or Kayce here behind me dies a painful death before your eyes.'

Gerry paused. He knew that Scott was serious. 'Let her go and maybe I'll entertain you.'

'You know I never lie, Gerry; I promise I won't harm her, now drink.'

Gerry looked at Kayce who now had tears silently rolling down her face. He looked at Scott, picked up the cup and downed the contents in one go.

'Satisfied? Now what? We just wait?'

'No, you know how this works. You have to die while my blood is in your system.'

Gerry looked up to the ceiling, exposing his neck. 'Get it over with.'

'Not like that, that's too easy, I'm afraid.'

Kayce watched impassively as Scott leaned across the table again and spoke directly into Gerry's eyes. A moment later, they both stood simultaneously. Scott turned and walked towards the front of the diner, stopping to face Kayce. Gerry walked around the other side of the counter and stopped at the deep fat fryer. Removing the baskets that usually held frozen French fries, he watched the boiling oil release steam that rose swirling up to meet his face, which was now leaning directly over the fryer, sweating profusely in panic at what he knew was about to do against his will.

Scott smiled into Kayce's eyes. A terrified scream was muffled and became a horrible gurgle as a head and upper body submerged itself in liquid fat. Unable to make a sound, Kayce closed her eyes, still streaming tears that dripped down onto her uniform. A moment later, the now lifeless body behind the counter slumped to its knees before falling to the floor.

Scott wiped away a tear from Kayce's face. 'I promised I wouldn't harm you, and I don't break my promises.' She looked relieved between the deep breaths she was taking. 'Poor Kayce, you've absolutely no idea what's going on, do you? Well, let me explain, Gerry is dead. But when he wakes, he'll be in excruciating pain and thirsting for blood. So, to cut a long story short, your life will be in his hands. He can choose to let you live and roll around the floor screaming in agony from his third-degree burns, or he can feed from you and heal instantly, stopping the unimaginable pain. Yeah, it's a tough one, I know. If he truly does care enough, you'll survive.'

Taking her by the shoulders, he kissed her on the forehead before enthralling her once more. 'Be a good girl: when he wakes up, take a knife, slice your hand and present it to him, let's see how strong his willpower really is.' He made his way to the door before stopping to watch a news bulletin on the TV.

'*... two more children have gone missing in the Green Bay area within the past 24 hours; police believe there is a connection to previous disappearances in the greater Wisconsin area ...*'

'Ah Green Bay, it's been far too long …' The door chimed as Scott opened it, slamming it behind him. Kayce stood silently holding a knife in her hand, waiting for a dead man to wake up and play a game for her life.

## Chapter 56

The sun was high in the sky later that same day as PJ entered Tallant cemetery. Homecoming was close, only one night away, and the apprehension and excitement from bagging the biggest job of his life was dominating his thoughts. Not to mention Rebecca Chambers. Going steady was a new experience. But he had questions and he needed advice. And who better to ask than his 600-year-old best pal? Surely with that lifespan, there was nothing Scott didn't know about the opposite sex.

Besides, Cartwright was being weirdly distant. Something was up; Dan didn't seem to have much time for Brad or Gary, either, and the group chat was eerily quiet. PJ thought it must have been a werewolf thing. He'd only spoken to him once since Scott broke the news about the Cartwright family. PJ being PJ had brought it up in conversation when they were alone, and Cartwright had shot him a warning look the likes of which he'd never seen. Knowing now what Dan was, he was nervous about seeing him again, anyway.. Being picked up by the neck with one hand and held against a wall while staring into glowing yellow eyes had made sure of that. This new supernatural world he'd woken up to was hard to swallow, but at least he felt safe with Scott having his back.

Passing the miracle bench as he crunched along the gravel pathway, he took his eyes from his phone long enough to glimpse Mr Coventry lying against a tree to his right. PJ shook his head and returned to his phone. 'Lazy bastard,' he said under his breath. After his social media update, he continued on towards the flat roof. Something on the path half-covered in loose gravel caught his eye. It was Mr Coventry's bunch of keys that he'd seen hanging from his belt on previous occasions.

'Hey!' he shouted over at Mr Coventry, holding out the keys. 'Mr Coventry? You dr–'. He stopped. Something wasn't right. Approaching from the side of a large evergreen, he first noticed the old man's rubber boots dangling above ground level.

'Mr Coventry? What the ...?' As he cautiously rounded the tree, the entire grisly scene unfolded before his eyes. PJ's mouth fell open. He pulled his cap from his head and clutched it tightly in front of his heart.

Mr Coventry was skewered through the chest with a pitchfork, pinning him to the tree behind. His head hung low; his open eyes stared blankly at the ground now pooling with his blood. PJ quickly turned and threw up into the grass verge. Things were easier when he hadn't known the truth. Sometimes ignorance is bliss. He knew that this wasn't a suicide, or a homicide by a random murderer.

This was revenge.

It was a sign. A sign that things had gone terribly wrong. That sense of trust he'd felt in Scott was replaced by a sense of dread. After all, he'd seen Scott's past. And even more disturbing was the fact that Scott had probably only shown him what he thought PJ could handle. PJ knew now that worse was to come.

## Chapter 57

'Nikky, can we have a little chat?' Ranger James Brennan broke the silence across the dinner table. Now that Beth had retired for the night, they were alone. It was as good a time as any to scratch the itch that had plagued his mind all day.

'You want *that* chat *now*? If you don't mind, could we postpone again, Dad? It's just that I'm heading out soon.'

'No, it's not about what you're thinking.' A more serious tone in his voice this time. He folded his arms, almost knocking his utility belt off the back of the chair.

Nikky scrunched her face in confusion. 'Okay … so what is it about?'

Brennan paused uneasily, unsure where to start. 'Your boyfriend dropped by my office today.'

Her face lit up. 'Scott went to see you? How did *you* know he's my boyfriend?' She felt proud that her father knew she was dating, but she was intrigued to discover why Scott had visited him.

'Because he told me.'

Another huge grin from Nikky

'Right before he gave me this.' Brennan reached into his trouser pocket and removed a small cardboard box, throwing it onto the table between them, where it landed next to the empty dinner plates. She picked up the box and examined it. It looked like some sort of medication.

'It's the morning-after pill, Nikky, he told me to make sure you took it today, before giving me a wink and leaving. Would you care to explain?'

She dropped the box back onto the table. 'I ... I, I don't understand? Why would he do that?' An awkward silence grew between them.

'That's exactly what I'd like to know.'

Her unbreakable smile had broken. Her heart raced and her cheeks flushed. She was speechless with embarrassment and confusion. Her father stood up, grabbed his utility belt containing his sidearm, and clicked it around his waist in a no-nonsense gesture.

'I have to go, we'll continue this conversation later, Nikky.'

Nikky sat gobsmacked, unable to make eye contact with her father before he left. She heard his pickup reversing down the driveway. The doorbell brought her back to reality. Then it rang again, and again. Walking down the hallway, she could see PJ's face pressed against the glass. When she opened the door, he almost fell inside on top of her, before he grabbed the door and slammed it shut. He peered through the glass into the dark, checking if he'd been followed, almost knocking down the vase filled with fresh sunflowers on the hall table.

'Hi PJ, feel free to come in, I guess?' Nikky waved her hands sarcastically. He turned and rested his back against the door. She could see something was wrong. PJ always acted weird, but paranoia was not his thing.

'Are you alone?' he said, out of breath.

'Grandma's upstairs watching TV; why, what's up? You're freakin' me out here.'

'Where can we talk in private?'

'Upstairs I guess, what's this about?'

Without saying another word, he charged up the stairs two at a time. She followed more slowly preparing herself for another of PJ's famous scenes.

'Honestly, PJ.' When she entered her bedroom, he was already sitting on the bed, looking frantically around him as if nowhere was safe. She closed the door, not knowing where to start.

'Make yourself comfortable, PJ, why don't you – oh wait you've already done that.'

'Lock the door.'

She shook her head and twisted the key in the lock. 'What's going on?'

He removed his cap and placed it on the bedside locker next to a sunflower sitting in a glass of water. He glanced to the door, then the window. 'It's about Scott, I think he's …'

'Scott? What about him?'

'Sshh!' He lowered his head along with his voice. 'I think he's ... gone bad again.'

She thought for a minute: perhaps this had something to do with the conversation with her father. 'What are you talking about? Why are you saying this?'

'It's, it's Mr Coventry, he's dead, Nikky, nailed to a tree by a pitchfork in the cemetery. It must have been Scott.'

'What? He's ... been murdered? But what makes you think it was Scott? Just because he's a vampire, PJ, doesn't mean–'

PJ cut across her. 'The old fart stabbed Scott in the chest a while back to prove to me that he couldn't die, now I'm guessing Scott returned the favour. Have you seen him lately? Is he ... does he seem normal to you?'

She frowned. 'Well, everything was fine last night but ... something happened today that was kinda *weird*.'

'Tell me?' he pushed.

No way was she going there, not with PJ. 'No, it was something bad but personal, PJ ... but there's no point jumping to conclusions until we know for certain.'

'Nikky, this whole supernatural thing is terrifying, and we've been dropped right in the middle. Our close friends are vampires and werewolves and now people are dying. I can see why Scott makes people forget what they've seen. But I'm telling you, Nikky, if he's gone rogue, nobody is safe.'

She didn't want to accept what PJ was saying. Not Scott, he couldn't, not after what they'd shared. He couldn't go back, surely, could he? Those bad days were far behind in his past. And, after all, Grandma was the best judge of character. And she'd given Scott the thumbs up. Even though she may have been a little biased.

An unexpected rap on the door caused PJ to jump up and bolt over Nikky's bed in a single leap before holding his hands up, crossing his index fingers into the shape of a crude crucifix. Nikky rolled her eyes again before turning to open the door. Her grandmother pushed past her with a serious look on her face, keeping one hand hidden under her yellow dressing gown. PJ exhaled heavily in relief and wiped his forehead with the back of his sleeve. Beth scanned the room before going to the window and peering into the darkness. She pulled the curtains closed and turned to face her granddaughter. More drama, Nikky thought. Just what this day needed.

'Grandma, you okay?'

'Where's your brother?' Straight to the point in an abrupt manner Nikky wasn't used to.

'Out with his friends, why?'

Beth looked from Nikky to PJ who gave her a half-assed salute with one finger, before looking at her granddaughter again.

'It's okay, Grandma, PJ knows about Scott.'

Beth accepted this news without comment. 'Have you seen the news?'

'No ... what's happened?'

'Several people have been murdered in Tallant, that's what's happened, and it looks ... very ...'

'... like Scott's work?' PJ finished.

Beth nodded slowly, still keeping one hand covered and out of sight. 'I think something's happened to Scott, something unexpected.'

'I've seen the results first-hand in the cemetery, he's gone back to being evil, and it's bad, *really* bad, for everyone.' PJ leaned over to pick up his baseball cap from the bedside locker before recoiling when he noticed that the sunflower was slowly withering and dying. 'Holy shit, did you guys just see that?'

Beth and Nikky looked at each other. They knew what this meant.

'Call your brother right now, Nikky!'

Nikky punched her phone. Caden answered right away.

*'Hey sis.'*

*'Caden, where are you?'*

*'Just outside, on the street.'*

*'Come inside right now, it's important.'*

*'Yeah I was just on my way in, anyway ... What? Okay.'*

*'Who are you talking to?*

*'Just Scott, he's –*

*'Oh God! You're with Scott?'*

Beth held her hand up to her mouth as PJ raised his hands to the sides of his head in terror.

*'Hold up sis, I'll be right in.'*

He hung up before she could say another word. She threw her phone onto the bed and ran to the stairs, surprised to see Caden walk through the front door alone.

'You're okay?'

He threw his jacket over the banister and continued upstairs, carrying something under his left arm. 'Why wouldn't I be?'

'Where's Scott?'

'Oh, he said he couldn't stay, told me to give you this; hi Grandma!' He took a small cardboard box tied with a pink ribbon from under his arm and put it into her hands as he passed, before going into his own room and closing the door behind him. Nikky went back into her room to see the relieved faces of her grandmother and PJ. Caden was safe.

'See? A gift from Scott. I think you guys are overreacting, making a big fuss over nothing.' Sitting on her bed, she began to open the box. PJ looked to Beth and shrugged his shoulders. Nikky pulled the ribbon open and lifted the top of the box away from the bottom, exposing a small paper card. It sat on top of pink tissue paper folded neatly over the contents. She read the inscription: *'FOR LUCK'*. She smiled, remembering her words at the funfair when she'd given Scott the rabbit's paw, as she pulled the pink paper aside to reveal her gift.

She released a harrowing scream and jumped to her feet, dropping the box and spilling its contents. The severed and bloodied brown paw of an animal lay on the floor for all to see. PJ knelt down and picked it up gingerly for a closer inspection. 'So, I'm guessing I'm right, which basically means we're all screwed.' He dropped it back into the box. Beth hugged Nikky tightly with one arm as she wiped away her tears.

'What are we gonna do, Grandma? You know him better than anyone.'

'There's nothing we can do, Nikky, except to go on with life like this never happened – we just need to take some precautions.'

'Go on as normal? But homecoming is tomorrow ... isn't there a way to cure him somehow? How was he cured the last time?'

'Time, which is something we haven't got.'

'Wow Nikky's-grandma-lady-who-seems-to-know-stuff, hang on just a second, you expect us to go back out there? Like nothing's happened?' PJ's voice shook as paced.

'From what I know about Scott's past, he liked to cause pain and suffering before getting around to the kill.'

Beth's matter-of-fact sincerity made PJ uneasy. 'Great, so basically he'll toy with us first before he kills us horribly? How can we defend ourselves against a 600-year-old immortal?' PJ paused. He clicked his fingers in delight. 'Nikky, I've got it: Cartwright? He'll help us, right? I mean, he's a werewolf, right? And he hates Scott … right?' PJ was already hating the way Nikky was shaking her head.

'Scott's immune to werewolves, remember?'

'Yeah but, he's strong, right? He might be the best option we have.' He spoke rapidly and nervously.

'There's a full moon tomorrow, PJ, Dan and the other Cartwrights will be locked up out of sight. I was talking to Amber earlier. She's pissed, said that Dan told her he wasn't going to homecoming this year, not that she knows the real reason why.'

PJ closed his eyes. 'So, we really are screwed then.'

'You mentioned precautions, Grandma?' Nikky turned to Beth.

'I know something that should help ... remember I told you I had a gift for you buried in my box of memories? Meanwhile I think your friend here should spend the night. Scott is weaker during the day and prefers to stay indoors unless absolutely necessary.'

'Gladly, Nikky's grandma, there's no way I'm going out there!'

Nikky sat on the end of her bed with her head in her hands. Beth looked at PJ and gestured for him to comfort her while she went to the window. She stuck her head through the gap in the curtains and peered outside. She knew Scott too well, and that he would stay around to witness the results of his carnage.

Outside, and barely visible in the darkness, hanging on the middle of the clothesline that joined the house to Caden's treehouse, was the body of a German Shepherd with one of its paws missing.

Buster.

In the blackness of the treehouse, Beth saw two glowing red eyes staring back at her, studying her reaction. But rather than recoil in horror, for the sake of her family, she took action. In defiance and without fear, from under her dressing gown she removed the silver crucifix she had kept from Scott's mausoleum and stood it on the windowsill.

The red eyes slowly receded into the darkness and disappeared as she pulled the curtains tight again.

Across town, Governor Cartwright sat behind the desk in his office sipping a glass of Scotch, contemplating tomorrow's plan of action for the approaching full moon. A second later, a deafening crash brought him to his feet. One of his family security team had been thrown through the double doors, smashing the ornate wood to pieces and landing roughly on the marble floor. A vampire followed, pursued by two more of the Governor's security detail.

Governor Cartwright held up his hand. 'Wait.' He studied the familiar face.

'I just thought you'd like to know: Scott's returned to his old ways.'

The Governor gestured his men to leave. He studied the contents of his glass and nodded before answering. 'That's … unfortunate, to say the least.'

Amdis approached his desk. 'But I happen to have some information that might help.'

Governor Cartwright sat back down into his chair and clasped his hands. 'I'm listening.'

# Chapter 58

'Ladies, gentlemen and everyone in between the big night is finally here, welcome to the Tallant Titans Homecoming Halloween Ball! And last night the Portage Panthers lost once again to the mighty Tallant Titans!'

A cheer erupted from the room.

'I'll be providing your musical entertainment for the night, and for any special requests, text them to the number displayed here and I'll do my best to accommodate you, if I approve and your requests aren't too lame: now enjoy!' A weaker cheer followed.

PJ stood at a desk of decks with computer screens on the balcony that surrounded the dance floor below, which was already filled with people in a variety of fancy dress. The school hall was decorated with orange and black balloons tied to makeshift pillars that joined in the centre to form the body of a giant spider. From one side of the balcony to the other, a thin fishing line ran the length of the hall, suspending a string of fake candles with flickering tea lights. The illusion was a sea of floating candles hovering above the dancers in the dimly lit venue. He'd impressed himself with how calm and professional he'd sounded, despite his fear. But he'd done all he could, and taken the necessary precautions as instructed by Beth the night before.

From the floor below, Rebecca Chambers gave him an inspiring thumbs up. She was dressed in a maid's outfit and held a clipboard listing final checks to perform. Her busy night was just beginning. Outside, a line of couples ran down the steps forming a crowd in the carpark.

On the dancefloor, the variety of patrons was increasing. Jack the Ripper chased Wonder Woman with a plastic butcher knife, trying to squirt her with fake blood. An inflatable sumo wrestler bounced off random people who passed where he stood next to a killer clown in a rubber mask and oversized pyjamas. Napoleon was deep in conversation with Dracula next to the drinks table while the Hulk tried his luck with Princess Leia in a corner. Opposite them, James Bond chatted to Mary Poppins, who had her eye on a lifeguard dancing in tight red shorts under the balloon spider.

It was organised chaos at its finest. PJ's hands shook as he eyed the door for the tenth time in the last five minutes. He still had a good view of Nikky at the far wall under the opposite balcony. Standing next to Amber, she wore a dark-green masquerade ball costume, an elaborate black curled wig hiding her blonde hair. She held a lime-green mask on a stick that she kept raised to her face in an effort to hide her identity. A large collection of emerald-green jewels hung around her neck, sparkling randomly in the flashing lights. Amber was dressed as Harley Quinn, pigtails, bubble-gum and baseball bat included. The venue was at bursting capacity now, the carpark empty apart from a police cruiser parked by the entrance. Three black SUVs pulled up outside. Inside the middle vehicle, Governor Cartwright spoke into his Bluetooth earpiece.

'I've just had a visitor: get ready for plan B and get there now, damn it! We can't take any chances.' The call ended. He dialled another number. 'Damien, where are you?'

Damien replied, 'At the town hall waiting for you guys, where the hell are you? Don't you know what time it is?'

'It's a long story, just stay there; if we're not back, lock that door.' He stepped out of the vehicle and was followed to the entrance by seven family members from his security team, who'd exited the other SUVs. The sound of music flowed through the double doors.

Police Officer Stanford greeted the group with a creepy smile, 'Have a nice night, Governor.' One of the Governor's companions grabbed him and threw him to the side before following Governor Cartwright into the hall. Stanford picked himself up and grabbed a heavy chain from the trunk of his cruiser. He closed the double doors, locking them tightly with the chain from the outside. Nobody else would enter. Nobody else would leave, alive.

On the balcony above the dancefloor, PJ wondered if he was delusional. He watched in astonishment, as a familiar figure approached. Dan Cartwright folded his arms and peered into the crowd below. PJ pulled the headphones from his ears and stared at the side of Cartwright's head for a moment, then shouted over the music.

'*What*, and I cannot stress this enough, the *fuck* … are you doing here, Cartwright? it's a full moon tonight, man!'

Dan didn't reply but watched his uncle who was standing on the opposite balcony, resting his hands on the rail as he scanned the crowd below. The other family members separated throughout the room, quietly observing the crowd, communicating with each other via hidden earpieces. The Governor spoke into his sleeve. 'Does anyone have eyes on the target?' This was greeted by a collection of negatives in his ear. At the DJ table, PJ punched Dan's arm for a response. Cartwright's head snapped in his direction.

'Oops! Sorry about that,' PJ said, realising he had just poked the bear. He gently stroked Dan's arm apologetically. Not knowing where to look, he prepared the next track to play. Cartwright moved closer and shouted into PJ's ear.

'Scott paid my family and me a visit a while ago, he used his mumbo jumbo crap to force us here tonight for the change, and I was given specific instructions to stand right next to you.' Frantically, PJ looked to the doorway, which was now closed. 'I'm afraid there's no escape, PJ, the door is locked tight from the outside and it's protected by a vampire. You know we had no say in this, right?'

'Yeah, that makes me feel much better before you tear me apart, thanks.'

'It's not over yet, my uncle has a plan.'

'Oh great. Aren't you going to fill me in?'

'Actually, he won't tell me, for some reason.'

PJ threw his hands in the air and looked towards the heavens. 'Scott's already here, isn't he?'

Dan exhaled heavily. 'Yep.'

'So he's probably looking for Nikky, right?'

'What's your point, PJ?'

'My point is that he once told me that vampires have highly advanced senses.'

'Again, get to the point?'

'What if we protect Nikky by screwing with his senses? Making it more difficult to find her in the crowd?'

'How do you mean?'

PJ pulled out his phone and sent a text. Nikky felt her phone vibrate.

*'Get on the dancefloor, I'll distract Scott.'*

Without explaining, she grabbed Amber and made for the centre of the floor, still hiding behind her mask and now surrounded by a crowd. It was PJ's turn next. He chose a dance song with a repetitive tone, set the strobe lights to randomise and turned the smoke machine to maximum output. The room became an artificial cloud. People flickered in slow motion between bursts of white light. As if she was suffering from a severe case of paranoia, Nikky watched every person who brushed against her on the dancefloor, her eyes moving from one to the other, preparing for the worst. Batman danced beside her with his hands up; an astronaut next to him struggled to hold his date in the air with her legs around his waist; Chewbacca was doing some fancy footwork; Dracula was busy biting the neck of his date in plain view, and Woody from *Toy Story* waved his cowboy hat over his head.

Nikky did a double take. What had she just seen? She put Batman between herself and the figure in the long black cloak and oversized collar. Watching closely, she noticed the girl's neck covered in blood as she fell to the floor. Dracula continued dancing.

She quickly sent PJ a text. *'Dracula is Scott!!!'* She looked up to see PJ relay the message to Cartwright, who ran to the other side of the balcony to inform his uncle.

'It's him, Uncle, he's Dracula!' Dan pointed to the figure in the black cloak.

Patrick Cartwright grabbed Dan by his shirt, pulled him close and shouted, 'We're not looking for him, you idiot! We're looking for your friend Nikky.'

'Huh? I don't understand?'

The Governor pushed him back and continued his search.

On the dancefloor, Nikky was still watching the girl who had just collapsed at Dracula's feet. She laughed and jumped back up and kissed her vampire boyfriend. False alarm. The crowd around her began to shift and Dracula was now out of sight; Superman replaced Batman and Elvis was moving in on Cinderella. Amber danced facing Nikky now, her baseball bat under her arm. She began to laugh, shaking her head in Nikky's direction.

'What's so funny?' Nikky mouthed.

Amber got close and shouted into her ear. 'Your worst nightmare is right behind you!'

Nikky smiled back awkwardly, confused, and slowly turned around. The killer clown was dancing right behind her. Nikky jumped with fright, accidentally dropping her mask to the floor. She pushed against Amber, putting space between them and Jack the Ripper. Amber laughed at Nikky's expense but stopped when she noticed Dan Cartwright watching from above.

'Nikky, I'll be right back.' Nikky stood alone in the middle of the dancefloor.

A sudden gap opened between her and the clown, with a clear line of sight. Killer clown stopped dancing. He stood still for a moment, watching her. In one slow movement, he reached up and pulled off his rubber mask, peeling it back over his head. Nikky's heart pounded in her chest.

Scott grinned from ear to ear before ripping the baggy pyjama outfit from his body and stepping out of his costume, leaving it in a pile on the floor. Within another burst of white, slow-motion strobe lighting, his vampire face with red eyes briefly flashed unnoticed by the dancers around him, before returning to normal. Nikky reached behind her neck to expose a small silver crucifix that was hidden behind her necklace. The grin on Scott's face quickly faded and when she blinked, he was gone. The Governor shouted into his earpiece and pointed down at Nikky.

'Target acquired! Move in!'

Wonder Woman danced across the room on an intercept course with Nikky. When she got within arm's reach, she ripped the wooden crucifix and necklace from Nikky's neck before throwing them across the floor and shouting into her face. 'He said you won't be needing that!' She danced away and merged back into the crowd. Four members of the Cartwright family materialised and surrounded Nikky, awaiting orders. The Governor shouted into his earpiece from above.

'What are you waiting for? It's her life or everyone else in here; do it *now*!' The two closest Cartwrights grabbed the combat knives sheathed on their belts and moved in for the kill. Nikky stood paralysed, unable to process what was happening. A fraction of a second before the first blade touched her skin, Scott appeared, holding her by the neck, with his head turned toward the Cartwrights, grinning. His face flashed into his vampire form before he spoke.

'Allow me.' He sank his fangs into her neck and fed until her body became limp. Her lifeless corpse dropped to the floor, earning him a round of applause from the unsuspecting crowd. The Governor watched on, feeling like all his birthdays had just come all together. Scott had just done their dirty work for them. Scott looked to the ceiling with his eyes closed and licked the blood from his lips, relishing the taste. He turned to face his Cartwright captives and tapped his wristwatch as his face became normal again.

'Tick tock, not long now,' he mouthed above the music. The Governor's smile vanished as quickly as it had arrived. Nothing had happened. He tapped redial on his earpiece and spoke rapidly, 'It didn't work, it's not her!' He paused as the voice on the other end spoke silently, then said, 'I understand,' before hanging up. Dan Cartwright turned to face a distraught PJ, who was staring blankly at the body of his friend on the dancefloor and shouting.

'Nikky! Are you okay? Nikky?'

'You need to get out of here, PJ, as quick as you can,' Cartwright shouted.

PJ slammed his headphones onto the desk, abruptly stopping the music, to the dismay of almost all present. Running down the stairs two at a time, his fear had now turned to anger. He ran through the Cartwrights and directly at Scott with vengeance in his eyes. Scott smiled and casually picked him up by the throat, leaving his legs dangling in mid-air.

'I was going to let Dan tear you to shreds, but what the hell, I'm hungry and I'm sick to death of your smart mouth.' His vampire face flashed again, but, unexpectedly, the smile disappeared from Scott's face. He resumed human form and lowered PJ back down to the floor. Scott dropped to the ground holding his head in his hands. He turned around on his knees to face Nikky and the damage he'd done.

'No! No! No!' Quickly he scooped her up in his arms, brushed the fake, black hair from her face and stared into her still-open, lifeless eyes. He roared to the heavens in his deep demonic voice, and the dancefloor cleared around him. PJ watched hopelessly. Scott sliced open his wrist with a fingernail, drawing blood, which he dripped into her mouth in an effort to cure her wounds. But nothing happened.

'PJ, CPR; do it!'

PJ knelt and began to pump up and down on Nikky's chest, tears pouring down his face. As all hope seemed to be lost, the wound on her neck begin to close. Nikky spluttered, sat up and coughed violently. She looked at PJ

'PJ? What happened?'

PJ didn't answer, he just hugged her tightly. She turned her head to see Scott and instinctively, she tried to escape, before PJ reassured her. 'It's okay, Nikky, he's back, he's back from the dark side; we're safe.'

'How?' her voice was weak.

'Honestly, I don't know,' Scott replied. All three stood up in unison. Nikky wrapped her arms around Scott.

Governor Cartwright arrived with Dan and his family members as the embrace ended.

'Apologies, gentlemen.' In a blur, Scott rapidly appeared in front of each of them, looked into their eyes and spoke then returned to stand next to PJ and Nikky. Onlookers were confused; some were too drunk to care, some continued dancing with no music, while the more sober among them panicked that the front doors were still locked, trapping everyone inside.

'Get to the SUVs, stat!' the Governor barked at his crew. Dan hugged Nikky and gave Scott a subtle nod before following his family to the exit. One of them stopped either side of the double doors and turned to the newest werewolf in town, with a nod of approval. Dan's eyes burned yellow. With a single kick, the doors burst open, shattering to pieces, and knocking the vampire cop Stanford to the ground. A torrent of students poured out, trampling the decorated pumpkins lining the steps as they stampeded past. As Nikky pulled the wig from her head, she felt her phone vibrate in her pocket.

'Dad?'

'Nikky, something has happened, come home right away.' James Brennan hung up with no time for a reply.

'Dad? Is everything okay?' But the line was dead. She turned to Scott.

'Go,' he said, 'I'll catch up with you later, I have to visit some old friends in the mountains.' Scott scrunched his face in anger, a momentary glow of red in his eyes.

PJ threw one hand into the air. 'Payback! Can I come along to see you kick some ass?'

'To a vampire lair in the mountains in the dead of the night swarming with the undead and at least four ancients, PJ?'

'Well, I guess, when you put it all romantic like that, Scott, I'll just get Nikky home safe instead.'

On the steps outside, PJ wrapped his arm around Nikky, gave Scott a nod and walked off toward the gate. Governor Cartwright gave Scott his own nod before climbing into his SUV and beckoning Dan to follow him. Scott grabbed the vampire cop by the throat and pushed him up against the wall, lifting him off the ground.

'I, I only did what you told me to do!' Stanford managed to protest with difficulty.

'Well guess what? You're going to do what I tell you to do one more time.'

'Wait, there's something you should know – it's Amdis, they just took her to the Great Hall this second, now will you let me live?' he coughed.

Scott pulled him close and looked into his eyes. 'Stand here on guard all night, until the sun rises and burns you to a crisp.' Scott released him and vanished. Inside the SUV, Dan Cartwright spoke.

'Straight to the Town Hall now, Uncle? We don't have much time.'

'Not exactly.' The Governor turned to his driver. 'Follow that pureblood.'

## Chapter 59

Amdis stood in the empty driveway of Nikky's house, rang the doorbell and waited.

It took some time, but a frail figure with a walking stick eventually opened the door, not looking surprised to see her visitor.

'Amdis.'

'It's been a while, Beth.' Amdis presented a neutral expression.

'Just like Scott, you haven't aged a day since I last laid eyes on you … I, on the other hand, well …' She tilted her head to the side while leaning on her walking stick.

'Actually, Scott is why I'm here. You need to invite me in, it's very …'

'Come in, Amdis, I invite you,' Beth cut in, and slowly turned, to make her way up the stairs. Amdis was thrown off by her instant acceptance. She stepped inside, checking behind her before closing the door. She followed Beth upstairs into the guest room, where she watched her sit on the edge of her bed, breathless, and waited for her to speak.

'I know about Scott, and I know why you're here.'

Amdis folded her arms and looked to the floor, uneasy. Beth continued.

'In order to break the spell, I have to die.'

'How do you know this?' A flat tone in the vampire's voice.

'Because it makes sense. When I met Scott, and we fell in love, I connected with him in a way that nobody else ever had, shattering what remained of the spell.'
Beth took a sip of water from a glass on her bedside locker and hung her walking stick from the bedpost. 'Now that the spell has been cast once more, permanently breaking Scott's connection to me could possibly shatter it again.'

'You're right. I'm sorry, but we don't have a choice. The witch told me how to break the spell. As much as I had fun with Scott in the old days, they were different times. I don't want Draven breathing down my neck or Scott turning this town into a bloodbath. I like things as they are.' For the first time in her long existence, Amdis was apologising for having to take a life.

'You don't need to explain yourself; my granddaughter's safety is reason enough for me.'

There was a pause before Amdis spoke again. 'If it's any consolation, and if Scott were himself, he would never allow this to happen.'

'I'm dying anyway, my dear. Scott knows this, and I've lived a long happy life. I experienced things with your son that most people could only dream of. I'm ready … and I'm glad my death has purpose.'

Amdis's phone vibrated. She answered. A hurried voice spoke on the other end. 'It didn't work, it's not her!' Her gaze moved sympathetically to the old lady sitting on her bed. Amdis knew what this news meant.

'I understand,' she replied and hung up.

Beth smiled again. She knew it was time. 'I know Scott better than anyone, and I know he'll take this hard. Please tell him that I wanted this and not to blame you, or himself.'

Amdis stood close to her. 'Of course. I will try.'

'Do one other thing for me, would you, Amdis?'

Amdis nodded.

'Tell my granddaughter Nikky to cherish every moment with Scott because it will never come again.'

Amdis looked to the floor guiltily, knowing that the phone call meant Nikky was dead and that her death hadn't broken the spell. She replied with something unexpected.

'I ... I want you to die knowing that your life was the best part of Scott's. Beth, you saw the monster he was, and you fell for the very thing he feared in himself, making him feel human.'

Beth took a deep breath and readied herself. 'Nothing lasts forever, even vampires, but I wanted Scott to be my nothing.'

As Amdis left the house, six vampires approached. One of them spoke.

'You and that silver crucifix are coming with us.'

**Chapter 60**

The moon was full as Scott approached the vampire hall hidden deep within the mountains northwest of Tallant. Surrounded by dense forestry, it was built into a cliff that overhung at the front to disguise the stone pillars and oversized wooden doorway ornately cut into the rock face beneath. Large blocks of stone forming a platform pathway rose above the forest floor like an oversized welcome mat to the entrance.

He was well used to the dark; for him it felt comforting. Darkness was an ally that served him well. Out of habit, he raised his hand to his brow, but the lack of light was cover. No need to hide: he could be his true self here. This was his domain, his sanctuary, and his poisoned chalice. It had been decades since he last set foot here, but it was unavoidable. The closer he got to that wooden door, the more his humanity slipped away through his fingers. He felt the vibrational hum start up in his chest. But this time it felt different.

Living in Tallant for so long had given him a reputation as its guardian, killing any and every vampire who came to town. It became common knowledge within vampire cults to avoid Tallant and the pureblood who guarded it. One, perhaps two, vampires might try their luck, limiting the hum in Scott's chest to a level that he became accustomed to. Never had that hum affected his ability to concentrate. Numerous vampires were close. More than he had been near for centuries. He knew he was outnumbered. But he was the pureblood. He had abilities that other undead could only dream of. Even the ancients were envious.

With the forest behind him, he stopped. Sounds came from the trees on all three sides and from the doorway as Draven appeared. Scores of vampires emerged into the clearing, leaving no escape. Dressed in random attire, black lifeless eyes stared in caution at the famous pureblood they'd heard about, their grey veiny skin barely visible in the moonlight. On the clifftop above Draven, more came forward, staring down from the edge. Scott glanced up before smiling at the ancient confronting him at the entrance.

'They look a little nervous, Draven, would you agree?'

Draven smiled. 'It's not too late to stand with us, Scott.'

Scott exhaled heavily. 'I disagree, Uncle. For centuries, all the countless lives I've taken because of you. I almost killed my friends because of you. It's time to fix this once and for all.'

'I let you live because of who you were: my own brother's flesh and blood.'

'You let me live because you were afraid of me but also wanted to use me when it suited you!' Scott roared in his demonic voice.

'Amdis agrees with me; she despises you; don't you know that? You killed the love of her life and she's never forgiven you.'

'Where is she?'

'She's inside right now cursing your name and the day you were born. Your father was an ancient, you took the only remnant that Amdis had left of him and buried it inside that time capsule. But unbeknownst to you, I reclaimed my brother's dagger years ago, and kept it until the time was right.'

'So you gave it to Amdis so that she could witness how I killed him again and again, a tainted vision each time she touches it to remind her of how much she hates me, how convenient.'

Draven grinned. 'In fairness, it didn't take much convincing, she saw what you are with her own two eyes over the centuries, I was just giving her a little reminder.'

Scott only looked at him silently.

'Scott, you and I are evenly matched in strength even without my army surrounding you, not to mention the three extremely powerful ancients inside. This can only end one way.'

Scott pulled his hands from his pockets. 'I'll take my chances.' His face morphed into his vampire self. From the darkness of the forest behind him, several pairs of yellow eyes glowed, accompanied by deafening howls and roars. Draven's expression changed instantly. His cockiness was replaced by uncertainty. Scott grinned before launching himself towards the ancient before him but the vampires from the rock face above leaped down to block his path as Draven escaped back inside the doorway and locked it behind him.

Scott flew at the vampires with his arms extended and burst through the chests of two of them as he bit the third on his neck. The now lifeless bodies punctured and hanging on his arms burst into flames. He held out their burning hearts aloft as a warning before shaking the bodies casually off his arms. Two more vampires attacked from behind, jumping on his back. The waiting game was over as the surrounding vampires began their frenzied attack. The pureblood was slashed and bitten; forced to the ground where he disappeared under a writhing pile of vampires.

Timed to perfection, several werewolves emerged from the forest, sending chunks of vampire flesh and limbs in random directions as they slashed their way through the vampire army. The pureblood remained pinned by sheer numbers. The air was filled with the roaring of beasts as the full moon lit the clearing that had become a ferocious battlefield. Fangs bit into furry flesh as some vampires attacked the werewolves from the rear, jumping on their backs before being clawed down and bitten to shreds in retaliation. Random patches of flame littered the stone platform as the undead met their demise.

    The bloodbath had begun.

***

Back in Tallant, in an alleyway behind Trevor's Diner, Gerry stopped feeding on an innocent victim and looked to the sky. His sire was injured; he could sense it. In the blink of an eye, he was gone.

# Chapter 61

Outside the Great Hall, the vampires covering the wounded pureblood exploded outward in all directions as Scott erupted upwards, gripping one of them by the neck. He flew into the air and hovered above the fight zone, staring into the eyes of his prey. His tattered leather jacket and clothes were covered in blood but the wounds on his face and body began to heal. This show of strength let the others know that he was not to be trifled with.

  He began to spin, still holding the doomed vampire, gaining momentum before releasing him in the direction of the entrance to the hall. The door burst open inwards with a crash, sending pieces of wood and splinters onto the stone floor in the narrow hallway behind. When Scott dropped back down, the vampires gave him a wide berth; some vampires fled, others continued the fight against their mortal enemies, but none had the audacity to try and stop him now. Entering the corridor, he smashed his foot down onto the head of the creature he'd used as a battering ram, leaving a burning pile lighting the way back to the entrance.

  The Great Hall was silent as Draven stood before the altar with Amdis by his side, facing the stone arch doorway, awaiting Scott's arrival. In her hand, she held the dagger once owned by Scott's father. Six burning torches hung from the balcony, and a flaming chalice on the altar lit the chamber, spreading light and shadows across the stone floor. Up above, three ancients stood ready and waiting. Red eyes appeared in the hallway outside the main hall as Scott slowly came into view. Scanning his surroundings, he stopped and looked from Draven to Amdis and back again.

Draven spoke. 'After six hundred years, your reign has come to an end, boy, you were nothing more than an experiment that–'–Before he could finish, Scott vanished from view. One by one, the torches were extinguished, leaving the chalice as the only light source remaining. Draven uncertainly looked to Amdis but she seemed as confused as he was. He stepped forward, nervously scanning the room to locate his nephew. From the balcony above, sounds of a skirmish drew Draven's attention for a moment before silence dominated the hall again.

The flaming chalice flickered, casting two long shadows from Amdis and Draven to the floor. In one simultaneous motion, three headless bodies tumbled over the balcony and hung by their feet, before combusting in the air. Now panicking, Draven spun about, searching desperately. He stopped suddenly and looked at the ceiling above him. Red eyes stared down from the blackness. Scott opened his arms.

Three severed heads fell onto Draven, bounced off him and landed with a hollow thud on the stone floor at his feet before bursting into flames. He recoiled, as Scott dropped to the ground. Slowly, he took three steps towards Draven, who quickly turned to the altar behind him, seized the flaming chalice of hot oil from the altar and threw the contents over the pureblood, igniting his body from head to toe.

Scott staggered and fell to his knees. His red eyes burned and regenerated in the same moment. Burning flesh melted into what remained of his leather jacket and his hair singed into charred skin. He fell forward on one outstretched arm and looked up at his mother, his body engulfed in flames. Draven pierced his chest with his dagger of the ancients before ripping it back out from his body. Amdis looked on, clasping the dagger of her fallen love tightly in her hand, telling herself that her son deserved this punishment. Draven looked to Amdis and smiled. He wasn't finished.

Reaching under his cloak, he pulled out the silver crucifix that Amdis has given him, wrapped in cloth which was preventing his own hand from burning rapidly. Scott fell back onto the ground behind him, blazing with flames – and with a mortal chest wound. The information Amdis had found in Scott's journal about his weakness to religious symbolism had served well. To the average vampire, the silver crucifix would have been little more than an annoyance. But to the pureblood, it was devastating.

Draven approached the pureblood with the clothbound crucifix held out in front of him. The closer he got to Scott, the more excruciating Scott's pain became. The skin on his face reacted to the crucifix like a hot knife to butter. It peeled his flesh causing him to scream in pain. The flames increased as Draven pressed the crucifix against what was left of Scott's face. His red eyes burned away, not regenerating this time, leaving empty holes in his skull. His mouth fell open, his teeth and jawbone now exposed as the power of the crucifix began to affect his entire body. His charred and partly skinless body collapsed.

Draven turned his head and shouted, 'Now is the time, Amdis, do it now!' Amdis pulled a wooden stake from under her jacket and looked at what remained of her son's skinless skull, his mouth opening and closing in silent agony.

'Do it!' Draven roared again.

Barely hesitating, she knelt and plunged the stake into the centre of Scott's chest. As a final act before death, a partly skeletonised hand grabbed her hand, with her fingers still wrapped around the stake protruding from his thorax. His eyes were gone, but he still had his sense of touch. A memory instantly flashed into her mind. But it wasn't her own memory – it was Scott's. She was in the Great Hall, but it was centuries ago. Through Scott's eyes she watched the memory unfold before her. Scott's abilities were still mostly unknown at that time and this scene was taking place in daylight. From high up in a shadowy corner of the ceiling, Scott hung upside down and watched two people discussing something that they both agreed upon. Standing by the altar, Draven and his brother spoke quietly to each other, safely knowing they were alone while the other vampires slept.

'It's not going as planned, the boy is too powerful – we can't allow him to reach adulthood, he would be unstoppable,' Draven whispered urgently.

'I've been watching him; he's ruthless with the beasts and his appetite for human blood is unquenchable. It's only a matter of time before my so-called son kills one of us,' Lauden replied.

'You must be the one to take care of it, Lauden, he's of your blood.'

'Amdis has no love for him, but she will not allow him to be killed.'

Draven sat back against the altar. 'In that case, brother, have you exhausted your time with Amdis, too?'

Lauden smiled. 'There's no shortage of women I can enthral. She's served her purpose; I'll take care of it personally.'

The vision inside Amids's mind dissolved and changed. This time it was a vision of herself as seen through Scott's eyes. She was sleeping, with Lauden standing next to her holding a wooden stake. Scott flew at his father and shoved him up against the wall. Amdis woke suddenly, in time to see Scott tear his father's heart from his chest, watching him burn as he dropped to the ground. As the vision ended, Amdis's expression changed, turning to one of horror and regret at how she had treated her misunderstood son, whom she now knew had saved her life all those centuries ago.

'What have I done?' she whispered to herself, as Draven stood, satisfied that he was now the most powerful vampire alive. She shook her head in disbelief. With her hand still clasped around the stake, she stood up, pulling it back out of Scott's heart. She turned to face Draven. He could see the new pain in her eyes, but he had expected as much. She flew toward him in a fury, vainly trying to puncture his chest with the blood-covered stake. He caught her by the neck and lifted her from the ground.

'Did you honestly think I'd have any use for you after he was dead?' he boasted. 'It's time to join your son, Amdis, you can tell Lauden that I said–' A trickle of blood ran from the side of his mouth. A bloodied fist pushed through his ribcage, holding his blackened heart. The grip around her neck loosened, dropping her to her knees. The silver crucifix pinged as it hit the floor, flipping over twice before coming to a stop. For one moment, Draven observed his own heart in front of his face, before his eyes rolled back into his skull and his body became engulfed in flames and fell, burning, next to Amdis.

Amdis looked up in confusion. Gerry stood holding the black heart in his hand before it too started to burn. He dropped it next to the corpse from where it came. Amdis had no idea who this vampire was, but she was grateful, nonetheless. She turned to her lifeless son and cradled his almost skeletal head in her arms. Gerry couldn't believe what he was seeing. Equally distraught, he dropped to Scott's opposite side, unable to comprehend what just happened, his human face gradually reappearing.

'I, I didn't know …' Amdis wept, touching Scott's face. Instinctively, Gerry sliced open his wrist with one of his long fingernails and dripped his blood over Scott's bony face and into what remained of his mouth. Angry at Gerry's stupidity, Amdis shouted, 'It doesn't work that way, you moron! Scott's blood cures, not yours!'

'His blood flows in my veins: move aside.'

'Whoever the hell you are, if he turned you, that doesn't mean you have his blood.' Amdis shook her head at this fledgling vampire's appalling ignorance. Gerry ignored her and continued to spill his blood onto Scott's face, until the wound on his wrist healed, whereupon he sliced it open again. Amdis knew that this was futile. Consumed by grief and guilt, she watched the stranger spilling his blood in vain over the remains of the son she had helped to kill. Seconds turned to minutes. They stared at Scott's remains in hopeless silence.

Very slowly, and unexpectedly, the charred fingers on Scott's left hand twitched slightly. Then his right hand moved. The bones exposed on various parts of his body began to regenerate. Layers of tissue and skin reformed, covering up the skeletal parts that had been exposed. The black skin changed back to its normal pigmentation. His hair began to re-grow and his face returned to its normal youthful self. He was perfect again, lying in his tattered, bloodied clothing. Amdis looked up at Gerry, who breathed a sigh of relief. Scott opened his eyes and looked into the eyes of his mother, cradling his head in her arms as tears poured down her face.

'You're okay, I can't believe you're okay. 'She looked to Gerry. 'How did you do that?'

'Scott's blood has flown through my veins since the day I was born – he healed my pregnant mother after a traffic accident where my father died.'

She looked down at her son whose eyes had not moved from hers.

'If a stake through my heart could kill me, I'd already be dead. I tried that long ago,' Scott said softly.

'I'm so sorry, Scott, you kept it secret for all these years; why didn't you tell me?'

'I like to play my cards close to my chest, or haven't you noticed?' He gave a small smile from one side of his mouth. The silence was broken as eight werewolves entered the Great Hall, their growling echoing off the stone walls, announcing their presence. They surrounded the altar in a semi-circle, breathing heavily and watching the trio of vampires. In an effort to protect his sire, Gerry moved to stand between Scott and the werewolves, showing his vampire face as he snarled in their direction. He was sired by the pureblood. Werewolves were no threat to him. Scott silently came to stand next to Gerry. Gerry's vampire face looked to Scott's human face and he spoke.

'We can take them.'

Scott turned and looked into the eyes of his friend. 'I'm sorry, Gerry, my old friend,' he said quietly. He shoved his hand into Gerry's chest and tore out his heart, watching as Gerry's confused look turned to flames. Amdis gaped to see her son kill the vampire who had just saved his life. Not to mention an ally against the enemies that had them surrounded. Scott dropped the heart of his friend to the ground and spoke for all the room to hear.

'I didn't expect the help, but I want to thank you.'

They roared in unison. Amdis couldn't believe her eyes. These beasts were Scott's allies. She truly understood now how little she knew about her own son.

The werewolves started to leave again through the door, knowing the battle was won. One of them approached Scott, his yellow eyes staring at his once mortal enemy. Scott nodded.

'I'll be seeing you, Dan, thanks.' Cartwright turned and followed the pack into the forest. When the Great Hall was empty, Amdis spoke reluctantly.

'Scott, there's something you should know.'

## Chapter 62

It was early in the morning and still dark outside. Two paramedics shook hands with Ranger James Brennan in his front garden before returning to the ambulance, packing away the equipment that had not been used. He went back inside to comfort his daughter who stood at the foot of her grandmother's bed, starting in disbelief at her dead grandmother lying peacefully on top of her bedclothes, her hands clasped across her chest giving the illusion that she was sleeping.

James Brennan stood behind his daughter and placed his hands on her shoulders. 'Nikky, she was dying, she made me promise not to tell you.'

Nikky sniffled and wiped away another tear. 'She lived a long life full of adventures, Dad.' He nodded and hugged her before leaving the room to start making the funeral arrangements.

From the rooftop of the house next door, Scott sat with an aching heart that couldn't beat, watching and listening to every word. He wanted to give Nikky the space that he felt she badly needed. Nikky left her grandmother's bedroom and went outside to Caden's treehouse, where she observed the full moon from the window. Scott entered Beth's bedroom window and sat on the bed next to her body. Brushing her hair to the side of her face with his hand, he leaned close and kissed her forehead.

'I'll tell the stars about you, now and forever.'

***

In the treehouse, Nikky was startled by Scott's sudden appearance. He sat on the floor facing her, looking out the same window to the moon above. Scott removed the silver bracelet from his wrist and handed it to Nikky.

'I think you should keep this; she'd want you to have it.'

Nikky shook her head. 'No, this was yours long before I was born. She gave it to you, and you should keep it to remember her.'

'I don't need a bracelet to remember her. I relive the memories every time I close my eyes. I want you to have it.'

'I know how much this bracelet means to you, Scott, it's, oh wait …it's a reminder, alright, but it's a reminder for me, isn't it? You're leaving?'

Scott hesitated. He knew this moment would haunt him forever, but something compelled him to continue. 'Listen, the only reason Beth lived so long and so happily is because she left Tallant, putting me behind her, and moving on with her life. Nothing good comes from being close to me, Nikky. Everything I touch reeks of death. It's better this way for everyone.'

'Scott, I've just lost my grandmother, I don't want to lose you too.' She reached forward and took his hand.

'People in Tallant died because of me, everyone at that homecoming almost died because of me, you need to do what your grandmother did and move away, putting this town behind you for your own sake and for the sake of your family. I'm sure you believe me when I say I'll never forget you.' In her heart of hearts, she knew he was right. The world was a much easier place to live in not knowing about its supernatural side. How difficult it must have been for her grandmother to leave him behind after everything they'd been through together.

'I suppose I've had a strange run of extremely bad luck lately, with everything that's happened.'

He held her hand tightly. 'Being with me can do that, Nikky, you're better off staying as far away as possible, I cast a never-ending shadow.'

'How can I go on living a normal life knowing how the world really is?' She moved across to lie against his chest. 'And how could anyone I meet in the future ever live up to you?'

'Beth could do it, and you're just as strong as she was. Where will she rest eternally?'

'With my grandpa in Green Bay.'

Scott stood up and, still cradling her in his arms, stepped out through the entrance, and glided gently to the ground.

'I will never be able to forget you, Scott.'

Scott hesitated before answering. He sighed heavily. 'Actually, Nikky, you'll forget ever meeting me in the first place. But I'll never forget you, I promise.'

'But you can't enthral me, remember? Wait, what was that?' She placed her hand on his chest. 'It felt like your heart was beating for a second?'

'I wish, but you're wrong. It's just the warning vibration.' Scott glanced over her head, directly behind her. Nikky turned around to see. She quickly turned back to Scott and thumped his chest.

'No, Scott! Please, don't do this! I love you!'

He took her face in his hands and kissed her. 'From a heart that cannot beat, I love you too.' Amdis moved to Scott's side and put her hand gently on Nikky's shoulder. Nikky stared deeply into Scott's eyes one last time and smiled. A moment later, Amdis stared into hers.

## Chapter 63

Outside the flat roof, just before the sun rose, Scott had questions for Amdis. She kept a close eye eastward, already able to smell the coming sunrise.

'How did you know how to break the spell?' Scott asked.

'The witch came to see me. Said she knew what the coven in Green Bay had planned for you; of course, I didn't believe her at the time. She told me that the love of your life must die for the spell to be broken.'

Scott sighed. 'Carol, yeah, I remember she said something before she died, about taking steps to break the spell. Did she intend to kill Beth?'

'No, she assumed Nikky was the love of your life.'

Scott scrunched up his face. 'But Nikky died, and the spell didn't break. Did she plan on killing Nikky before I did?' The horrible memory stuck in his throat.

'I'm not sure, she just said leave it to her, she'd do what needed to be done.'

'I'm afraid she won't get the chance to do anything ever again.' He sighed. Another memory he could do without. He looked at his mother, contemplating how to say his next words. 'I've caused enough damage here to last a lifetime. Think I might disappear for a few decades, let those who remember me try to forget.'

Amdis nodded. 'I'll know where to find you. But Scott, Beth told me to tell you not to blame me or yourself for what happened, and that she welcomed it; she was dying with not much time left.'

'That sounds like her, alright. And I don't blame you, Mom. You saved Nikky and everyone at that homecoming.' Amdis hid a subtle smile, unable to believe what he'd just called her. Scott said one more thing before he went inside.

'Anyway, I blame myself for all of it.'

# Chapter 64

At nine o'clock the following morning, Scott sat outside the Governor's office in the pouring rain. With the collar of his leather jacket pulled up, he watched as two black SUVs pulled up to park in their designated parking spaces right outside the front door. The tinted rear window slid down, revealing a familiar face.

'I didn't expect to see you so soon?' the Governor shouted from the opposite seat. Scott shrugged as the rain pelted his face.

'I didn't expect the help.'

'Won't you get in?' the Governor gestured. Scott opened the rear door and climbed in next to him. The Governor spoke to the driver up front. 'That'll be all.' With a nod, the driver got out and ran up the steps into the building, leaving them alone.

The governor spoke first. 'You know, my sources tell me that the persons behind the Tallant kidnappings were found dead in Green Bay? Horribly mutilated, along with all the members of that coven. Ring any bells?' Scott eyed the rainwater running into the drain on his side of the vehicle.

'Shit happens, I guess?'

The Governor grinned and shook his head. 'You've saved a lot of lives, Scott.'

'It can never make up for the lives I've taken in the past, so to me that means nothing.'

'The witches are no more, and any remaining vampires will think twice about coming near this town again, thanks to you.' The Governor studied the family crest on his ring. Things really had come a long way since the days when vampires and werewolves were mortal enemies. Scott watched a solitary leaf drop to the ground then be washed into the drain before responding.

'I'm leaving Tallant for a while, don't know when I'll be back, maybe not within your lifetime.' The Governor knew this was a good thing and Scott knew he'd be happy to hear those words, but he wasn't finished yet. 'But I need you to do a few things for me, Governor.'

'I don't usually do personal favours except for family, but for you I might make an exception.'

A half-smile escaped from Scott's mouth. 'Make sure your people are locked up when the moon is full, I won't be around to patrol the forest.'

'That's always done.'

'And tell your nephew that PJ won't remember anything after today.'

'Done. Anything else?'

'Yes. I believe you were in touch with Amdis recently about breaking the spell?'

'What about it?'

'I want you to keep an eye on her for me.'

'Do you mean keep an eye on her to stop her killing innocents or keep an eye on her to keep her safe?'

Scott said nothing. He turned and shook the Governor's hand, then stepped back out into the rain. A moment later he was gone.

\*\*\*

Later that same day, PJ stood soaked outside the Maglace mausoleum in the empty cemetery. Scott stood next to him.

'When you leave this cemetery, you will not remember encountering me or my kind, and the supernatural world does not exist.'

PJ nodded. 'Do you really have to do this, man?'

'Yes, my friend, for your own safety.'

'Are you really sure you wanna go through with it?'

'It's for the best, believe me.'

'What about Nikky and her grandmother's funeral in Green Bay tomorrow?'

'I've said my goodbyes to Beth, she'd understand me not being there. And Nikky won't remember a thing, either.'

'I'm gonna miss ya, man.'

Scott smiled at his friend. 'Actually, you won't.' PJ grabbed Scott and hugged him tightly. His eyes welled up as he turned and entered the tomb.

'You ready?'

Scott nodded.

'What am I supposed to do?'

'When I'm lying down, place the crucifix into the slot inside the lid, then slide it back where it belongs, sealing me inside.'

PJ nervously nodded. 'So, this is really it?'

Scott nodded. 'And PJ, make sure you lock the door from the outside when you leave.'

PJ took the cap from his head, wiped away a tear, and handed the cap to Scott. 'For whenever you wake up, whatever century it is, so you'll remember me.'

Scott smiled and grabbed PJ by his hand, thumbs looping. 'I never forget my friends, that's the problem.' He placed the cap on his head, gave PJ a wink and lay down into his concrete casket. Tears poured down PJ's face as he removed the silver crucifix from his pocket and placed it into the holder.

Already, Scott could sense its presence.

PJ pushed the lid with all his strength, sliding concrete on concrete until the casket was whole again, sealing the best friend he'd ever had inside. Within the casket, flesh became charred skin, and charred skin became bone, but the bones were still dressed in a black leather jacket along with a baseball cap for eternity. PJ bolted the door from the outside as requested. He took more time than was necessary to reach the northern gate, contemplating everything that happened. Stopping at the gate, he looked back one last time, knowing it would all be gone in just a few steps.

'Back to my boring old life, I guess.' As he passed through the gate, he raised his hand to his head in confusion. 'What the hell happened to my baseball cap?'

## Chapter 65

The next day, Nikky stood alone at her grandmother's freshly dug grave after the other mourners had left. Her father and Caden waited in the pickup, sheltering from another day of nonstop rain. She needed this time to say goodbye. First her mother, now her grandmother. Bad luck seemed to follow her.

She placed a sunflower on the mound of earth and returned to the car where her family waited.

The journey home was quiet. Rain hammered relentlessly against the windscreen. Nikky searched her small black handbag for another tissue. Wiping her nose, she reached inside again and pulled out a keyring photograph of her mother, smiling back at her. Putting it back inside, she pulled out her hand again, finding something that she had not placed there. In her hand lay a small piece of tattered cloth, tied at the top with a leather string. There was a strange symbol on its side that looked oddly familiar.

At that moment, a black cat ran across the street in front of the pickup truck. Tyres screeched on the wet surface as the vehicle locked into a hard turn to avoid hitting the cat but collided with an oncoming van and flipped over, rolling twice before coming to a standstill on its flattened roof.

There were no survivors.

Four hours later at the Green Bay mortuary, a mortician tied a name tag around the toe of one of the victims of a tragic motor vehicle accident earlier that day. The mortician removed a silver bracelet from the victim's wrist and placed it with other personal belongings, including a small hex bag in the form of tattered cloth, into a chrome container for collection by relatives. Removing his disposable apron and gloves, he threw them in the rubbish on his way out as he switched off the lights, leaving the room cold and dark. The hum of refrigeration units was the only company for the deceased. That is, until the blonde girl on table 3 opened her eyes. Their original sapphire colour was gone.

Her new pale complexion came second only to her glowing red eyes.

Printed in Great Britain
by Amazon